Some
Kind of
Forever

A FORT BENDER NOVEL

LAYNA JAMES

For those who are worried it's too late. It's not.

CONTENT NOTES

This story is intended for adult readers 18+ and contains elements of familial secrecy, familial death (off page), explicit language, racial micro-aggressions/racism, alcohol usage, and brief open door scenes.

Fort Bender
N
W
E
S
THE BLUFFS ESTAT
FORT BENDER
VISITOR'S CENTER
AND MUSEUM
MAIN STREET
LIBRARY
CRYSTAL BEACH

R BOTANICAL
GARDENS
SHOWER TREE LODGE
YOUTH CENTER
CAMP BENDER
FORGET ME NOTS
WILLIS NEIGHBORHOOD
WALLER TREE FARM
RRIS ORHOOD
BENDER ELEMENTARY
BENDER SECONDARY
HERBERT'S HOLE

KAYLA

I drink in the cool sea air as yellows and pinks paint the morning sky. The breeze whispers through my hair, and the waves in the distance lap at the shore, humming a peaceful melody I've missed while being away. This is my happy place.

Home.

The colors melting into the clouds are mesmerizing enough that when my phone beeps, I jump, jolting back to reality. The first batch of muffins should be ready in five minutes. That's plenty of time for me to get down from the roof of Patti's Place to grab them out of the oven. As I reach into my pocket, movement flickers on the ground.

"Kayla, girl. Don't jump," my best friend, Ashlie, calls up from the sidewalk. Her dramatic performance shakes the golden-brown coils piled on top of her head. "I need you to make me some coffee first..."

"Like *you* need any more energy," I reply, standing from the crates I piled into a makeshift stool.

"If I want to make it through this summer, I do." She slaps a hand on her hip. "Who wakes up at five in the morning for a summer job anyway? Oh, wait..." A smirk spreads across her lips as she points a finger up at me. Ashlie's given me a hard time about my work ethic ever since she found out I was working split shifts in high school. The teasing has only increased as more responsibilities pile onto my plate.

With one last look at the now orange-tinged sky, I turn toward the ladder at the end of the roof. The sea breeze flaps my jacket open, making a shiver travel across my shoulders as I rush to pull it closed. Fort Bender, California, is a bit colder than I'm used to at my home away from home, Salima State University (SSU). They're a little less than three hours apart, but the stark difference in temperature and scenery makes Fort Bender feel like it came straight out of a storybook about the Fae. Between the thick redwood forest and the craggy cliffs flocking the ocean, my town is a chilly little oasis in the Golden State—cozy and magical.

The rhythmic beeping from the oven sounds right as I make it into the kitchen, and I swap my jacket with my navy-colored apron on my way to silence it. I've been working for my boss, Ms. Patti, since high school. Slipping on this apron, with its worn embroidery on the pocket, always takes me back to those simpler times. Working at the diner back then planted the seed in me to pursue my dream of being an event planner. The amount of detail and organization that goes into working at the diner gives me a rush that I sometimes miss when I'm at SSU, so I happily take on shifts whenever I come home. It keeps me busy—gives me a routine—and busy routines keep me productive.

The sweet, steaming aroma of blueberry muffins fills the air as I flip the pastries onto the cooling rack. There are two more batches to get started before we open at seven, and it's just past six.

Right on schedule.

I should be able to get both batches done, and the fruit for today's pies prepped with time to spare. I pop another tray into the oven, reset the timer, and flip on the coffee maker as I pass it on my way to unlock the front door. Falling back into the opening routine for the diner is as easy as making my bed, seeing as I'm the one who introduced the idea of a diner checklist to Ms. Patti in the first place.

"Hey, girl!" Ashlie says, pulling me into a hug. She's wearing her cobalt blue tracksuit labeled *Swim Team Captain* and yawns as she wraps her arms around my neck. The puffiness surrounding her eyes tells me she rolled out of bed and came straight to the diner for her morning fix.

"I've missed you! How was the drive from LA?" I ask, hugging her back.

"Long and winding. I forget how twisty the coast can be," she says, reaching into her bag and pulling out a compact mirror.

It's been five months since I've seen my best friend. She looks the same as she did when we met in high school, down to every last freckle splattered across her amber cheeks. While I decided to stick closer to home for academics, Ashlie went and got herself into the University of Los Angeles on a swimming scholarship. I'm able to make it home whenever I feel homesick, but a nine-hour drive means she only comes back for holidays and summer vacation.

As she checks the damage the wind did to her curls, I grab a mug from the shelf. Another yawn overtakes her when I slide the coffee over. "But I'm here now and ready to make sure all the tourists *'fall in love'* with the history of Bender, as my boss likes to say." Her voice takes on a flowery, mystical tone, like she's trying to enchant the future visitors.

"*Ugh*, tourists! Don't remind me." I groan, moving around the counter to set condiments on the tables. "The audacity will be at an all-time high. You get cute retired couples looking for history and antiques. I have to deal with demands for diet water and BLTs without the B or the T."

"That lady was so sure her lettuce sandwich would taste like a BLT too..." She giggles. "And then had the nerve to ask what you did to it to make it taste nasty!"

"The lady ordered a *wish* sandwich, so that's what I gave her. I bet she *wished* she kept the bacon and tomato on it," I say, giggling right back.

We came back just in time for my least favorite season in Bender. Memorial Day weekend marks the start of summer vacations and the arrival of people who are used to getting big city accommodations with their entitlement. I'm professional, but the infernal rage I feel inside when someone asks for the manager wears on a girl.

Ashlie's phone chirps, and she rolls her eyes.

"How's Bryan?" I ask.

She sighs, slipping the phone out of her pocket. "He's... stressing me out. We agreed to do the long-distance thing. But he only graduated a week ago, and I can't walk two steps without my phone going off. I knew he was clingy before, but this is next level."

I cock my head to the side. "You were both pretty clingy at Christmas. If attached at the hip was a couple, it was you two."

"Well, that was before he started talking about marriage and babies," she says quickly, before sipping from her cup, fixing her widened eyes at the brim.

"Girl!" My mouth falls open.

"*I know*! I thought he just wanted to take the next step, but something about meeting my parents flipped a switch. Every conversation we have now involves some form of fortune telling. 'Our kids will be so cute. You would sound good with my last name. Wedding. Wife.' *Ugh*."

"Ashlie Christensen *does* have a nice ring to it," I tease. She gasps and makes a gagging sound I can't help but laugh at. Ashlie's mostly bubbly personality is a mixed bag of humor, sass, and a whole lot of attitude. Whoever pins down my best friend is going to have their hands full, and it doesn't sound like that person will be Bryan.

"I love him, I do, but I'm too young. I have things I want to accomplish. Places to go. People to...do. Speaking of, who are *you* doing lately?" She waggles her eyebrows, taking another sip of her coffee.

I snort and shake my head. "I'm *doing* a lot of different jobs this summer and don't have time to worry about a *who*. I have to put all my energy into landing that internship, on top of working to pay for next semester."

I have my shifts at the diner, the odd babysitting gig, *and* I'll be a camp counselor for the first session at Camp Bender. Added to that is a trial catering event at the end of summer that will determine if Ms. Patti extends one of her catering internships to me. I can't afford to get distracted. That internship is my Holy Grail.

"Ah, yes, because burning out by graduation is a great way to get your start in the real world," she says, scrunching her lips to the side. "I'm just saying, maybe a little 'hit it and forget it' won't hurt you this summer."

"I'm pretty sure that's not the saying..."

"Whatever. You know what I mean." She waves her hand in the air like she's trying to swat away my attempt to change the subject. "How long has it been anyway?"

"Since what?" I challenge with a blank expression. The beeping timer sets me in motion.

"Since, ya know..." She makes an *O* with one hand and sticks her pointer finger through it with the other.

"Oh, that... Since Evan," I mumble, turning around to avoid her wide-eyed stare. I scurry back to the kitchen and turn the muffins onto the cooling rack, reset the timer, and slip in the last batch.

"*Evan*? Like freshman-year-in-college Evan? That Evan? That was three years ago!"

I face her as I come back around the counter and lift an eyebrow. She knows exactly which *Evan* I'm talking about. She's the one who helped pick me up off the proverbial floor after what happened with him. "Yes. That Evan. Thanks, by the way. I love to be reminded of how that all went down. Top ten, all-time favorite memory," I deadpan. "And I've been busy!"

"Busy for three years? No one in college is that damn busy." Her side-eye full of sass makes me roll my eyes.

"Well, I am. And why are we talking about this when I'm at work?"

She shrugs, biting her lip nervously. "Sorry! I was just surprised. Three years is so long ago I assumed you'd gotten back in the game. You know, gotten Prince Charming out of your system. And he was charming," she rambles. "Evan charmed the pants right off your roommate." She tries to hide her joking smile by pinching her lips closed as I glare at her, the giggles overtaking her short frame.

I met Evan Matthews at freshman orientation. He was tall, dark, and handsome—everything a naive eighteen-year-old me was looking for. A football player for Salima State, he was charming, affectionate, confident, and I was enamored...until I was catapulted straight out of the clouds and dropped face-first on the ground.

"Okay, buh-bye now." I narrow my eyes at her. "Don't you have some maps to pass out?"

"Yeah, I should get going. But, Kayla, *girl*, you really need to get back out there." She glances at the clock on the wall and stretches her legs before standing. "Text me when your lunch break starts."

Once the jangling from the bell above the door stops, I'm left to enjoy the last few moments of the quiet diner. Ashlie scored the front desk position at the Fort Bender Visitor's Center and Museum across the street. She gets to relax behind a desk all summer with a good book, hand out maps, and remind everyone to sign the visitor's log. I get to run around town like a beheaded chicken with its wings on fire. *Relaxing? What would that be like?* I'm only a little jealous.

CHAPTER TWO

CHASE

"Torture. That's what this is. I thought we were friends, but *this*? Unforgivable." Hunter huffs as he looks out the car window, face scrunched tight.

"We didn't know how to tell you." I hold back a chuckle as I drum my hands on the steering wheel. "Besides, Fort Bender's got some cool things going on. Give it a chance."

"I'm looking for the *things*... There *are* no *things*! A tree. Another tree. *A third tree*," he groans. "We're in California! Where's the beach? The sun? *The beach*?"

"I said there'd be camping..."

"Yeah, but I thought you meant *on the beach*!" His voice raises in pitch the more frantic he gets, green eyes widening as I laugh at the ridiculous tone his voice has reached.

Hunter and I have been friends since he was born. I'm a year older, but that bit of age difference hasn't stopped us from being close. Our families are close too. We've vacationed together for as long as I can remember. This year, his dad picked Fort Bender and Hunter is *stressed*.

"It could be worse," I say, switching the radio station. "We could be stuck working that EdTechU convention booth again. At least this place has some character." Our dads met in college, where they started a small educational technology company called EdTechU. It's grown to be one of the largest tech support firms in the country. It's always been my dream to work for the family business, and now that I've graduated, I'm ready to embark on that journey. All I want to do this summer is take it easy and have a good time in this small town which, according to my best friend, is the worst thing in the world.

"I'm just saying, you could have warned me," Hunter continues, his short dark curls swaying against his light brown skin as he shakes his head.

"I sent you a map, details for our volunteer hours at camp, and the rental info. What more do you need?"

"Bruh, a *beach!*"

We turn down Main Street, and the ocean comes into view. "There's your beach," I offer, pointing straight ahead. This view of the Pacific Ocean is amazing. Paired with the overcast sky, it seems like the perfect place to relax this summer.

"Nope." He juts out his jaw. "That's the ocean with a bunch of cliffs and rocks. The beach has sand and sun and—"

"Some bikinis?"

"They can wear whatever they'd like," he says, a smirk sliding across his face. "I can appreciate it all. I'm just saying, I didn't sign up for a dry summer."

I've known Hunter long enough to know he's not upset about the beach, so much as who usually frequents the beach. He rotates through relationships as quickly as he refreshes his timeline. I don't relate to that approach.

"Think of it as a palate cleanser. Take the summer to clear your head before next semester's flings. Besides, there are interesting people in small towns. Maybe stop thinking with your di—"

"That's easy for you to say. You're Mr. Charming wherever you go. You could make friends with a plastic spoon if you wanted to. I don't have the patience for that."

Charming. This isn't the first time someone's called me that.

Sure, I make friends easily and like meeting people from all walks of life. I follow the Golden Rule and try to help when I can, but I don't set out to dazzle people with my personality. I just try to be a good person. If that means I have charm, then so be it.

My stomach growls, and I glance at the clock. We haven't stopped to eat real food since we got breakfast on our way out of LA, and a person can only eat so many granola bars. "Hey, look up some restaurants around here," I say abruptly. "We still have an hour before check-in."

"Restaurants in NoBeachTown, USA. Got it," he says, exaggerating the tapping of his thumbs on the screen. "There's a Rosa's Pizzeria, Seaside Tacos, Nando's Fish & Pasta, SandWishes Deli, and—"

"Patti's Place," we say simultaneously as I spot the large building straight ahead. It's a rustic-looking diner with weathered wood siding and dark stained trim along the roof. It looks more like a cozy cabin than a diner. The words *Patti's Place* sit right above the entrance in bold white block-style font, and a giant neon red sign blinks the word *DINER* in the parking lot.

Hunter looks up and shrugs. "Sounds good to me."

A bell tinkles overhead, signaling our entrance. The place is nearly empty. It's around two o'clock, and only a few patrons sit at the counter.

"Hey, guys! Seat yourselves. I'll bring menus in a sec," the waitress booms from behind the counter. She's a short woman, probably in her mid-fifties, with dark brown hair. Glasses hang onto the tip of her nose, and she wears a navy-blue apron with the name *Patti* on the pocket. "Bert, you ready for that pie yet?" Her voice projects across the counter as she looks toward an older man in suspenders.

"Don't rush me, Patti!" Bert shakes his head and grumbles, "I'm retired now. I can take as much time as I want."

Patti chuckles and grabs the pie tin, slicing and dishing up a hearty piece. She sets the plate in front of Bert and winks, saying, "I'll just leave this here for whenever you're ready."

Hunter heads toward a booth, eyes down at his phone while he walks. I take in the decorations around the eatery as I follow behind. Sepia photos of surfers and framed news articles of people fishing cover one wall, while brown and white striped surf boards are anchored along the other. The booths sit along large windows, and the brown vinyl seat squeaks as I ease onto my side of the table.

Patti sets down two glasses of water and plastic-covered menus. "You here for vacation?" she asks.

Hunter nods, and I smile at her. "Yeah, we're here for the summer. I'm Chase," I say—reaching for her hand—"and this is Hunter."

I kick his foot, and he pops his head up, offering a thin-lipped grin.

"You must be the famous Patti. It's a nice place you've got here," I say, winking.

With a chuckle, she grabs her apron at the corners and gives a small curtsy. "Well, aren't you a charmer! I sure am Patti. Here for the whole summer, huh? You must be staying in those fancy long-term rentals at The Bluffs. Where'd you come from?"

"We drove up from LA this morning," I say, nodding.

Her eyes widen as she says, "Los Angeles? Bender's a different world than what you're used to, then."

"Yeah, it is." Hunter snorts, suddenly interested enough to add to the conversation. "A different universe...with no beaches..."

"Well, welcome to Fort Bender. I'll give you a few minutes to decide." She beams a smile before walking away.

"Bro," I say, kicking his foot again.

"What?" He kicks me back.

"Would it kill you to talk to people?"

"Yes," he says flatly, eyes fixed to his screen.

My stomach rumbles again, and I'm flipping through the last of the menu pages when Patti returns. Only it isn't Patti's voice that says, "What can I get for you?"

The scent of spiced vanilla overtakes my senses as I look up into the boldest jade-colored eyes I've ever seen. My jaw drops before I can catch myself, and warmth spreads through my cheeks. Straightening up in the booth, I kick Hunter and try to regain some composure.

"Bruh, kick me again..." he warns before looking at the new waitress.

"Um." I clear my throat and pretend to look back at the menu.

"You're not Patti..." Hunter says, interest piquing. He quirks an eyebrow and smiles, moving the phone to his pocket.

"Sure, I am," New Patti says. She shifts on her feet and tips her head to the side. A few dark locs frame her deep bronze face, the rest pulled up into a swirled bun. "I'm Patty with a *Y*. You met Patti with an *I* before," she continues with a lilt of humor.

The sound of her voice is enough to set my heart pounding. It's smooth and warm, and suddenly, my throat is dry, like I've never tasted water. I reach for my glass, unable to look away, and almost knock it over. Hunter flicks his eyes to the table, making sure I don't need help with the cup. As I gulp for relief, I glance at the top of her apron. Sure enough, *Patty* is spelled with a *Y*.

"Stay here long enough and Pattie with an *IE* will show up too. But you probably want to eat before the dinner rush, so... what can I get you?" She taps her pen on the rose gold ring on her thumb. The worn green polish on her short fingernails is nothing compared to the color in her eyes. She's breathtaking, and it's becoming more apparent that I'm staring. I look down at my menu again and take a deep breath, ready to order. My heart pounds in my ears, making it hard to hear my own thoughts.

"I'll take the bacon cheeseburger, fries...and your name for my friend here." Hunter smiles, ignoring another kick under the table. "Your *real* name. I'm Hunter, by the way."

Patty puts a hand on her hip. "I'm Patty," she insists, her smile slipping for a second. She turns to me and asks, "And you?"

"I-I'm Chase," I stammer. People don't generally make me nervous, but something about the cool confidence she carries herself with has me in knots. She sends another smile my way, and my internal dashboard short circuits. I'm done for. Death by dazzling smile was unexpected, but what a way to go.

"I meant, what can I get for you?"

"Oh, hmm," I hesitate, trying to buy the time my mouth needs to catch up to my thoughts. "I'll take the chicken Caesar salad," I manage to squeak out.

Patty nods and grabs both menus. "Anything else to drink? More water? I have a pump out back, directly from the Pacific if you need it," she teases, gesturing to my mostly empty glass. I nod, trying to think of the words *yes, please,* or *thank you,* but none of them come to mind before she's heading back to the counter to fill up a pitcher, shaking her head and laughing to herself.

"You good? Need a little pep talk? You know how great I am at talking to people." The smart-ass smirk on Hunter's face makes me shake my head.

My heart's pounding is returning to its normal pace, and I chance a look behind the counter. I can't help but notice the curve of her waist as Patty balances a tray full of plates on her hip, clearing the dishes left by Bert. I'm intrigued, enthralled, and I can't look away. Another deep breath and I realize my fingers are tapping on my knee, exploding with the anxious energy I feel. She turns, looking back toward our booth, and damn it, I'm still staring.

CHAPTER THREE
KAYLA

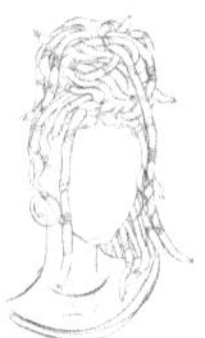

I turn around from clearing dishes to see the cute guy at the booth, staring with the same intensity as when I took his order. At least the Black guy, Hunter, made small talk. Mr. Tall, Blond, and Blue-Eyed didn't even hint at a smile. Looking at him now, his hair isn't all blond. An even mix of light brown breaks up the paler strands falling over his eyes in a way that makes me wonder, for a split second, how soft it would feel on my fingertips if I brushed it out of his face.

What the hell?

Maybe Ashlie's right if I'm imagining running my hands through the hair of a perfect stranger. I shake the thought from my head, turning away from what's-his-name. *Chance? Chad?* It doesn't really matter. Summer vacationers only stay a few days here before heading to warmer, sandier California shores. These two, with their matching gray Gradford University shirts, seem like they're just passing through. I'll turn up the hospitality and suffer through the pleasantries, and then they'll be on their way.

Balancing the tray of food on my upturned palm, I grab a water pitcher and head back to the booth. "Okay. Burger for the mighty Hunter," I tease, passing his plate to him. "And a salad for the tranquil gatherer." I smirk at the blond. Hunter snorts a laugh, earning a smile from what's-his-name.

"Chase," he says, the smile remaining this time.

"Ah, that's it!" I snap my fingers. "I knew it was something primitive."

He's staring again, but this time with a crooked grin plastered to his lips. The blue in his eyes gets deeper the longer I look at him, so I avert my attention down, landing on the spread of facial hair covering his chin. I swat away another thought of running my fingers down his jaw. *Oh, he's attractive, all right. And he probably knows it too.*

Hunter clears his throat. "I was just telling Chase I've never met another Black person with green eyes, aside from the people in my family. It's pretty rare."

"Yeah." I bob my head. I can't go a day without someone interrupting me just to tell me about my own eyes. "I hear that a lot, actually. Enjoy your—"

"Maybe you can help us out." The words rush out of Chase like he's been dying for a chance to speak.

"With what, exactly?"

"Hunter here is convinced Fort Bender has nothing fun to offer. That can't be true."

"There's tons to do here. We have Crystal Beach, Bender Botanical Gardens, Redwood Rail Bikes, hiking, bonfires on The Bluffs, so many museums, and the Herb Train that goes to this cool little outdoor bar."

"Herb? Like, *herb*-herb?" Hunter asks, pinching his pointer finger and thumb together and tipping them to his mouth with hopeful eyes.

"No." I shake my head, laughing. "The man who designed the rail system was named Herbert. Hard *H*. Herb. That type of train wouldn't have been legal yet. You might be able to leave a suggestion card now though."

"A puff-puff train is right up Hunter's alley," Chase ribs, grinning so wide it shows off his impossibly straight teeth.

"Alright, alright, maybe it won't be so bad here," Hunter concedes. "So we'll see you around this summer, then? You sound like the perfect tour guide."

"Oh, me? Naw, not really. I'll be working."

"All summer?" Chase asks earnestly. His eyes bore into mine so intensely I have to look away again.

"I—"

"Patty," my boss calls from the back office. "Come here a sec."

"Yep, all summer. I'll be your cashier at the counter whenever you're ready. Enjoy!" I scurry back to Ms. Patti's office.

Saved by the boss.

Patti's gimmicky idea to give everyone who works in the diner the pseudonym Patti evolved out of an abundance of caution to protect us waitresses from overeager tourists. Our town is small enough that almost everyone knows everyone's name, but to visitors, we're all known as *Patti*. Or *Patty*. Or *Pattie*. I'm pretty sure we've had a *Pat* in the past too. Her foresight has saved me a time or three, and right now, I silently thank her for the fallback. Cute tourists equal distractions. As my mom would say, *Ain't nobody got time for that.*

"Hey, Patti, what's up?" I slip into a chair next to her office door.

"I'm finalizing details for the internship interview at the end of the season. Seaside Catering has been hired to service a shareholders' event for a tech company called EdTechU. You're still going for the internship, right?"

Definitely.

Catering isn't my final destination, but this internship, along with my degree in event management, will give me the last bit of experience I need to make my dreams of becoming an event planner come true. I love planning, organizing, and executing ideas. Taking a vision and watching it come to fruition. Even the contracts and budgets are something I enjoy. My kaleidoscope of responsibilities has helped me gain exposure to some of those other skills, but *this* opportunity would be the cherry on top. I've wanted it for as long as I can remember. Now it's so close I can almost taste it.

"Yes. Absolutely. One thousand percent yes," I say.

"Great!"

She's aware of how hard I've worked for this. Like me, Patti grew up here in Fort Bender. She left to receive a degree in restaurant management and returned here to renovate an old hardware store into the Patti's Place of today. A few years ago, she created the offshoot Seaside Catering, which has become a top catering service for the northern coast of California.

This diner holds a significant spot in my memory. It's where we came to celebrate all my milestones—awards, post-game team bonding, graduations—you name it. When I reached junior high, I came after school most days for a milkshake or a piece of her most popular apple pie. I asked for a job in high school, and she said yes on the spot. She teased I was there every day anyway, so she might as well pay me for it. Ms. Patti got to watch me grow up, and it feels fitting to embark on my professional journey under her guidance.

Her expression shifts as she puts her businesswoman face on. "There are two positions this year, and three of you vying for them. We'll need to be all-hands-on-deck with everyone's head in the game, so to speak. It looks like we'll be in San Francisco, so I need you to mark your calendar for August 5. When I have the final details, I'll let you know."

"Okay. Got it." I slide my phone from my back pocket and enter the date into my overflowing calendar. "What can I start working on now?"

"Is it okay, Kayla?" she asks with furrowed brows. "I know how hard you're working this summer. It's a lot, and I don't want the stress to get to you."

"I can handle stress. It's no big deal."

"The diner, camp counselor, babysitting, and who knows what else you've taken on." She leans back in her office chair, lacing her fingers over her midsection. "You're young and still need to live a little… So no, I'm going to wait to give you details until after you're done with camp. You'll still have plenty of time to get things ready after that."

"I'm fine, Ms. Patti," I urge, trying to keep the irritation out of my voice. "Really. I'll be fine." I have a lot on my plate this summer, but it's nothing I can't handle. Where most people would crumble under the pressure of a packed schedule, I've found compartmentalizing to be easy. I can stick things on the shelf in the back of my mind, putting the worry on ice until I have to deal with it again. Some might call it avoidance. I call it efficiency. It works well for me and makes focusing on the task at hand a lot more manageable. Getting ready for this internship is something I've been looking forward to since I decided to apply. I'm itching to get my foot in the door, and her withholding the information because she thinks I'll crumble under the pressure is annoying. I know what I can handle.

"No." She shakes her head, setting her final words in stone as she sits up in her chair. Like someone hit a switch, her face relaxes, and her eyes glint mischievously. "Speaking of *fine*, did you see the guys at the booth? *Whew*!" She fans herself. "Talk about a hot boy summer."

I chuckle and groan. "That's not what that means, Pat!"

"Well, it should. I may be old, but I've got eyes. They're right around your age too. Maybe living a little could include one of them." She wiggles her eyebrows, giving a shoulder shimmy.

The bell next to the cash register dings, and I'm on my feet, headed to the door before she tries out any additional out-of-pocket lingo. "I don't have time for boys this summer."

"That's the whole problem!"

Just as I reach for the doorknob, she puts a hand on my forearm. Her brows furrow like before. "You'll let me know if it's too much, right? We can always cut back hours here at the diner."

"I'll be fine," I say again. And after her repetitive questioning, I *think* I'm still telling the truth. This summer is packed, but that's how I've always liked it in the past. Busy helps me stay on top of things. Busy keeps me safe. I don't waste time thinking so much when I'm running around putting out everyone else's fires.

When I get up to the register, Chase is standing there, alone, drumming his fingers at his side as he smiles at something on his phone. That smile probably helps him get away with a lot, paired with that hair and...everything else.

"It'll be $20.75. We take everything except check," I say, glancing over to the empty booth. "Is Hunter out on the prowl?"

He slides his phone into his pocket and smiles at me while fishing for his wallet. "With him, anything's possible. I wouldn't be surprised if he's halfway back to LA by now."

"He's not a fan of Bender so far?"

"He just hasn't given it a chance yet. Hunter's more of a sandy beach, sunshine, girls everywhere kind of guy."

"And you're...?" My voice trails as I internally kick myself for sounding interested. I have no business asking that kind of question to a cute stranger who's been staring at me for the last hour.

"I'm the kind of guy who can wait patiently to learn your real name." He smirks.

His sudden confidence is a stark difference from earlier, and it throws me off guard. My mouth gapes as I struggle to think of a response, and the butterflies surging through my core are no help. Cute, shy tourists are one thing, but confident, charming ones scream *danger* to everything inside of me. I wish he would skip the flirting, pay his bill, and get out of town so I can finish my shift in peace.

"I'll be here all summer," he adds. "Plenty of time to bump into each other and get acquainted."

With my pulse hammering in my ears and the flutters scattering throughout my chest, I almost miss what he said.

All summer?

I have to see him around town for the next three months, with *that* smile and *those* eyes? "I guess it'll be your lucky day, then." My attention drops to the register screen.

"Oh, it definitely will be."

From the corner of my eye, I watch him slip something into the tip jar on the counter. "Thanks!"

"Sure. The food was great, and the waitress was..." He pauses, waiting until I flick my eyes up to his before he says, "phenomenal." He winks at me. *Winks.* Like he's used to girls melting at the expression. I wouldn't call what happens to me melting. Maybe a slight warming. And yeah, my face flushes. He can't see it, but he smirks like he can.

"See you next time, *Patty.*"

Once he leaves through the door, I puff out the breath I've been holding and lean back against the counter. Since when does winking turn me stupid? I've been winked at before, and it's never made me blush. Yet here I am, fanning my face, thinking about his ocean blue eyes and crooked smile. That thing could brighten up any space, especially paired with the tiny sense of humor he seemed to find before leaving. Hopefully, he and his friend find another restaurant to frequent while they're here and he can wink at some other unsuspecting waitress.

I notice one of Patti's white business cards in the tip jar, tucked under the cash Chase slipped in. I contemplate putting it right in the trash, but when I pick it up, there's a phone number and one sentence scrawled on the back:

Next time, try not to steal my breath away.

—Chase.

CHAPTER FOUR

CHASE

The fresh air breezes into the wide-open French doors of my bottom floor bedroom while I enjoy the view from the deck. As I take in the calm, waves crash against the cliff. This place is amazing, perfectly peaceful. I'll enjoy some much-needed relaxation after the way I powered through my last semester before graduation.

The Bluffs Estates is a set of four coastal style beach houses curved into a cul-de-sac overlooking the Pacific. The property owner rents the houses for the summer, and between my family and Hunter's, we've rented out three of them. My parents and sisters will stay in one, Hunter's dad and sister in another, and Hunter and I in the third. The fourth, as far as I know, is still vacant.

Hunter snagged a room upstairs, and the heavy bass thumping from his music rattles the windows as I come back inside to unpack. I'm transferring clothes from my suitcase into the drawers lining the wall when my phone rings.

"Hey, Dad," I answer, pressing the video icon and flopping on the bed.

"Hey, kid! You two make it in okay?"

"Yep, just getting settled into the rental now."

"Great. I found out I have to fly to New York for a week to speak at a conference, and then to Chicago for another the following week. Your mom and sisters will get there tomorrow evening. Make sure they get settled in for me, okay?"

"Sure, Dad, no problem," I assure him.

"Enjoy this summer, Chase. You worked hard at Gradford, and I'm proud of you."

"Aww, thanks, Dad. I'm proud of you too!" I tease.

"Hey, at least someone is," he says with a wink and a smile. "I've got to run to the office, but I'll check in on you tomorrow. I love you, kid."

"Love you too, Dad," I say, waving as he clicks off the video. Sometimes, looking at him can feel a little weird, like I'm seeing myself in twenty years. We definitely look like father and son, except for his cropped hair and brown eyes.

My parents, Russell and Christine Wilmington, were high school sweethearts, and they strive to embody a close-knit family unit. We have game nights, annual vacations, and Sunday dinners. Showing up for one another comes naturally, so Dad asking me to help Mom and my sisters get settled really is unnecessary. It's something I'd do anyway.

I move back to my open suitcase and finish loading clothes into the dresser when my phone rings again. I don't recognize the number, and my heart skips a beat, remembering the bold message I left for the captivating waitress at the diner.

"This is Chase," I answer with a tentative edge to my voice.

"Hi! This is Claire Roberts, director at Camp Bender. Have you, by chance, made it into town yet?" she asks sheepishly.

"Oh, hi! Yeah, I got here a few hours ago."

"Good, good! I have a big ask... One of our certified camp counselors broke their wrist last week and won't make it to the first session of camp...doctor's orders."

"I hope they're okay," I reply, still wondering what the question is.

"They should be right as rain for the second session, but I

need a fill-in for the entire first session. Looking at the volunteer list we have for the summer, you meet the qualifications to become a certified counselor."

I take a beat, considering whether I want to dedicate an additional three weeks of my summer vacation to this. "What all would I need to do to become certified?" I ask.

"Well, since you already submitted your background check, you would just need to join our other counselors for first aid and CPR certification starting tomorrow at the youth center. Then on-site training up at Camp Bender next week. The kids for session one will show up the week after that, and then week two campers would be your last group. It will fly by." She speeds through her spiel like she's worried I'm about to turn her down.

"That sounds reasonable..."

"Oh, and you'd have weekends between camping groups all to yourself back in town."

My reasoning for signing up to volunteer this summer was to give back to the local community. Changing my status to *camp counselor* would come with a paycheck I don't need, defeating my sole purpose for volunteering in the first place. "I'd love to help you out, under one condition."

"Okay... I'll do what I can. What's your condition?"

"Would it be possible to donate my wages to a scholarship fund for campers who need it? Anonymously?" I pull at a loose thread on my jeans, feeling the unease about money talk creep into my gut.

"That's...very generous of you. Are you sure?"

"Absolutely. I was planning on volunteering anyway, so this feels like a good way to keep that spirit and give back."

"Oh, Chase, what a great idea. I can definitely do that, but you're sure you want to remain anonymous? We usually list donors on the camp website."

"Yeah, knowing a couple more kids will be able to experience camp is recognition enough."

"Well, if you're sure... Thank you so much! You're a lifesaver!"

She lets out a relieved breath as a keyboard clacks in the background. "I'll send you the counselor informational email. See you tomorrow!"

"No problem. See you tomorrow." I hang up the phone and toss it on the bed behind me.

"Already roped yourself into a philanthropic venture, huh?" Hunter shakes his head from the doorway. He pumps his arm into the air like a superhero. "Chase to the rescue!"

"It's called helping." I grab the leather toiletry bag out of my suitcase and toss it on the bed. Wherever we go for summer vacations, I like to find some kind of cause to help with. Giving back is fun for me, but I prefer to really get in there and experience things instead of relying on monetary donations. Hunter doesn't share the sentiment and likes to give me a hard time about *saving the world*. "The director for Camp Bender called and needed a last-minute camp counselor. It's for the kids, and we were going to volunteer anyway—so why not?"

"You're wasting half your summer working with annoying little kids. That's why not. You just graduated after busting your ass to get dual degrees. This is your last summer of freedom."

School wasn't hard for me, so I wouldn't call it *busting my ass*. But there were plenty of nights I wished I could have gone out and let loose instead of staying in to study. Enrolling in Gradford University's dual degree program seemed like the best solution to get where I wanted to be at EdTechU. But by the end, my motivation dragged, and the last few months were some of my hardest. I did it though, getting both a bachelor's degree in business management and a master's in information systems. This summer is supposed to be all about enjoyment and relaxation before diving into the corporate sphere. Serving others is something I enjoy.

"It's not a waste if I like doing it." I move back to the dresser with the last of my clothes.

Hunter's eyes widen. "Does this mean I have to go early too?"

"Nope." I close the top dresser drawer and zip up my suitcase. "Your volunteering schedule hasn't changed."

"I'm only doing it for that stupid service-learning credit Gradford makes us earn before graduation."

"Yeah, and if you wouldn't have put it off until your last year, you could've had your pick of organizations to volunteer with." I tuck my empty suitcase into the closet and lean against the wall next to him.

"Why do it now when I can do it later?" he jokes.

That's probably the biggest difference between us. Hunter's spontaneous, impulsive, flighty. Procrastination is his middle name, and school is not his friend. I plan, calculate, and scrutinize. I don't like leaving a lot of things to chance. If I can figure out a strategy beforehand, I almost always will, or persist until I find a solution.

"I guess this will give you a good chance to explore Fort Bender. Maybe hit up the puff-puff train while I'm busy at camp."

"I'll need a good puff-puff to make it through the summer in this boring-ass town. Why did my dad pick *this place?* Make it make sense, bruh."

"I don't know. It doesn't seem so bad to me." I shrug, remembering the pretty waitress at the diner. I think if I could spend a little more time around her this summer, it will be anything but boring.

CHAPTER FIVE
KAYLA

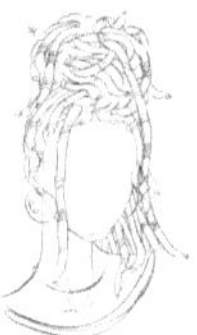

Pulling a double shift probably wasn't the smartest way to start off the summer. I'm worn out from talking to people, my feet ache, and I just want to fall into bed. My house is close enough to the diner that I usually walk. Today, it feels like I'm trudging through wet cement, each step heavier as I make my way up the sidewalk. To my surprise, Mom's car sits in the driveway. She should be at the hospital for her night shift.

"Mom? Is everything okay?"

"What?" she calls from the back of the house.

I hang up my bag by the door and slip off my shoes before trailing my hand across the back of the worn leather couch. My toes sink into the plush beige carpet as I head to her bedroom. Mismatched nursing scrubs hang out of an open suitcase, with toiletries scattered all over the bed. She's digging through the back of her closet, black curls piled high into a puff on her head.

"Mom"—I try again—"doesn't your shift start soon?"

"I start my summer caseload in the morning. Pretty sure I put it on the calendar…" she trails off distractedly.

She didn't. I check our shared calendar daily. I would have noticed this schedule change. It's not the first time she's forgotten, and I'm sure it won't be the last. But it's annoying enough for me to point it out today.

"Mmm, nope. Not in the calendar."

"Oops. Have you seen my green scrubs?"

"They're in the laundry room." I step out of her way as she leaves the room. "How long is your first contract?" My mom, Karla, is a nurse at Fort Bender Hospital. During the summer, she takes on travel nursing contracts.

"This first one is in Sacramento for four weeks, then I'm home for a week. I swapped shifts so we could get groceries before I left. Plus, I need some travel snacks." She grins, her glasses raising slightly on her rounded cheeks from the movement.

If my feet could do it on their own, they would run away. Grocery shopping is the last thing I want to do tonight, but I've barely seen Mom since I came home a week ago—and now, she'll be gone another month. My back cracks in several places as I straighten it out, urging the aches from the day to go away for a couple more hours.

I take my time getting ready, jumping in the shower to let the hot water loosen up the tension in my back and shoulders. The warmth from the stream might have made me even more tired. When I head back to my room, I slip on a SSU sweater with some black leggings. I resist the urge to fall into my bed and sleep until my early morning shift tomorrow, instead moving to the wooden desk in the corner of my room. I hope the sustained focus required for me to repaint my nails will help keep me awake.

When I enter the living room with my lotion, Mom has finished packing and is rustling around in the kitchen, making something that has my stomach rumbling. She's still wearing her navy-colored scrubs, and a few wispy curls frame her bronze face.

"Beef Stroganoff?" I ask, leaning over the pots on the stove. White cabinets swing open and closed as she gathers plates and cups.

"Yeah. I thought I'd go all fancy for our last dinner together. You didn't eat at the diner, did you?"

I shake my head, stomach growling as the steam from the savory sauce reaches my nose. By the end of my shift, I was ready to leave and put my feet up. The diner is like my second home, but sometimes a girl just wants her actual home.

"Tourist season has officially started. Anything interesting happen on your first day back?" she asks, sticking her head in the stainless-steel fridge.

My mind flashes to the business card in the tip jar, and I bite back a smile. I don't talk to Mom about this kind of thing, and I'm really not starting now. She's too nosy. If she gets even a whiff of any kind of gossip, she'll never stop asking me about it. "Nope." I shake my head. "It was busy, but nothing out of the ordinary."

"Well, the hospital was outrageous. Even with my short shift today, I could barely sit down to rest my feet before another emergency came in. Tourists come into town and lose their minds." She dishes up the food and hands it to me, plopping a fork on my plate as she nods for me to go sit at the table. "And let me tell you about Sarah and the new doctor!" While we eat, she fills me in on all the hottest happenings from behind the scenes at Fort Bender Hospital. I mostly pay attention, only tuning her out toward the end.

When we finally make it out the door, the first stars are appearing in the dusky sky. Music blasts through the speakers as soon as she turns on the car, and I race to turn down the '90s R&B blasting through the speakers. She likes her music loud, but with the headache creeping up the back of my neck, I don't need that shock to the system right now.

"Don't you touch my music, Kayla. This is my jam!" She shimmies her shoulders from side to side, singing loudly and off-key as she backs down the driveway. Any song that hit the charts before the year 2000 is her "jam," but I like this one and don't plan to argue. I giggle, shaking my head at her solo dance party as I dance along with her.

The grocery store parking lot is packed with cars from up and down the coast, making me brace myself for the crowd we're about to face inside. I scan the list saved on my phone while we head to the front doors, hoping to get in and out as fast as possible.

"I forget how crowded it gets on Memorial Day," Mom grumbles, sliding past a cart left in the middle of the cereal aisle. She hates the summer season as much, if not more, than I do. "Can you grab the bread, milk, and eggs? I'll meet you over there. Divide and conquer might be our best strategy for getting out of here alive," she says with a grimace.

"On it," I say, turning in the opposite direction. The checkout lines flow into the aisles, forcing me to sidestep distracted families and confused retirees every couple of seconds. "This is ridiculous," I mumble under my breath, wishing I would have gotten groceries earlier in the week.

Milk and eggs secured, I maneuver to the bakery. By some small miracle, the bread aisle is vacant. I take a centering breath, enjoying the quiet before locating the bread I like. The farther I walk down the aisle, the emptier the shelves become. It would be just my luck if this basic grocery necessity is sold out for the one week I actually need to pack a lunch.

I lean my head back to grumble at the empty shelf when I spot one solitary loaf at the top, pushed to the very back. Tipping on my toes, I stretch to reach the bag with one hand and fall short. Sliding the milk and eggs on an empty shelf, I hop and attempt to grab the bread again. I'm tall, but not tall enough to reach, and my jumping shakes the entire rack. A crash and a chorus of voices respond in surprise as something falls off the shelf in the next aisle.

"Sorry!" I call with a grimace. Hands on my hips, I stare at the bread loaf in defeat. This isn't a big deal, but I'm grumpy and tired and it *feels* like a big deal.

"Everything okay?" Mom asks, coming down the aisle with the shopping cart. "You exploded a jar of pickles over there."

"Perfect." I grit the front of my teeth to try and grind out some of the frustration I'm feeling. "Everything is great. I'm tired, my feet hurt, and the bread I need for my lunches this week is stuck up there," I whine. Mom looks between me and the bread briefly before her eyes slip past me and widen. "What's wrong?"

"Here you go," a voice says from behind me. I turn and a tall Black man hands me the loaf. "That must be some special bread. You narrowly missed me with those pickles over there." He gestures to the next aisle with a bright smile stretching across his deep umber face.

"Sorry about the pickles," I say, offering a forced smile. "And thanks for the bread..." I take a step back toward Mom, whose head is down now, shaking from side to side as she rummages through her purse.

The man looks between us both and smiles again. "Not a problem. Someone's over there cleaning it up now. Have a good evening." He turns back the way he came and disappears around the corner.

"You good?" I ask Mom.

"Umm, yeah. I think I left my phone in the car, and I'm on call until eleven tonight. Take my card and check out. I'll meet you outside." Her words are rushed, and she's seemingly out of breath as she swiftly walks toward the doors.

"...Okay. See you in a few hours," I say to myself in a sarcastic tone, remembering the checkout lines from earlier. I make it through quicker than I thought I would, and before I know it, I'm knocking on the trunk of the car.

When I get in the passenger seat, a new '90s R&B song plays through the speakers. This one I've heard plenty of times before, crooning through the walls at night after she's had a glass or two of wine. Mom sways side to side, looking up at the moon through the windshield. She hums along this time, and as I reach for the volume knob to turn it down a few notches, she shoots a glare sideways. "Let me guess," I say. "This is your jam too..."

CHAPTER SIX

CHASE

It's early when I pull up to Patti's Place for coffee—hopeful *Patty* with a *Y* is working again this morning. The calming breath I take while walking through the nearly empty parking lot clears my head as I mentally prepare to see her again. If I want to make an impression, I can't afford another speechless encounter like the one at lunch yesterday.

"I'll be with you in a minute," Patty calls over her shoulder, keeping her eyes on whatever task she's working on in the kitchen.

I slip into a seat at the counter and wait, watching her prep another pot of coffee. Her hair is pulled up in the front, flowing down her shoulders in the back. My heart beats a tick faster at the thought of seeing her face again. She turns to greet me, and my breath hitches in my throat.

"What can I...?" She pauses, halting her steps. "Oh, hey, *Gatherer.* Didn't expect you back so soon."

"Chase," I say. I think she's messing with me, but the polite grin on her face betrays nothing.

She nods, trying to hide a smirk. "Oh, I remember."

"Yeah... I was sent to pick up some coffee. The grocery store was fresh out."

"I saw that last night on my search for bread. That place was packed. What can I get for you?"

I list the order sent to my phone and settle back into the stool. "I also wanted to apologize."

"Apologize? For what?" she asks, back turned again as she prepares the drinks.

"For yesterday. I'm not usually that reserved…"

"I figured." She faces me, and my eyes follow the path of her hand as she puts it on her hip. "Quiet guys don't leave me their number in a tip jar." Arching her eyebrow, she presses her tongue against the inside of her cheek, an adorable attempt to keep from smiling. I can tell she wants to, so I lay it on thick.

"Would you believe me if I said it was low blood sugar?" I ask.

"Are you diabetic?"

"No."

"Hypoglycemic?"

I shake my head, smiling. "Nope."

"Then nope." She grins back politely and places the four small to-go cups in a drink carrier before sliding it over to me. "That'll be $10.25."

I slide my card to her and our fingers brush as she picks it up, leaving tingles where we touch. Her skin is so damn soft, and I notice the new color on her nails—a bold sky blue, my favorite. When she returns, she holds my card out to me, and I keep her gaze. Her hand hangs in the air with the plastic between her fingers, her eyebrows dipping like she's trying to figure out why I won't take back my card. But I have her attention, and that's all I want right now.

"What I wrote on that business card yesterday…" I say.

"What about it?"

I bite the inside of my lip with a sigh and nod. "You managed to do it again."

She takes a deep breath and looks away, eyes wide.

Mission accomplished.

Slipping the card out of her fingers, I wink as I say, "See you around, *Patty.*" I chuckle at her reaction and stroll out the door, coffee in hand. This diner is about to become my new favorite restaurant.

THE RECEPTIONIST CHATTERS AWAY ON THE PHONE when I arrive at the front desk of the youth center. She holds a finger up to me before typing furiously at the keyboard in front of her. I smile and nod, recognizing the signal for what it is, and take in the large ocean mural on the wall behind her while I wait. The painting shows a panoramic view of Fort Bender's landscape, rendering the ocean bluffs on the edge of the city, the shops downtown, and ending with the dense redwood forest on the other side.

The young woman greets me as she hangs up and points me down a long hallway to my left, opposite the squeaking noise of sneakers on vinyl coming from the gym. The shrill ringing of the phone next to her sets her in motion again, and I thank her as I turn to walk down the hall. When I stop at the doorway marked Conference, there's only one person in the bright white recreation room—a small blond woman in cargo pants and a Bender Youth Center T-shirt, sorting through first aid materials.

"Claire?" I ask cautiously.

"Yes, that's me," she says, looking in my direction.

"I'm Chase. It's nice to meet you."

"Chase! Oh! Let me thank you again, in person, for helping us out last minute." She steps closer and lowers her voice as she leans in, saying, "Since no one is here yet, I want to tell you that we were able to offer two campers a spot with your generous donation."

"I'm glad I could help," I say, flashing her a smile before looking around the room. I don't want to be rude, but I really don't want to put more attention on the money either.

A picture window taking up half of the wall frames Fort Bender's beautiful landscape, showcasing the town in a way that is almost identical to the mural out front. The only difference is the wind adding an animated effect to the swaying trees and crashing tide. The view is even more amazing on this hill.

"Everyone else should start filing in soon, and we'll get started," Claire says as she digs into her supplies.

I turn back toward the smooth glass, walking closer to see the breathtaking view. Moody ocean waves lapping at the cliff's edge whisper millions of years' worth of wisdom toward the thousand-year-old redwoods. Paired with the gloomy sky, it all makes for an ethereal view. I really could get used to this place.

"I forget how different Bender looks from up here," an energetic voice says next to me. "You can barely see Main Street. Hi! I'm Ashlie."

"Chase." I stick out my hand, and she shakes it. "Nice to meet you."

"Wow, your eyes are *really* blue," she gasps, gripping tighter as she steps in close and peers into my face. "Like, deep, dark blue... Sorry." She smiles apologetically as I lean back in surprise. "I forget about the personal bubble sometimes."

With a chuckle, I respond, "No worries. I could sit down if that makes it easier to see them..."

"Is that a short joke, Chase?"

I pinch my fingers together. "A little bit," I tease again.

She wheezes a laugh and bumps my arm with her shoulder. "You're lucky you're cute," she says. "And funny. Where are you from?"

"I grew up in LA, but I just finished school down at Gradford."

"Ooh, private school. You're *fancy*-fancy! I'm from here, but I go to ULA."

"Born and raised?" I ask, wondering if she knows the mystery waitress at Patti's Place. A couple more people have filtered in, and they sit in the chairs set up in the middle of the room.

"Nope, we moved from Vegas when I started middle school—"

"Let's get started with some housekeeping items," Claire calls from across the room, closing the double doors to separate us from the noise down the hall. "Kayla's on the way with lunch, and then we'll do icebreakers and begin first aid certification." She stands in the middle of the semicircle of chairs as we all gather, reading from an itinerary on her clipboard. "Tomorrow, we'll do CPR, Thursday is both survival skills and mindfulness day, and Friday we'll head to the art museum."

I take a chair on the end, and Ashlie sits down next to me. "Since you're from here, have you worked at this camp before?" I ask.

"Ew. No. I'm not a camper. The whole bug thing just…ew." She shivers, sticking out her tongue. "I'm not even working for Camp Bender. I needed to renew my 'certs' for the museum, and this was the only training in town. After tomorrow, I'm all done."

"Oh, nice. Which museum? My buddy and I are looking for things to do here."

"The one on Main. The Visitor's Center and Museum, across from Patti's Place—"

The slow creaking of the heavy metal door as it eases open across the room turns our attention. "*Ugh*, this stupid cart!" The door closes and creeps open again, the person on the other side clearly struggling. I make my way over and hold it open, standing behind it to hopefully help with the process. "The wheel is stuck. Hang on…" the voice says in an exasperated tone.

I peer around the door and freeze as the familiar scent of vanilla washes over me. Her back is turned, but I recognize the locs flowing down around her shoulders.

"Patty?" I ask, smiling wide.

She turns slowly, brows creased in the middle. "What are you doing here?"

"I'm one of the camp counselors," I explain, moving back to make way for the cart.

"No..." Shaking her head, she glances over her shoulder at the group. She moves the cart over the threshold, toward the long tables on the wall, and expertly arranges disposable plates and utensils around the table. "Where's Seth?" she asks, looking between the group and me, aluminum pan in hand.

"Hey, Kayla!" Claire bounces toward us. "Seth broke his wrist while backpacking in Iceland. Chase here so graciously stepped in last minute." Changing gears, she looks toward the lunch spread out on the tables. "This food looks amazing! Dig in, guys!" Claire calls to the group.

"Kayla, eh?" A sly grin settles on my face.

She scrubs her hand over the frustration on her face and sighs. "Yes, Kayla. My name is Kayla. Surprise..." She makes a less than enthusiastic *ta-da* gesture with her arms. "Why are you looking at me like that?"

"Like what?"

"Like the cat that ate the canary."

"This is just how I look." I shrug. My smile grows as I'm struck by how well her name suits her. Those piercing green eyes, the warm scent of spiced vanilla, and something else I can't place, with one stray loc falling against her cheek. *Kayla*. I like it, and my fingers twitch just thinking of brushing that hair from her face.

"Hey, girl!" Ashlie sidles up to us.

"How do you know Kayla?" I ask.

"Uh, she's my best friend." She throws a sassy hand on her hip. "How do *you* know Kayla?"

Kayla groans while watching the exchange. As she brings her hands together, I notice she scrapes at one thumb nail with the other.

"We met yesterday at the diner," I confess, smiling at both of them.

"*Wait!*" Ashlie gasps dramatically. "This is 'Tip Jar Guy,' isn't it? Shaggy hair, tall, blue eyes a mile deep..."

With a grimace on her face, Kayla rubs the furrow between her eyebrows. I don't know if she's flustered or irritated or both, but either way, this is entertaining. She shoots a threatening glare at Ashlie, who's none the wiser as she grabs a plate.

"A mile, huh? That's pretty deep, for eyes." I turn my attention back to the enchanting green ones. "You told your friend about me?" Raising my eyebrows, canary-eating grin plastered on my face, I wait for her answer.

"I didn't tell her about *you*. I don't even know you. I just told her about a thing that happened at work."

"And the thing was me...?" my voice trails as I waggle my eyebrows playfully. That earns an eye roll from her. Oh, she's definitely flustered, and I have to admit, it's fun watching her squirm. She gets cuter the more ruffled she is, like she isn't used to being put on the spot like this. "Well, *Kayla*, I guess today really is my lucky day." I wink, and she heaves a long sigh, pursing her lips before turning back to the lunch spread.

We've just finished eating when Claire leads us through a few icebreakers. Claire, Kayla, and a man-bun-wearing guy named Samson have worked at Camp Bender before, while Sami, her twin brother Kyle, and I are new this year. Ashlie, of course, is just here for certification.

"The goal this summer is for the campers to create lasting memories and bond with each other," Claire says. "There's no better way for us to encourage that than to do the same things ourselves. During training, this week and next, I encourage all of you to get to know each other, make friends, and create bonds. We want the campers to feel like we're all one big happy family. Let's go around the circle and share two interesting facts about yourself."

Since I'm sitting on an end chair, everyone turns toward me, waiting for me to start. I stand, giving a little wave. "I'm Chase, I work in tech, and I've been told I have blue eyes a mile deep." Ashlie snorts next to me, and I get a peek at Kayla. She's two chairs over, shaking her head and biting her cheeks to keep from laughing.

"I'm Ashlie, I work at the museum, and I think all y'all are weirdos for camping out in the woods for weeks on end." That earns a laugh from the group before all eyes turn to Kayla. A smile spreads across my face as I watch, waiting to learn anything about her.

"I'm Kayla, I was born and raised here, and I work at Patti's Place."

Damn. Nothing new. Everyone else turns their attention to the next in line, but my eyes linger on Kayla. She fiddles with her thumb while Samson introduces himself, and must feel my eyes on her because she looks my way. Just as quickly, she slides her eyes back down to her thumb. My mind is stuck on this mystery girl who appears to be a completely closed book. The more I encounter her, the more I want to read the first page. I'll even settle for the blurb on the back cover if she'll let me.

CHAPTER SEVEN
KAYLA

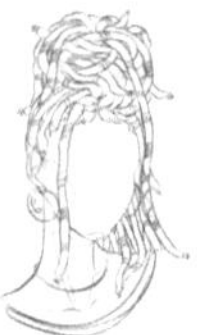

I walk into the conference room early at the youth center and almost walk right back out. The room is empty except for Chase, leaning back in a chair with his outstretched legs crossed at the ankles. He laughs at something on his phone, and I dig my fingernails into my palm to keep my thoughts from drifting toward how good he looks with that light blue polo stretched across his shoulders. It's only Thursday, but he is everywhere, all the time, making it hard for me to forget he exists. He has infiltrated the diner, camp training, and even the gas station. Bender's a small town, but I never realized how small until now. Sure, he's cute and funny, and probably *would* be my type if I had time for any of that. But I *don't* have time, and won't have time, which makes the intensity in his eyes whenever he looks at me that much more annoying.

I'm about to step backward through the doorway when he sees me. "Oh, hey, *Kayla*." He smirks, sitting up in his chair. Even the way he says my name is intense. "No Ashlie today?"

"Nope, she's back to work at the museum." I'm trying to think of some excuse to leave, but my brain has decided to quit on me—and betray me, apparently, seeing as it's telling my feet to move closer to Chase and farther from the hallway.

"That's right, she did mention something about that. I guess it's just you and me then..." He looks right in my eyes during the last part and smiles, and my stupid knees wobble.

In my distraction, my toe catches on the carpet in front of his chair. I lurch forward and reach out to catch myself just as he stands up to catch me. His hands wrap around my upper arms as I land against him, my palms flat on his chest.

We freeze.

Slowly, his thumbs stroke my upper arms, and I know he can feel my goosebumps rising. He smells good—woodsy and fresh—and the impulse I had to run in the opposite direction has flipped, urging me to lean in closer to him.

"You okay?" he asks, smiling down at me. I manage to nod, looking down and dropping my hands from his chest. With his thumbs still caressing my arms, I mistakenly glance into his eyes again, and I'm trapped. I can't look away, and he's already proven he won't look away first. He licks his bottom lip, smiles wider, and asks, "You already falling for me?"

And that little bit of charm is all it takes for me to snap out of the trance I stumbled into, allowing me to take a step away. I laugh, attempting to shake the nerves from my body by shaking my head. "Not yet," I say before thinking. My mouth falls open, and he chuckles.

"Not yet, huh? So there's a chance..." He tips his head, a glint of amusement flickering in his eyes.

"I meant, not likely. Not ever."

"But you *said,* 'not yet,' which means—"

"Hey, guys!" Claire calls from across the room. I've never been so happy to see the camp director in my life. I drop my bag on a seat, leaving an empty chair between me and Chase, and scurry over to talk to Claire.

"Need any help?" I ask, almost jumping with enthusiasm. I glance over my shoulder, and by some small miracle, Chase has stayed put. Sami and Kyle, the twins, stroll in as Claire places a stack of notebooks in one of my arms and a bag of pens in my hand to pass out to the group.

By the time I make it back to the seats, Sami has posted up next to Chase, talking a mile a minute. Her long black ponytail sways back and forth down her back as her short legs swing under her chair. Emphasizing whatever she's talking about, her hands swirl in the air while Chase smiles and nods. Sami's a cheerleader at Oregon Central and has the energy to prove it. She's friendly, charismatic, and I don't think she has a mean bone in her body. Kyle sits on the opposite end of the semicircle, thumbs plucking away on his phone. They have the same face but couldn't be more different. He's tall with a buzz cut, and a lot gruffer than his sister—sarcastic and stoic.

"Hey, Kyle!" I hand him a notebook and pen. He looks up from his phone, tips his chin in greeting, and tucks the notebook on his lap without a word.

Samson slides into a seat next to Kyle, yawning while he ties his dark brown hair in a messy knot on the top of his head. He's been a counselor for Camp Bender a little longer than I have, starting a few years before me when he was right out of high school. I've never seen him any other way than he is right now, always rolling in at the last possible second and yawning his way through the day.

"Thanks," Samson mumbles as I pass his book over to him. He crosses his ankle over his knee and leans his head back against the chair, using the notebook to cover his face.

Circling around to Sami and Chase, I drop a notebook and pen next to my purse before turning to them.

"Oh no, were you sitting here?" Sami gasps.

"Nope, you're just fine right there." I smile big, encouraging her to settle into the chair separating me from Mr. Charm. While handing over her writing supplies, I notice Chase nodding his head from the corner of my eye. When I look up to give him his notebook, he's already looking back at me. His pointer finger rests over his upper lip, nodding still, like he's impressed with my ability to curve him. I've won this round, and we both know it.

CHAPTER EIGHT

CHASE

I pull into the youth center, parking next to the large white eight-passenger van waiting out front. We're headed to the museum today for ideas on incorporating the history of Fort Bender into our arts and crafts at camp. I'm early, as usual, but since the hazy sun is making a rare appearance in the morning sky, I wait outside on the hood of my car.

Kayla usually shows up early, too, and what I wouldn't give to have a couple of minutes alone with her, just to try and chip away at some of those walls she has up. She's stunning, sure, and that's what first caught my eye at the diner, but something else keeps me drawn to her. With her gentle confidence and the unbothered way she navigates the space around her, I'm not even sure she knows how captivating she is. I've spent all week frequenting the diner and trying small talk during training, and all I've managed to get is a few fleeting moments and seeing how she interacts with everyone else. It's just enough information to keep me wanting more.

"Hey, Chase." Claire waves, grasping a clipboard to her small frame as she walks toward the van. I turn a smile her way, walking the short distance from the hood of my crossover to meet her near the van's sliding door.

"Hey! Do you need help loading anything?" I ask, looking into the van to see if she's already loaded it. "You mentioned sack lunches yesterday."

"Nope, we're just waiting for everyone else. Kayla offered to make the sack lunches at Patti's, so she'll meet us at the museum and bring those over at lunchtime."

Damn. Another lost opportunity. Since she won't be meeting us here, I go for the easy alternative—asking her boss about her. "You've known Kayla for a while, right?"

"Oh, yeah. I was one of her camp counselors when she attended Camp Bender. She's so funny! And a patient teacher. When I became director, I knew she'd make an awesome counselor herself. Kayla's great!"

"Yeah, she seems like it..." I nod casually, even though I'm busting to ask more. Sami and Kyle pull up, silencing any other questions I could have asked. I climb into the back of the van and wait for the rest to file in.

Sami slides in next to me, ready with an entertaining story about how the rental she and Kyle are staying in lost power last night. She's talking fast, and I nod, trying to keep up. She's nice and all, and I don't want to make her feel bad. But, man, can she talk.

Samson finally clambers into the van, yawning like he just woke up. He says hello, tips his head back on his seat, and laces his hands over his lap. I'm pretty sure he's out by the time we reach the end of the parking lot.

The museum looks like a two-story lodge, with a dark green roof framing the honey-colored wood siding. The entire front of the building is made of glass windows, tinted dark to keep the sun from shining in too brightly. It's like we're about to go inside some kind of rustic bed-and-breakfast. Walking around to the front, a large wooden sign welcomes us to Fort Bender Visitor's Center and Museum. Sami has turned her motormouth to Samson, and I take the opportunity to walk ahead and hold the door open for everyone. Claire is the last one through, and when I step in behind her, my eyes take a few seconds to adjust from the brightness outside.

Looking around the main floor from the entryway, I wonder if they really did make this place out of a lodge. The split-level interior includes a wide-open main floor with a long hallway of rooms upstairs. Folded maps you'd expect to see in a visitor's center line the wall immediately to my left with display cases against the surrounding walls. Behind the information desk, the main floor opens to a large exhibit showcasing the wonder of redwood trees.

My eyes finish their sweep of the room and land at the front desk where everyone is gathering. Kayla leans against it, hand under her chin, talking and laughing with Ashlie. She's wearing her standard Patti's Place uniform, minus the apron, and it's the first I've seen her look so relaxed. Her genuine smile—not the polite grin she gives to me, but *that one*—nearly knocks the wind out of me. It's not even directed my way, and I'm hooked. I'm making it my new mission this summer to get her to smile at me that way.

"Alright, everyone," Claire calls. "Sign the visitor's log, and then you're free to explore the museum. We'll meet for lunch on the patio at noon."

I step in line behind everyone, waiting for my turn to write in the log. When I get up to the desk, a large group of retirees enter through the door behind me.

"Hey, Chase!" Ashlie greets me with a smile, her curls dancing in the ponytail piled on the top of her head. Kayla looks at me, flashes the polite smile, and heads across the room to the stairs.

"Hey!" I respond. "So tell me about this place. Where should I start first?"

"Sure thing. Do you want the whole spiel or the abbreviated version?"

"Whatever you have time for." I shrug. She goes into the history of the building, confirming my suspicions about it being a former lodge. They gutted and remodeled the inside ten years ago, but the town voted to keep the exterior the same to match the historical accuracy of the other buildings downtown.

"The main floor is all about the history of Fort Bender, and everything upstairs is local art." She leans in close with a knowing smirk on her face. "I'm pretty sure Kayla went upstairs..."

I smile back and glance toward the staircase. A touch on my arm brings me back. "Hey, Chase..." she says quietly.

"Yeah?" My eyes snap back to hers, wondering about the sudden change in her tone.

"Just...keep trying," Ashlie says. I tilt my head, trying to decipher what she means. She continues, "I've seen the way you look at her. My best friend doesn't open up easily, but she's worth it. Just keep trying."

"Oh, I plan on it." I glance back toward the stairs. The group of retirees looks to be growing restless behind me, so I wave at Ashlie before making my way to the second floor.

I weave in and out of rooms filled with taxidermy, sea fossils, and local plants before I find Kayla. She's standing in front of a large black and white portrait of an older woman whose short curly hair forms neatly around the deep wrinkles in her face. It looks like the entire exhibit is pottery and sculptures by this woman—Pearle Harris. I watch as Kayla stares at the portrait for several minutes before she moves on to look at some of the pottery.

"So you're into ceramics..." I say from behind her.

Kayla jumps, whipping her head around. "Oh, God! Do you sneak up on everyone like that?" She holds her hands to her chest, taking a deep breath to regulate herself. The rose gold ring on her thumb glints under the track lighting overhead as she lowers her hand.

"Sorry." I chuckle as I walk across the small room to stand next to her. "So...ceramics?" I try again.

Kayla glances at the door behind me, trying, I assume, to plot an escape. She's good at that, finding ways to avoid me. But instead of leaving, she sighs and squints at me. "Yeah, I guess you could say I like ceramics." She turns back to the exhibit and walks slowly from the wall of pottery to the tall displays showcasing sculptures. I follow along next to her, focusing my attention on the intricate formations of clay.

"Like...you *make* ceramics?" I ask, trying to get her to engage with me.

"No." She snorts. "I'm not any good at sculpting. I'm strictly an admirer." A soft smile lands on her face, and she glances back at the portrait on the wall.

Behind us, a small group of retirees pile into the room, talking loudly as they fill the space. An overzealous couple sweeps in near us to peer at a sculpture, and my hand instinctively presses to the small of Kayla's back as we step closer. She goes rigid, and our eyes lock, both of us holding our breath at the intimacy. I didn't mean to do it, but when the couple moves on to the next display, I have a hard time moving my hand away. Just the act of this innocent touch sends an electric jolt through me that makes me want to savor it.

"Hey, you two," Claire walks toward us quickly. Kayla clears her throat and steps sideways, looking down into the display case in front of her, making my hand fall limply to my side. "I knew I'd find you in here, Kayla. Has she told you all about this exhibit yet?"

"Um, no." I turn to Kayla, raising my eyebrows expectantly. She grimaces as she taps her fingers on the glass display case.

"Of course not. Really, Kayla, you're so modest," Claire says before turning back toward me. "This was all made by her grandma. Kayla's basically Bender royalty."

"My great-grandma, actually..." Kayla says quietly. A wistful look falls over her face as she looks at the portrait again.

"Oh, that's right. Anyway, she could probably tell you all about Pearle's sculpting process. I have to go check on the other counselors. Enjoy!" Claire swirls on her heel and bounces out of the room, her long braid swinging behind her.

"Well, *your highness,* were you going to tell me you were famous?" I tease.

She rolls her eyes and wrinkles her nose. "I'm not famous..." Shaking her head, she crosses her arms over her chest. "Or Bender royalty, whatever that means."

"Local celebrity is still celebrity," I say, smirking. "So tell me about Pearle's process. What put her on the map?"

Kayla looks at me for several seconds, pressing her tongue against the inside of her bottom lip as she decides whether she's going to take the bait. Finally, she drops her hands and moves back toward the vases. "Okay, look up here at these." She points to a collection of simple, unglazed ceramic vessels, ranging in color from light gray to a rich rusted red with intricate designs carved into the earthenware. "These are her earlier pieces—simple and delicate. Compare them to these over here," she says, moving around me and a few stragglers to the wall behind us. The stoneware on the display shelves is much more colorful. Shiny blues, greens, and whites swirl through the vases and platters, reminiscent of the waves crashing into the ocean bluffs outside.

"Wow, it looks like the ocean."

"Exactly. She ground up the sea glass from Crystal Beach to get the colors, and heating up the glass during the firing process would melt it down. That's where the pooling and swirls of colors come from." A faint smile teases her lips as she looks back at the pieces, seemingly lost in a memory while she fiddles with the rose gold band on her thumb.

"Did you spend a lot of time with her?" I ask softly, not wanting to disrupt the nostalgic expression on her face.

Kayla nods, looking down at her hands. "She helped raise me. I used to collect the glass for her when she couldn't make it down to the beach anymore. She tried to show me how to do it all, but I was too young to be any good. And I..." Her voice trails as she looks back at the portrait.

I wait, hoping she'll continue. This glimpse of vulnerability, the first I'm learning anything about her besides the bare basics, leaves me intrigued with this mystery girl. I sense pushing will only make it harder to get to know her, and I *definitely* want to get to know her. So I wait.

She takes another look at me, and her eyes have shifted back to the cool mask she wears. "I should go grab the lunches from Patti's," she says.

"Do you need any help?"

"No...no. I'm good." She moves around me and walks right out the door. As frustrated as I feel that she ran again, I can be patient with this. With her. I think I'll have to be if I want to make any kind of progress.

CHAPTER NINE

KAYLA

After a full week of camp training and a weekend of diner shifts, it's nice to get into the woods. It's still work, but being out in nature makes the job a little more peaceful. I pull through the Camp Bender entrance gate and follow the winding dirt road to the cabins. The tinge of nostalgia I feel from my days as a camper makes me smile as I park. A large activity building sits front and center, wooden logs stained dark, giving it the perfect summer camp aesthetic. The boys' and girls' cabins flank either side of the main hall, set back farther into the redwood forest and stained the same dark hue.

I step from behind the wheel, breathing in the relief of the fresh mountain air before grabbing my bags from the trunk of my silver sedan. When I walk into the mess hall, Claire is standing on a table, trying to hook an oversized Welcome banner on the wall.

"Need any help?" I grab the other side to keep it from sweeping the ground and hold it steady until she sidesteps across the table to grab my end.

"Actually, yes. You know how finicky the copier is in the office upstairs? Can you make copies of this week's training itinerary, please?"

"On it!" I turn and walk right into Chase.

"Hey there," he says playfully, steadying me with a hand on my shoulder. "We missed you at the diner this morning."

"Oh yeah?" I shrug, acting like bumping into him didn't just send my stomach belly flopping into my toes. "It must not be your lucky day then..." I don't wait for a response before heading upstairs to the office.

Chase and Hunter have come into the diner at least once a day for the last week for coffee, meals, dessert, directions, you name it. They sit at the counter, taking their sweet time eating, finding ways to get me to engage.

"Hey, Kayla, what's better: books or phones?"

"Hey, Kayla, who would win in a fight: a bear or a shark?"

"Hey, Kayla... Kayla... Kayla."

It's juvenile and irritating, and sometimes a little hilarious. Patti thinks they're a hoot and eggs them on. Ashlie will join in if they happen to be there for lunch—turning into a trio of laughing distractions. Before they leave, Hunter always heads to the car while Chase hangs back to try and work his charm. And charming he is, but I'm immune. *Mostly*. He usually asks some form of, "Do you have any free time?"

And I consistently disappoint him with my standard response of, "I'm working." It doesn't stop him from trying though.

The copier jams for the umpteenth time, and I give it a swift kick in the side. It spits out the rest of my copies, and I take a few extra minutes to crisscross the papers for easier sorting. I took the initiative of printing out the schedules for next week, too, so the stack of papers has grown larger than I anticipated. Carefully shifting the massive pile over my forearm, I reach for the stapler with my free hand before leaving the copy room.

Almost everyone else has arrived. The twins sit at the windowsill, having a thumb war, while Claire briefs Willie, the kitchen manager, on the dietary restrictions of the incoming campers. Then there's Chase, holding a broom while he chats with Bo, the groundskeeper. Chase says something that makes

Bo's head fall back with laughter as he sits in a chair and rubs his knee.

The papers in my hand shift, dangerously close to falling on the floor, so I slam the heavy stack down on the end of a long cafeteria-style table. I may have been a little too ambitious with this project, but I'll adjust. If needed, I can work during lunch and finish up while Claire gives the opening remarks for the day.

I move pages across the wood grain tabletop and organize the piles for stapling. Samson strolls through the door, looking like he just rolled out of bed with his messy hair and puffy face. He sits on the opposite end of the table right as Claire calls out a five-minute lunch warning.

"Hanging up your counselor hat already?" I gesture at the broom as Chase slides in next to me.

"And miss my chance at spending a week with you? Never." He winks with a smirky grin on his face. My cheeks light on fire, and I suddenly notice how close he is. If I take too deep of a breath, we'll touch shoulders. I clear my throat, hoping to settle the fog in my head, and focus on stapling the schedules in front of me. He continues, "No, I saw my buddy Bo limping around and asked if I could help him out. Turns out, he fell last week chasing his cat. I told him to direct me to the mess and take a load off."

"Your buddy?" I swear this guy knows everyone. Even at the diner, he greets the regulars like he's been coming there for years. In a week, he's made friends in all my spaces.

"Well, he is now." He smiles at me. Before I can stop myself, I look into those dark blue eyes. He takes a deep breath, our shoulders sharing the lightest touch, and my heart threatens to catapult right onto the table. "Need any help?" he asks, looking over the piles I'm working with.

"Nope. I have a system."

"I'm pretty good with systems..." he tries again. The persistence this guy exhibits would be impressive if it was directed at anything besides me. *Why does he insist on trying to help me with simple things I can handle on my own?* I don't really have a system beyond *pick up papers, staple papers, stack papers*...but accepting his help feels like I'm letting him win some unspoken challenge between us.

"I'm good," I say, shaking my head. As a hint for him to leave, I try to act like I'm distracted. He doesn't leave though, taking another deep breath instead, and it takes a hell of a lot more concentration to keep my mind focused on this easy task of stapling papers instead of the brushing of our shoulders.

AFTER LUNCH, CLAIRE GATHERS US OUTSIDE AT THE ropes course. The sounds of the forest sing around us as we stand at the base of a large redwood. A platform and stairs have been built up the side of the tree, anchored next to a climbing wall. One side has handholds and footholds for climbing, and the other side has flat, wooden slats to rappel down.

"There are two things we want our campers to remember about the rules. Stay with your buddy, and don't go higher than you're comfortable with. Pair up and let's get started with rappelling."

As I look around the circle of counselors, my eyes lock on Chase's across from me. I don't mean to look at him. I've spent a week trying not to notice him, and yet, here we are, our eyes bolted together. Just when I think he's about to walk over, Sami sidles up to him.

"Wanna be partners?" she asks, smacking her gum and bouncing on the balls of her feet.

"Sure." He smiles, turning toward her. An unexpected wave of disappointment hits me, and I shoot my eyes down to my scuffed hiking boots to try and hide it. It doesn't matter. It *shouldn't* matter. This is for the best. The pang of unwarranted jealousy as I watch him pair up with Sami should be enough of a warning to my system that I need to refocus. *Sami's doing me a favor. I don't need to be getting any closer to Chase this summer anyway.*

I turn my back to them and pair up with Samson, trying to ignore that pesky feeling in the pit of my stomach. We do rock paper scissors to see who's going first, and he scrunches his face in defeat when he loses. Sending a big smile his way, I grab a helmet and climb the ladder to the top of the platform.

Claire is up here with Kyle, handing out gloves and showing him how to secure our ropes. I've done this every summer since I was a camper, so I take a minute to enjoy the view and listen to the birds chirping in the trees. When Claire finishes her instructions, I double-check my ropes and peek over the edge, spotting a messy head of blond waves. Chase was already heading down the wall when I reached the platform, so I shouldn't have another run-in with him until I'm down on the ground.

"Rappelling!" I yell down to Samson on the ground.

"Rappel on," he answers, letting me know he's ready to spot me. I test my feet on the edge of the wooden platform while standing backward. Crouching down low, I move to a sitting position with my break hand gripping the ropes tightly. I take a deep breath and ease my way down slowly.

Making it a little over halfway, I look down and see eyes on me. To my left is Chase, sitting comfortably in his ropes like he isn't hanging from the side of a wall. Lowering myself a little more, I stop when we're almost eye level. *This better not be a ploy to get me alone.*

"Fancy meeting you here," he jokes.

I tip my head to the side, wondering why he isn't moving. "Everything okay?"

He gestures to his feet, and that's when I see his shoelace wedged in between two of the wooden planks, making his left leg cross over the right. "Think you could help me out?" He smiles sheepishly.

"How did this even happen?"

"I think I bobbed when I should have weaved, and my partner

isn't really the guiding type." He tips his head down to Sami on the ground, who's turned toward Samson, talking with her hands. "My shoe slipped, and the next thing I know, I'm sitting pretty," he explains with a shrug.

"Everything okay down there?" Claire asks, peering over the edge.

"Just a little stuck, but I think I got it," I call back. Moving sideways slowly, I place my feet next to his, reaching to pull on the shoelace with one hand while clinging onto the rope with my braking hand. The lace doesn't budge. I try again, yanking harder, and almost lose my balance.

Taking a minute to think, I reposition my feet and scrunch up my face, looking at his shoe. I need to get some leverage, but there isn't enough space for him to shift to the left without releasing his ropes. And I can't use both of my hands without releasing mine. "I think I need to sit in your lap," I say seriously, completely missing the blaring double entendre. His eyebrows shoot up suddenly, and color fills his cheeks as I try to explain. "I didn't mean... I just can't get a good grip unless I—"

"Sit in my lap..." he finishes with a smirk. "Got it. I never thought you'd ask. Be my guest."

Rolling my eyes, I release my rope a little more until I'm level with him. Slowly stepping side to side, I maneuver around his twisted lower half until my legs straddle the stuck shoe. His left arm encloses mine, and I have to choke down more butterflies. "You'll need to hold my rope and yours at the same time," I warn. He nods, brushing my gloved hand to grab the rope in my lap. Even with clunky gloves on, the flutters inside me abound. I look over my shoulder. "I'm serious, Chase. If you let go, we're going to—"

"I got you," he whispers. His warm breath fans over my ear, leaving goosebumps trailing down my arms. The scent of sandalwood and something earthy wraps around me as his arm settles on my hip. I take a deep breath to try and release the excitement rumbling around in my belly. Bracing myself against him, I lean forward to grip his shoe and feel shifting underneath me.

"Really, Chase?" I say under my breath as I try to reposition out of the path of his bulge.

"Not exactly a choice right now..." he grits out.

With another breath, I yank hard, and the lace breaks, leaving a flimsy gray remnant as the only evidence of what just happened.

Silently, I wrap my hand around his and grab my rope from him. "I'll-um...see you down at the bottom," I choke out nervously, moving slowly to my side of the wall. He's watching me, and I keep my eyes straight ahead to avoid looking at him. I can't make it to the ground fast enough as my body tries to recalibrate after that sensory takeover. His arms, his cologne, his...well... *him* underneath me, it was a lot to deal with all at once. Hitting the ground, I get a high five from Samson, and Sami mentions something about being fearless. But all I can think about is the tickle of warm breath on my neck and the strong arms that were wrapped around me.

I'm not fearless, proven by my heart skipping several beats as Mr. Sandalwood lands next to me. The jolt to my senses while being that close to him, feeling the hair raise on my arms at his whispered breath in my ear, that's exactly what I'm afraid of. Chase is getting under my skin, and I need to nip it in the bud.

"What did we learn?" Claire asks as she climbs down from the platform behind Kyle.

"Kayla's a badass, and Sami talks too much," Kyle chides. Sami punches him in the arm before mouthing *sorry* over at Chase.

Claire nods thoughtfully, looking between Chase and me. "You two made a really good team up there. Calm, cool, and collected. Great job! Sami, a word."

Chase catches my eye and smirks. Suddenly, nothing is more interesting than the rock I'm staring at on the ground. I kick at it with my boot, trying to rid myself of the nervous energy coursing through me. *This is so, so bad.*

CHAPTER TEN
KAYLA

A clap of thunder shakes the ground outside, making me jump just before I reach the doors to the mess hall. The girls' cabin isn't far, but my jacket is already soaked, leaving my green camp counselor tee damp underneath it. I'm freezing, but the rain is pouring down in sheets hard enough that I'm not running back through it to get my heavier jacket from the cabin. According to today's schedule, we're supposed to be practicing survival skills outside—building fires, making shelter, purifying water—but with the lightning being a liability, I doubt Claire will let us venture out there.

After peeling off my sopping jacket and hanging it on a hook by the door, I head straight to the food line. Hopefully, a hot cup of coffee will take the chill off enough for me to stop shivering. Distracted by the involuntary shaking in my shoulders, I don't notice Chase grabbing his breakfast in front of me until I'm standing right next to him. *Great.* I managed to avoid him for the rest of the night yesterday and had plans to do the same today. I didn't like the twinge of jealousy I felt when I watched him interact with Sami, and I'm trying my hardest to convince myself I didn't like the way he wrapped his arms around me up on that stupid wall.

"You okay, there?" He laughs at the shimmy coursing through my body. His gray Gradford U zip-up is dry as a bone.

"I'm fine," I say through chattering teeth.

"Uh-huh..." His voice trails as he watches me.

I avert my eyes down, grab a tray and mug, and wait for him to move out of the way.

"Here," he says, and the next thing I know, he's placing the hood of his sweatshirt over my head and pulling the rest around my shoulders.

He adjusts the sleeves on his long sleeve tee as I look at him, shaking my head. "I'm really okay. I just need coffee," I say, putting down my tray before sliding the jacket from my shoulders. It's warm and smells like him, and these reminders of yesterday are doing nothing to help me forget about the wall.

"You're clearly freezing," he says, pulling the sweater back over my shoulders. He puts his hand through the bottom of the sleeve, grabs my fingers, and guides my hand back through the hole with his. "Just wear it until you warm up." He works on the other sleeve, grabbing my hand and pulling it through. Then he flips the hood over my head and zips it up for good measure, smiling. "There."

I stand stiffly, my mouth hanging open as I decide whether I want to feel annoyed or flattered. The kindness in the act isn't lost on me, and under any other circumstance, I'd probably think it was sweet. He gave me his jacket and zipped me up in it like a burrito, and the longer I wear it, the less I want to take it off. "Thanks..." I say.

"Sure. Besides, it looks good on you." He winks before walking off to sit at a table, sending flutters surging through my stomach. *What am I supposed to do with that?* I'm wrapped in his warm, amazing smelling hug of a sweater after he manhandled me in the sweetest way possible, and then he *winks?* I have no words —no thoughts except for taking a hit of the sandalwood scent coming from the fabric of this hoodie.

I make it to a table with my breakfast, sitting as far away from

Chase as I can without it seeming weird. My thoughts are already swirling, and I don't want to find out what a double dose of being close to him will do to me right now. Luckily, Kyle is sitting at one of the table ends, and I plop my tray down next to him. He looks at me, tips his chin up in greeting, and returns to his eggs and bacon. I'll take silent company over the unpredictable jacket giver over there.

"Well, it looks like we're stuck inside today," Claire announces across the mess hall. "The forecast says the rain won't let up until sometime tonight. We'll pivot to wellness activities today and move survival to tomorrow. Meet me upstairs in ten for journal work."

I take one last sip of my coffee, load up my tray, and head for the kitchen. If I get upstairs before the others, I can claim the little nook by the window. It's just big enough for one person, the perfect spot to box me in, away from blue-eyed distractions.

The loft upstairs is open and cozy. Large brown floor pillows lay scattered around the hardwood in front of the crackling fireplace, and a foosball table is across the room, near couches by the windows. Claire hands me a notebook and pen, and I scurry to the corner, a little relieved I'll have some room to breathe. The nook has one small window overlooking the forest behind the building, and the storm puts on a hypnotizing show as I turn to watch through the raindrop-streaked glass.

It's a lot warmer up here, so I shrug off Chase's hoodie and hold it to my nose one last time before laying it across my lap.

"Dear Diary, the cute girl at the window just sniffed my sweater..." Chase says.

Damn it.

He stands next to me with his head turned slightly, pretending to write in his notebook. An amused look has settled on his face like he's fighting the urge to smile. "Does this mean she likes me?"

"Why would I sniff your sweater?" I ask, trying to deflect as I turn to face him.

"Why *did* you?" He smirks, and I bite my cheek to keep from smiling back. *He's cute and I hate it.* I hand him the hoodie and swear he purposely grabs it in a way that our hands touch, watching me expectantly, waiting for an answer.

"I'm trying to figure out what's mixed with the sandalwood," I finally admit, looking down at my hands.

"Cedar," he says, tossing the jacket over his shoulder. "You like it?"

"I...it's—"

"You can admit it. I won't tell anyone you were sniffing my jacket," he says, the smirk from before changing to a full smile. "But just so you know, it sticks around for a while. You'll probably smell like me for the rest of the day..."

I roll my eyes, sucking my teeth. He's having fun with this, and I don't know why it's bothering me so much. "I wasn't sniffing it; I was smelling it."

"Mmm, and there's a difference?"

"Yes."

"Which is...?

"Was that your plan all along?" I fold my arms, raising an eyebrow as I attempt to change the course of the conversation. "Force me into your clothes and mark me with your scent?"

"Nope." He chuckles as he shakes his head. "I was just being nice. Everything else is a perk."

"A perk? What kind of perk?"

"Two perks, actually. One: I got to see the way you look in my hoodie, which definitely lived up to the fantasy. And two: now I have the satisfaction of knowing you'll smell like me all day, hopefully thinking about me as much as I'll be thinking about you." He *fucking* winks again—and I don't know what my problem is —but my breath catches in my throat while my cheeks burn. Maybe I'm not as immune as I thought I was.

He chuckles the entire time he walks over to the couch across the room, fully enjoying the rise he just got out of me. I groan to myself when I realize he was right. I do smell like him, and I can't make myself hate it.

CHAPTER ELEVEN

CHASE

We're on day four of training at Camp Bender, and we've been stuck inside for the last two because of the rain. There are only so many crafts and mindfulness prompts you can do before going a little stir crazy. And If I see another board game, I might just lose it. Today, though, the sun shines through the windows of the mess hall while I try to fully wake up for the day.

"Looks like we're getting sun today!" Sami says in a singsong voice, black hair swinging behind her. She bounces on her toes as she walks toward the table, and I have no doubt her energy will be a great fit for the campers next week.

I nod while sipping on my coffee. "I hope so. We're running out of things to do in here."

"Hopefully, we can find some dry wood out there for the survival stuff." She crosses her fingers on both hands. "Hey, Kayla!"

Kayla waves and heads to the food line. Her hair is pulled away from her face, exposing her neck in a way that has my eyes tracing the curve of her shoulder, down her arms, until they land at the dip in her waist, remembering. I had to stay up on that damn wall for an entire minute before I was decent enough to rejoin the group. It's been days and I still can't get the feeling of my arms wrapped around her out of my head, the scent of vanilla and apples etched in my brain. I realized it was apples that night, after lying in bed stewing over the fragrance for a full thirty minutes.

She comes to the table and, to my disappointment, sits across from me and far enough away that talking to her would be awkward. She did the same thing yesterday, spreading out her craft supplies to take up the space around her, and the day before, spending the entirety of the mindfulness activity alone in a corner. She's been doing this since our moment in the air, putting distance between us, avoiding being alone for too long. I hate it. Tapping my fingers on my leg mindlessly, I remember the wall all over again. I liked having her close to me, and I'm running out of ideas on how to get closer. She interacts with everyone else, helping when she can and openly laughing and telling jokes, until I join in. When I'm added to the mix, she shuts down and bows out of the conversation. I don't get discouraged easily, but she's comfortably sitting behind a solid brick wall with barbed wire circling the top, and I have no footholds to help me breach it.

"Good morning, everyone," Claire says cheerfully, walking into the mess hall from outside. She carries a backpack over one shoulder and stops at the head of the table. "Good news! We'll be training on survival skills today. Thanks for being flexible with the weather." She grabs items from the storage cabinet on the wall and stuffs them in her backpack as she talks. "Meet me out by the firepits in twenty," she says, bouncing out the door.

We trickle outside and walk down the trail leading to the firepits. Birds chirp with the early morning dew, and the sun rays on my shoulders give me the boost I've needed since Monday.

"Hey," I say, sidling up to Kayla.

She slides a quick glance over to me and back to the ground. "Hey…"

"Come here often?" I tease, trying to get her to smile. She does, finally, and it lights up her face. I think making her smile might be one of my favorite things.

"Only on days that end in *y*." She looks my way again, green eyes glinting in the sunlight.

"Any fun plans this weekend?" I ask, hopeful she'll say no.

"Yep. Working."

Damn. I think this is becoming our thing. I hint at asking her out, and she shuts me down with work. She's done it every single time, like it's the only pastime she has. "I said *fun* plans..."

"Working *is* fun for me," she says, mimicking my intonation.

"You don't take any time off?"

"Nope."

"Ever?"

She shrugs. "Not really. I need all the help I can get during the summer to pay for SSU. Unless I'm sick or injured, I'm working."

We reach the clearing where Claire has set up smaller firepits surrounding the large one. "A little bad news," she says, puffing out her lower lip. "The big firepit was filled with water. I bailed out what I could, but it's unusable this morning. The good news is, this is a great time to tell you the final partner pairings for camper groups one and two—Sami and Samson, Kayla and Chase, and Kyle, you're with me. Get with your buddy and pick a pit."

I turn to say something witty, but Kayla is halfway to the other side of the clearing. The reserved way she acts around me sometimes leaves me confused. *Am I saying the wrong things? Am I doing the wrong things? Why won't she give me the time of day?*

I follow behind and stand next to her awkwardly. When she sits, I sit. When she crosses her legs, I cross mine. This is the closest we've been in days, and I can't make my brain form coherent thoughts. The sun shines off the high bun in her hair and down her shoulders as she tips her head back, face up, eyes closed. A smile creeps across her lips, and suddenly, watching her like this is another one of my new favorite things. I enjoyed it before, but *this?* This is different. Before, she was a mystery to be solved. Now that I know a tiny bit more, now that I'm around her almost every day, I want to be closer.

She sighs, eyes still closed. "This is nice. Warm. I forget how gloomy it gets when it rains up here."

Still watching her, I nod in response. I can't get my eyes to look anywhere else, or force words out of my mouth, so I nod and watch.

Claire interrupts my thoughts by dropping a box at my feet. "Here's your flint, steel, and dry tinder," she says in passing. I reach for the box and inspect the contents, just for something else to do other than look at Kayla.

"Wanna have a race?" Kayla asks. Surprised, I snap my head back to see her eyebrow arched over an intense, challenging stare.

"What do I get when I win?" I ask, like I've ever made a fire from scratch before. We use lighters in LA, but how hard can it really be? Hit a rock with some steel and make the sparks hit the dry stuff. *Easy.* And she's engaging with me for once. Of course I'm going to say yes.

She chuckles at my confidence. "Loser makes s'mores for the winner at the closing firepit tonight...all night."

"Hope you're good at making s'mores then," I tease back. We set up our respective piles of tinder, and on the count of three, we're off. I'm on my knees, hitting the steel key against the rock furiously with guitar strumming motions, trying to get a spark to land down on the dry leaves. Striking faster and closer to the ground, I grit my teeth in determination. Glancing sideways at Kayla, I see her grinning from ear to ear with her hands on her hips, squatting next to a small flame. I sit back on my haunches and laugh. "Cheater. You do this every summer."

"Here." She squats next to me. "Hold the flint horizontally and place a little kindling on top." Moving her hands around mine, she positions the rock in my palm. "Then strike down with the steel perpendicular to the flint, like this." She guides my hand, imitating a strike against the flint. I shiver as her warm breath dances across my arm.

Kayla sits back, seemingly realizing the intimacy in her proximity. I clear my throat, trying to break up some of the tension.

Trying again, her way this time, I get one good hit on the rock and the dry leaf lights up in a flash. "Yeah! Good! Now add that leaf to the rest and blow lightly, like you're whistling." She stands, hands on her hips again, with the biggest grin shining down on me. The kindling isn't the only thing sparking on fire.

Tipping her head to the side, brows creased, she asks, "Have you ever made a fire before?"

"Not without a lighter."

"Then why did you accept the challenge like you knew what you were doing?"

"You were talking to me again." I shrug.

"I—what? When was I not talking to you?"

"You've been avoiding me ever since we got down from the climbing wall, and finally you weren't. So..."

"I wasn't avoiding you, Chase. I just..." She exhales loudly. "On the wall, when I had to, you know—"

"Sit on my lap?" I offer, shooting her a sly grin.

"Yeah. That. It just made everything awkward."

"Would it help if I said I enjoyed it?" I bite my lip in mock embarrassment.

"Oh, I felt how much you enjoyed it." She laughs and hides her face in her hands. "*Ugh*, Chase. This is the problem! You say things like *that*, you force me into your sweater and look at me with those eyes, and then you make me laugh. And don't get me started on the winking..."

"These are *bad* things? I'm confused..."

"It's not bad. It's...you're cute, and funny, and..."

"And...?" I prompt her.

"And charming."

"Charming is a bad thing?" I say slowly, trying to understand the path of her logic.

"Believe it or not, yeah." She puffs out her bottom lip and a shadow flickers in her eyes. "*And* you're leaving at the end of the summer. We both are." She shrugs, as if to convince herself as much as me.

"So...I'm cute?" I ask, amused at how open she's being with me right now.

"You *would* latch onto that one thing..." She shakes her head, laughing.

"Hey, those were *your* words, not mine." I grin as she bumps my shoulder playfully.

I bring Kayla her second s'more of the evening while everyone chats around the fire. The sun dried out the ground enough that our last night of camp training will be spent around the flames. Tomorrow, we clean up and head home for the weekend before coming back Monday morning to meet the first group of campers.

"Thanks," she says, making cute little grabbing motions with her hands as I walk toward her.

"A deal's a deal." I hand over the s'more, and the smallest drop of melted chocolate drips onto her pinkie. My eyes follow her hand as she licks it off, my heart racing the longer I stare at her lips. *Do they feel as soft as they look?* Noticing my gaze, Kayla clears her throat, snapping me back to the present as she looks down toward the flames. I drop my eyes and sit down on the log next to her, shoving my hands into the pocket of my hoodie. *Damn it.*

Kyle tunes his guitar across the pit and strums slowly, deciding which notes to play. He plucks a couple of songs, which gets the group swaying as we talk to each other. After a while, I recognize the simple chorded tune from a '90s Britpop group my dad used to play frequently. Claire sings along, and Samson's humming buzzes next to me while he taps his foot on the ground. Sami and Kayla's voices join in, creating the kind of harmony that makes campfires magical. I don't sing, but I appreciate the atmosphere. Hearing Kayla's honeyed voice sends a frisson up my spine and goosebumps down my arms. I watch her as she sings, the smile growing wider on her face, and I'm thankful for the sheet of darkness that hides the color heating my cheeks. I'm realizing how multi-dimensional this girl is. If I thought I couldn't be more captivated by her, I was dead wrong.

The song ends, and Kyle strums another, this one more upbeat. "Your voice is beautiful," I whisper. "Which makes sense, considering..."

She giggles and turns to me, rolling her eyes. "Thanks, Sir Flirts-a-lot. I think it's time for another s'more."

"You got it."

I glance back and see Kayla watching me across the pit as I toast a new marshmallow, unsure if the fire in her eyes is from the literal flames between us or something else. I feel it, but the jury is still out on whether she feels it too. The progress we've made today could all be in my mind, changing in the morning as quickly as the fickle Fort Bender weather.

"Well, I'm spent," Claire says through a yawn, stretching her legs.

I make my way back to the log and hand the s'more to Kayla, trying not to blush at the smile she sends me.

"Kayla, you're still on firepit duty tonight?" Claire asks.

"Yep, on it!" Kayla answers cheerfully.

Samson stands and says, "I think I'm gonna turn in too." And the charge in the air has shifted. Sami and Kyle are opposite Kayla and me, singing and strumming in their own little twin-connected world. Kayla shifts, hugging her legs to her chest before resting her cheek on her knee.

"You gonna make it?" I ask.

"Yeah, I'm not tired. Just enjoying the fire," she says casually, staring into the flames. I'm transfixed by the peaceful look on her face, and my fingers twitch at the thought of stroking her exposed jawline.

"Well, we're gonna head in too," Kyle says, walking toward us with guitar in hand.

Sami follows close behind, and when she passes me, whispers,

"You're welcome." Her eyes dart over toward Kayla in an obvious way, but Kayla's stare is still lost to the flames.

The cool breeze blows through my hair, making me shiver as I pull my hood up. "You could go in, too, if you want." Kayla's tranquil voice coats the tension between us. "I'll be fine out here."

"Gotta stay with my buddy, remember?" I tease, recalling the camp rules. "S'more time?"

She pops her head up and flashes her teeth in a nervous grin. "Maybe just one more, if you don't mind."

"Hey, you won these fair and square. I'll make as many as you want." I head back to the marshmallows, roasting two this time. Maybe if my mouth is full of melted sugar, I won't make a fool of myself. Two s'mores later, we're sitting side by side, shoulders touching, watching the fire burn lower and lower. Our intimate quiet game will be over soon, and even though we aren't talking, I don't want this night to end. I turn to her, moving my legs to either side of the log.

"Wanna have a thumb war?"

She gives me a full-bodied laugh and looks in my eyes. "Really? That's the line you're going with?" A fit of giggles escapes her as she rocks back on the log.

"Wha—that's not a line." I smile, chuckling.

"Oh, it so *is*. You mean to tell me a thumb war isn't your attempt to hold my hand?"

"I mean, the nature of the game is to hold hands. I don't make the rules, I just follow them. Scared you'll lose?" I raise my eyebrows in a challenge, staring at her. She gazes right back, and after several seconds, slowly turns her body to face me, her toes touching mine on either side of the log. She holds out her right hand, and when her eyes meet mine, they reflect the last simmering flickers of the flame. I hold my palm next to hers, and an electricity rivaling the burning embers in the ground surges through my hand as she slides her fingers against mine.

"One, two, three, four, I declare a thumb war," we chant in unison. Our thumbs dance in the low light of what's left of the fire. Kayla bites her lip in concentration, I lose focus, and she pins my thumb under hers.

"Ha!" she yells, triumphant. "I win—"

"You have some chocolate…" I whisper, pointing to her lip. She takes her free hand, and my eyes follow the line she traces across her lips.

"Did I get it?" she asks breathlessly. Based on the surprised look in her eyes, I think she realizes just how close our faces have gotten. I shake my head and reach with my thumb, tracing the same line across her lips and down her chin, until my hand rests in that crease between her jaw and pulse. War hands still locked in an embrace, jade green eyes staring into my blue, I lean forward. Our breath waltzes together the closer I inch, and just before my lips press to hers, she lets go. Breathing a heavy sigh, her hand swipes at her brow and she scoots backward.

"I can't believe I almost fell for that one," she muses out loud. Her face twists. "You're good… Did I even have chocolate on my face?"

I shrug. "I…uh…guess we'll never know." *Smooth, Chase. What the hell was that?*

Kayla stands and grabs the shovel leaning against the table, before mixing up the ashes in the pit. She throws water on what's left of the smoldering embers, dousing the glow and drenching the tendrils of whatever just happened between us. I grab the left-over dessert supplies, and we walk silently to the mess hall, a significant distance between us. Inside the activity center, the dark hallway all but consumes her retreating form as I wait by the exit to escort her to her cabin, like a good little camp buddy. I need to find a way to salvage this night—hell, this whole week.

Walking to our cabins in silence, we stop just short of her building. "Goodnight, Chase," she says with finality, not chancing a look at me as she turns toward her door.

I grab her hand, turning her to face me. "Kayla, wait." I pull her toward me, my hand finding the dip in her waist. Having her this close again is mind-numbing, and it's all I can do not to capture her mouth with mine. She doesn't pull away, but she doesn't look at me either. As I cup her cheek, my heart beats rapidly in my chest. "I—"

"Chase, we can't," she whispers. But I don't miss her tongue darting out over her bottom lip.

"Why not?" I lean in, feeling pulled into her orbit.

"Because we...work together..." her voice trails breathlessly.

My hand drifts from her cheek to her chin, lifting her head until our eyes meet. I want a taste of her so damn bad, but only if she wants it too. "Okay, fair enough," I whisper. She looks at my mouth as she bites her lip. "I can wait for you. But I think you should know..." I dip down close enough that the tip of our noses touch. "I have every intention of falling for you this summer."

She inhales sharply, eyes widening as she lowers her head toward the ground. Feeling satisfied, I drop my hands and walk backward to my cabin. "Night, Kayla."

CHAPTER TWELVE

KAYLA

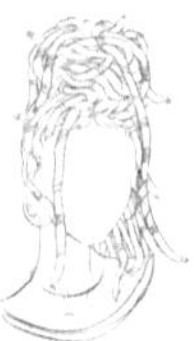

"Girl..." Ashlie starts as soon as she walks into the diner. "I need help." She slides onto a stool, curls bouncing when she plops down.

I grab her a cup of water and prop my elbows on the cool counter. "It's just lunch, Ash. We can figure this out," I deadpan. It's Saturday, the rush is about to start, and I really don't want to get into some drawn-out story with a bunch of customers coming in.

"Stop playin'. This is serious!" Her eyes grow wide as she slumps on the stool.

"Are you going to tell me or...?"

"Bryan wants to come visit," she says dramatically.

I cackle at the anguish on her face. "You need my help because your *boyfriend* wants to come see you?"

"*With his parents!*" she whisper-screams.

I gasp, clutching my heart with wide eyes. "The horror!" She glares at me and sucks her teeth before rolling her eyes over a sip of water. "Look. No guy is worth all of this. If you're not happy, break up with him."

"That's easy for you to say. You don't care if you end up alone. Your great-granny did it. Your mom's doing it. You have strong examples of how to do it. Besides, I want the things he wants. I just don't want them *yet*."

Her words cut a little. She's right. I do know *how* to be alone. I've been on my own since I was little, but I wouldn't say I'm indifferent. It's not something I strive for, and I don't necessarily want to end up alone. I just don't have time to deal with the inevitable drama that comes with relationships, and I'd be lying if I said I wasn't scared of getting hurt again. Being alone is easy— safe.

"Girl, if you don't want those things with Bryan, then what are you doing? Maybe just tell him how you feel." The bell over the door jingles.

In walks Hunter, phone in his face, and behind him, Chase. I drop my eyes to the counter, breathing in sharply as my heart pounds in my chest. I didn't have to see him yesterday, after our way too intimate night by the fire, and I was not prepared for the parade of elephants barreling through my belly at the sight of his shaggy hair.

Ashlie looks from me to the door and back again. "Maybe *you* should take your own advice..." she whispers, side-eyeing me as she sips her water. I haven't told her about anything that happened at camp, and I don't know if I want to. Talking about it would be the opposite of pushing it down and acting like nothing happened, and that's all I want to do. Act like nothing happened.

"Hi," Chase says, a smile sliding across his lips.

"Hi," I say, biting my own growing smile. "Hi." I wave a hand at Hunter.

"Hi." Chase nods toward Ashlie. She looks at Hunter, and they both laugh.

"You two sound ridiculous." Hunter shakes with laughter as he slides onto the stool next to Ashlie.

"Just like those seagulls in that fish movie." Ashlie giggles. They mimic the exchange together, varying intonations with every *hi*.

I roll my eyes at their two-person comedy show and turn to fill more water cups.

"You left early yesterday morning," Chase says when I return.

"Had to work." I shrug, passing menus to Hunter and Ashlie while they chatter away. "Are you going to sit, or did you want something to go?" He takes the seat next to Hunter and drums his fingers on the countertop.

"Did you ask her?" Hunter asks Chase.

"Hey, Kayla, do you think I could ride back with you at the end of the week? Hunter needs my car to get back each night, and it doesn't really make sense for him to come up on Friday just to pick me up..."

Alone in a car, for an hour, with a guy who has not only tried to kiss me twice but also shared his sole intention to fall for me by the end of the summer? *That* wouldn't be dangerous at all. I should tell him no. Nip this in the bud right here and now and be done with it.

"Uh, sure, that makes sense," I hear myself say. *Why?* Beats the hell out of me. I'm just as surprised at my answer as the three people shooting shocked looks back at me.

CHAPTER THIRTEEN

KAYLA

All the camp counselors are lined up outside, waiting for the first bus of campers to arrive. The four volunteers we have for the week, Hunter included, are inside setting up icebreaker activities. We'll have twelve campers—six boys and six girls—and the week will follow the same schedule it did during training, weather depending.

"Here they come," Claire sings, bouncing on the balls of her feet. A large black charter bus angles around the narrow dirt road, kicking up dust behind the wheels. I see the excited faces of the campers, aged between seven and twelve, pressed against the windows.

"Welcome!" Claire grins as the kids spill out of the charter. "We're so excited you're all here. Let's head inside, where I'll introduce you to your counselors."

Chase and I have four campers. Two boys—Aiden and Caleb, and two girls—Katie and Liz. We teach them a couple of camp songs and chants, and then dive into the icebreakers.

"If I could be any animal, I'd be a giraffe," Chase says. The kids snicker.

"Who picks a giraffe?" Caleb responds with a forceful guffaw, knocking into Aiden, who's laughing just as hard. I can't help but laugh along with them, tipping my head to the side to see whether Chase is serious.

"Why a giraffe?" I ask with genuine curiosity.

He shrugs. "They just seem nice..."

Another hooting laugh from the boys gets us all smiling.

"Plus, they're tall, smart, and loyal." Chase looks right at me, like his list of giraffe qualities double for qualifications to an unspoken job listing between us. I shake my head, giving him a warning look before taking my turn.

"Well, I'd be a hummingbird," I say. "Because their wings flap so fast they can hover in the air, and they're impossible to catch."

"Fitting..." Chase quips, nodding slowly.

"That's *almost* as bad as a giraffe," Caleb snorts. "If I were an animal, I'd be a lion, that way everyone would know I'm the king." He stands and flexes his skinny arms, mustering all the confidence a nine-year-old can, while nodding his head, his afro bouncing up and down. From what I've seen, he's a funny kid who lights up whenever he makes the group laugh.

Once he sits, we learn Aiden would be a bear and Liz would be a swan. Katie chooses not to answer, her dark hair falling over her face like a thick black curtain, and we don't push her.

Some campers need a while before they come out of their shell. She reminds me of myself the first year I came to Camp Bender.

"Well, I'm excited to hike up Bender trail to see the waterfall," I say, moving into the next icebreaker.

"I'm excited for the ropes course!" Aiden exclaims, his brown hair falling into his eyes as excitement courses through his body.

"Ooh, yeah!" Caleb agrees.

Liz taps her chin with her pointer finger, twirling one blond pigtail with the other. "Hmm, I'm excited for the arts and crafts, I think."

Katie plays with her laces, not answering.

"How about you Katie? What are you excited for this week?" Chase prompts. She shrugs and continues looking at the floor.

"That's okay." His smile is kind as he taps a finger on her shoe. "You'll find something when you're ready."

Of course he's good with kids. Charming, helpful, funny, and now this? I can't catch any breaks here. It's like the more I learn about him, the closer I'm pulled toward the caution tape.

Chase turns to the group and says, "I'm excited to get to know everyone." His eyes shoot to mine, blazing briefly before he smiles at the kids, and it takes everything I have to keep from biting my lip in response.

THE ROPES COURSE ROTATION GOES OFF WITHOUT A hitch. Our campers chatter excitedly as we switch out the group for rappelling. Claire secures the ropes for Aiden and Liz on the platform, while Chase is up there double-checking helmets and tightening gloves. There's no mistaking the rapport he's built with the kids—encouraging when they doubt themselves and being energetic when they need motivation. He smiles, giving Aiden a high five as he jumps with excitement at getting all the gear on. I grin to myself while watching the exchange before turning to Katie and Caleb, making sure they're ready to spot their partners with Kyle's guidance.

"Wow... I can't believe he's up there," Hunter says, shaking his head as he comes to stand next to me.

"What? Why not?"

"Your boy up there doesn't do heights. I'm surprised he isn't clinging to the ledge, hyperventilating."

I ignore the clear prodding at his use of "your boy," and concern myself with the hyperventilating part. Scrunching my nose, I look back up to the platform to see Chase tightening Liz's helmet, smiling with ease. "He seemed fine last week when his shoe got stuck," I say.

"Shoe got stuck? Where?"

Pointing to the left side of the wall, I say, "Up there. You can still see half of his shoelace dangling."

"He went down that wall?" Hunter's eyes widen, mouth gaping.

"Rappelling!" Liz yells hesitantly from the top of the platform, her pigtails dangling out of the helmet as she peers over the ledge.

I move toward Katie, who looks at me with unease filling her expression, and I whisper a few words of encouragement. "Rappel on!" she squeaks. I stay beside her, pointing out ways she could direct Liz down to the ground. In no time, shoes hit dirt, and the girls share an embrace.

"You did so great!" Liz says to Katie, making her break out into a wide smile.

"You girls were awesome!" Hunter says from beside me, slapping high fives to both of them.

As they take off their gear, he continues our conversation. "Last year, we went to Mexico, and Chase had a panic attack on the zip line platform. Both of our dads had to carry him back down the ladder. I don't know what happened last week, but he doesn't do heights." He shakes his head. "Anyway, I have to head back to town. See ya tomorrow."

I look back at Chase, who's watching us with a questioning gaze in his eyes. Flashing a smile, I give a thumbs-up and shrug. He sends Aiden down, and I coach Caleb in the same ways as Katie. Aiden's feet hit the ground just as the dinner bell rings.

Our four campers race to the mess hall, and Chase's steps fall next to mine. "Did Hunter give you any good dirt?"

"Apparently you're afraid of heights?"

"Ha!" He throws his head back as he laughs. "He *would* tell you that. Let me guess, panic attack in Mexico?"

"Yeah...but I'm confused. You were fine up there last week."

"Eh," he says, tipping is hand over side to side. "I wouldn't say that..." He bumps my shoulder with his as we walk. "The whole reason my foot slipped is because I realized how far from the ground I was. You found me mid thought spiral. Pulled me out of it, actually."

"How did I do that?" I ask, confused about how anything I did last week would pull him out of a panic attack.

"You, uh...well, you talked to me." He rubs the back of his head.

"I—huh?"

"Your voice. It's soothing. You asked if everything was okay, and suddenly everything was..." He shrugs.

I stop walking. "Why did you even go up there, knowing you would panic?"

"Not sure. Maybe I wanted to impress you, be around you. I *like* you, Kayla. I'll spend the time any way I can take it. Why do you think I'm at the diner every day?"

"I..." I start, not sure what to say to that. He's always so direct with his words—bold in the way he expresses his interest in me—and it catches me off guard. Evan always gave me the runaround, so I'm almost at a loss for how to handle Chase's candor. Deciding on avoidance for now, I march past him. "We have to get in there with the campers."

He jogs to catch up, walking quietly beside me as my own thoughts spiral while I mull over his confession, weighing the gravity of my own floundering feelings.

CHAPTER FOURTEEN

CHASE

"You guys were the best group here," I say, holding my hand up for the collective handshake we created during the week. Everyone leans in, snapping their fingers twice, and then slapping high fives to each person next to them. The boys turn to me, pounding fists and bumping elbows as a goodbye.

Liz leaps across the circle to give Kayla a hug, and I hear her say, "Ooh! I'm gonna miss you, Liz!" Kayla turns to Katie, holding up a hand for a high five, but Katie wraps her arms around her waist instead. Kayla's eyebrows shoot up in surprise as she pats her back. "I'm so glad you had fun, Katie."

I squat, holding out my hand to the girls. Liz slaps my hand, and I'm almost knocked off my feet by another unexpected hug from Katie. "Thank you for helping me find my brave," she says quietly.

My heart cracks wide open with pride. Watching her come out of her shell this week has been such a gift. "Hey, you were already brave, I just helped you remember it." I pat her shoulder as Claire calls the kids over to take attendance. When our four run off, I look up to see Kayla watching me. Her eyes aren't guarded for once, and her arms aren't folded. She's just staring at me openly. "What?" I ask.

"That was adorable," she teases, a smirk landing on her lips.

"Yeah, well, that's what camp is all about, right? Gaining confidence?" I shrug, falling in step next to her as we walk back to the main building.

She kicks at a rock on the ground. "It is…"

The three-hour clean up goes by quickly, and I'm hauling my small duffel bag over my shoulder before I know it. When I get to the parking lot, Kayla's leaning against the side of her car with the trunk open, scrolling through her phone. I drop my bag in the trunk, snapping her attention from her screen.

"Ready?" I ask. She nods and climbs into the driver's side. When I get around to the passenger door, I fold myself into the front seat, looking for the adjustment lever underneath. My knees are up against my chest as I lean forward, and there's no way I can close the door and ride like this the entire way.

"I'm sorry." She giggles, looking over at the spectacle that is me, smashed in her car. "Ashlie was the last one over there. The button is on the side of the seat. It's automatic, so just push it backward."

"*Whew*," I breathe out dramatically, and she laughs again as the seat eases back. We ride in silence for a few minutes as we make our way down the dirt road. I've got her alone for an entire hour, and while I'm dying to ask her questions, I don't even know where to start. I'm not sure if she wants me to start *anything*.

"You can listen to whatever," she says, nodding at the radio. Her thumbs tap on the steering wheel to the beat of the R&B song, and it looks like she's resisting the urge to bob her head and bounce her shoulders. She adjusts in her seat before relaxing behind the wheel.

"This is good," I say, trying to decide how to break up the silence. "You can dance if you want. I won't tell anyone."

"Mm-hmm, just like you didn't tell anyone I was sniffing your jacket?" she asks. The corner of her mouth curves up as she keeps her eyes on the road. Last weekend, I let it slip to Hunter and Ashlie at the diner, and they did not let her live it down. I almost felt bad until she told them how much I've been staring at her, and they turned it around on me. "I'm not falling for that again. And you're staring...again."

"So you admit it. You *were* sniffing my jacket... I could give you another whiff when we get into town if you want," I tease.

"You're really funny." Her tone oozes with sarcasm, but she looks at me with a real, genuine smile on her face. *The* smile. It's warm and inviting, like I can feel the rays of the sun directly inside my chest. Far too quickly, her head moves forward, her eyes on the road. I want to earn that smile back. If I could have her smile directed at me at all times, in all forms, I'd do just about anything.

"What can I say? I like seeing you smile," I respond, like it's not the cheesiest thing to say. But it worked because she laughs and looks over at me again while shaking her head.

"That line was so obvious! Does it ever work for you?"

"Yeah, more often than you'd think. Not as well as some of my others though."

"Well, let's hear them..." She waits expectantly, and I don't care if the laughing is at my expense right now because she's actually opening up. *Finally.*

"You know what my shirt's made out of?" I lean over the center console, getting close to her ear. She turns slightly so she can see me out of the corner of her eye. "Boyfriend material," I whisper, waiting for her reaction. The laugh builds in her throat, and she slaps a hand over her mouth, trying to keep from completely losing it. I smile, sitting back in my seat. "That's in the top three."

"That's so bad!" She tries to contain her giggles. "What are the other two?"

"No, no. Now it's your turn." I shake my head. If I'm going to keep her talking, I have to turn this into a game. I've seen her joke around with everyone else, so I know she has it in her. We've even had *some* light banter between us. I'm so close to wedging my foot in the door with her, I can feel it. But then she rolls her eyes, and the smile drops from her face. *Damn it.*

She moves her tongue along the inside of her bottom lip, staring straight ahead. "You know..." she starts, shaking her head with a rueful look on her face, and I really start to think I pushed too much. "...I know your name is Chase, but...can I call you 'mine'?" She sticks her tongue in her cheek, holding her smile until I realize she's playing along.

The full belly laugh that rips out of me has me slapping my knee. "That delivery was perfect. I thought I'd messed up there for a second."

"Naw, this is just for fun. Now what's your number two?"

I only need a second before I say, "There's something wrong with my phone... Your number's not in it..."

"Okay, but that one I could see working. It's cute." She nods, jutting her lip out in appreciation before firing another one back. "You know what I'd look great in? Your arms..." We're at a stop sign, about to ease onto the main highway, when she turns and gives me a flirty wink. And even though I know we're just playing around, the flutters in my stomach sure don't.

"Ooh, nice. I'll have to remember that one. Okay, now for my number one, top pickup line." I rub my hands together, ready to deal an unfairly flirtatious hand in this otherwise friendly game. She's still looking at me, an eyebrow quirked up as she waits. I look her square in the eyes, lick my bottom lip, and say, "If there was no gravity here on Earth, I'd still fall for you..."

Her eyes flash wide for the briefest second, letting me know the line landed just how I wanted it to. That one wasn't just for fun, and we both know it. I want her to know, with absolute clarity, that I don't see her as just a friend. What I want from her is more than that, if she'll give me the chance.

Kayla whips her head back and forth to check the road and presses her lips together as she turns through the stop sign. "I, um... I can see why that's your number one..." She clears her throat and focuses on the road ahead of us.

The car fills with silence, save for the repetitive beat coming through the speakers, and my phone buzzes, breaking up some of the tension as I dig it out of my pocket. I tap out a response to Hunter's message asking for my ETA before sliding it into the cupholder. Ahead of us, the forest gives way to the ocean on the horizon. It won't be too much longer before she's dropping me off at the diner and the comfortable banter we had going ends. I don't want it to. I've gotten the smallest glimpse into her, and I'm aching for more.

"So... I was thinking..." she says carefully. "It doesn't make a lot of sense to leave Hunter without a car all next week. I could take you up to camp and bring you back. If you wanted. If it's easier..."

She wants to do this again? Two whole hours, just me and her? I look at her to see if she's joking, but the only tell is her nibbling on the inside of her lip. For weeks I've been trying to get close to her, and now she's offering me a chance.

"Yeah, I—that would be... I'd like that." *Pull it together, man.* I'm a bumbling mess, so I stop talking and just nod. She turns a small smile in my direction, and if I weren't already having a hard time with words, I definitely would be now.

CHAPTER FIFTEEN

KAYLA

"Well, well, well, fancy meeting you here," Chase says, slipping into my passenger seat. Hunter honks twice before leaving the Patti's Place parking lot in Chase's car.

Monday came in the blink of an eye. I yawn, hoping the steaming hot sips of coffee kick in before we hit the highway. The inky dawn looms around us as the dome light fades in my car. "Good morning," I say, reaching for the second cup in the center console. "I got you some coffee..."

"You...did?" He looks surprised as he reaches for the cup and takes a swig. "You memorized my coffee order?"

"I mean, you come in several times a week for coffee, and you always make it the same way up at camp... It's not that big of a deal."

"If you say so." He smirks, and the glowing console gives enough light for me to see his eyebrows raise as he takes another drink.

Okay, maybe I *did* memorize his coffee preferences, and maybe I've noticed he might really be a nice guy. We can be friendly. There's nothing wrong with being friends with a cute tourist who's good with kids and has told you, under no uncertain terms, that he will fall for you by the end of summer. Doesn't mean I'll fall for him. Just friends. *No problem.*

I turn the radio to a soft rock station and hum quietly to the melody as I pull out of the parking lot. With the soft glow of the lights from the dashboard, I notice Chase tapping his fingers on his knee as stares out the window. The sun will crest over the mountain by the time we reach the highway, but for now, the car is enshrouded in darkness.

"Do you like this kind of music?" I ask, breaking the silence. If we're going to be friends, I better get used to initiating conversations with him.

"Yeah, it's what I grew up on. But I'm okay with whatever. What kind of music do you like?"

"Everything." I shrug.

"Country?"

"Yep."

"Classical?"

"Mm-hmm. And opera...sometimes. I have to be in the mood for that."

"Rap?"

"Seriously, Chase?" I laugh, wondering what about the word *everything* lends to his confusion.

"Hey, I don't want to assume." He chuckles, putting his hand up in defense. "My assumptions about you have been wrong so far. You're an enigma."

"Am I?" I challenge, knowing full well I've been giving him nothing to work with. I've purposely kept him at arm's length so he couldn't know more, but something about him calling me out on it makes me feel defensive.

"Kayla, most of what I know about you has been through watching you interact with everyone but me. There's nothing wrong with that, it's just—you're a puzzle, and I want to learn how all the pieces fit together."

His words hang in the air, leaving me speechless. *He wants to learn how all of my pieces fit together? How do I even respond to that? What does it even mean?* We've been in the car for less than five minutes, and my *just friends* mantra is disintegrating due to a cheesy metaphor.

"The music thing... You sure you like *everything*?" he asks.

"Scan the radio, and I bet I can sing the words of 90 percent of what comes on."

"If it's a bet, what do I get when you lose?"

"What do you want to get?" I ask, not realizing how wide-open I just left that opportunity. My eyes flash in a panic as I look over at him, and he laughs.

"Hmm. Your number."

"...That's it?"

"Do you want there to be more?"

I shake my head.

"Okay, then. We'll go through ten songs, and you can miss one. Any more than that and I get your number. Deal?"

"Deal."

The first few songs are easy, as the radio cycles through the Top 40 and popular hip-hop stations. Chase keeps count of the songs on his fingers, nodding his head along to some of them. I hesitate slightly when we reach the oldies and hard rock stations, but I still manage to string the lyrics together before the radio switches. I've gotten all eight songs right so far, and I smirk over at Chase, meeting the amusement in his eyes.

We lose reception as we drive farther into the mountain, causing the radio to cycle back to the beginning. "I don't know this one..." I say, shaking my head at the fuzzy Mariachi song crackling through the speakers. He smiles and I smile back, finding myself enjoying his company despite the silly bet we have going on.

"Okay. Last song, and then you get to hand over your number," he teases, rubbing his hands together. The radio settles on the final station, and by some miracle, it's landed back on R&B. I turn, animatedly serenading him in triumph as he strokes the hair on his face. "*Ugh*, I was so close!" He hangs his head in defeat, shoulders shaking from his laugh.

"Told you." I laugh back, turning off the highway onto the mountain road. The sun crests the horizon ahead of us, and I reach over to nudge his shoulder. "Look at the sunrise," I say, pointing to the muted yellow-gold breaking through the pink and periwinkle tinted dawn. "The sunrise is another one of my favorites. Now you know two things about me..."

Chase looks from the sky to me and takes a deep breath. "Beautiful," he says, looking right into my eyes. And as much as I want to believe he's talking about the horizon, I know, deep down, he isn't.

CHAPTER SIXTEEN

CHASE

"Are you two dating?" Harper, a thirteen-year-old with braces, asks from across the table. She's looking between Kayla and me like we're a math problem to be solved. And maybe we are. I don't know what's happening, but something has shifted between us this last week at camp. Our other campers—Jack, Cameron, and Sarah—sit across from us, chatting away.

With a wink and a smile, I say, "Not ye—"

"No." Kayla steps on my foot, and I bite back a smirk. "We're just friends," Kayla assures her, shaking her head.

"Friends, huh?" I question, raising my brows in mock surprise. "That's new. I'll take it!"

Kayla rolls her eyes, knocking into my shoulder. We're sitting close enough that our knees bump occasionally, and the brush of her arm on mine sends tiny jolts through my skin. We've landed in some kind of valley where we're past the acquaintance stage, but not quite more. It's a fragile friendship. She knows where I stand, and she hasn't kept her distance like she was doing before. But her cool, calm, collectedness has me floundering sometimes. I don't think I've ever had to work this hard to convince a girl to give me the time of day.

Outside, damp earth spreads under my hiking boots, not quite dry from the drizzle of rain last night. We have one last hike with our campers before they load the bus and go home.

"Alright, guys, this hike isn't very long," Kayla announces from the trail opening. "But with the rain last night, the path will be a little more slick than normal. Please, watch your step. We don't want anyone going to the infirmary or worse."

She takes the lead, and we sandwich the campers between us, hiking our way up the spongy path. Bright green trees covered with moss flank the trail. I look up in time to watch Kayla crest the hill, the morning sun casting an ethereal glow over her. It triggers the memory I have of her basking in the sun weeks ago. Just like then, I'm having a hard time looking away. Jack stumbles in front of me, snapping me out of my reverie. "You okay?" I ask, grabbing his shoulder.

"Yeah, just got distracted..." His voice trails. I follow his gaze to Sarah, who stands next to Kayla in the sunlight. They slap hands and celebrate, acknowledging the feat of climbing up the steep hill.

"I know the feeling..." I say wistfully.

We reach the waterfall in record time, and after teaching the campers how to build shelter and craft fires, it's time to head back. The sun has dried up the trail some, but slick spots still surprise us as we slowly wind our way down the hill. The clearing behind the cabins comes into view, and before I know what's happening, Harper has slipped, sliding into Sarah, who launches at Kayla's back. Kayla yelps, trying to catch herself, and her head hits the side of a lichen-covered log as she goes down. How it happens so quickly and in slow motion baffles me as I watch from the back of the trail, unable to do anything.

I leap around the boys, quickly assessing which of the three girls needs attending to first. Harper's in shock, standing frozen as she stares ahead. Sarah sits in the mud, holding her knee to her chest, blood trickling down to her ankle. Kayla isn't moving, her body splayed face down on the ground.

"Jack, Cameron, find Claire," I shout over my shoulder. "Tell her we have a camper and a counselor hurt. *Run!*" They take off in between the cabins toward the main building as I slip and slide over to Kayla. She's breathing, and quiet moans slip past her lips, but her eyes stay closed. A gash dribbles bright red above her eyebrow. "Kayla…" I shake her leg, attempting to wake her up, then carefully turn her over to rest on her back.

"Sarah, are you okay?" I call over to her, shaking Kayla's leg again. She groans but still doesn't open her eyes. I grab her pack and rip into the small first aid kit, using my teeth to tear open the package of sterile bandages. Applying pressure to her forehead, I wait, stroking her other cheek.

"I think I'm alright, just scratched up," Sarah answers, voice shaking. "Is Kayla okay?"

God, I hope so. "I'm not sure yet," I reply honestly, eyes scanning over Kayla for any other injuries. "Harper, you okay?"

She doesn't answer.

"Harper?"

I look up to see her staring at the scene, her eyes wide as she shakes her head back and forth. "I didn't mean to," she whispers repeatedly.

Claire and Samson come running from the building, first aid supplies in hand. Samson checks on the campers, guiding Harper to a rock before attending to Sarah.

"We need to get her inside. Can you lift her?" Claire asks, bending next to us and lifting the gauze to check Kayla's wound.

"Yeah, I just don't want to hurt her."

Kayla stirs under my hand, her eyes fluttering open. "Wh-why is my face wet?" she asks.

"Hey, just lie still," I say. Before I can stop her, she reaches up to the gash above her eye and looks at the fresh blood on her fingers. Her eyes widen before rolling into the back of her head.

"Chase, inside! Now!" Claire booms.

I lift Kayla in my arms, and her head falls limply on my chest as I heft her to the infirmary. After laying her down on the closest bed, I grab gloves and more gauze to swap out the crimson-soaked cloth on her head. The bleeding has slowed some, but it's a deep cut, one that needs proper medical attention.

With shaky hands, I rip open the fresh pad and promptly drop it on the floor. "*Damn it...*" I mutter and reach for another pad. Taking a deep breath, I try again, still trembling as I drop another one. "*Shit!*"

"Chase," Claire steadies my hand. "Let me do that. Sit."

"I can do it!" I snap, shaking my head as I grab the side of the bed for support.

Claire puts both hands on my arms and walks me over to a chair against the wall before plopping me down in it. My vision blurs at the edges, and I link my gloved fingers on top of my head, my chest heaving as I try to slow my frantic breathing. When that doesn't work, I lean forward with my elbows on my knees and close my eyes. Images roll into each other in my mind of Kayla falling, her helpless yelp as she went down, my inability to reach her fast enough.

After several minutes, my breathing steadies, and I've calmed enough to notice I'm still wearing the blue gloves on my hands. A lamp in the corner dimly lights up the space. The soft whir of the refrigerator as it kicks on in the corner helps bring my focus back to the room. Claire is standing next to Kayla's bed, dressing her wound. I'm almost scared to see how bad her injury is. Watching her fall like that, seeing her crumpled on the ground, I can't get the image out of my mind.

"Where's Sarah and Harper?" I ask.

"You passed them in the hallway. Samson thought it would be better to keep them out of the room in case Kayla's injuries were dire."

"I guess I was a little preoccupied…"

"It happens," Claire says softly. "I need to call the parents of your four campers to see if they want to pick up their kids, since they saw everything. Are you okay to sit with her until the paramedics get here?"

I nod. "No problem…and I'm sorry for snapping at you earlier."

She waves her hand, dismissing the thought. "If any time were a time to snap, this is it." With a reassuring smile, she heads out the door.

I move my chair next to the bed and wait. Even with the bandage taped to her face, Kayla looks as beautiful as ever. Her long eyelashes curl up at the crest of her cheeks, full lips parted slightly. Not able to resist, I put my hand on hers and stroke the smooth skin with my thumb. Her head moves side to side, her eyes slowly fluttering open. "Where…what happened? Where are the kids?" She attempts to sit up on her elbows, and I gently guide her shoulder back down.

"Hey, it's okay. The kids are alright. I can explain it all later, just rest."

She shakes her head, then grabs it in agony before lying back down. "Ah, my head hurts."

"Yeah, you hit your head out on the trail. Just…lay…down," I say as she struggles against my hand.

"I'm fine, Chase. If you would stop moving around, my head wouldn't be pounding like this."

Despite the somber circumstances, I can't help but smile. "I'm not moving. That's the concussion talking."

She lays back down in defeat, closing her eyes and wincing at the pain in her head. For the next thirty minutes, she dozes in and out of sleep, and it takes everything in me not to reach for her hand again.

With a tap on the door, a slender bald man flips on the overhead light as a younger red-haired woman walks to the bed with a flashlight in hand. Kayla groans at the sudden brightness, shielding her eyes. I take a step back and let them work.

The young paramedic clicks off her light and peels back the sopping gauze, tsking as soon as she sees the wound. "Looks pretty deep, Todd."

Todd takes a quick look and hands his partner a small bottle of saline, some cotton swabs, and a sterile bandage from his pack. "Eh, I've seen worse." He turns a friendly smile to Kayla while his partner gets to work on the cut. Todd wraps the blood pressure cuff around her arm, saying, "Kayla Harris, I haven't seen you in ages. Tessa here's gonna clean you up." Air hisses as he squeezes the pump in his hand. "Now what's this I hear about you slapping logs with your head?"

"Hey, Todd." Kayla grimaces a grin, flinching with each dab Tessa presses on her wound. "Any chance you could patch me up right here?"

Tessa shakes her head as she secures a new bandage over Kayla's eye before glaring over at Todd. "She really needs to go in for stitches and observation, ASAP." Todd chuckles like it's an overreactive assessment, but after seeing how Kayla hit her head, I'm siding with Tessa. The sooner she can get to the hospital, the better.

He puts a hand on Kayla's knee, smiling while he fishes his penlight out of his shirt pocket with the other. "Afraid not, doll. Falls like this need a proper workup. Follow my finger." Shining the light in her eyes, he slides his pointer finger from left to right in front of her. "Tessa's right. You gotta go in. But I'll save you the ambulance ride if your friend here can drive you. Sound good?"

"*Ugh, fine,*" Kayla mumbles.

"Sure, no problem," I say quickly, feeling a little relieved at Todd's recommendation after his nonchalant bedside manner. Helping Kayla right now is my top priority.

Kayla groans and draws her knees up. "I don't have time to sit at the hospital."

"Thanks to that cut on your head, now you do." Todd

squeezes her shoulder and sticks his light back in his shirt pocket before turning to me. "Since you saw the fall, you relay that information to the doctors. Like I said, I'm okay if you want to drive her there, but make sure she stays awake the entire time."

"Absolutely. I'll do whatever she needs."

"Great!" Todd turns back to Kayla and pats her knee. "Tell your mom *hello* for me." He zips up his pack while Tessa tosses the used first aid supplies in the hazardous waste bin. I step to the side and thank them while they shuffle toward the exit.

From the doorway, I watch as Kayla sits up straight and loosens her hair from the usual bun. Black locs cascade around her, framing her shoulders and halfway down her back. She catches my stare. "What?"

"I don't think I've ever seen your hair down," I say carefully, hands in my pockets.

"It helps with the headache..." She grimaces, turning to face me.

"The girls want to see you before we go, if that's okay." Sarah and Harper peek around my back, and Kayla forces a smile, scrunching her nose in pain as she does. I leave them while they hug and cry and reassure one another, off to find Claire to figure out logistics. My steps echo through the long hallway connecting the infirmary to the mess hall.

To my surprise, Kyle meets me in the large dining hall with my bag and Sami with Kayla's. Sami hands me Kayla's car keys, and I thank her before heading out to stick the bags in the trunk. When I come back inside the dining area, I'm shocked to see Kayla sitting at a table, talking to Claire.

"Don't worry about the cleanup or anything. I want you to get on the road and get checked out. Chase already put your bags in the car, and he'll be driving you. We can worry about the incident reports later," Claire says, giving way too much information to someone with a concussion. And yet, Kayla nods like she's following every word.

"Ready?" I ask, helping her to her feet. She grabs my hand,

and I slide my arm around her, gripping her waist as she finds her balance. While having my arms wrapped around her again has been high on my list of experiences, this is not the way I imagined. She sways, bumping into me, and I grip tighter. "Don't worry, I got you," I whisper, trying to keep my thoughts from spiraling with worry.

I load her into the passenger side, and as we head down the road, she lays her head back and closes her eyes.

I shake her arm to get her attention. "Nope. You gotta stay awake, dear."

"Dear? *Ew.*" She scrunches her face, eyes still closed.

"Honey?"

"Ugh! That's bad too."

"Bae?" I chuckle.

"*You're* making my head hurt now," she groans, but a smile tugs at her lips. I blast the cold air in her direction, and that gets her eyes open. "Are you going to be this annoying the entire drive?" she asks, turning her head toward me.

"Probably."

She makes it a few more miles down the road before closing her eyes again, and I lace my fingers in hers, shaking her arm to wake her a second time. "Kayla, sweetheart, you gotta stay awake." Her eyes pop open, but she doesn't object to that one. She doesn't move her hand away either until we pull up to the hospital an hour later.

CHAPTER SEVENTEEN

KAYLA

I wake to a rhythmic beeping noise. My head throbs, pounds, as I pull myself up to sit. Turning toward a curtain-covered window, I make out a form dozing in the chair opposite the bed. I blink the bleariness from my eyes and clear my throat, looking for my phone and wincing when I turn my head.

"Hey, girl." Ashlie sits up, wiping drool from the corner of her mouth.

"Where's my phone? I should call my mom..." I croak. The dry, metallic taste in my mouth has me searching for water.

"Claire already called her. She had to finish her overnight shift, but she's on her way back now." She hands me a water-filled paper cup from the table by my hospital bed, and I drain it quickly.

"What time is it? What day is it?"

She grabs her phone from the chair. "Eight-thirty a.m. and Saturday," she says, laughing and shaking her head at something on her phone.

"Care to share with the class?" I quirk the wrong eyebrow and wince again. Holding her phone out to me, she walks toward the bed. The notifications show five missed texts from Chase, with a sixth one chiming in while I hold the phone.

CHASE

Thanks for staying with her.

Is she sleeping okay?

Can you give me her number?

Wait, no, give her my number.

Is she awake yet?

What kind of flowers does she like?

"You got that boy *stressed*," Ashlie blurts with a giggle. "It's pretty cute."

Staring at the phone, I recall everything I can from the last twenty-four hours. I don't remember the fall, but I remember Chase in the infirmary, concern etched across his face as I opened my eyes. The way he laced his fingers around mine to keep me alert during the drive here. Waiting with me until Ashlie got off work. Letting me squeeze his hand in response to the numbing needle, and staying while the doctor sewed me up. I remember him calling me sweetheart, and that thought gets my heart pounding in time to the pulsing in my head, making a nice rhythm for the gymnastics routine happening in my belly.

"Well, you should probably answer him then," I say, nodding at the phone.

The nurse comes in with breakfast and a painkiller for my head. No sooner than I finish the limp microwaved bacon and scrambled eggs, there's a knock at the door.

Chase stands in the doorway, carrying a bouquet of pink lilies, wearing a smile. Without the energy to find restraint, I allow myself to fully take him in for the first time since the day we met. The hair falling over his forehead, his crooked grin, the way his eyes glint when they meet mine, it's enough to set my heart pounding.

Again.

"That was quick," I say.

"I may or may not have been up and at 'em by six-thirty this morning..."

Ashlie shifts in the chair, grabbing her phone before standing. "And that's my cue." She shakes her head, laughing. "I'll be back in a bit. You two have fun." I watch her go, waiting for the door to click before looking back at Chase.

"How are you feeling?" His tentative steps match the nervous grin on his face. When he sits in the chair beside my bed, the thought crosses my mind that it's not close enough.

"Like I hit my head on a log," I tease. His smile falls, replaced with a look of concern. "Sorry. It's probably too soon to joke about it." The words stumble out of my mouth as I register the vulnerability flashing across his face.

Hesitating for the briefest moment, he reaches for my hand. The buzz of a billion atoms flows into our touch, and warmth spreads through my body as his thumb trails over my skin. "I was so worried about you... I'm sorry I couldn't get to you in time."

My breath hitches at the look in his eyes, and I'm lost to the deep blues staring back at me. "I...I'm okay. You don't have to apologize." I know he saw everything happen in real time, but his haunted look makes me question just how much I've underestimated his feelings for me. The look in his eyes shouts more than flirting and attraction. He looks at me like he cares about me, like he cares *for* me. And I have to admit, it's not the worst feeling, being cared for. "So...are those for me?" I nod toward the flowers.

"Yeah. Yep... *Yesss.*" He nods and puts the bouquet on the desk next to me. Thumb hooking under my palm, he shifts his fingers over mine, his voice taking on a husky tone as he says, "Kayla, I—"

The door swings open and in comes Mom, still wearing her scrubs from her travel nursing night shift. The concern in her eyes changes to surprise and then confusion as she looks between Chase and me.

"Hey, Mom," I say, my voice increasing an octave as I move my hand from under his.

She eyes him before asking, "Who's your friend...?"

"I'm Chase," he answers for me, standing to shake her hand. "I'm one of the counselors at Camp Bender."

"Yeah, he's the one that saw what happened. He carried me back to camp and drove me here."

"Well, I guess I owe you a thank you," Mom says politely, taking his outstretched hand.

"Oh, no thank you needed." Chase waves a hand in the air. "I'm just glad I was there to help." Mom tips her head, looking at him while we all fall into an awkward silence. "Well, I should probably let you rest. I just wanted to check on you." He smiles over at me, says another "Nice to meet you" to my mom, and walks out the door.

Mom turns around, arching her eyebrow as she comes to stand next to my bed. "He's cute..."

"He's just a friend." I shake my head, biting my cheek to keep from smiling. I don't even believe myself when I hear the words slip out of my mouth.

"Uh-huh, and I was born last night..."

It's Tuesday evening, and I'm already crawling out of my skin. My head hurts occasionally, usually when I try to do too much, but I'm itching to be productive. Mom is doing everything in her power to keep that from happening, including hiding my car keys and locking the vacuum in her bedroom. She wants me rotting on the couch, and I'm trying to do everything but.

A knock on the door has me jumping from my spot on the sofa. Mom comes rushing from the kitchen, giving me a look of warning when she says, "Sit down, Kayla Marie." I roll my eyes at her back as she opens the door. She'd keep me lying on this couch until I get my stitches out on Friday if she could.

"Hey, Ms. Harris," Ashlie says as she walks through the door, carrying her hair box in one hand and a box of sushi in the other. "Hey, girl." She turns toward me on the couch. "How you feelin'?"

"Bored," I say, shifting a side-eyed look over to Mom who throws her hands up in the air, shaking her head like she's exasperated. She walks back into the kitchen without another word.

"Well, let's get into this hair," Ashlie says, standing behind the couch and handing me the food. She's been doing my hair for as long as I've known her, and she's the one who encouraged me to get locs back in high school. I maintain my hair on my own when I'm away at school, but Ashlie helps me retighten my locs whenever we're both back home. Since we don't have many essentials for Black hair care here in Fort Bender, it's been nice having someone to share the load with.

I turn toward the TV as she sections off the bottom row of my locs. She begins weaving the strands until they're tight against my scalp.

"So..." I say. "How are the guys?"

"*Chase* is fine. He keeps asking about you." Her hands loosen the silk scrunchie at the top of my head long enough for her to pull down the next row of hair.

"And what do you tell him?"

"Do you want me to give him your number so you two can talk and leave me out of it?"

Do I? That remains unclear. Everything after my fall has been different, and I've been trying to reconcile the friendship we cultivated at camp with the *something more* I've felt since waking up in the infirmary. I still feel the warmth that spread through me as he laced his fingers around mine in the car. Flutters surged through my core each time he called me sweetheart, and I liked watching him walk through the door of my hospital room with a smile and flowers, just for me. But it's been a few days, and having some distance from him has given time for doubts to slip in. Something in me wants to leave that experience, and all the warm fuzzies that accompanied it, under lock and key in my memory so nothing can taint it. "I-I'm not sure. I don't know." I shrug.

Ashlie sighs, dropping her hands from my hair, prompting me to turn and look at her. "Do you like him?" She watches my face for any nuance. I can't even admit it to myself right now, and saying the words out loud will cement them into canon in a way that feels detrimental to my carefully crafted dignity.

"We're just friends," I answer with finality. She squints at me, quietly calling my bluff, before shaking her head and leaving it alone. I turn back around, digging into the sushi and pretending I'm fully invested in the show on TV. My mind, however, is trying to sort out feelings I've been avoiding for weeks.

CHAPTER EIGHTEEN

CHASE

"Hard no." Ashlie shakes her head as she leans around Hunter to look at me. It's Wednesday afternoon, and we're at the diner like we would be on any other Wednesday. Everything's like it normally is, except Kayla isn't here. Pattie with an *IE* is nice and everything, but she's no Kayla.

"Ashlie, please..." I beg. "I just want to check on her. It's been days."

"She's at home with her mom, who's a nurse. And I saw her last night. She's fine."

"Ashlie—"

"Uh-uh, nope. I'm not hopping over that boundary. If she wanted you to have her number, she would have given it to you." She turns back to her food, shaking her head again.

I look to Hunter, and he shrugs back before checking the newest notification on his phone. "*Ugh*, okay. You're right." I give up, blowing out a breath and scrubbing my face in my hands. This is literal torture, going from talking to her every day to radio silence. "Can you tell her I was asking about her, at least?"

"I did, last night. And the night before."

"And...?"

Ashlie growls in frustration, shooting a glare over at me.

"Bruh, chill," Hunter finally chimes in before turning to Ashlie. "He wants to know if she's asking about him, too, but he's too scared to say it."

I clench my fist and tap it on my leg, thinking better of slugging him in the arm. *What the hell, man!*

"Sorry. Girl code," she says, pushing back from the counter. "And now, *I'm* taking my lunch to go because *you* are driving me nuts with your one-man lovesick, puppy dog show over there. She's fine. She'll be back to work on Saturday." Ashlie stops at the counter to pay for her food and rolls her eyes over at us before waving and walking back to the museum across the street.

I kick Hunter's foot from the stool ledge. "Speaking of, what ever happened to guy code, Hunt?"

"Oh, I'm *sorry*. With all the whining you were doing, I didn't realize you were trying to hide your feelings for this girl. *My bad.*"

Shaking my head, I let out a breath and focus on lunch. Pattie with an *IE* asks how we're doing, and all I can think about is how much better I'd be if I could talk to Kayla.

I TAP MY KNEES, TRYING TO FOCUS ON THE DETECTIVE show on TV. It's good, one of my favorites, but I can't concentrate when my thoughts keep straying to Kayla. How is she doing? *What* is she doing? Fidgeting is the only way I feel like I'm making something happen, when I know I can't do anything until she's ready to see me—talk to me, even. Shifting on the couch, I lean back into the cushion until the energy coursing through my body forces me to sit forward with my elbows on my knees. I finally stand, stretching my back and walking into the kitchen for a bottle of water. Needing something to do with my hands, I tap the bottle lid on the counter a few times. It doesn't help.

"You're all over the place," Hunter says from the couch. "You need to go for a run or something? You're driving me crazy."

I breathe out a long sigh while tipping my head up toward the ceiling. "I know. I can't sit still. I just need to move."

"You like this girl that much? What happened up at that camp that has you doing all this?"

"Nothing, really. She's just—something about her has me—I just like her."

"She's under your skin."

"Bad. It's like, I felt drawn to her from the beginning, but now that she's starting to open up, the pull is magnetic. I can't get her out of my head."

He scrunches his face, shaking his head like he's about to do something he'll regret. "Okay, I'm gonna give you some info, but if you tell Ashlie I said anything, I'm gonna call you a liar."

"Why did Ashlie give *you* info?"

"Because we hung out while you two were doing whatever up at camp, and she's cool. Do you want the info, or do you wanna ask more stupid questions?"

"Info," I say, rubbing the hair on my face.

He puts his phone down and looks at me while he delivers the news. "Kayla's been asking about you too."

"She has?" I breathe a sigh of relief, feeling like my heart's about to burst right out of my chest. It's not a detailed revelation, but it's enough.

"Yeah, but you gotta chill all the way out, man. You gotta move slow or you're gonna scare her off. She'll be back to work on Saturday, so take the next few days to calm the fuck down."

I nod slowly, feeling the first few edges of calm enter my thoughts since seeing Kayla at the hospital last week. She's been asking Ashlie about me, which isn't huge, but it's something. Something that has me a little more hopeful than I have been since meeting her at the beginning of summer.

"I'm gonna go for that run. You coming?" I ask Hunter.

"I'm down." He stands from the couch and walks upstairs, nodding while he slips his phone in his pocket.

Feeling the cool breeze whip through my hair as I pull fresh air in and out of my lungs is exactly what I need to help get some clarity. My mind still filters through thoughts about Kayla, but I've come up with some strategies to hopefully move our fragile friendship into something more. I'll give her space until Saturday, and I'll feel her out then. But I can't carry on pretending like we're friends when I want to be so much more. I'm determined to shoot my shot at least a few more times before throwing in the towel.

Hunter keeps up beside me, heavy bass thumping from his earbuds, and I'm reminded of all our years on the track team. He needs the noise to run, but I prefer the silence when I need to clear my mind. Something about hearing my breathing and my pulse in my ears helps bring me inward. Give me music for training days, but not when I need to think.

The pounding of our footsteps slows as we return to the bottom of the hill under The Bluffs. I tip my head to the sky, sucking in the fresh air as I prepare to run up this hill. Hunter bends at the waist, holding his side.

"You good?" he asks, turning his head toward me.

"I will be when I beat you up this hill." I take off, stretching my legs past him to try and get a head start on this impromptu race. Hunter still runs track for the Gradford team, while I stopped after high school, but I wouldn't say I was ever faster than him, even back then.

"Motherf—" He takes off after me, my long-legged stride no match for his speed. I'm halfway up the hill by the time he's right on my heels. When we reach the rental, I'm looking at his sweat-stained T-shirt back. He turns around, grinning wide at his victory. "Gettin' slow there, Chasey boy," he says, laughing and whacking me in the arm.

Chuckling, I sit on the porch steps, running my hands through my sweat-slicked hair and feeling more relaxed than I have in a while. I needed this, even if only to sort out my thoughts surrounding how I want to move forward. I'll pump my brakes and follow Kayla's lead. Slow and steady wins the race, right? I've proven that with the progress I've already made.

Hunter leans against the porch banister, looking down at me when he asks, "But seriously, you good?"

I nod quietly and look out at the trees swaying in the breeze down the hill. I'm good, and on Saturday, I'll be even better.

CHAPTER NINETEEN

KAYLA

The doorbell at Patti's Place jingles over my head as I walk in for my first lunch shift since my fall. My stitches were removed yesterday, and apart from a thin scar, you can barely tell I lost a fight with a log. Patti threatened to fire me if I didn't take the entire week off to recuperate. I had to negotiate only working a half shift before she agreed to let me come back today, and I'm ready to hit the ground running.

"Hey, Patti." I smile at the familiar feeling of being back at the diner. As tired as I am at the end of my shifts, I've missed this place.

"Ooh!" She rushes over to give me a side hug. "How are you feeling?"

"Good! Better. I haven't had a headache since Thursday."

She purses her lips, eyes scanning mine, before she finally says, "I have half a mind to send you back home another day or two. I'll be in the back for your entire shift today. If you feel so much as a tingle in your head, you'd better let me know."

"Sure thing, Pat." Slipping behind the counter, I head down the hallway to replace my purse with my apron. I make it back out just in time to watch Ashlie stroll in, followed by Hunter and

Chase. Grabbing menus from the register, I tuck them under my arm and head toward the water dispenser.

"I'm just *saying,* it's the last day of June, and we haven't done anything. Not even the 'puff-puff train'." Hunter taps his hands on the counter.

"The *what-what* train?" Ashlie's head juts back as she looks at him like he's sprouted another head. Chase laughs while Hunter tries to explain again.

"You know, the 'Herbal Train,' or whatever it's called."

"The Herb Train?" I ask, placing water and menus down on the counter.

"Hey," Chase says.

"Hi." I bite my lip, suddenly feeling timid as heat creeps up my neck. Chase's wide smile almost pins me in place. I know he's been asking about me, and I'd be lying if I were to say he hasn't been on my mind all week too. But I just don't know what to do about him. Taking the week to think about it was supposed to help me clear my mind, but it's hard to do that when my mind has been swimming with the possibilities of the charmer sitting in front of me.

"Here they go again..." Ashlie laughs as Hunter shakes her hand, repeating their comedy bit from weeks ago.

"How are you?" Chase asks, putting his hand on mine. Going from being around him almost every day to nothing for an entire week has left a bit of a void in a place I didn't know he had staked a claim. Between camp and daily diner visits, we haven't needed to, but now...now might be the time to give him my number.

"I'm good." I smile back. The bell over the door rings again. "Working," I say, tipping my head toward the sound, enjoying the warmth of his hand over mine. Suddenly, I don't want to move from this moment. This quiet intimacy we've established feels nice—right. The anticipation I feel whenever he gets close enough to touch is exciting and new, and I kind of like it.

A loud gasp turns all of us toward the door. "Chase Wilmington, is that you?" says a petite brunette. Her hair waves down around her bare, olive-skinned shoulders, stopping short of the belted waist of her sundress. Her tall friends, blond buns high and tight, glide in behind her. All three seem to float forward, feet flitting gracefully. "Your mom said you might be here…" Her voice trails as she looks down at his hand on mine.

Hunter mumbles something about ballerinas under his breath.

"Hey, Maggie," Chase says with a polite smile on his face. He doesn't move his hand from mine, and his thumb strokes the back of my fingers idly. "Where'd you see my mom?"

"Oh, back at the rental. We had to finish our semester, but Daddy rented out the fourth house at The Bluffs Estates for us." Maggie looks around the restaurant, scrunching her face as she folds one arm over her chest, her handbag tucked in the crevice of her other elbow. Her upturned palm hangs pointed in the air as her eyes finish their sweep and land on me. "This is such a… kitschy little diner."

"You're staying here?" Hunter asks, his own look of disgust bolstering the animosity in his eyes.

"Oh, hey, *cousin*," she says coolly, sneering back at Hunter.

"Hey, Maggot," he bites back with a smirk. Ashlie chokes on her water at his response, while Chase mashes his lips together, stifling a laugh and shaking his head.

"Anyway…aren't you going to give me a hug? I haven't seen you in forever!" she lilts back to Chase, placing long dainty fingers on his arm.

"Uh…" He pauses, looking over at me. I slide my hand from under his, my sudden self-consciousness occupying the space of the intimacy I was feeling moments ago. A flash of unease fills his eyes when I move away, and I look down to avoid it. He's clearly got some kind of history with this girl, and she came in hot with the territorial vibes. I turn around to grab menus and water for the newcomers, taking a couple of deep breaths before fixing the disappointment on my face. When I turn back around, I try to ignore the festering pit in my stomach.

"...Sure." Chase stands for the embrace and Maggie melts into him, slowly stroking his back and smirking in my direction. I try to shove down the jealousy simmering in my chest by reminding myself we aren't together. In fact, I told Chase we couldn't be together. Besides, I'm working. *I'm working.* This is my job, and I don't have time for whatever is happening right now.

Snapping out of my internal spiral, I return to the counter with a smile. "Welcome to Patti's," I say to the trio. "Feel free to sit at the counter, or pick a booth. I'll be with you in a minute." And thankfully, they pick a booth, leaving me with my friends at the counter.

"So are you going to order or...?" I say, staring down at my notepad, avoiding looking at any of them.

"Burger and fries," Hunter says smoothly, breaking the silence.

"I'll do a BLT," Ashlie chimes.

I turn toward Chase, keeping my eyes fixed on the paper in my hand, and I wait.

And he waits.

"What do you want, Chase?" I ask, frustration poking through the calm in my voice. I peek up at him, and those deep ocean waves watch me, appearing to be contemplating something that has nothing to do with his lunch order.

"What a loaded question..." he says, looking right into my eyes. "I'll start with a turkey wrap and see what else looks good." He eyes me up and down with a desire-burning gaze.

"What was *that*?" Ashlie cackles, shaking her head. "You're getting rusty there, Chase."

"So, train? Tonight at five? These two are already in," Hunter cuts in, looking at me.

"Oh, me? I don't know. I don't think I'll be home by then."

"You will," Patti's voice says from behind me, grinning from ear to ear. "She'll be there, boss's orders!"

CHAPTER TWENTY

CHASE

We pull up to the train depot a little before five p.m. and wait for the ticket booth to open. Wrought-iron gates surround it, set against a backdrop of redwood trees. A brown and burgundy steam engine sits just beyond the ticket counter, pulling three mustard-colored train cars behind it.

I glance at my phone to check the time again and look around the parking lot, hoping to see a silver sedan pull in. What I see instead makes me groan internally, my scalp prickling with irritation. Maggie St. Clair and her cronies drive by in a jet-black luxury SUV, looking out of place next to the smaller, fuel-efficient cars in the parking lot.

"Did you invite Maggie tonight?" I turn to Hunter, tipping my head in their direction.

"Why the hell would I do that?" he asks, missing my gesture while he cranes his neck to look down the track. I kick his foot and he looks up, instantly grimacing as disgust floods over his face. "No, I didn't invite her. You know I can't stand her."

Hunter and Maggie may be cousins, but you wouldn't know it. They look nothing alike and share a mutual disdain that only escalated once Hunter's parents divorced. Where Hunter likes to have fun and live carefree, never taking himself too seriously,

Maggie embodies poise and discipline, oozing with pretentiousness. They're oil and water personified.

"Ashlie and your girl are here though." He nods behind me.

"She's not my girl..." I shove my fidgeting fingers in my pocket, the word *yet* hanging off the tip of my tongue.

"But you want her to be. And she wants to be...or she did, before you hugged Maggie at lunch." He shivers, scrunching his face like he's just tasted something bitter. I regretted hugging Maggie as soon as I agreed to it, and watching Kayla's face drop as she pulled her hand away from mine was like a punch to the gut. Maggie doesn't get along with many people, and I guess I feel bad for her. But in my effort to be friendly to someone I really don't care for, I may have harmed what little chance I have with someone I do.

Kayla's hair is down tonight, her locs deeply parted and flipped to one side, fanning around the dark denim jacket on her shoulders. An olive-green tee hugs the dip in her waist before giving way to ripped, skin-tight black jeans. I've never seen her style outside of a waitress uniform and camp counselor shirts. This newest glimpse into her personality only fans the flame. She bites her lip and looks down at her boots, and I realize I'm staring again.

"Before you two start your little 'hi' routine, the ticket booth is open," Hunter says, the smirk returning to his face as he watches the tension between us.

The four of us make our way onto the train, with Hunter leading us back to the middle car. Warm yellow lighting against cream walls creates a path along the ceiling, and brown vinyl seats, just wide enough for two people, face together next to large windows.

Hunter takes a seat, and I grab the one across from him. Ashlie catches on and heads toward Hunter. "Boy, if you don't slide over and give me the window..." She nudges his shoulder until he moves to the opposite end of the seat.

Kayla plops down next to me, her hip pressing into mine. I

drum my fingers on my knee as I struggle to keep my hands to myself. "Do you want the window?" I ask casually, trying to expel my nervous energy through small talk.

"I'm okay." She smiles, placing her hand on mine, stilling the rhythm of my tapping. She doesn't move away, so I take it as a good sign and flip our hands over, knitting our fingers together.

"*Okay*! Progress! Progress!" Ashlie claps her hands in a silent applause, nodding approval at our newest milestone.

It takes about an hour to get from the depot to the outdoor bar. Ashlie and Hunter keep the conversation light and flowing while I steal glances over at Kayla. Seemingly relaxed and happy, she laughs easily at the banter between our best friends. She hasn't moved her hand away from mine, and I know with complete surety I'm not letting go first.

We arrive at a large green barn with sparkling lights lining the places where walls used to be. A small gazebo sits toward the back of the property, overlooking a trickling stream. Lawn games are scattered over a grassy grove across from firepits surrounded by Adirondack chairs. The sign at the entrance gate reads Herbert's Hole, with an inscribed history of the establishment.

"Herbert's Hole?" Hunter fakes disgust. I just know he's about to make this into some kind of innuendo. "They couldn't think of a better name? We're playing all night in Herbert's Hole?"

Kayla snorts a laugh next to me, while Ashlie shoves his shoulder playfully.

"Hunter, that's disgusting!" a familiar voice snarls from behind me. I turn to see Maggie, flanked by her friends, whose names I forget. Cami and Tami? Carly and Tara?

"Why are you even here, Magma?" Hunter asks, shoving his hands in the pockets of his jacket.

Maggie's lips fall into a thin line as she rolls her eyes at the misnomer. "Your dad asked if we were going on the train ride, and we thought it sounded fun."

"You wouldn't know fun if it bit you in the ass."

"You're so crude," she replies, staring him down.

"And we"—Ashlie cuts in, pointing to Kayla and herself—"are going to get our drinks. Maybe you two should stay away from each other tonight, hmm?" She lifts an eyebrow at the dueling cousins, links arms with Kayla, and pulls her toward the bar. Kayla shrugs back at me, and I watch her walk away.

"She's right. You two should probably keep to opposite corners tonight. We came to have fun," I offer diplomatically, which seems to be the role I play whenever they go at each other's throats.

"Sounds good to me," Hunter huffs. "Make sure you get your kiddie wristband, Maggot," he sneers over his shoulder as he walks toward the bar, referencing the fact that Maggie is still under twenty-one.

I turn to follow when Maggie grabs my hand. "You can come hang out with us when you get sick of their juvenile joking."

"I'll keep that in mind," I say, taking back my hand and shoving it into the pocket of my sweater. I jog to catch up to Hunter, leaving the imposing ballerinas to make their own fun.

CHAPTER TWENTY-ONE

CHASE

We settle in chairs around a firepit, close to a stage where a large speaker and portable screen are set up on the concrete platform. A middle-aged redhead is singing karaoke to a popular country song, her hair swinging around as she shimmies her body to the beat. People bob their heads along to the music, keeping their separate conversations alive despite the performance. When the song ends, whooping and hollering sounds from all around the bar. She takes a bow and runs back to her seat, joining a table full of laughing women.

Just as I'm about to turn toward Kayla, she hands her drink to Ashlie and walks up to the stage. I look to Ashlie for an explanation.

"Oh, you're in for a treat," she says, nodding toward the stage. "Kayla's a karaoke master."

She adjusts the microphone stand on stage and straightens her jacket. The music to a slow blues ballad starts, and she closes her eyes, cradling the length of the stand in her hands. *What I wouldn't give to be that microphone right now.*

Her body sways to the soulful melody, and the smooth sound of her voice washes over me as she croons the first words of the love song. I'm entranced, frozen under her spell as her voice lilts and swells around me. I couldn't look away if I wanted to, the words of the chorus striking me right in the heart:

> *Sometimes*
> *What you've lost, you'll find*
> *And you'll fall in kind*
> *To some kind of forever.*

The silence of the crowd when she finishes is a stark difference from the performance before, ending abruptly when Ashlie and Hunter whoop and clap. The rest of the patrons follow suit, and Kayla smiles, taking a bow before heading back over to us.

"Amazing," I say, giving her a smile. I reach out to squeeze her hand, and she beams at me. I don't let go, she doesn't pull away, and my determination to take things to the next level with her has multiplied tenfold.

After a couple of drinks and several rounds of horseshoe, our group of four has separated. Hunter and Ashlie are battling it out at a giant four-in-a-row game, laughing and joking like they've been friends for years. I spot Kayla standing in the gazebo, gazing into the water. The sun has gone down, and the twinkling lights strung along the ceiling cast a warm yellow glow over her. I weave my way through the guests enjoying their night at the firepits, around the twinkle lit walls of the bar, and straight back to her.

"Hey," I say, stepping beside her, breaking whatever thought she was lost in. Leaning my arms against the wooden railing, I peer over to the water below.

"Hey," she says breathily, jolting slightly in surprise. I scoot closer just to feel the warmth of her arm against mine. She looks down at our touch and then right into my eyes, biting her lip. "I... think you should have my number..."

"Oh?" I grin. "And why is that?"

"Maybe I missed seeing you last week..." She flips around so her back and elbows rest on the railing.

"Maybe or definitely?"

"Definitely maybe," she teases, looking up through her lashes. My heart skips several beats as I contemplate pulling her close and pressing my lips to hers, a month's worth of tension finally washing away. "We have an audience," she whispers, nodding her head forward. I look over my shoulder to see Maggie watching us from the firepits.

"Ah, yeah. Maggie." I nod, turning back to the water. "She's intense."

"She's been watching you all night, Chase."

"Has she?" I ask. "I've been a little distracted and haven't noticed." To make her smile, I wiggle my eyebrows. It works, with an added eye roll before she tilts her head to the side.

"She clearly likes you. She damn near peed on your leg at the diner trying to mark her territory." Kayla watches me, and her cool mask slips briefly as a moment of anxiety flashes in her eyes.

I rub my fingers against my forehead, trying to ease the frustration that has settled there. This is *not* what I want to be doing right now, talking to Kayla about Maggie. I don't want to be talking about *anything* with Kayla right now. I'd rather be kissing her. Dropping my eyes to the water, I focus on the languid trickle as it flows past, hoping to gather my thoughts well enough to redeem myself. "I know. It's been like this since we were little. She has it in her head that we'll end up together eventually, and no amount of me brushing her off gets the point across."

"Wrapping her in your arms doesn't help get that point across either..." There's an edge to Kayla's voice, one that has me nervous about glancing over at her.

"I... Yeah. I know. And I shouldn't have hugged her." I stand, turning to face her.

"Then why did you?"

"I guess I was just trying to be nice. She doesn't get along with a lot of people, as you saw." I finally get the courage to slide my eyes up to her face. She's looking at me with that same guarded expression I worked so hard to break through at camp.

"And you've never...been with her? Wanted to be with her?"

The look in her eyes is killing me, thinking that I could possibly want anyone but her in this moment, let alone Maggie.

"Nope. Never. She's the furthest from anyone I could see myself with." I place one hand on each of her shoulders, turning her toward me. "Kayla, I—"

"Train leaves in ten!" The bartender calls from a loudspeaker, cutting off my words and any other chances I had at resolving this conversation.

"We should probably go find the other two." Kayla pulls away, kicking at the ground. I nod, and while we walk back toward the train together in silence, the gulf between us feels wider than it did when we first met. We find Hunter and Ashlie waiting at a firepit, talking animatedly about something I can't hear because I'm stuck replaying my fizzled moment in the gazebo.

The last train car is mostly empty, except for a cozy couple in the corner. Ashlie and Hunter are still debating over fruit filled donuts vs. custard filled when we sit. Their volume, assisted by the drinks at the bar, gets louder and louder as they volley back and forth. Kayla has her hand covering her mouth, and she shakes her head as she watches their passion-filled pastry argument.

"I'm going to get some air." I point to the train car balcony. "Do you wanna—"

"Please!" She widens her eyes, looking at the two across from us.

As I stand to leave, she reaches for my hand and we make our way outside. The crisp night air whips around us as the train breezes past trees, the leaves leaving whispers in their wake. The moonlight glows through the branches overhead, raining silvery beams on Kayla's face.

"You were amazing up there, singing..." I say again, remembering the chills I got from listening to her honey-sweet voice. This feels like a safer conversation to have than the one we left in the gazebo, and I just want to focus on her right now.

"Thanks," she whispers, flashing a grin before biting her lip.

She leans against the end of the balcony, closing her eyes and tipping her head back, smiling the same way she did in the sunshine at camp. At this moment, I realize it doesn't matter if it's in the sunlight or moonlight. That smile will always steal my breath away.

"I never thanked you for staying with me after the accident. Carrying me inside. Keeping me awake in the car. Making sure I was okay... Thank you, Chase." She looks right at me, eyes betraying the calm in her voice. A vulnerability I've never seen or heard from her sets me in motion. I move closer, unable to stop my feet, even if I wanted to. Slowly, I reach one hand to the scar on her brow, the other landing on her hip.

"How's your head?" I whisper, my voice turning husky as the scent of spicy apple-vanilla overtakes my senses. My thumb traces down to her cheekbone, across the ridge of her upper lip, and lower, until I find myself lifting her chin. Her hands pull me in at the waist, and we dip close enough that I feel her breath swirl with mine.

"Yo, Chase!" Hunter yells, busting through the train door. If there were ever a worse moment for my best friend to come around, this was it.

"I'm gonna kill him..." I whisper, tipping my forehead to hers. She giggles, breathing out the lingering passion between us, and takes a step back. My hand clings to her waist, refusing to let go.

"Ooh, my bad!" he says, realizing what he just interrupted.

"Way to go, Hunter. You ruined the moment." Ashlie pulls on his arm. "I told you to give them a minute!"

Another giggle slips out of Kayla.

"I said I was sorry! Besides, who makes out on the balcony of a train?"

"Not us, apparently," I say, shooing him with my hand. "Do you mind?"

The train door opens again and out walks Maggie. She sees my arms wrapped around Kayla and her eyes narrow, mouth set in a scowl. Kayla's giggles have turned into outright laughter at the scene unfolding. The more people who spill through the door, the harder she laughs, and I can't even blame her. The comedic timing of everything happening right now isn't lost on me, but it would be funnier if I wasn't the one being stunted.

As Casey and Lacey—or whatever their names are—squeeze through the door, Kayla taps her palm over my heart. "Maybe next time, Chase," she says with a sigh, still half laughing while pulling away. She steps around the five interruptions and back into the rail car.

I hang my head in defeat and inhale the night air, wondering what the hell just happened. This entire night should have been different—easy. Not full of disruptions and ballerinas. Blowing out my exasperation, I march across the balcony of the train and move through the gaggle of chaos still staring at me. With each determined step I take, I know what I need to do. If I don't do anything else tonight, I'm getting Kayla's number.

Marching inside, I head straight to the row of seats where Kayla's staring out of the window. I clear my throat to get her attention, and her eyes meet mine, a small smile on her face. She bites the inside of her cheek to keep from laughing, and I lose it, tipping my head back with a shoulder-shaking chortle at everything that just happened. Her shoulders shake in time with mine as she giggles, and I cover my laugh with my hand and give her my phone. The addition of the phone only adds fuel to the fire as her snickering turns into a boisterous cackle, making her double over. I sit down across from her, taking a couple of breaths to try and quell my laughter.

When we've calmed enough to look at each other, I lean forward, putting my hands on her knees. "Hey, so...there's something wrong with my phone..." I nod toward her hands. She raises an eyebrow as she looks at me, waiting for me to continue. "Your number's not in it..." I finish my tried-and-true number two pickup line.

She nods, biting the smile sliding across her lips. "See. I told you that one would work," she says, before typing her number into my phone. *Finally.*

CHAPTER TWENTY-TWO

KAYLA

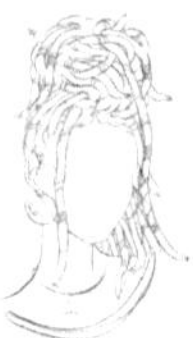

"So let me get this straight," Ashlie says, sitting on my couch. We came right from the train to have a mini girl's night sleepover at my house. She sits cross-legged on the cushion, facing me, while our favorite trashy TV show plays in the background. "Chase has almost kissed you not once, not twice, but *three* times? And this is the first I'm hearing about it?"

"Yeah...sorry." I wrinkle my nose. "But to be fair, two of those were on the same night up at camp, about twenty minutes apart..."

"Girl!" She reaches forward and nudges me on the knee. "Start from the beginning. What happened at camp?"

"Besides sitting in his lap on the climbing wall? Nothing," I say casually, watching her eyes widen.

"Was this a planned sitting or...?"

"No, I didn't plan to sit in his lap. I didn't even plan to see him after the tip jar incident, but he's been everywhere." I tell her about the awkwardness on the wall, the thumb war around the fire, and the intense moment in front of my cabin. She listens, eyes intensely taking in each anecdote like it's straight from the gossip column.

"And you like him," she says, squinting her eyes at me.

"I...don't know."

"Oh, don't give me that. You held his hand the entire way to the bar tonight, and you almost kissed him out on the balcony. He's cute, he's your type, and he likes you too."

"My type?" I ask, raising my eyebrows skeptically. "And what is 'my type'?"

"You know. Cute, funny, tall, Chase... Your type." She waves her hand in the air to get her point across.

"*Ugh!*" I sigh into my hands. "He is my type, and I hate it." I *do* like him. Despite all my attempts to thwart all *his* attempts, I like him.

Ashlie laughs, shaking her head at my undoing. She nudges my foot with hers. "Why do you hate it? He's a nice guy."

"Evan was a nice guy..." I say. I see the humor drain from her face as she realizes what all my hesitation has been about.

"Nice to look at, maybe, but you know damn well Chase isn't anything like Evan."

I look at her, quietly waiting for her to convince me otherwise.

"For starters, Chase *actually* likes you. He's spent almost every day at the diner just for a couple of minutes to talk to you. Evan only liked the fact that you liked him—always asking you to drop what you had going on to spend time with him and then making you feel bad if you didn't."

I sigh, knowing she's right. Chase even said as much up at camp, and logically, I know this. But emotionally, I'm ready to tuck my tail and run. Three years is a long time, but not long enough for me to forget how hard it was to get back to myself after freshman year.

"Has Chase ever tried to convince you to call out of work?" She gives me a look that tells me she already knows the answer.

"No," I say quietly.

"Has he ever made you feel bad for being a workaholic?"

"I am not a worka—"

"Yes, you are. Answer the question."

"No," I whisper again.

"And what did he do when you told him you couldn't kiss him up at camp?"

I roll my eyes, catching on to her logic. "He respected it and backed away."

"Exactly. Evan may have been a 'nice guy'"—she throws her fingers up in air quotes— "but Chase is a *good* one. He's met you where you are, patiently waiting for you to let down some of those thick-ass walls when other guys would have been long gone by now. The question isn't whether you like him. The question is if you're brave enough to do something about it." She leans forward and puts a hand over mine, stilling the fingers picking at my thumb. "You deserve to be with someone who treats you well, girl. Evan can't be your 'Happily Never After' forever."

I let her words settle in around me, relenting to the fact that I can't hide from my feelings about Chase anymore. My phone buzzes on the coffee table beside me, skittering across the smooth glass at the same time Ashlie's goes off under her leg. I grab mine, opening it to find a group message.

> CHASE
>
> Hey there. Are you two busy on the 4th?
>
> My family is having a BBQ and I wanted to invite you.

I look up at Ashlie, who's already watching me with a smirk on her face.

"Hey," she says, holding her hands up in a surrendering pose. "It's up to you. If you want to go, I'll go with you. If you don't, I can text him back with some bad excuse."

She's giving me an out, testing me to see if I'm brave enough to step away from the shadow of my last failed relationship. I mull it over for several minutes, trying to play out the worst-case scenarios in my head. On one hand, I could give in, give Chase a chance, and get my heart broken.

Again.

On the other hand, I could cut and run, and always wonder what if.

"You're forgetting to think about the third possibility..." Ashlie's voice breaks through the mental argument I'm having with myself.

I tip my head, wondering if I was talking out loud without realizing it. "How did you—"

"You might have everyone else fooled, but I've known you for almost eight years. You're a pessimist and thinking you're either going to get your heart broken or wonder what could have been. I'm saying, there's a third possibility you're not considering."

"Okay... Are you going to enlighten me or...?" I ask.

"It could all work out. You could end up happy." Shrugging before leaning over the back of the couch, she digs in her overnight bag. "And here." She tosses me a small box. I catch it, and immediately throw it back at her upon realizing it's a box of condoms.

"What the hell, Ash! I don't—that's not happening anytime soon." I fumble my words as I try to recover from the flustered feeling creeping up my neck.

Doubled over, she's laughing so hard her shoulders shake. "You should have seen your face!" She mimics my expression before cracking up all over again.

I roll my eyes, shaking my head at her before giggles overtake me as well. After a minute, she slides the box back toward me.

"Seriously though, just in case. You've got too much going for you, and we're breaking that Harris family pattern."

I leave the box against my knee where she's pushed it and pick up my phone.

ME

We'll be there. Can I bring anything?

CHASE

Apple Pie *smiley face*

CHAPTER TWENTY-THREE

KAYLA

"Wow, these houses are bigger than I realized," Ashlie says, eyes widening as she peers up at The Bluffs Estates from the open door of my car. These houses were built after we left for college, and it's never really been an interest during our visits home to drive across town and check them out. Until now.

Ashlie's white sundress contrasts with my light blue one, matching today's Fourth of July color scheme. I start walking up to the door, Patti's apple pies in hand, when she stops me. "Hey, if I need to find a ride home tonight, so be it." She wiggles her brows playfully, and my eyes widen at what she's implying.

"That won't be happening." I hand her a pie and push the thought from my head.

"Bet it does, girl." She bumps my hip and walks ahead of me to the front door, leaving my thoughts racing at the idea that things would progress so quickly with Chase tonight that she'd need to find a ride home. She's almost to the stairs by the time I snap out of it and scurry after her.

"Hey!" Hunter flashes a grin and steps back to let us in the house. The inside is coastal, white, and open concept, giving it a fresh feel. Stairs on our left lead up to a loft and a couple of rooms, while the hallway on the right is lined with what I assume are more bedrooms and a bathroom. The kitchen is front and center, with an expansive picture window in the dining area that showcases the estate's namesake.

"Everyone's out back. You can leave the pie on the counter." He begins to lead us outside when a door opens to my right. Chase, wearing a sky blue polo and khakis, steps out. A wide grin spreads across his face when he sees me. "Well, aren't you two cute... Did you plan this?" Hunter asks sarcastically, referencing our matching outfits. Hunter and Ashlie head out the door while I place the pie on the counter next to a spread of fruit trays and salads.

"He's right," Chase says, placing his hand on the small of my back. "We do look pretty good together."

I turn to face him, biting my lip to hide the ever-growing smile as we stand suspended in the moment. "Hey," I say, looking down.

"I'm glad you could make it," he whispers, lifting my chin until our eyes meet. It shouldn't be this nerve-racking, talking to him this close, being that we see each other nearly every day. I shouldn't have this crescendo of butterflies in my stomach every time, and yet, something in the small ways he touches me melts any logical thought I have. I expect him to kiss me right here, but he lowers his hand and laces his fingers with mine instead. "Is this still okay? Holding hands?" He rubs his thumb over mine.

I nod, and with a smile, he pulls me across the kitchen. We make it out to the deck, where we're immediately greeted with loud music and laughter. Ashlie and Hunter are sitting on the banister with drinks in hand, swaying side to side, watching three young girls play with sparklers. Maggie and her friends are at the far end of the conjoined deck, sitting with a slender woman whose graying light brown hair is pulled up into a loose bun. A tall blond man wears an apron while standing at the grill, smiling over at a Black man sitting in a chair. The Black man looks familiar, but I can't quite place where I've seen him before and assume it's from the diner. Chase clears his throat, and the two men turn their attention toward us, still smiling.

"Everyone, this is Kayla," he announces, turning toward me. "This is my dad, Russell Wilmington, at the grill, and Hunter's dad, Kendall Jackson." I give a self-conscious wave and they say friendly 'hellos' and 'nice-to-meet-yous' before returning to their conversation. "My mom is over there with Maggie," Chase continues, pointing across the deck. "And the two blond girls over there are my sisters, Avery and Hadley. The third one is Hunter's sister, Artemis."

I turn to him with an overwhelmed smile on my face as I realize what I just walked myself into. I'm meeting his entire family, on a holiday, and I don't even know what he and I are doing yet. Hell, we haven't done *anything* yet.

"Don't worry. I'll be here the whole time. I got you." He gives my hand a squeeze, seemingly reading my mind, and leads me toward our friends.

I meet Chase's sisters—Avery, the long-legged fourteen-year-old with braces, and Hadley, the eleven-year-old math genius with pigtails—who are actively trying to see who can hold on to their sparklers the longest before chickening out. Hunter's sister, Artemis—Artie for short—is ten. Loose brown spirals frame her face as she talks excitedly to Ashlie, having abandoned her sparkler. Ashlie motions for me to come closer.

"Don't Artie's curls pop? I told you that hair mousse would fix you right up! You gotta leave that hard cast on our hair type. No scrunching it out like the straight-haired girls or it gets frizzy."

"Yeah!" I say, understanding the assignment. "It looks great! Ashlie's a pro with curly hair. She used to do mine all the time." Artie turns to me, green eyes lighting up with excitement as we hype her up.

"Artemis, you really should let me straighten your hair," a disappointed voice scolds from behind me. "Your mom would hate to see it looking so..." Maggie waves her hand around her head before finishing with "...wild." Artie, so excited before, slumps her shoulders and kicks at the ground. I see the little boost of confidence she'd acquired shrivel and wither away.

"Magnet"—Hunter mimics with a bite to his voice—"you should really stop being such a b—"

"Watch it, son," Kendall warns, deep voice rumbling as he walks up to stop the ensuing battle. His voice tickles at a memory I can't quite place. "Artie-girl, you look beautiful. I love your curls," he reassures her lovingly. Maggie turns around in a huff, and suddenly, the bread aisle comes vividly into my mind.

"You're the Pickle Guy!" I say, like everyone knows what I'm talking about.

"Excuse me? The what, now?" Hunter's eyes go wide. He looks over at Chase, who shrugs and tips his head to the side as he looks at me.

Kendall takes a beat before recognition spreads across his face. "Ah, Bread Girl." He nods knowingly with a smile. Everyone's looking at us like we're speaking some alien language. Giving a chuckle, he dives into the story of how he was shopping for condiments when a jar of pickles jumped off the shelf and crashed in front of him. When he tried to turn around, more pickles smashed to the floor, like a classic paranormal movie. "That's when I heard grumbling from the next aisle over."

"I couldn't reach the last loaf of bread and was trying to launch myself up the shelves to get high enough," I continue for him. "I was this close to throwing my shoe when he came over, handing me the bread and telling me I almost knocked him out with a pickle jar."

"Pickle Guy and Bread Girl sounds like some defunct super-hero team." Hunter snorts a laugh.

Ashlie chimes in with a goofy announcer-like voice, "And with their powers combined, they can make...*sandwiches*." We all lose it at that, laughing with ease like we've known each other forever. The nerves I was feeling at the thought of being around these strangers dissipate, and Chase has been true to his word, never leaving my side.

"The food is ready!" Russell calls from the grill, closing the lid and placing a plate full of burger patties on the elongated table. Everyone migrates to their seats when Chase steers me off to the right. He grabs his mom's arm as she passes, turning us into a cozy little trio. "This is my mom, Christine," Chase says with a smile. "Mom, this is—"

"Kayla." She smiles, looking back and forth between us. Her eyes match the dark blue of the ones smiling next to me. "Chase is right. You are breathtaking. It's nice to meet you."

Startled by her frank phrasing, I stammer, "I...th-thank you. It's nice to meet you too." She pats my arm, and the three of us continue to the table.

The fruit and salads have made their way to the table outside, as well as just enough chairs to account for everyone. Kendall and Russell take the ends of the table, with Christine sliding into an empty seat right next to Russell. They instantly reach for each other in a way that shows they've been doing it forever. Ashlie is between Artie and Hunter, next to Chase's sisters on one side of the table, while Maggie and her friends—twin sisters Camryn and Tamryn—are on the side of the table closest to me.

One empty chair flanks the three of them on each side, creating a seating dilemma. Maggie turns and looks right at me, offering a thin-lipped grin that doesn't reach her eyes. My steps falter, and Chase looks to me before glancing at the table where Maggie sits with a satisfied smirk on her face. He clears his throat, getting the attention of his mother.

"Oh, Magnolia, could you move?" Christine says nonchalantly. "You're in Chase's seat. Your spot is next to your Uncle Kendall."

Maggie goes rigid, cheeks burning bright red as everyone turns to look at her. Hunter chokes on his drink, prompting Ashlie to clap his back with one hand, hiding her laugh behind the other.

"Oh, yeah, sure," she says politely, moving three seats over. Chase squeezes my hand, leading me to the seat by his mom, before taking the one next to Camryn...or Tamryn. I can't really tell them apart until one of them speaks. Camryn's voice is high pitched and airy, while Tamryn's has a much deeper tone.

I glance over at Christine, and she smiles warmly, patting my hand. She winks, and when I turn toward Chase, he winks. I'm sure Russell would do some winking of his own if I were to look at him. It must be a Wilmington family trait because I've never been winked at more in my life.

We all dive into the food, passing around sides and making small talk while eating. Feeling eyes on me, I catch Maggie's glare across the table before she looks back down at her plate. Christine and Russell ask me about school, my jobs, and my family—nothing too detailed, just enough to get a general sense of what I have going on. Chase squeezes my knee, leaning in to learn about all the things I've yet to share with him.

"How's it going at NYSOB, Magnolia?" Kendall asks loudly enough to make this a table topic.

"What's NYSOB?" I whisper, turning to Chase.

"New York School of Ballet," he whispers back, his warm breath leaving goosebumps on my skin.

Mouthing the word, *oh*, I nod. That bit of context explains everything, from the high, tight buns on Camryn and Tamryn and the flitting way Maggie walks, to their ramrod posture as they sit in their seats. Pretentious ballerinas makes perfect sense.

"It's going well. I'm in the running for a spot in the ballet company after graduation next year."

"That's amazing, Maggie." Kendall smiles warmly. "You'll have to tell me when your first performance is."

"Sure, Uncle Kendall."

A tap on my hand turns my attention back to Christine. "Could you help me bring out dessert?" she asks, eyes twinkling.

I nod, and she loops her arm in mine as we walk toward the kitchen. She hands me a knife when we reach the counter, and we slice the apple pies together.

"This is still such a magical town. Kendall, Russell, and I vacationed here for a month, back when we were still in school. Not much has changed. You said your family is from here?"

"Yeah. Well, kind of. I was born and raised here, but my mom moved here to live with her grandmother when she was five."

"And your dad?"

"Unaccounted for. But it's all worked out," I say, smiling. "Can't miss what you've never had, right?"

"Oh, I don't know about that. Speaking of missing someone, Chase sure missed you. The week after your accident, I don't think I've ever seen him that restless before. I'm glad you two could finally figure it out."

"Oh... I... We're just friends."

"Uh-huh..." She gives me the look that mothers give when they don't believe a word you're saying. "'Just friends' don't look at each other the way you two look at each other..." She picks up her pie and walks to the door, and I'm too stunned by her assessment to do anything other than pick up the other pie and follow.

"You two talking about me in there?" Chase smiles, taking the pie from his mom.

"Who else would we be talking about?" she teases, swatting his shoulder as he swipes a stray glob of filling from the tin. I set mine on the table.

In our absence, a full-blown dance party has started. Music blasts from the integrated speakers on the deck while the sun makes its descent, giving way to the first stars appearing in the sky. Lanterns blink on around the property, illuminating the dance floor, while Kendall and Russell sit back in their chairs by the grill, watching the fun. Hunter and Ashlie have started a dance circle with the little sisters, and Camryn and Tamryn dance together in the corner. Maggie is nowhere to be found. Quite honestly, I'm glad she's taken a break from trying to behead me with her eyes.

I'm about to step across the deck when Chase grabs my hand. "Do you want to go down to the beach? We have a little bit before the fireworks start..." The eager look in his eyes and the warmth of his hand in mine seeps through my body. Nerves settle in my stomach at the thought of being alone with him again. He almost kissed me on that train the other day, and I have no doubt he'll try to kiss me again tonight. And in light of my latest confession to myself, I really think I might just let him.

I nod, and he flashes a smile before leading me down the stairs at the end of the deck. We walk for a little while, hand in hand, letting the sound of the waves settle over us with the music and laughter of the party in the background.

"Your family is fun," I say, picking a small boulder big enough for both of us to sit on. "Thanks for inviting me."

"Sure thing. My motives were purely selfish, though." He bumps my shoulder with his, and I smile while looking out at the water.

"Figures. You'll do anything for some of Patti's *famous apple pie...*"

He laughs loudly, throwing back his head. "It is good pie..."

I slide my eyes over to him, noticing the way his hair falls over his brows. Suddenly, I don't want to be talking about pie or anything else anymore. I reach my hand up to brush the hair out of his eyes, the soft strands feathering across my fingers as I stare into those midnight blue waves of the deepest ocean. I like him, I want him, and I'm tired of trying to convince myself I don't. With the last shred of my resolve to keep him at arm's length melting away, I palm his jaw and kiss him softly.

It starts slow and timid, as we explore this new dynamic together. The tip of my tongue darts out, searching for a little taste of him, and when he meets me, I swear our hearts beat as one. A gentle sigh slips from his lips, drawing me in like a tether from his heart to mine. It speaks to me, the faintest whisper echoing the refrain, "*Finally.*" He wraps his arm around my waist and pulls me in, easing the strain as our lips ladder together, like we're climbing to heights we've only imagined thus far.

"*Woo!*" Hunter whoops, and Ashlie cheers from the top of the bluff. We break apart, and I giggle, looking at our best friends jumping around and cheering us on.

Chase tips his head to mine, his signature crooked smile replaced by flushed cheeks and desire burning in his eyes. "Come on," he says, pulling me up from the rock, leading me determinedly toward the toe of the bluff.

"Chase, what—"

He crushes his lips to mine, guiding me back against the cool, jagged bluff face. His hands rove through my hair, down my shoulders, and around my waist frantically, like this moment will be ripped away from him at any minute. I can't say I blame him, considering how many times he's tried to kiss me. Right now, with the way my skin blazes under his touch, I'm wishing I wouldn't have waited so long to let him. Our tongues swirl wildly, setting a much faster pace than before. When he pulls back, the intensity in his eyes makes the pounding in my chest skyrocket.

"I'm tired of being interrupted," he whispers. "Can we go inside?"

CHAPTER TWENTY-FOUR

KAYLA

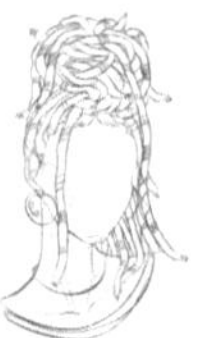

With a nod from me, we're running up the steps of a different staircase, leading us past the last house in the estate, across front yards, until we reach his doorstep. Chase leans back against the door, pulling me in with a smile. He traces the seam of my lips with his thumb, drawing a shaky breath from me before pushing the door open behind him.

The house is dark, except for the light of the party going on outside. I follow him down the hallway, and he nudges me through the doorway ahead of him. The dim light from a floor lamp fades on as I hear the flip of the light switch. When I turn around, Chase is leaning against the door with his hands behind his back, watching me.

Waiting.

He's put all his cards on the table several times. This choice—this movement forward—is mine to make. Uncertainty clouds his eyes as I step closer to him.

"I want you, Chase..." I say, pulling out the first words that come to me. That's all it takes. He reaches me in two steps, our lips colliding as the last of my reservations disappear. Tipping on my toes, I pull him into my mouth deeply while he palms the back of my head. Our tongues twirl in a dance meant just for us, and

I'm wondering why I resisted this for so long. *Why did I deprive myself of this?* We spin around the room, finally landing with him pushed up against the wall. My hands wander under the hem of his shirt, the ripple of muscles smooth against my fingertips.

And then he's pulling my hands away, holding them at the wrists. "Wait, wait," he says breathlessly, touching his forehead to mine.

"I thought..." I start to pull away. A thousand paths of doubt swirl through my head as I try to make sense of his sudden halt. I thought he wanted this. I thought he wanted *me*.

"Don't..." he says softly. "Don't run, just...give me a minute. Let me catch my breath. Form some thoughts." After what feels like forever, head still tipped to mine, he drops my hands and cradles my face, stroking my chin with his thumb. He looks at me, unblinking, and smiles softly. "I want to know you, Kayla."

I drop my eyes, suddenly feeling a little too bare, too intimate. Wanting someone in a moment of heated passion and wanting to know someone are two vastly different things, and I didn't account for the latter.

He lifts my chin until our eyes meet again and smiles. "I want to know your favorite things, and your hopes and dreams. I want to know about your family, about your past. I want to know why you look down whenever I say something too direct and what makes you scratch at the side of your thumb. I just...need you to let me in a little bit. Okay?" Bringing my hand to his lips, he kisses my thumb, then my wrist, and looks up expectantly. Watching. Waiting.

"Okay." My voice is barely a whisper, but the spread of his bright smile rivals the light show beginning in the night sky behind me.

"Let's watch." He turns off the lamp and guides me to the bed, right down into his lap. I lean back against his chest, and his arms wrap around me, feeling just as nice as they did on the climbing wall. The French style doors across from us make a perfect frame for the fireworks outside as the *boom-crackle-hiss* fills the silence we've fallen into. He nuzzles my neck and breathes me in before kissing my shoulder. "You smell like apple pie..." He chuckles quietly.

"What?" I giggle, shaking my head. "You really are getting rusty."

"You do. Like vanilla...cinnamon and apples," he says between the kisses he places up and down the side of my neck. "And butter..."

"*I do not!*" I snort, twisting to look at him.

Laughing then, he pulls me back against him. "Okay, maybe not that last one." He laces the fingers of his left hand over the back of mine and plays with my thumb ring.

"Do you always wear this?" Chase whispers.

I nod, temporarily losing my ability to speak as warmth spreads through me at the feeling of his breath on my ear. "It was my great-granny's. I never take it off."

"Mmm." He brushes his lips against my shoulder again, making my breath shudder. Colors explode and sizzle outside the glass doors—red and bright white fading into the dark night sky —and none of it rivals the simmering anticipation here in this room.

"What's your favorite color?" I ask, realizing there are so many basic things we don't know about each other. So many things I've avoided out of fear.

"Green, like your eyes." He snuggles into my shoulder, kissing my neck again.

The hair on his face tickles against my skin, and I giggle, shaking my head. "I'm serious. What's your favorite color?"

"Blue—but light blue. Sky blue," he says. "What's yours?"

"Green, like my eyes..." I joke.

He laughs, his chest vibrating against my shoulder as I snuggle in closer. "Makes sense. You look good in green... You look good in blue too." He brushes his lips over the skinny strap of my light blue dress. "Everything, really..."

Turning my chin with his finger, he tips my face up and kisses me slowly, taking his time like he's savoring all of it. I break away, spinning in his arms to fully face him, before pressing into his kiss again. Now that I've admitted to myself that I like him, now that I've kissed him, I can't get enough. When he finally pulls away, I'm breathless.

"Tell me about your family," he whispers, brushing his thumb along my jawline.

"There's not much to know about. It's just Mom and me. Mom works a lot at the hospital and always has, so I had a lot of alone time growing up."

A look of understanding reaches his eyes as he nods. He doesn't pry, and I like that he's satisfied with whatever bits of information I'm willing to give. No pressure or guilt-tripping. "So that's how you became so independent," he says.

"I didn't really have a choice." I shrug, looking down at the buttons on his shirt. "It got better once I met Ash, and Patti's been around since I was little. Great-granny, too, when I was younger. I had people, just not very many." He lifts my chin again, and I wonder how annoyed he must be that I keep looking away from him. But when I look into his eyes, all I see is that warm, intense desire I'm learning to become accustomed to. He looks at me the same way he's been looking at me for weeks, and it's easy to get lost in it now that I'm here in his arms. I kiss him again, sighing into him as his fingers tighten around my waist.

"What about you?" I say, pulling back for a breath and trying to keep myself from feeling too vulnerable. "Tell me about your family—what didn't I learn tonight?"

"Well, Mom and Dad are high school sweethearts and act like it." He chuckles, shaking his head. "They're never *not* touching if they can help it."

"I noticed. It's sort of adorable."

"You think so? Some would call it intense."

"Oh, it's intense, but in a cute way. You can tell they've been together for a while."

"Yeah..." Chase shrugs. "It's normal to me, I guess. All my

past girlfriends commented on how comfortable I am with affection. One even called me the 'PDA King.'"

"The king, huh?" I tease, raising an eyebrow.

He smiles, shrugging again. "I guess you can be the judge of that," he says, pecking the tip of my nose before leaning back against the headboard. "I dunno, I just...when I like someone, I show it. I don't know any other way." His fingers trail over my shoulders. "Is that okay with you? PDA?"

"Yeah...it's okay." I bite my lip.

Chase pulls me against his chest. "That's good. It's been hard enough not touching you before now."

I look up at him through my lashes as he traces lines up and down my back with his fingers, staring back at me. I'm positive he's leaning down to kiss me again, but when he gets close, he bites his lip and whispers, "What's your favorite food?"

A surprised laugh escapes me, and I cover my mouth with my hand. We could have blasted through this information weeks ago if I would have been honest with myself and let him in sooner. Such a basic question paired with our heated energy tonight makes the simplicity seem silly.

He laughs, too, and I tip my head to his chest, my shoulders shaking. His arms circle around me, and we're lost in a fit of giggles, spending the rest of the night talking and laughing, kissing and learning. And when the early morning comes, I'm still wrapped in his arms.

"*So...how was your night?*" Ashlie wiggles her eyebrows as she sips her early morning coffee at the diner counter. Hunter gave her a ride home last night, seeing as I was otherwise preoccupied. I smile, remembering everything from the night before. "Girl, if you don't just tell me..."

"It was good...nice. We slept together."

"I mean, yeah, I figured that out."

"No, I mean, we fell asleep. We kissed and talked and slept."

"Oh," she says, smile dropping off her face. "I thought you two would have had fireworks with a side of *fireworks* last night. 'Nice' doesn't sound good at all. What happened when you left this morning?"

"I...snuck out."

"*Girl!*" Ashlie says with wide eyes.

"*Ugh*, I know." I cover my face with my hands. "Last night was good, but when I woke up this morning with his arms wrapped around me, I panicked. I don't know what my problem is."

"I do." She smirks between sips. "You like him. He gave you intimacy, *real* intimacy, and you freaked." I know she's right. She's been right this whole time. I was fully prepared to give it up to him last night, and when he stopped me, when he poured out his heart, it threw me for a loop that I'm still reeling from.

"He said he wanted to know me."

"Like, biblically?"

"No, Ash, like get to know me...be with me."

"Aw." She puffs out her bottom lip, her brown eyes giving me an oh-so-cute look. "So, you're together, then?"

I shrug. "I think...maybe. Yeah."

"*Woo!*" she shouts, shooting her arms up in the air. "Mission accomplished. I won the bet with Hunter. Now he owes me."

"Owes you what?" I laugh, not at all surprised our best friends had a bet going against us.

"I haven't decided yet." She smirks, pulling out her phone and shooting off a text.

CHAPTER TWENTY-FIVE

CHASE

Waking up to the bed and my arms empty, I half wonder if I dreamed everything from last night. The kiss. *Kisses.* Lots of kisses and watching fireworks from my bed. Feeling Kayla's laugh vibrate against my chest. Her touch. I sit up and run my hand through my hair, looking around for my phone, when I see it on the floor, next to her bracelet. A late-night memory hits me of her giggling. Her trying to untangle the chain from the snag in my shirt collar before ripping it off her wrist and throwing it on the floor, diving her lips back into mine. Nope, no dream could compare to last night. I reach for my phone, swiping the bracelet up with it and shoot off a quick text.

ME

You snuck out on me.

KAYLA

Had to work and didn't want to wake you.

ME

Dinner tonight?

KAYLA

Can't. Working a split shift and have to close
tonight.

Coming in for coffee today? There's still time
for breakfast…

ME

Work meeting this a.m. What about lunch
today?

KAYLA

Babysitting for my neighbor at lunch.
Tomorrow?

ME

I can't wait until tomorrow. Even if it's just five
minutes, I want to see you.

KAYLA

Okay… I have a 15 min. break after the dinner
rush. 8:00?

ME

I'll be there *smiley face* This is our first
date… should I be nervous?

KAYLA

Definitely. And then you can stare at me and
leave your number in the tip jar with some line
about stealing your breath away. Oh, wait…

MY PARENTS ARE EATING BREAKFAST WHEN I WALK
into their rental. Dad has his arm draped lazily over the back of
Mom's chair, holding his phone away from his face to read whatever is on the screen. Avery is sitting at the kitchen bar, typing
furiously on her phone. I ruffle her hair as I walk by, and she
swiftly elbows me in the back.

"Cut it out, Chase!" she says, smoothing her mussed-up ponytail.

"I missed you, Av! Gotta make up for lost time." I wink, and she rolls her eyes at me as she turns back to her phone. "Where's Had?" I ask, leaning against the countertop, looking around the room for my youngest sister.

"She slept over with Artemis last night. They haven't seen each other in so long, I can't tear them apart," Mom answers, looking up from her word puzzle. "Speaking of last night...how'd it go?"

"Leave him alone, Christine, before you get details from your precious baby boy that aren't so innocent," Dad says.

"Oh, he didn't have sex with Kayla. He likes her too much to rush into that." She stares at me over her readers, daring me to challenge her.

"Oh?" *Challenge accepted.* "And what makes you say that?" I volley back at her. I've told her bits and pieces about my journey to capturing Kayla's attention, but never details that would give her any notion of my bedroom habits.

She folds her arms, tipping her head as the glare in her eyes intensifies.

"It's the way you look at her, Chase," Dad intercepts, putting his phone down on the table and crossing one ankle over the other. I rub my fingers across my forehead, wondering how I walked into this battle at nine-thirty a.m. "Your last girlfriend from a year ago...what was her name? Lucy?"

"Lacie," Mom says, helping him.

"Right. You never looked at her that way. Or the other one, Carly."

"Kylee..." Mom helps him again.

"What would I do without you?" he asks, leaning down to kiss her temple.

"Lose your head, that's what," she teases back, smiling up at him and cupping his chin. They lean in to share a kiss, and I hear my sister gagging behind me.

"Ew! Your room is *right there*!" Avery points down the hall-way, her face scrunched up like this is the most disgusting thing she's ever seen.

"And yours is upstairs." Mom shrugs, kissing Dad one more time. Avery hops off the stool and stomps up the stairs, mumbling something about the kitchen being a place where we eat. I shake my head and take her seat, watching the unabashed love my parents share. They've been this way forever, never leaving the 'high school sweetheart' status behind, and I admire them for it. I strive to emulate it.

"Anyway, I think when you meet someone who makes you look at them the way you look at Kayla, you do whatever it takes to keep them," Mom says.

She turns and gazes into Dad's eyes, a scene I've witnessed so many times before. This is just the way they look at each other, but something about this time, this glance, gives me a new perspective.

"And in what way do I look at her?" I ask, hoping to be told what I already know. I anxiously rub the hair on my face while I wait.

Dad answers this time, eyes still fixed on Mom. "Like there's no rush, and you can see forever."

GETTING TO THE DINER AT SEVEN FORTY-FIVE FEELS like the cool water at the end of a long race. I'm early, but I just couldn't wait any longer. Bert sits in his spot at the end of the counter, reading the paper as he sips on his decaf, like he does on most nights. I look around the warmly lit diner for Kayla, spot-ting her at the end of the room, past the row of booths. She layers plates and cups on a tray and maneuvers around a chair, walking behind the counter and dumping the stack through the kitchen window. She hasn't noticed me yet, and just like usual, the casual way she navigates the space around her, graceful and confident, sets my heart racing. When she turns and sees me, she smiles and it's bright enough to melt me down to bare bones.

"Staring again?" she asks, coming around the counter to stand next to me.

"Guilty," I say, reaching to pull her closer. She stands between my knees, palms flat against my chest.

"Patti's sick today, so I have to take my break out here." She flashes her teeth in a nervous grin.

"That's okay. Is she alright?"

"She thinks the new fish place down the street gave her food poisoning a couple of days ago. She's on the mend, but needs me to open in the morning too."

I stroke her cheek, rubbing my thumb down to her jaw. I just want to press my lips to hers, but Bert's still over there, sipping away in the corner. Even though we talked about PDA last night, I don't want to make her uncomfortable at work. "I missed you today," I whisper, tipping my head to hers as I reach into my back pocket for her bracelet.

"I'm sorry I snuck out," she whispers back, running fingers up the back of my neck and into my hair. Capturing her hand and bringing it between us, I hook the bracelet around her wrist and press a kiss to her thumb. "I didn't want to wake you up that early," she continues, peeking up at me.

"Wake me up. Always wake me up. I don't care what time it—"

The bell above the door rings again, and she sighs, straightening out her back and stepping away. "That's my cue," she says, rubbing her face with a sigh. "Can I get you anything?"

I shake my head and watch as she greets the couple making their way to a booth. I didn't know a "dessert rush" was a thing, but five more groups shuffle in, demanding one form of pastry or another. Except for touches that are far too brief as she walks between the kitchen and the customers, I don't get another minute with her until the booths empty out again. With the last group walking out of the diner, she leans over the speckled quartz countertop, planting her elbows as she dips her head. She rubs her eyes like she's trying to wipe the last hour from her face.

"Twenty minutes," she sighs. "Twenty minutes and I can lock the doors."

"Think he fell asleep over there?" I jut my thumb to the corner, taking in the suspenders fitting too tightly against Bert's white button-down shirt. His bowler hat sits on the countertop next to his newspaper.

"Oh, Bert? Naw, he's always here this late. He comes in early too. Patti pays him in free food to make sure no one causes problems."

"So he's a bouncer?"

Stifling a yawn, she nods and walks in his direction.

"Hey, Bert, you can head out early tonight if you want. Chase will stay with me while I clean up."

He whips his head over to me, eyes narrowing as I give a little wave. "Alright, Kayla, but you call me if you need anything. I'm just around the corner."

She nods, giving him a thumbs-up.

"Any more pie left?" he asks, craning his neck to look at the dessert display.

"Fresh out. That last group took the rest of it to-go," she tells him, grabbing his empty cup and plate.

"Ah, well, I can't say I blame them." He stands, places the bowler on his head, and strolls right over to me before putting a hand on my shoulder. With a pointed look, he tells me, "She walked today. You make sure she gets home safe."

"You got it, Bert." I nod back at him, and he claps my shoulder twice before walking out the door.

Kayla's already gotten to work, wiping down appliances and countertops, flipping display light switches off as she goes. She stifles several more yawns as she makes her way to my end of the bar. When she gets close enough, I grab her hand, slipping the wet cloth from her fingers.

"Let me do this," I say, reaching for the spray bottle in her other hand. She steps back, just out of reach.

"No, Chase, I got it. It'll take me fifteen minutes, tops." She reaches forward to grab the towel, and it's my turn to lean back.

"You're tired. Let me help you so you can get home and sleep. It's my fault you were up so late anyway." I smirk.

She stares at me, exhausted and exasperated to be losing this battle of wills, and hands over the spray bottle slowly. Grabbing more towels from under the bar, she directs me to the booths and tables while she tackles the dishes. Fifteen minutes turns into seven, and before I know it, she's locking the front door. She places a box of dirty towels in my arms, and I follow her to the back to dump the towels in the washing machine.

"Let me just grab my stuff, and I'll be ready to go," she says, slipping the *Patty* apron over her head. She throws it in the washer with some detergent, preparing it to be run in the morning.

I wait for her by the back door, and when she finally reaches me, my arms can't go around her fast enough. Lifting her chin, I graze her lips with mine.

"Thank you for helping me." She nuzzles her face into my chest.

"Of course." I rub her back.

It's a short drive to her house, through the neighborhood across from Patti's Place. Even in the darkness outside, I see a large tree beside the small, rambler style home. After parking in the driveway behind her silver sedan, I turn to her.

She looks down at her hand in mine, rubbing her thumb over my index, and quietly asks, "Can you come in for a little bit?"

"Thought you'd never ask." I raise her hand to my lips before getting out of the car.

She leads me up the path to her front door and flips on a tall floor lamp as soon as we enter. I take in the overstuffed mahogany leather couch next to a low, glass-covered coffee table in the living room. Beyond the couch is a round dining room table, big enough for four, with a speckled granite countertop separating it from the kitchen.

"Let me take a quick shower before you tell me I smell like pie again," she teases, patting my chest and handing me the remote to the TV. I flash a smile and sit on the supple leather couch as she disappears down the hallway. She makes it back to me in under ten minutes with a blue silk scarf wrapped around her hair. Green shorts peek out under the oversized black T-shirt hitting her thighs as she maneuvers around the room. Carrying a bottle to the coffee table, she sits on the couch and spreads the vanilla scented cream over her arms and legs.

"That explains the vanilla..." I say, drumming the hand on my leg, wishing my fingers were the ones traveling across her skin.

"The apples are from my shampoo," she says, rubbing the last bits of lotion into her hands. She bites her lip and pulls me toward her end of the sofa. Noses touching, I breathe her in before diving to find her lips. They're soft and warm, greedily wrestling mine in a whirl of resolved anticipation before she pulls back, yawning.

"I'm sorry..." She scrunches her face before yawning again.

"Sweetheart, you're tired." I smile down at her before sitting up and grabbing the lotion from the table. "Lie down," I say, placing her foot in my lap.

"What are you—ahh, mmm." She moans as I rub the lotion across her sole, making concentric circles with my thumbs. She makes a halfhearted attempt to take her foot back before sinking into my hands again.

"Just relax and let me do this for you," I say, grabbing her other foot. "Besides, you've been running through my mind all day. These things must hurt."

She lets out a giggle, covering her eyes in the crook of her arm while I work. "How was your meeting this morning?" she asks, relaxation settling into her voice.

"It was good. Dad and Kendall decided I'll start at the new EdTechU headquarters in San Francisco while it gets up and running."

"EdTechU?" She shoots up from the couch, peering at me with wide eyes.

"Yeah... You heard of it?"

"I'm catering for them in August..." she says slowly, eyes narrowing.

I tilt my head slightly, wondering why she looks confused. "I've never said I was working for my dad?"

"No, you did, but you never said a company name. So he's like, one of the higher-ups?"

"More like the highest up. He and Kendall are co-founders. CEO and CTO, respectively. They founded EdTechU during undergrad at CUT—"

"*CUT*? Like California University of Technology? Like, only super-smart geniuses go there?"

"Yeah... You didn't know this?"

"How would I know this? Isn't EdTechU, like, a really big company?" Her eyes widen with every bit of information I confirm for her.

"...Yes..." I hesitate, unsure where she's going with this.

"I... You're..." She shakes her head, grabbing her phone. "That's like, one of the top technology companies..." Her mouth drops open as she looks down at her screen. "It's worth a ton!"

There it is. The reason for the panic. We stare at each other while she processes the fact that I'm the son of a technology-genius multimillionaire.

"But...you had a job up at Camp Bender..."

"I didn't, technically. I signed up to be a volunteer at first and didn't need the paycheck, so I took the position without pay. Claire used the money to offer scholarships to two of the campers." The way she's staring, slack-jawed, makes me wonder if I've sprouted three heads. I move to cradle her face in my hands, not sure what else to do. "Hey..." I say softly. "I'm still me. I haven't changed in the last five minutes. My family just has a little more money than most."

"*A lot* more money than most. You're millionaires! Why

didn't you say anything? I met your family, met your *parents*, and just treated them like regular people. I gave them mediocre small-town pie!" She leans back against the arm of the couch, folding her arms with a bewildered look in her eyes.

"Three things," I say, laughing at her quip about the pie. "One: they *are* just regular people. My parents didn't grow up with money and like to stay as grounded as possible. Two: that apple pie is better than any expensive dessert I've ever tasted, and three: I didn't say anything because it's not something I go around advertising."

She studies me, trying to make sense of everything spoken in the last few minutes. I take her hands in mine, pulling her close enough to wrap my arms around her waist. "Look, my family is wealthy. I use it when I need to—want to, even—but I try not to let it affect me. I don't talk about it because it's not the most interesting thing about me." Her face softens, and I breathe a sigh of relief, sensing we've made it past this millionaire sized hurdle.

"You should have told me."

"You're right. Surprise," I tease, squinting an eye as I flash my teeth in a nervous grin. She laughs, and I peck a kiss on her lips.

"So you're moving to San Francisco? Not back to LA?" she says up through her lashes.

"Yep."

"That's only an hour away from SSU," she whispers.

"Yep," I smile, moving in for another kiss. Her fingertips trail down the muscle in my jaw as she kisses me back, sweetly at first, and then more urgently, until another yawn breaks us apart. "Come here." I chuckle, lying back on the couch and bringing her to rest on top of me, head to chest. I play with her fingers, recalling that night at camp when our hands locked together after a thumb war. Being that close to her back then was amazing enough, but *this,* having her body curled around mine, is something I don't ever want to end.

"Can I ask you something?" I ask. The words come out cautiously, and I don't know if I actually want to hear her answer.

She nods against me.

"Up at camp, you said being charming was a bad thing. Why was that a bad thing?"

She breathes a deep sigh before propping herself up to look at me. Her eyebrows dip, and her eyes seem to glaze over as she stares down at my chest. "Because it was."

She recounts the story of her last boyfriend, his charm, the way he made her feel special, her abandoning her grades to spend time with him only for him to betray her trust in the worst possible way. Her resistance toward all my hints and flirting makes perfect sense now. I reminded her of him.

"I took a trip to see Ashlie for spring break, and when I got home, I found him in my roommate's bed. With my roommate. Alone together." She twists her fingers around themselves, voice shaking. "I should have known better. He was always flirting with other girls and then reeling me back in with empty promises whenever I got upset. Not to mention, we just didn't make sense. He was the wealthy star football player, and my roommate was on the cheer squad. They fit inside each other's worlds. I very obviously did not."

"So what did you do?" I try to keep my voice steady, but searing heat fills my chest. My back teeth grind together at the thought of Kayla being mistreated. I'm angry for her. Pissed that someone would do that to her, make her feel less than the beautiful person I know today. Upset that someone would take advantage of the fierce loyalty I've seen from her.

She shakes her head as a crease forms between her eyes. "I did nothing. I didn't stand up for myself. I just walked out and avoided them. I was devastated."

With a clearing of her throat, her voice comes back strong, confident, the way I'm used to hearing. "I spent the rest of the semester in the library, trying to salvage the nine months of school I'd neglected. With help from my advisor and caring professors, I worked my ass off to get the extra credit I needed, and I made it happen. It was hard as hell, and I promised myself I'd never let a guy get in the way of my future again. So I work and avoid distractions." She bites her lip, uncertainty shadowing her face as she looks up at me.

"And I was a distraction..." I say, as I piece together every moment we've shared up to now. After everything she just told me, I can see how my efforts to get her attention would have pushed her farther away. I reminded her of some asshole who broke her heart and destroyed her confidence in the process.

"Yeah." Her voice is barely a whisper.

"What changed?" I ask, searching her face for a glimmer of hope for a future with her. Hope that I've shown my character enough for her to know I would never treat her that way. But the hope I seek doesn't come from the look on her face. It comes from the way she lies back on my chest, head to heart, and curls her body into mine.

"You were there for me," she mumbles, on the edge of consciousness. I wrap my arms around her and hold her tight. In no time, her breathing slows, signaling her transition from awake to fast asleep. Stroking her back, I hear the faintest sigh, and a memory of her smiling in the sunlight is the last thing on my mind before falling asleep myself.

CHAPTER TWENTY-SIX

KAYLA

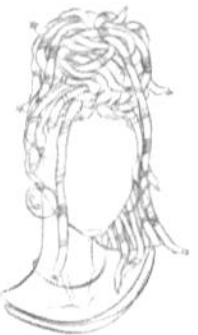

"*Shit*!" I hiss, scrambling up from the couch in my living room. "Shitshitshitshit*SHIT*!" I throw magazines and remotes off the coffee table in front of me, looking for my phone. The alarm didn't go off. Or I didn't set it. Did I turn the sound back on after work? I was so tired last night; I don't even remember.

"What's going on?" Chase yawns from the couch. I drop to the floor, seeing if my phone bounced underneath the sofa.

"We fell asleep, and my alarm didn't go off. I'm supposed to be at the diner at five to have breakfast started by six, but I can't find my phone." The words rush out of my mouth as fast as the racing pulse I feel spreading through my chest. My mind is hazy from sleep, and heat rushes to my face in my panic. I'm about to start throwing couch cushions when Chase stands and grabs a hold of my shoulders.

"Hey, breathe." He strokes my cheek, reaching for his phone in his pocket with his other hand. "It's five-fifteen. Grab your stuff, and I'll meet you in the car." He leaves a quick kiss on my forehead and heads outside.

I race to my room and throw a bra and uniform shirt and

pants out of my closet and onto myself as if I'm going to miss a flight. After stumbling into the bathroom for a haphazard tooth brushing, I leave the toothbrush unrinsed on the sink and run back through the house. Grabbing my shoes and bag from the entryway, I hurry outside, barefoot, pausing briefly to lock the door.

Chase is tapping away on his phone when I get to the car. "Hey..." He reaches up, loosening the scarf tied around my hair. It drops to my shoulders, and I snatch it up and stuff it inside my bag. I quickly wiggle my feet into my shoes. My finger scrapes away at the cuticle on my thumb as we round the corner out of my neighborhood. Chase must notice it, too, because his hand snakes around mine, and he lifts my thumb to his lips, kissing it lightly before moving our conjoined hands to his cheek. "Stop. Breathe. It's going to be okay."

He drops me off in the back lot of Patti's Place. I manage to remember to squeeze his hand and thank him before running toward the door. Muscle memory takes over, and my arm is halfway up to the light switch before I realize the lights are already on. Was I so tired last night I didn't turn them off? Momentum takes me into the supply room to start the preloaded washer, which is also already running.

Weird.

I walk slowly down the hall, confusion settling in the closer I get to the dining room. The smell of freshly dripped coffee permeates the air, and the mixer in the corner whirs away with muffin batter. Patti stands at the prep station, cutting up fruit for pies as she dances to whatever song is in her earbuds. I put my hand on her arm, wondering what she's doing here.

"Oh! Kayla!" She jumps, clutching at her chest before slipping out an ear bud. "You scared me! What are you doing here? I gave you the day off..."

"Um, no? You called me yesterday during lunch saying you needed me to open..."

"I woke up around ten-thirty last night feeling wonderful, so I sent you a text with the schedule change. I thought, worst-case scenario, you'd see the message when you woke up."

"I lost my phone," I say, wondering if this is some kind of stress dream I'll wake up from and realize I really am late for work.

"Well, get your buns back home and take a nap or two. Maybe spend the day with your friends out there." She nods her head toward the window where, to my surprise, Ashlie is standing next to Hunter and Chase. "Go have fun. You deserve it," she says as she nudges me toward the door.

I walk out the front door with my face scrunched, holding onto the strap of my bag like it's a lifeline to reality. I'm still not completely convinced I'm awake.

"What's going on?" Hunter says with a yawn.

"Apparently, I have the day off..."

"Bruh." Hunter turns to Chase. "You woke us up at the ass crack of dawn, and she doesn't even have to work?"

Chase shrugs, looking to me for the answer.

"I did have to work, but I guess Patti texted me to cancel my shift last night. And I lost my phone, so I never got the message..." I lift an eyebrow at Chase and ask, "Why *did* you call them at the ass crack of dawn?"

"My girlfriend was panicking, and I thought she could use some reinforcements." He shrugs, grinning like his explanation is the most logical conclusion to come to at five-thirty in the morning.

"*Girlfriend?*" three voices say at once. Ashlie's smiling, Hunter nods with approval, and I, well, I'm speechlessly slack-jawed, staring at Chase as he quirks his eyebrow back at me.

"Besides..." Chase continues. "...I think the better question is why they were *together* at the ass crack of dawn." Ashlie's smile falls, and Hunter kicks at the ground, suddenly fascinated with the cracks etched into the sidewalk.

"We were just hanging out and fell asleep..." Hunter says, glancing at Ashlie. His face is unreadable, and Ashlie looks everywhere except at me.

"Uh-huh," Chase says suspiciously. "And that hickey there on your neck is just what? A mosquito bite?" He points right at Ashlie's collarbone. Her eyes widen, and she tries to cover up with her jacket.

"*Spill it!*" I gasp, looking between her and Hunter.

"Can we not do this here?" Ashlie whines, bouncing her knees. Her eyebrows knit together, the slightest quiver taking hold of her upper lip. She's about to break down, and to spare her the embarrassment, I let it go.

"Yeah. Okay. Give me a ride home?" I ask.

She nods and ambles over to wait in her car.

"What? Wait." Chase turns to me. "You have the entire day off. I was thinking we could spend it together..."

"That's what you get for being a snitch." Hunter snorts.

"Hey, why don't you go wait in the car?" Chase grabs his keys from his pocket and tosses them at Hunter, nodding toward the black crossover parked next to Ashlie's. Hunter takes the hint and strolls toward the car, and as soon as he gets there, Chase turns back to me. His hands circle my waist, drawing me into him before he captures my lips in an embrace. "I really can't take you home?"

"I think Ashlie needs me right now..." I say, remembering the tortured look in her eyes.

"Okay. I get it. I should probably check on Hunter too. But I called you my girlfriend..." He bites his lip. "Is that okay?"

"I'll let you know when you pick me up for our date," I say, kissing him quickly and stepping backward toward Ashlie's red hatchback. "Crystal Beach. Three o'clock." A goofy grin slides across his face, and if this is all a dream, I think I'll be okay with it lasting a little bit longer.

Ashlie backs out of the space before I can click my seatbelt in, quietly navigating the familiar streets of my neighborhood. Pulling up to my house, she shifts into park and lets out a shaky breath. I look over to see tears free-falling down her cheeks, leaving wet marks on her jacket as they flow. Whatever is going on is big.

"We broke up," Ashlie says, voice shaking while we sit in my driveway talking about Bryan. "We had a fight last night about him coming here with his parents next week. He kept telling me what he thought I needed to do instead of listening to what I was saying, and I went off."

"I'm sorry, Ash," I say, rubbing her back. "What did you tell him?"

"That I didn't want to have his ashy babies."

I cover my mouth with my hand, trying to keep a serious look in my eyes while I hide my smile. "Oh, no..."

"It's okay, you can laugh. Hunter laughed, too, when he heard me say it. I don't even know why I'm so upset. Bryan and I haven't been on the same page in so long. But after two years together, I thought we'd figure it out."

"So you broke up with your boyfriend and went over to Hunter's place...?"

"I was already over there because we're friends now...*were* friends... I don't even know anymore. I...messed everything up." Tears flow freely from her eyes as she sobs, all traces of her bubbly personality overcome with grief.

"Messed it up how, Ash? I'm confused."

She shakes her head. "I know this is a really shitty 'best friend' answer, but I don't want to talk about it. Ever."

My mind swims with possible answers for what she got into with Hunter last night, but I let it go for her sake. "Do you want to come in? We could have a girl's day with junk food and trashy TV."

"No, girl. I think I gotta put my big girl shoes on for this one. I should get home anyway. Mom's been blowing up my phone all night."

I point at her. "Okay, but you call me if you need me. I'll check on you tomorrow?"

She nods and shoos me out of her car, swiping at her cheeks as she checks her face in the rear-view mirror.

After hanging my bag by the door, I start searching. My feet sink into the plush beige carpet in my living room as I stoop to clear the rummaged chaos I left in my panic this morning. I find my phone wedged between the cushion and back of the sofa, with the missed message from Patti and a good morning text from Chase sent two minutes ago. Scenes from last night flow through my mind, and a smile spreads across my face.

We had some big revelations on this couch last night. Between the EdTechU son-of-a-multimillionaire shocker and my ex-boyfriend sob story, I could have easily let it come between us. We're from different worlds, much like how it was with Evan. But at the end of the day, Chase is still just the helpful guy trying to care for me. He rushed me to work after being jolted awake by my panic. He called my friends to come help me. He calmed me. How I ever found similarities between him and Evan is beyond me. Chase is in a class all his own.

THE DOOR THUDS AS IT CLOSES, AND I BOLT UPRIGHT. Through the bleariness in my eyes, I can barely make out the large, fluffy coils wearing scrubs and glasses. "Mom?" I say, rubbing my face. "What are you doing here?"

"My Bakersfield contract got cut short, but I'll be heading to LA in two days for a new one. No work today?"

"Nope. Patti gave me the day off."

"Good! You work too much anyway, Kay."

"Says the lady speeding all over California for a living."

"I guess you came by it honest. I'm going to shower and then, let's get groceries? Maybe lunch?"

"Yes, to groceries, but lunch has to be quick. I have a date." I stand from the couch and inch toward the hall.

"A *date*?" she teases. "It's that cute white boy from the hospital, isn't it?"

I shrug, wiggling my eyebrows while walking backward to my room without answering. I'm not giving her any information before I have to. She'll find out when Chase picks me up later anyway.

Navigating the store today is so much easier than the last time we came together. The lines are within the range of normal, and the bread is fully stocked. We don't have to split up this time, so I push the cart, hopping up with my feet on the basket to glide down the aisles. Mom is in the middle of telling me all about the drama between her coworkers in Bakersfield when she bumps into someone tall. The glasses fly off her face and slide along the floor.

"Oops, I'm sorry. Let me grab those for you."

"Kendall?" I say, recognizing Hunter's dad immediately.

"Kayla, hey," he says distractedly, handing the glasses back to Mom. He freezes once he finally gets a clear view of her face. Mom cleans her lenses on her shirt, scrunching her nose as she slides them back over her eyes.

"This is my mom, Karla," I say. "And this is my friend's dad, Kendall."

He sticks his hand out, looking at her intensely despite the smile on his face. "Nice to meet you."

Mom stares down at his outstretched hand for a couple of seconds before clearing her throat and giving it a shake. Her eyes flick up to his and then back down as she takes a step backward.

"Is Chase bringing you over for dinner tonight?" He turns his smile on me.

"Yeah, he just texted me about it."

"Great," he says, nodding and looking at Mom again. She's distracted herself with a cracker box on the shelf, so he turns back to me. "Well, we'll see you later then."

"See you later!" I wave as he leaves. Kendall looks over his shoulder once more before moving to the next aisle. Turning to Mom with raised eyebrows, I ask, "Not your type?"

"No one's my type, Kayla. I've got bills to pay," she snaps, throwing the crackers in the basket and grabbing the cart out of my hands with a huff.

CHAPTER TWENTY-SEVEN

KAYLA

I'm checking myself in the mirror in the far corner of my room when three swift knocks hit the front door. Hustling out to the living room, I see Mom lounging on the couch, feet curled under herself. We look at each other for a split second before she leaps off the sofa to answer the door. I spring from my spot in the hallway, making it a second too late.

"Let me meet him," she says, laughing.

"You already met him." I roll my eyes, grabbing my purse behind her. She's such a "Nosy Rosie" sometimes, and I don't want her sticking her nose in this early. "Please, Mom, just let me open the door..."

"You could *both* open the door," Chase says from the other side. I widen my eyes at Mom and point my head to the couch, mouthing the word *stop*. She wiggles her eyebrows, reaching for the doorknob and yanking it open. Sliding past her, I close the door on her slipper before nudging her foot back into the house with my own.

With a big exhale, I turn and bite the smile that appears when I look at Chase. The sun beams down on us, and his light blue polo matches the bright sky. He bends to kiss me, but just before our lips meet, I hear an excited squeal from the other side of the peephole.

"Hey, Chase!" Mom yells from behind the door.

"Hey, Ms. Harris!" he calls back, shaking his head with a smile.

He gives me a quick peck and leads me down the steps. Once we get inside his car, Chase tangles our fingers together, kissing the back of my hand twice before placing our hands on my knee. Comfortable silence fills the car while he taps his thumb on mine to the beat of the music on the radio. The oldies station filters through several upbeat popular tunes before playing the slow ballad I sang at the outdoor bar a week ago. I look out the window, watching neighborhood trees give way to ocean waves, thinking about everything that has happened in a week.

"Hey," he says with a gentle squeeze of my hand. "What's got you thinkin' over there?"

"Just...this song," I say.

"It's the same one from the bar." He nods, smiling over at me.

"You remember it?"

"How could I *not* remember it? I don't think it's something I'll ever forget." He pulls our hands up to his lips, pecking kisses on my thumb before setting them back down on the center console. It's cute and romantic, and even though this is a new thing, I like the little ways he touches me. I feel desired. It makes me feel like maybe Ashlie was right, and this *could* end well.

Despite it being prime tourist time, the beach is nearly empty. Sparkling pebbles glimmer in the sunshine as we walk hand in hand along the beach. "So where did all these crystals come from?" Chase asks, stooping to fill his hand with the stones and letting them sift through his fingers.

"Garbage." I sit down on a nearby boulder at the water's edge, taking off my shoes and letting the waves tickle my toes.

"Garbage?"

"Yeah. Literal trash. This place used to be a dumping site."

He tilts his head, eyeing me with a skeptical look. "How does garbage turn into crystals? Are you messing with me?"

"Nope. It's glass from old broken bottles that were dumped off boats at sea. The sand and sea water smooths out the glass and deposits it back onto the shore."

He studies the pebbles in his hand, letting them sift back down to the ground through his fingers. "They're so small, though. Shouldn't there be bigger pieces?"

"There used to be a lot more, but tourists kept taking them as souvenirs. Now it's illegal to take glass or anything else from this beach, but the damage has already been done. Tourists leave with something shiny, and all we're left with are tiny pebbles."

"What a shame. There's something about the ocean taking trash and turning it into treasure that feels poetic. Magical. It fits Fort Bender perfectly." He stands, wiping his hands on his jeans as he comes to sit next to me.

"Speaking of magic, Bender lore says the blue glass is the rarest to find on the beach. Whoever finds a blue pebble will have all their dreams come true."

"But..." he says, pulling me close and nuzzling my nose. "My dreams have already come true..."

"*That* was the cheesiest line you've fed me yet," I say with a giggle.

He leans down and kisses me until the smile wipes off my face. It starts off slowly, but soon, we're grasping at each other, chests heaving as we sit here in this beautiful place, water lapping at our feet. When we pull apart, our noses stay snuggled together as his thumb caresses my side.

"I missed you today."

"Oh yeah? What did you miss?" I arch my brow.

"Everything. I've gotten used to being around you."

"Me too," I whisper, leaning in for another kiss.

After a while, he sighs, pulling back enough to say, "We could skip family dinner tonight..."

"And miss hearing embarrassing stories about you? Not a chance."

"I haven't embarrassed myself enough around you? Now you need sources?"

"Yep." I pat his thigh before wiggling on my shoes and standing. "Sources and references. Maybe a bibliography too. Have to make sure you're fully vetted." I wink, and he laughs as he slips his hand into mine.

This feels good, spending time with Chase and letting myself like him without restraint. Opening up to him—sharing about Evan and letting him into my world just a little—has tunneled out some capacity to be at ease around him. The nerves I used to feel have turned down to a low, manageable simmer. He told me he would spend the summer falling for me, but I think, unwittingly, I've been falling for him too.

"Kayla..." Chase says from the seat next to me, breaking up the pleasant "what if" thoughts that have been scrolling through my mind the last several minutes of our drive. I blink, shaking my head to clear the haze and realize we've pulled up to The Bluffs Estates.

"What's up?"

"About earlier, I know I called you my girlfriend and we didn't really talk about it beforehand...or after, for that matter, and—why are you looking at me like that?" His forehead creases in response to the side smirk creeping up my face.

"No reason. Go on..."

"Summer will be over soon, and I know you'll be busy with school and the internship, and I'll have a new position at work to figure out but..."

"But...?" I encourage him. He's rambling, which is adorable

because I already know the answer to the question he's about to ask.

"But... I want this. I want you to be mine, and I want to be yours. So...will you?"

"Will I, what?" I tease, trying to keep a straight face while I watch him squirm. This feels like good payback for all the times he's flustered me out of speech. Plus, he's cute when he's nervous.

He blinks. "...Will you be mine?"

"Oh, um, no, Chase. I can't," I say, shrugging while I force an apologetic look on my face.

He opens his mouth and closes it again, confusion settling into every line of his face. "You...can't?" He knits his brows together as he stares straight at me.

"Nope."

"...Why?" he asks quietly, rubbing the back of his head like it will help him make sense of this conversation.

"Because..." I whisper, pulling him by his shirt so we're eye level. "I already have a boyfriend." I smile, poking my tongue into my cheek while I watch the realization ease the pinching on his face.

"*God*, Kayla..." He puffs out a deep breath, slapping his hand to his chest and flinging his head back against the headrest.

I lose it with laughter in the passenger seat, and I'm still in a fit of giggles when Chase pulls me out of the car and leans me against the side. He steps in close, grazing my nose with his. "You scared the hell out of me, baby," he murmurs. "I thought you were serious."

"*Baby*?" I ask, feigning shock. I like the way the simple word rolls off his lips, like he handcrafted it just for me. Pet names have never been my thing, but he could call me *baby* for an eternity and I don't think I'd get sick of hearing it.

"Yep." He lifts his hand to the crook of my neck. "Baby."

I tip up on my toes, giving him the apology for my prank in the form of a kiss.

Two kisses.

Okay, three, for good measure.

"Hey, whenever you two are done sucking face, dinner's ready!" Hunter yells from the porch while looking down at the phone in his hand. He slips back inside the house, and Chase sneaks one more kiss before we head inside.

The smell of something heavenly flows through the air. Avery, Hadley, and Artemis are draped across the couches, watching TV while waiting to be called to the table. Hunter walks down the hallway toward us, finishing up a conversation on his phone.

"Dad said he probably won't make it back in time. Something about having some business to finish up," he announces to the room.

"Then we'll get started," Christine says, placing a stack of plates on the white marble countertop, next to the cups and silverware. "Hey, Kayla! Glad you could join." She flashes a friendly grin.

"Oh, thank you for inviting me over again. I had a blast last time."

"No Ashlie today?" Russell turns to Hunter.

"Naw, not today. She said she couldn't make it." He kicks at a scuff on the tiled floor, which I'm learning is one of his tells for when he's uncomfortable.

"Well, dig in." Christine motions from the sink toward the food she prepared. Salad, breadsticks, and the heavenly smelling chicken parmesan are spread in the middle of the table. Chase reaches his arm around my waist, grabbing a plate and slipping a little kiss on the top of my shoulder. Looking back to give him a smile, I catch Christine watching, nodding knowingly.

Once we've mostly finished eating, I turn to Chase's parents and say, "I was promised some embarrassing stories."

"*Ugh,*" Chase groans playfully, squeezing my knee. The girls get up and head to the loft, and Hunter excuses himself to go back to his rental.

"Oh, we have plenty of those!" Russell chimes in with a wink. I learn about the stuffed bunny Chase slept with until second grade, the time in junior high when his first kiss led to two sets of stuck braces and the paramedics being called, and him inviting a homeless man to dinner who turned out to be a college kid off work from a construction job.

"Oh, and don't forget Janet!" Christine says, clutching at her chest while she laughs. "When these three were young, I hired a housekeeper to help me keep up on things. One day, when Chase was about seven, I couldn't find him anywhere. I finally asked Janet if she had seen him, and she told me he was in the laundry room. He had locked her out so he could fold the clothes and she could get some rest."

Chase shrugs, smiling at his mom. "She was limping all over the house, and it looked like she could use a break."

"Our little humanitarian over here demanded she get a raise and a break every hour to put her feet up. He made me cross my heart before he would open the door."

"You're forgetting the part where you actually met my demands." Chase chuckles.

"Of course I did. She was limping and needed the breaks!"

We all laugh, and I turn to look at Chase, remembering how he swept up the mess hall while Bo rested his sore knee at camp. *This guy's been authentic all his life.*

"Well, as much as I've *loved* reliving all of my worst moments, it's time for me to get you back home." Chase squeezes my knee.

"Yeah, probably should. I have work in the morning."

"Okay! Well, I'm sure we'll see you around here more often." Christine winks before clearing the rest of the dishes from the table.

Russell heads to the kitchen sink, rolls up his sleeves, and grabs a sponge. "Good night, Kayla!"

The moon inches higher in the sky as we drive through town to my neighborhood. Pulling into the driveway behind my car, Chase parks but doesn't move to turn off the engine. He plays with my hand, slowly twirling his fingertips around mine like he's memorizing each fingerprint. I lean toward him, drawing on his lips lightly with my own. The short hairs on his face tickle my palm as I run my hand down the muscle in his jaw.

His fingers trail up my arms, smoothing over my shoulders until they're tangled in my hair. Right as I adjust in my seat to get closer, deeper, he pulls away. With a long sigh, hands still in my hair, he touches his head to mine and whispers, "You're killing me, Kayla." His thumb ghosts over my bottom lip, and he sighs again. "Let me walk you to the door before I get ahead of myself."

Once we're on the porch, I tip my head back, reaching up on my toes and looping my arms around his neck. He bends to meet me halfway, hands wrapped around my hips, pulling me flush against him. After another deep, slow, goodnight kiss, I look up into his eyes. "Are you coming into the diner tomorrow?"

"Of course I am." He squints like the notion of not coming to see me is absurd.

"Then I'll see you in the morning," I say, smiling. I turn toward the door, and right as I touch the knob, he pulls me back to him. His thumb caresses the spot behind my ear as he nudges my lips open with his, the ebb and flow of our breathing working in tandem—rising and falling, giving and taking.

"Goodnight, baby," he whispers breathlessly, nuzzling his nose with mine. Heat surges up my neck, and I bite my lip, heart leaping in my chest at him calling me *baby* again. I like it, and I really like him.

Stumbling through my front door, I close it quietly behind me in case Mom is asleep. My lips tingle as I lean against the smooth, patterned glass, and I find myself reaching up to soothe the buzzing, smiling like a fool.

I take a step toward the hallway, and that's when I see her. Mom sits at the dining room table, still as stone. She stares at me, glasses in her hand, the remnants of tears and sniffles still present on her face. I haven't seen her like this since her granny passed.

"Mom? Everything okay?"

"Kayla," she says with a trembling breath, shaking her head and looking down at her hands. "I'm so sorry." I take in the scene at the table, trying to figure out what she could possibly be apologizing for when I notice there are two coffee mugs instead of one.

"Kayla," a deep voice says from the darkened hallway. A voice I recognize, but one that's entirely out of context in my house. I freeze, confused, as I hear him say, "You should probably sit down."

CHAPTER TWENTY-EIGHT

CHASE

Despite the storm clouds outside, I whistle heading into Patti's, hoping to catch a few stolen moments with Kayla before the coffee orders start rolling in. Last night, the afternoon, everything the last few days has been beyond what I could have imagined for us when I first laid eyes on her. I wouldn't change how any of this played out if it all meant she and I ended up here. Prepared to see the girl of my dreams as I stroll into the diner, I hesitate at the sight of Patti.

"Hey there, Chase! Grabbing something for Kayla?" she asks with a smile, wiping up coffee rings from the countertop.

"No... She's not here?"

"Oh. Nope, she called in sick last night. I figured she would have told you."

Weeks of seeing Kayla work herself ragged gives me enough basis to know this is unlike her. Kayla doesn't call into work sick, and she was fine when I dropped her off last night. "Uh, no, I haven't heard anything..." I check my phone notifications. Empty. "Thanks, Patti," I say, turning around and heading back to my car.

My mind reels with worry as I battle every intrusive possibility for why she wouldn't tell me she was sick. Sure, she didn't answer when I texted her goodnight before bed, but I figured she had already fallen asleep.

Trying to stay calm, I shoot off a quick text:

ME

Hey…everything okay?

Are you home?

I sit and wait for what feels like forever, tapping my fingers against my leg to try and keep the anxiety at bay. Not able to resist, I call Kayla's phone, and it goes straight to voicemail. My heart drops into my stomach. Fleeting hope surges when my phone immediately vibrates in my hand.

HUNTER

Hey man, you with Kayla?

ME

Looking for her now. What's up?

HUNTER

You should probably talk to her…

ME

Why? What happened?

HUNTER

Kayla should tell you.

ME

Tell me what?

HUNTER

Bruh, just find her.

I toss my phone on the passenger seat, trying to swallow down the frustration-filled lump in my throat. How does Hunter know what's going on with Kayla before I do, and why won't he tell me? I slam the car in reverse, angle out of the parking lot, and turn into the neighborhood across from Patti's Place. If something's happened, I need to know about it. Check on her. Make sure she's okay.

I hesitate when I pull up to her house, considering more intrusive possibilities. What if she doesn't want me here? What if I misread everything about yesterday, and she really doesn't want to be with me? I slipped into relationship mode too quickly. What if I scared her off and this is her attempt at running? I check my phone again—nothing. Before I can talk myself out of it, I take a breath, open my car door, and walk up the steps of her porch.

After a knock and a brief wait, Ms. Harris opens the door. Deep-set bags above her cheeks bolster the red tinge in her eyes. "Sorry, I know it's early. Is Kayla here? She's not answering her phone," I say, trying to slow down the words as they rush out of me.

Looking down at the weathered doormat, she shakes her head. "No, she packed a bag and left last night." Tears well in her eyes, and she quickly swipes them away.

"Left? Where'd she go?"

"Maybe Ashlie's?"

"Can you tell me what happened?"

She shakes her head again. "Kayla should be the one..."

That again. What the hell happened in eight hours that has everyone acting like I'm asking for government secrets. *And why am I the last one to know about it?*

"Okay...thanks..." I turn to head back to my car when Ms. Harris stops me.

"Chase, when you find her, could you tell her I'm leaving early for my next contract? I'll be gone by noon today."

I nod, no inkling of why she can't tell this to Kayla herself, and climb back into my car. Done with the waiting game that comes along with texting, I call Ashlie. I drum my fingers on my jeans while the phone rings.

"...Hey, Chase," she answers, hesitating slightly.

"Hey, is Kayla with you?"

"Uh, hold on."

This morning might possibly be the most agonizing thing I've ever experienced. If I could just find Kayla and figure out what the hell is going on, I could start crafting a plan. The frustration rising in my voice while I try to figure out what's happening is apparent as I say, "Look, Ashlie, I just want to make sure she's okay. I don't know what's going on, but I'm worried and she's not answering her phone. Is she with you or not?"

"...Yeah, she's here."

Relief floods over me, but the anxiety creeps back in slowly as I contemplate the reason for Kayla's radio silence. "Can I talk to her?"

"She's shaking her head no, but I'm going to send you my address anyway. It's just around the corner from her place." She hangs up, and after too many seconds, my phone buzzes with the message.

The short drive brings back the long form questions from before. If she doesn't want to talk to me, I'm positive she doesn't want to see me either. She's with her best friend, so she's clearly okay and just ignoring my messages.

I pull up in front of a two-story house wrapped in graying weathered wood siding, and I wait. If she's changed her mind and doesn't want to do this, doesn't want to be with me for whatever reason, I can try going back to being just friends. I'm head over heels for her, but if that's what she wants, I'll do it just to keep her in my life. Several more minutes pass before I convince myself that I just want to make sure she's okay. I'll check on her, and then I'll leave if she wants me to.

I head toward the door, and Ashlie opens it before I reach the porch.

"She's in my room." She leads me up the flight of stairs in front of us, my heart thumping with the anticipation of what I'm about to walk into.

"Ashlie, what's happen—" The bedroom door is open, and there's Kayla, sitting up in the bed with a blanket wrapped around her shoulders, tears streaming down her cheeks. Her eyes meet mine, and just as fast, she buries her face in her hands. Fierce sobs break through the space between her fingers. Seeing her like this and not knowing what's wrong, not knowing how to help, not knowing if she even wants me here is pure torture.

I stand in the doorway, unsure of what my next steps should be. Ashlie nudges me from behind, prompting me to sit next to Kayla on the bed. When I do, her body stiffens beside me, and I look toward Ashlie for a little direction. Nodding, Ashlie motions for me to put my arm around Kayla. When I reach around her shoulder, the rigid stiffness that terrified me seconds ago melts into my touch. She curls into me, making it easier for me to scoop her into both of my arms. I swing her legs across my lap and rub circles on her back, comforting whatever tragedy is brewing inside her world.

"Do you want me to leave?" I whisper the words, hoping with everything I have that she says no.

Shaking her head, she nuzzles into my neck, and I breathe a sigh of relief with the first glimmer of assurance that this isn't about me. Something is terribly wrong, and seeing her this way breaks my heart. But she wouldn't be clinging to me right now if she didn't want me here.

"Okay. You don't have to tell me anything if you don't want to, but can I talk?"

A nod against my chest prompts me to continue.

"Your mom wanted me to tell you she's leaving for her next contract at noon today. Do you want me to take you home so you can see her?"

She shakes her head as another sob threatens to rip through her body.

I give her some time to let the fresh current of tears slow before asking, "Do you want me to take you after she leaves?"

A sniffle and a nod, paired with calmer breathing, lets me know that this wave is passing.

"Can I get you anything?"

"Water," she whispers.

"You got it."

I kiss her forehead and carefully shift her body back onto the bed. When I get downstairs, I find Ashlie in the kitchen, back against the counter, rubbing her face.

"Kayla wants some water..." I say.

Quietly, she walks to the fridge and hands me a cold bottle before reclaiming her spot against the counter. "I've never seen her like this, Chase. I don't know what's going on, but she hasn't slept at all. She showed up last night with a bag and has been inconsolable ever since."

Looking at her without the lens of panic, I notice the dark bags under her eyes, proof of a night of no sleep for her either.

"She wants me to take her home after her mom leaves at noon."

"Her mom already left. She texted me a few minutes ago saying she couldn't get a hold of Kayla and asked me to pass it on."

"I'll get her home so you can get some sleep, then."

When I get back to the room, Kayla's exactly where I left her. I crack open the bottle of water and hand it over, watching her sip, then gulp. "Your mom's already gone. Do you want to go home now?"

She nods, and I stoop to grab her bag before offering her my hand. Landing on the main floor, Ashlie stops us to give Kayla a hug. "I'm sorry," Kayla whispers, sniffling.

"Girl, don't you dare apologize. Text me after you get some sleep."

Kayla dips her chin and stares down at the floor as I guide her to the door with my hand on her back.

The drive back to Kayla's house is a stark contrast from our drive yesterday. Dark clouds roil in the sky, masking the sun. While I'm still holding her hand, the energy is sadness instead of excitement. The hitched breathing comes from prolonged tears instead of kissing. Songs from the radio are replaced with post-crying hiccups.

At the door, she sticks the key into the lock and goes rigid, hands trembling. "I got you," I say with a squeeze on her arm, unlocking the door and pushing it open. The curtains are drawn, making the house dark to match the dreary mood of the morning. Propelling her forward enough for me to close the door, I reach for the switch on the wall and flip it on. Warm yellow light illuminates the entryway.

"Can you stay?" She looks up at me, eyes bloodshot from crying and lack of sleep. One arm hangs loosely at her side while the other is slung across her body, hugging her elbow.

"Of course. If you want me here, I'll stay…"

The crease forming between her eyes as she registers my words tells me how unwarranted my fears were this morning. "Why wouldn't I want you here, Chase?"

"I…don't know." I rub the back of my head, trying to unscramble my thoughts. "I couldn't get a hold of you, and no one would tell me what was going on. And then you didn't want to talk to me when I called Ashlie, and I just…don't know what you want." It comes out rushed and messy, as I lay my anxiety at her feet.

I watch as the crease of confusion fades from her face into a look of contrition. Tucking her chin, her shoulders slump as she takes a deep breath. She scrubs a hand over her face and, without saying another word, reaches for me and leads me down the hallway to her room. Placing her hands on both of my arms, Kayla nudges me to sit on the light blue bedspread. She kicks off her shoes and climbs in next to me, turning her back to lean against the headboard. I mirror her, kicking off mine and turning to face her across the bed. We sit, knees touching, not saying anything.

Placing my hands in hers, she takes a deep breath and looks into my eyes. "I'm not used to relying on people," she starts with a shaky voice, eyes never leaving mine. "I do things on my own, figure things out on my own so no one needs to worry about me. Even with Ash, I don't always lean on her like a best friend should. I'm the one with solutions—cool, calm, collected—not the one who falls apart, and I didn't—" Her breath hitches as tears stream down her face. "I didn't want you to see me like this." She waves her hands over her body, briefly dropping mine before grabbing them again.

"You can't just disappear. If this is going to work—"

"I know."

"The running is…" I pause, looking down at our hands as I feel the surge of emotions I've been pushing away all morning. I want this to work out with her so badly, but I don't think I can deal with another morning in the dark like this. I can't be the only one willing to communicate. She squeezes my hands reassuringly, waiting for me to finish. "The running is tearing me up inside, Kayla. I can't handle it if you're going to keep pulling away. I need to know what's going on in that head of yours. Even if you just want some space. I need to know."

"Okay." She sits up on her knees, dropping my hands to cradle my face. "I'm sorry I made you worry—made you question this." She brushes my lips with the lightest touch of her own. "I want you to stay, Chase. You're my blue pebble, and I want you to stay."

I lean forward, kissing her more fully while the smile grows on my lips. "Look who's being cheesy now…"

As the tiniest smile appears, the tired lines on her face remind me she hasn't slept. I move across the bed to lie down on her pillow, pulling her along with me. She snuggles into my chest, arm draping across me, and with hardly any time passing, I can hear the deep breathing of sleep take over.

We lie like that, entwined together for hours. Her asleep, and me drifting in and out. Catching me mid-doze, I feel her shift at my side. I glance down at her face to see her eyes wide-open, staring at a spot on the wall. I rub gentle circles on her back to let her know I'm with her.

"Kendall's my father," she whispers, holding on a little tighter to me. I take a beat, trying to make sense of what she's just said.

"That's what happened last night. I opened the front door to find my mom and Kendall."

"Kendall Jackson? Like, Hunter's dad?"

She nods against me, drawing shaky breaths. The floodgates open again, and she tells me everything that happened after I dropped her off last night. How they sat her down at the table, her mom explaining how they met in Fort Bender twenty-two summers ago. Her mom found out she was pregnant but didn't look for Kendall, despite knowing how to contact him. Karla panicked and left when they bumped into him at the store the first time, but Kendall hadn't seen her face then. He recognized her immediately when he saw her yesterday morning.

"She lied to me. My entire childhood, she told me she didn't know who or where my father was, but she did. She saw an article about EdTechU when I was little and recognized him then. She lied about it a month ago when we first bumped into him at the store, and she lied again yesterday. I felt ambushed at that dining room table and just needed space...so I left and turned off my phone." Kayla sits up on her knees suddenly, wiping tears from her cheeks. "I'm so angry at her. This whole time I could have had a dad, siblings to bond with. I wouldn't have grown up feeling so alone."

I listen and I wait, partly from not knowing the right words to say, but also because as she tells her story, she sits a little taller. Her voice grows a little stronger with each word, and the tears flow a little less. This is helping her feel better, and I'll listen and wait forever if it's what she needs to feel better.

KAYLA

Today is the first day in almost a week where I feel like myself. I've pushed through my shifts at Patti's, and the crying happens less frequently. Today, I feel good. I feel capable. Happy even. The bell tinkles above the door at the diner, and in walks my own personal brand of sunshine, smiling widely when he sees me. I grab water and a menu and meet him at the counter.

"Hey, Ashlie," Chase says, taking the stool next to her. She waves at him from behind her book, silently turning the pages of her current thriller novel while she chews on her turkey wrap. I come from behind the counter, and Chase wraps his arm around my waist, pulling me into his lap.

"Hey, baby." He nuzzles his face into my neck, leaving kisses along my jaw.

I turn, pressing a quick peck on his lips. "No Hunter again today?" I ask. He hasn't been around much since that day in the parking lot with Ash, and after my mom's bombshell confession, I can't say I blame him.

"Nope. He's trying to give you both some space." His head tips over at Ashlie, whose eyes are wide as she finishes up her chapter. "I think whatever happened between them gave our little

Hunter a bit of a conscience," he says, rubbing circles on my hip with his thumb.

"Whew, okay. I'm done. Hey, Chase," Ashlie says, closing her book. "Where's Hunter?" Her voice is light, but the way she looks around the room shows me she's nervous about running into him.

"I don't think he's coming back until you start talking to him again." Chase shrugs. "So, you gonna tell us what happened?"

"Why are you two in my business?" Ashlie rolls her eyes.

"Because your *business* is just starting to fade from your neck," I say, before turning to Chase. "She won't tell me anything either."

"He said he doesn't want to make things worse, but that's all I've been able to get from him," Chase says.

"Ash, if you won't talk to me about it, at least talk it out with Hunter. You said you were going to talk to him…" I say.

"No. I said I *should* talk to him. Big difference." She holds her hand out, inspecting her nails to avoid my eye roll.

"Okay, *why* won't you talk to him?" Chase tries again.

"Oh. Easy. Because I don't want to."

The door chimes again, and I look over my shoulder just in time to see Maggie and her friends walk in.

"Here we go," I say under my breath, loud enough that Chase snorts in response. He kisses my shoulder, keeping me in place with his arm.

"*Ugh*, see, this is why I hate coming here. The service is horrible." Maggie glares right at me. If I weren't at work, I'd have some words for her.

"Then leave," Ashlie sneers at the ballerina, crossing her arms in a "try me" fashion.

"I would, but Daddy wants to try this *famous* apple pie everyone keeps raving about for my twenty-first birthday tomorrow."

"Your dad's here?" Chase asks.

"Oh, Chase, hey," she answers sweetly. "Yes. Daddy arrived

last night for some founders' meetings with your dad and Uncle Kendall."

Chase nods, and I steel myself for the interaction I know I've got to have with her.

"Now that I'll be twenty-one, maybe you can take me for my first drink..."

Oh, please.

"Did you want anything else with the pie?" I ask, standing and moving toward the dessert display.

"Just the pie." She rolls her eyes like I'm bothering her, like she didn't walk into *my* diner. Boxing up the dessert, I watch her move in closer to Chase.

"He actually wants to talk to you while he's here," she says, looking up from her lashes, hinting at something. What? I have no idea, but I *do* know she can take several steps backward. She's a little too close to my boyfriend for my liking.

"I'll have to see if I can catch him then." Chase's voice is uninterested as he offers her a polite, tight-lipped grin.

"It'll be fourteen dollars." I drop the pie box on the counter between them, getting a little satisfaction out of the small jump she takes backward. Chase flicks his eyes up to mine and stifles a laugh, sticking his tongue in his cheek. I slide over to the cash register and wait for the ballerina, who I'm realizing reminds me way too much of my former roommate.

Maggie turns an icy glare toward me, maintaining eye contact the entire time she fishes her wallet from her handbag. She hands me a twenty, and when I give her the change, she grimaces and juts her chin toward the tip jar. Looking me over one more time, she turns on her heel, grabs the pie, and flits out the door with Camryn and Tamryn close behind.

"Couldn't be me..." Ashlie glares at the trio in the parking lot.

"Maggie's harmless. She can be annoying, but she's all talk." Chase shakes his head.

"She can catch these hands is what she can do. Cartoon and Tampon too." Ashlie seethes.

I cover my mouth, laughing at the newest nicknames for Maggie's friends. "You know that girl's name isn't 'Tampon.'"

"Might as well be. She gets pulled along by a string like one." Ashlie shrugs, stuffing her book in her bag before leaving. She hasn't had a good thing to say about Maggie since she deflated Artie's ego on the Fourth of July. I can't blame her either, seeing as every interaction I've had with Maggie has been insufferable.

Before Chase leaves, he bites his bottom lip, trying not to smile. He pulls me in close and says, "You're cute when you get jealous."

"Jealous of Maggie? No." I scoff, shaking my head.

"I'm pretty sure that pie would disagree..."

"It slipped," I say. "And she needed to take a step back."

"Uh-huh." He drops a kiss on my lips. "Whatever you say." He winks, kisses me on the forehead, and strolls out the door.

I wouldn't label that feeling as jealousy. Mild possessiveness, maybe. Annoyance, for sure, but not jealousy. After learning a little more about Maggie, I know pigs would fly before she ever had a chance with Chase.

THE REST OF MY SHIFT GOES BY WITHOUT TOO MUCH drama, and I'm walking home before I know it. The sun is shining, and my shuffled playlist is playing all the right songs as I make my way up the sidewalk. Lost in my own little world, I almost miss Hunter sitting on my porch. He lifts a couple of fingers in a wave, and my steps waver as I try to decide what to do next. Slipping off my headphones and looping them around my neck, I slowly walk up to the porch and sit down next to him.

"Hey, sis," he says, kicking at the cement.

"Hey..." We sit silently, awkwardly trying to figure out how this conversation is supposed to start. Not only do I have a brother, but *he's* my brother. I'm his *sister.*

"I told you I've only seen the green eye thing in my family," he teases, trying to lighten the mood by bumping my shoulder. Offering a lopsided smirk, I can't seem to make words come out of my mouth. "I want you to see something..." He digs in his pocket and pulls out a small photo, letting me look it over.

The face I'm looking at is my own. With shorter hair and a slightly rounder face, the woman in the photo has the same green eyes and dip of the nose as I do. The same full lips spread across her face. "That's my—*our*—great-grandmother. You look like her..."

"You just carry a picture around of your great-grandmother?"

"Naw, but Artemis does. She has an album she takes every-where. She started after the divorce. I think it helps her feel connected."

Nodding, I play with the ring on my thumb. I've never really looked like my mom, and seeing this photo makes it a little easier to fathom being related to the Jacksons.

I hand the picture back, and Hunter shakes his head. "Naw, that's yours. Artie had two of them, and she wants you to keep that one. She's pretty excited to finally have a sister, by the way."

"I... This is—"

"A lot. Yeah... We've been trying to give you some space to process everything. I do have something else, though." He scrunches his face. "You can say no, we totally get it, but Dad wanted me to invite you over for family dinner on Saturday. He's hoping the three-day lead will give you some time to consider it."

I take several seconds to answer, unable to decide what I want to do. On the one hand, I've already met them and know that I get along with them. On the other hand, being a long-lost daughter and sister changes the context a little bit.

Hunter continues, "Chase and his family will be there, too, if you want. Or not, if that's too many people. You can bring Ashlie if that helps. Basically, whatever you're comfortable with, that's what we'll do..."

"I'll think about it." It's the best answer I can give right now. Going from just mom and me to a sudden insta-family feels like a big transition. They're all eager to get to know me, but I have the task of trying to build new relationships with the three of them. It's a lot right now.

Hunter nods, gripping the banister to pull himself up. "Fair. I should get back..."

"Hunter?" I ask as he heads down the path leading to the driveway. "Who's older, me or you?"

He turns around to face me, slowly walking backward to the car. "Oh, it's me. Older *and* wiser." The smart-ass smirk I've become accustomed to seeing spreads across his face before he turns and climbs in the car. To my surprise, he turns down the street toward Ashlie's house after backing out of my driveway.

KAYLA

Friday sneaks up on me, and I'm already struggling through the second part of my split shift when Patti calls me back to her office. I cover a yawn and head down the hallway.

"Alright, Kayla. They've requested a formal setting for the EdTechU event, so let's talk about the things you need to have in your portfolio for the interview."

"Okay, go for it," I say, grabbing the pen and pad out of my apron. I stifle another yawn. This is the moment I've been waiting for. I need to get my head back in the game after my romantic detour and family drama.

"First, you need to research the company—their mission, their culture, logo, colors, etc., and come up with a color scheme for the venue, as well as attire for the catering staff. Look up Trancy Hall so you can decide on table placement for the venue. Brush up on your formal table setting knowledge and get some ideas for menu course offerings. I'll need all of this by August 1, nicely formatted in an online presentation so it can be shared with the internship board before the event."

I nod, writing everything down furiously as she speaks. When I think I have it all, she starts again.

"And Kayla..."

"Yep, I'm ready. What else?" I finish my notes and peek up at her, waiting for the next bit of information. The emotion in her eyes catches me off guard, and I put down my pen, giving her my full attention.

"I'm proud of you. You've worked hard to get here, and you're going to do great." She wipes her eyes and shakes her hands, looking around the room for a tissue. "Ooh, I'm such a baby!"

"Thanks, Patti." I smile back at her, handing her the box of tissues next to me.

"It's true, Kayla. You work so hard and do so much for everyone else. I don't think you get enough recognition for it. You deserve a little something for yourself too."

"*Ugh*," I say, shaking my head and blinking away tears. "Pat, stop trying to make me cry! I have to get back to work." We both laugh at that, fanning our faces to dry up the tears as I stand.

"Yeah, you're right. Get back to work!" She jabs a finger in my direction as I leave, pretending to be the hard-ass we both know she isn't.

It's the calm before the dinner rush, so I grab some clean dishes to practice my formal place setting skills while I wait for the next customers. After twenty minutes of moving silverware around and adding and removing plates and cups, I stare at the puzzle in front of me. This shouldn't be so hard for me to remember, but looking it up on my phone feels like cheating. It's mostly right—but some small detail is wrong—and I can't for the life of me figure it out.

"What's this?" Chase asks, standing across from me while I stare at the place setting. I didn't hear him come in and look around the diner quickly to make sure I didn't miss anyone else.

"I have to practice formal place settings for my portfolio. We haven't gone over those in school since my first semester, and something's missing. It looks wrong."

He comes behind the counter, puts his hand on the small of my back, and looks at the dishes before me. "Butter knife," he says confidently, before walking back around. He sits on the stool directly across from me, smiling.

"*Duh*! A butter knife. I've been looking at this for so long, everything's starting to merge. How did you spot that?"

"One of the perks of etiquette classes." He shrugs.

"You took etiquette classes?"

"Yeah. How else would I have become so charming?" he teases, wiggling his eyebrows.

"Okay, Mr. Charming." I roll my eyes, chuckling. "You're early. The dinner rush hasn't even started yet."

"Good, that means I can kiss you now instead of having to wait."

"Oh, is that what that means?" I load my place setting dishes into the dish return behind me.

"It does if you ever get over here to say hi." His eyes follow me as I move around the counter and stand between his knees. Wrapping his arms around my waist, he pulls me in close enough that I have to tip my head back to see him. "Hi," he breathes over me, making my heart tick a beat faster. I've mostly gotten used to the way he makes my heart flutter, but sometimes, like right now, he'll catch me off guard and I have to look away just to think a proper thought. As I lower my chin, he lifts it back up with his finger. "Don't do that," he says softly.

Those piercing dark blue eyes stare straight into my soul before he presses his lips to mine, and I swoon. If he wasn't holding me, he'd have to pick me up from the floor. "I'll let you get back to work," he whispers, steadying me while I find my feet. The smirk on his face shows he knows the exact effect his kiss had on me. I take a deep breath as tingles surge from my lips down to my toes.

The bell above the door chimes, breaking my trance and setting me in motion to seat the two booths worth of people who just came in. As I get them settled, three more groups file in, creating a revolving door of customers until the dinner rush ends.

At the end of the night, Chase grabs the spray bottle and

cleaning rags, wiping down tables, while I head to the back to prep the washer. I free my hair from the bun on my head, relieving the tension headache I've been battling for the last hour. Leaning against the storage room wall, I stretch out my back as Chase drops the dirty rags in the washer. "Done already?" I ask, eyes half closed from exhaustion.

"Yeah. I had a little motivation..."

"Oh?" My eyes pop open, watching him take slow steps toward me. "And what was that?"

He lifts the apron over my head, tosses it in the washer across the room, and wraps his arms around me. "Not what. *Who*. You might know her...tall, green eyes, breathtaking."

"The Statue of Liberty?" I gasp, looking behind the door.

He laughs, running his fingers up my arm. "I'm trying to be romantic over here, and you've got jokes."

I slide my hand along his jaw, pulling him down onto my lips. A deep longing that has been building all evening floods over me. "Take me home?"

By the time we reach my porch, I'm buzzing. Chase kisses my neck from behind as I struggle to get the keys in the lock. Each new kiss sends a shock through my overloaded senses, making me fumble a total of three times.

"Chase..." I say on a giggle. "I can't focus when you—"

He reaches forward, slipping the key into the lock on his first try and propelling me inside the dark entryway. He nudges the door closed with his foot, locking it behind him, giving me enough time to toss my bag on the couch. The back of his fingers caressing my cheek is all it takes to regain momentum before his hands are tangled in my hair, lips frantically kneading with mine.

"I've been thinking about touching you all day," he says against my lips.

My fingers run down his sides, and I slip my hands under his shirt, reminiscent of the Fourth of July. Only this time, he doesn't stop me as we spin in a passionate waltz through the house, losing shoes and shirts and belted pants all down the hallway to my bedroom.

I walk him backward to sit on the bed and slide my knees around his hips, holding his face in my hands to control the tangled mess of our tongues. He sighs, and I smile against his mouth, feeling his elation build beneath me. The surprising excitement I felt sitting in his lap on the climbing wall is nothing compared to the heated frenzy I feel now. In this moment, the only thing I can think about is getting closer to him. I just want to be closer. My fingers slide down his chest, catching on the rippled edges of a smooth scar.

"Baby..." he pants between kisses.

"Later."

"Babe."

"Shh!"

"Kayla," he tries again.

And I pull back, looking into his eyes with a huff. I just want him, want to feel his hands on my body, and he insists on talking.

"We left our socks on."

I look down, past our underwear clad bodies, and something about my frustration mixed with how ridiculous we look wearing socks on our feet sends a chorus of titters through my body. I cover my face with my hands, unable to stop them from building. He leans in, chuckling into my shoulder, and we're both gone, lost in a fit of giggles over socks.

Chase moves my hands away from my face, sweeping a stray loc behind my ear. He kisses me slowly, sweetly, like he's got all the time in the world, and lifts me from his lap to place me on the bed. We lose the socks and everything else.

I stretch to open my nightstand, grabbing a condom from the box forced on me at girl's night, silently thanking my best friend for her foresight. Chase's eyes flash, blazing with the heat we both feel for each other in this moment. The grazing of his lips on mine, trailing down to my neck, is ambrosia to my soul, healing parts of me I didn't know were aching to be healed.

"Do you realize how beautiful you are?" he asks, dropping kisses across the base of my neck.

"I...um...don't really think about it," I answer breathlessly while his lips glide across the expanse of my collarbone.

"I think about it enough for the both of us." His breath dances over me as he lets out a soft chuckle. Goosebumps race across my skin, a moan escaping my lips when he swirls the tip of his tongue around my nipple. "You like that, sweetheart?" I nod as the room grows hazy. "And this?" He sucks on the other side, smiling at the quiet gasp that slips from me. "You're so sensitive. So responsive." He blows a light stream of air over me, and I bite my lip in response.

"Mm-hmm. I like when you touch me."

Chase's lips deftly course down my body, hands smoothing over every other inch of me. I'm ready to burst by the time he reaches my thighs. "Chase," I whimper, rolling my hips toward his face.

"Give me a minute, beautiful. This is my new favorite thing. Let me taste you?"

I nod quickly, but he keeps his kisses above my center.

"Words, Kayla."

"Yes, I...want you to." The words work out of me while I try to hang on to some semblance of control. He teases my clit with the tip of his tongue, sending a curl-inducing zap straight down to my toes, and all that control goes out the window. "Chase, please," I say, loving the torture but needing release. "Ch—"

"Shh, I'm working," he mumbles, and his chuckled moan barely registers before he strokes me with the flat of his tongue. I grab a fistful of his hair and hold on for dear life. "God, your taste, baby. You're perfect." He swirls his tongue, and my hips roll upward, seeking more of him. "Relax. You deserve to be treated like a queen, Kayla," he whispers across my skin, triggering a series of shudders. Slipping two fingers inside me, he pumps them in and out before curling up, hitting that delicious spot that makes me cry out his name. The more I moan, the more earnestly he laps me up, licking and sucking until I'm writhing beneath him. "That's it. Right on my tongue. You're doing so well for me, sweetheart."

As much as I didn't like the talking at first, right now, I don't want him to stop. The careful way he holds me—grazing my skin with the tips of his fingers, his gentle hands working the sensitive parts of my body—it's like I'm his most precious discovery. I come alive under his touch, and when he brings me to that wondrous ecstasy, I know there is nothing—past or future—that can ever compare to this moment with him. Though, the next moment comes in as a close second.

LYING TANGLED IN THE SHEETS, ENJOYING THE FEELING of being wrapped up against his warmth, I trace my finger down the faint scar cutting across half of his chest and down his side.

"What happened?" I ask quietly.

"I fell out of a tree." He strokes my back lazily and speaks with a low, relaxed voice. "When I was nine, Hunter and I were climbing a dead tree at my grandparents' house. I jumped up to reach the next branch, breaking the one underneath me, and fell all the way down, hitting almost every branch on the way. The branch that caught my fall did it by impaling me in the side before it broke."

"You—what?" I prop up on my elbows. "Are you okay?"

"I think the last hour has shown I'm more than okay..." He smirks. "Hunter had to leave me alone under that tree to get help, and I was rushed into surgery. They got the main branch out of my side, but it punctured my lung and splintered just right that the imaging couldn't pick up all the pieces. I would stabilize, go to a room for observation, and then bleed internally or get another infection. After the fourth time, they made a long incision and pulled out six different wood fragments."

"That's why you're afraid of heights?" I ask, wide-eyed.

"That's why I'm afraid of heights." He nods. "I was in the hospital for almost a month. But it wasn't all bad, and I got to stay out of school for weeks after. I wasn't too grumpy until they told me I couldn't play sports for a year."

"A grumpy Chase?" I tease. "I can't see it."

He gives me a quick kiss. "It's not often. The tree scale helps with that."

"Tree scale?"

His eyes sparkle in the dim light of my room as he chuckles. "Yeah, so whenever something bad happens or I'm stuck on making a risky decision, I ask myself, 'Is this worse than falling out of a tree?' It puts things into perspective for me."

"Sounds like an easy way to face your fears. Maybe I should use the tree scale."

"Yeah, I mean, in a roundabout way, it got you sitting in my lap up on that wall, so...I think the tree scale works pretty well."

That memory seems so distant. I never thought I'd be here, with him in my bed, but I'm thankful for whatever cosmic forces lined up to make it happen. I'm happy I took the chance on him.

He brushes his lips on mine again briefly. "Hey, Kayla..."

"Hmm?"

"I told you I was going to fall for you this summer..."

"And...?" I wait, watching the look in his eyes change from fiery passion to a fierce vulnerability.

"Baby, I'm free-falling."

CHAPTER THIRTY-ONE

CHASE

Kayla looks so damn delectable in this olive-green dress I have half a mind to call off dinner myself and throw her on the bed behind us. But everyone has put a lot of time and energy into planning tonight. They would kill me if we didn't show up.

"You look great, baby," I say to her frowning face in the mirror, wrapping my arms around her waist and pulling her against me. I drop a kiss on her neck.

She shakes her head, pulling at her clothes before adjusting her hair. Shrugging away from me, she takes another dive into her closet.

"You've met all of them before..." I say, trying to appeal to her logic.

"But that was as your not-yet-but-almost girlfriend. This is different. Now I'm their long-lost daughter, new sister. What if they hate me—?"

"Whoa, whoa, whoa." I grab her hands, pulling her away from the closet of doom to keep her attention. "No one's hating anyone. Especially you. You're too amazing for that to happen." I move her over to the bed, nudging her to sit while I kneel in front of her. Trying to think of a good way to help ease her worry, I look into her eyes and ask, "Would it help you to know they're just as nervous as you are? Well, not Artie... She's pure excitement, but Hunter and Kendall."

"What do they have to be nervous about?"

"Hunter wants to make sure you're as comfortable as possible. He's been hounding me all week about your favorite foods and flowers, music taste, hobbies... I'm sure he's been driving Ashlie nuts too." That gets a little smile out of her, so I continue. "Kendall's worried about pushing you too fast too soon. He's ready to welcome you into the family with open arms, but doesn't want to scare you off. And me..."

"You? You're nervous?" She tilts her head, a confused line settling between her eyes.

"Yeah... I'm worried I won't be able to keep my hands to myself all night." I wiggle my eyebrows, leaning in for a kiss. She lets out a round of giggles, shaking her head at the cheesiness of it all. Her lips are soft against mine, and as I lean her back on the bedspread, she kisses me slowly, weaving her hands in my hair before pulling away.

"Baby, we can't..."

"*Baby*? Did you just call me *baby*?" Kayla hasn't used a pet name with me before, and hearing her say *baby*, knowing it's just for me, gets my stomach fluttering.

"Is that okay?" She lifts her eyebrow.

"Why don't you say it again and we can find out together...?"

She bites her lip and looks at me through her lashes. Leaning up, she grazes her nose against mine, whispering, "Chase, baby," and the shiver that runs through my body short circuits my brain. Her nails graze against my scalp as she lays her head back down to look at me, smiling like she already knows she's left me speechless.

She pulls me down into featherlight kisses, and slowly, my brain comes back online.

I love you.

Those are the only words I can think of right now. It's too soon to say anything, and I'll need to keep this to myself for a while. I told her I was falling for her last night, but I've already fallen, splattered on the ground at her feet. I'm done for. But she's about to have a life-altering dinner with her dad and new brother and sister, and I don't want to add to the overwhelm.

To keep the words from spilling out, I bury my head in her neck and pepper kisses at her pulse. She moans as I maneuver down to her shoulder, and I cross her clavicle before she stops me again.

"We really do need to stop. I already have to fix my hair…and makeup."

"You're welcome," I say with a wink and a smile. She rolls her eyes but gives me one more peck before getting up.

Moving back to the large mirror on her dresser, she smooths out the lines in her dress and swirls the front of her hair into a twisted knot. I could watch her get ready for an eternity and be just as mesmerized as I am now. The way she sweeps the bottom half of her hair across her shoulder, the swipe of her finger under her lip after reapplying lip gloss, the vanilla perfume… I'm completely spellbound.

I love you.

It hangs off my tongue, and I bite down on my back teeth just to move past the urge to say it.

We walk through the door of Kendall's rental, and Artemis charges toward us. Kayla gasps as Artemis wraps her arms around her waist, giving her the tightest hug a ten-year-old can muster. "You came!" She holds on tight, and Hunter moves toward us, flowers in hand. My parents stand together in the kitchen, while Kendall settles in front of the dining room table.

"Artie, we said, 'Be cool.' In what world is this keeping it cool?"

"Shut up, Hunter. I've always wanted a sister, and now I finally have one!"

"Well, give her a little bit of space. Personal bubble." He breathes heavily, trying to pry Artie off. Stepping in between them, he hands Kayla the bouquet of pink lilies with a hand-written card hanging from the top that says Welcome to the Family.

"Hey." He gives a sheepish grin. "We got all of your favorites." He steps from the entryway to showcase the food spread out in the kitchen right as my sisters emerge from the loft upstairs.

"I...wow. This is...wow." Kayla's mouth gapes as she takes in the assortment of food.

"Ashlie and Chase told us which places you liked, and Christine made it look all fancy," Hunter continues. "But Dad and I were the ones who put everything together."

"We wanted a glimpse into your life here and thought there was no better way to start than for us to experience some of your favorite things for ourselves." Kendall's wide grin shows his excitement, but he stays in the kitchen. Kayla turns toward me, mouth still open, her feet never having left the entryway. I squeeze her hand and nudge her forward.

Mom comes from the kitchen and gives her a side hug before setting the bouquet on the counter. "Welcome to the family. Now where should we start?"

"Um...definitely the crab cakes from Nando's." Kayla smiles, taking a breath and grabbing a plate. We load up and move to the table.

I drop a peck on her shoulder as I slide into my chair, and she gives a small grin. Wanting to feel close, I place my hand on her knee under the table. When I look up, I catch both my mom and Hunter watching us. Hunter sits with his tongue pushing the inside of his lip, trying to hide a smart-ass smirk, and Mom's eyes twinkle as she nods an *I-told-you-so* at me.

"So, Kayla, I know you're at Salima State, but I don't think I know what you're studying," Kendall says from across the table.

"Oh, my degree will be in event management. I'm hoping to land an internship at the end of summer to give me some experience in the catering world."

"Ooh, event management sounds right up my alley!" Mom chimes in cheerfully. "Is your focus more on the management or the planning side?"

"Planning, I think. I kind of do a little of everything right now, but I really like watching the details come together."

"When does your internship start?" Hunter asks between bites.

"If I get through the interview, it will start in October and run through May, with another full year after graduation."

"What does a catering internship interview look like?" Dad asks, fully invested in the conversation.

I feel Kayla tense next to me. "Maybe we could take a break with all the questions…" I say.

She smiles, putting her hand over the one I have on her knee. "It's okay. My interview will be the EdTechU event coming up in San Francisco, actually. I have to submit plans for place setting ideas, color schemes, the menu, and staff uniforms."

"What a small world," Kendall says. "But I think Chase was right about the questions. Do you have anything you want to know about us?"

"Everything really. I just don't know where to start."

"That's alright." Kendall flashes a bright smile. "There's no rush. We're just glad you're here."

After going back for seconds and dessert, everyone has migrated to the living room. Funny stories about the Jackson family get passed around, while Kayla laughs easily as she learns about them. Artemis hasn't left her side all night. It sounds like they're becoming fast friends.

"Can I show you some pictures?" Artie asks Kayla during a lull in the conversation.

"Yeah, I would really like that."

She bounds up the stairs to her bedroom, coming back down

shortly with a large burgundy photo album. "This is our family," she says, opening to a picture I've seen a thousand times. It used to hang in the Jackson's foyer. A young Hunter and baby Artemis sit in front of their parents, everyone smiling in the posed shot. "That's my mom, before the divorce." She turns pages and points out young Kendall, his parents—Wilson and Audra, and finally stops on a face that looks eerily similar to Kayla's.

"Wow," I say, looking between the picture and my girlfriend. "You look just like her."

"That's our great-grandmother, Betsie. I noticed you looked like her on the first day you came over, but everyone tells me to mind my business. So I did," Artie says with a satisfied edge to her voice.

"Hey, kid. Let me steal you for a minute." Dad claps me on the shoulder and motions for me to follow him outside. I squeeze Kayla's hand before walking out behind him. The cool evening breezes around us as the sun falls below the skyline. "How do you think it's going in there?" He juts his thumb toward the house.

"Pretty good, I think. The funny stories definitely helped."

"Good, good. I had to discourage Kendall from a few grand gestures, so I'm glad they kept this casual." Dad taps his fingers on the banister, and I can almost feel the nervous energy radiating from him. "...How has your summer been? You been able to relax at all?"

He's stalling and not doing a very good job at it. "What's up, Dad?"

With a long sigh, he explains, "Well, we met with William earlier today, and the board has decided they want the sales team up and running in San Francisco before the shareholders' event in August. Since you'll be one of the managers on the new team, you'll need to get there about a week beforehand for training and gathering the projected sales numbers for the region."

I prop my arms against the banister, scrubbing my face in my hands. "And why am I just hearing about this now?"

"Sorry, kid. With everyone on vacation, it's been a task trying to get the board together for a meeting."

Dread steamrolls through me as I mentally calculate what that means and how many days I have left with Kayla in Fort Bender. *I'm supposed to have another four weeks. Now I only have one?* I already wasn't looking forward to the one-hour distance we'll have after summer, but now I have to tell her I'm leaving next week. And it's three hours away? I need more time to prepare for this. *We* need more time.

"The good news is that after the event, you'll have another two weeks before your contract begins. Should be enough time for you to wrap up any loose ends." He pats me on the shoulder and heads back into the jovial noises coming from the beach house, leaving me alone to stew over the newest hitch in my schedule.

I should go in, too, but my frustration needs a little time to simmer. My need to figure out a sensible plan reverberates, and I don't know if a week is enough time to do that. I need time to figure out how to break the news to Kayla, to assure her we can make this shortened timeline work. Time to tell her I love her. I just need more time.

CHAPTER THIRTY-TWO

CHASE

"Hey," Kayla says, taking careful steps toward me. I turn, leaning back against the railing as a smile creeps across my lips. I'll tell her about leaving when I take her home tonight. Right now, I just want to enjoy the time I have. "Is everything okay?"

"Yeah, just...work. How are things in there?" I ask. She comes close enough to slide her arms around me and then tips up on her toes to reach my lips, kissing me far too briefly. "What was that for?" I grin, pulling her closer.

"Just a thank you for being you. Kendall told me this was all your idea."

I hang my head, trying to hide the flushing on my face. "He wasn't supposed to tell you that."

"He told me that too..." She kisses me again, wrapping her arms around my neck—and maybe it's the urgency I feel from the news my dad shared—but those same words from earlier try to slip through my teeth. "Kayla, I—"

"Chase, nice to see you. Glad I could run into you while I'm here." William St. Clair walks across the conjoined deck from his rental. Kayla sidles away, and I pull her back to my side, holding her in place with my arm. I don't want her to leave yet. She can hear whatever he has to say.

I clear my throat, trying to lighten some of the huskiness I know has settled there. "Nice to see you again, Mr. St. Clair. This is my girlfriend, Kayla. Kayla, this is Maggie's dad, William."

"Nice to meet you." Kayla holds her hand out to shake his.

"Likewise," he says dismissively, holding the tips of her fingers like a used napkin.

"I'll...give you two a minute," Kayla says, moving my hand off her hip and walking back into the house. The last place I want to be is stuck out here with this asshole, but he was the biggest seed funder of EdTechU and remains a current shareholder. So I'll suffer through it for the sake of networking.

"Your dad tells me you'll be joining the new sales team in San Francisco. I think that's the perfect place for you."

"Uh, yeah... Thank you." I nod, not sure why he's cornered me out here. The fact he's been wanting to talk to me gives me pause. He's a tall, dark-haired man with a permanently pinched look on his pallid face. The coldness radiates off him as he stands with his hands clasped behind his back like he owns the place, making it unbearable to be near him for too long.

"I'm going to speak openly here, Chase." He brings his steepled hands forward, exerting misplaced power over this conversation. "I know my nephew likes to immerse himself into the urban lifestyle, and there's nothing wrong with that while you're young. We've all done it. I think Hunter's a little too far gone to be saved, but I wanted to give you some friendly advice."

"About the *urban* lifestyle?" I ask with a slight edge to my voice. I've known William to be less than politically correct, but I really hope he's not steering this conversation in the direction I think it's going.

"Yes, well, urban culture seems to be a popular trend these days. I don't blame you for getting wrapped up in it. College years and all of that." He waves his hand in the air, as if the action will clear away the offensive notes in his message.

"You keep saying *urban*. Are you talking about Black culture?"

"Oh, Chase, I wouldn't be so crass as to use that term."

"Well, *William,* you really should say exactly what you mean…" I'm not in the mood for this right now. I'm still irritated with having to leave early, I've got my girl waiting for me inside, and now this bastard wants to insert himself into my business like he knows the first thing about me.

"I'm encouraging you to get it out of your system while you're young. Have your fun with the ethnic girls now, for as long as you need to. And then, when you're ready to settle down, you and my Magnolia will make a worthy pairing."

I grind my back teeth together and remind myself to breathe. "You're being serious right now?" I huff, running my hands through my hair to try and dissipate the rigid rage creeping up my spine. "I don't need any of your advice, William."

He places a hand on my shoulder, gripping a little more firmly than is necessary. "There's no need to get upset. I'm trying to help you. Give you a leg up. Walking into the corporate world with the right woman on your arm will only help you climb the ladder more quickly. My Magnolia—"

"There's not a snowball's chance in hell that *your Magnolia* and I will end up together." I spit the words, glaring into his face, ready to haul his ass to the ground.

He doesn't drop his hand from my shoulder, staying right inside my personal space. My fingers flex, and I flatten them against my leg to keep from curling them into a fist. It's offensive that this towering waste of space thinks we can relate about anything, and the red haze seeping in to cloud my vision is urging my logic to the backseat. The more he says, the harder it is to keep my feet from propelling me forward. The longer he talks, the bolder his vile words become, and I'm livid this man thinks he and I have any kind of understanding.

"We'll see about that. I can be persuasive when I need to be." He finally takes a step back, clasping his hands behind him. "I understand there's a certain novelty to the colored girls, especially if they can cook, but it doesn't last. Whenever it fades out with this one, my Magnolia will be waiting. You understand?"

Before I realize what's happening, I'm in his face. "Say one more thing, you racist motherfucker, and I swear you'll be tasting every single one of your goddamn veneers."

"Whoa, hey…" Hunter grabs my fist, stepping between us and moving me back toward the railing. I must have missed the door opening twice because Mom is out here too.

"Really, Chase, the thug act isn't becoming. I expect that out of Hunter, but never from you. Don't let that Black girl ruin the good head on your shoulders."

I lunge again, and Hunter pushes me back, stepping to his uncle. "You might be family, but I won't hesitate to shut your mouth for you if you won't shut the fuck up."

"That's enough!" Kendall booms from the door. "Boys, go for a walk." We don't move, watching as he saunters up to William, leans in close, and sneers a few words before turning around and pointing to us. "Go. Cool off," he says, before strolling back into the house.

Hunter pushes me toward the stairs leading to the beach, but not before I hear my mom saying, "William, you disagreeable son of a—"

"Bruh, since when do you get into fistfights with old men?" Hunter asks, his hand on my shoulder like he's worried I'll try to make a break for it.

"You didn't hear what he said… He's foul. Disgusting."

"I heard enough, and you know he's like this. Why'd you let him rile you up?"

"Did Kayla hear any of it?"

"Naw, your mom is the stealth queen. She grabbed me when she saw what was happening outside. Then she had Avery get my dad. Last I saw, Kayla and Artie were busy bonding over music."

"Good. I don't want her to hear any of that shit."

"She's going to hear that shit though, and probably already has before. You can't protect her from that kind of stuff, Chase."

"I can try!" I say, adrenaline making my voice more forceful than I mean it to be. Lacing my fingers at the back of my head, I blow out a puff of air as I pace, trying to rid myself of the pounding energy coursing through me.

"You love her, don't you?" His question catches me off guard, and I don't answer, choosing to stare at the sand and toe the edge of the bluff. "Have you told her yet?"

I shake my head.

"*Why* haven't you told her yet?"

With a deep breath, drawing out the exhale, I run my hands through my hair. "It's too soon. The timing's not right."

"I mean, sure, if you'd only spent a few days together. But it's been almost every day for the last two months, working together, saving her from a nasty fall, *and* supporting her through a family secret that left her devastated. If you're feeling it, maybe it's not too early." Hunter kicks at the ground, watching the spray of sand.

I shake my head again, trying to breathe out the rest of the aggression in my body. "I can't. If I tell her now, she'll run, and I don't want to lose her," I say finally, swiping my hands through my hair.

Hunter nods, watching me as I unravel in front of him. "Fair enough, but maybe no more boxing, eh?" he jokes, punching my shoulder. We stay out on the beach for several minutes, listening to the whirring of the tide until I feel calm enough to rejoin the party. The chaos from outside has left me extremely tired, and when we get back to the house, all I want to do is fall into bed.

Finding Kayla, I wrap my arms around her from behind, breathing her in. "Can we stay over here tonight?" I ask, hopeful she won't make me drive her back across town. She nods, and we make our way around Kendall's place to say goodbye.

My arm flies to my wide-open mouth as I stifle a yawn at the sight of my bed. I kick off my shoes and catch Kayla watching me. She tilts her head before putting her palms on my chest, wheeling me backward until I'm sitting on the bed. "You're sleepy, so let's go to sleep," she says, slipping off her shoes and letting the bun out of her hair.

"I'm okay. I need to talk to you about something first." Unable to catch myself, I yawn again.

"It can wait for the morning." She moves around the bed, plumping up pillows and turning down the bedspread. "Lie down."

Shaking my head and trying to keep my eyes open, I mumble, "It's gotta be tonight."

"Okay, well, let's snuggle, and then you can tell me. Deal?" My exhaustion can't really argue with that logic, so I lay back on the pillow, arms open, waiting for her to climb in. As soon as her head lays against my chest, I cling to her, resting in her warmth as my heartbeat slows. All the worry dissolves under her touch, and the only thing I'm concerned with is being here, right now, with her. Maybe my message *can* wait until the morning.

I start to doze before my eyes pop open, remembering what I needed to tell her. "I have to leave Friday," I murmur, waiting for her to tense beside me. She doesn't move, taking so long to answer that I wonder if she's fallen asleep. "Baby?" I crane my neck to peek at her face.

"Okay. We'll figure it out in the morning." She squeezes me a little tighter, and there's only a few deep breaths between me and sleep before I'm out.

CHAPTER THIRTY-THREE

KAYLA

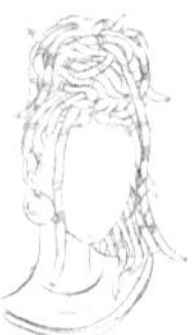

The morning sun streaming through the curtains wakes me. I don't know the last time I slept in this late, but it's nice to feel rested for once. Family dinner last night was better than I could have ever imagined. Even though things are still a little awkward between us, I'm excited to learn more about my newfound family.

Blinking to help the room come into focus, I look up to see Chase is still asleep, his lips parted slightly. The rays cast angelic golden highlights across his mussed hair, making it almost impossible for me to look away from the unbelievably caring soul beside me. He gave them the idea for dinner last night. *For me.* For my comfort. That thought alone makes me feel giddy inside. I like the way I feel when I'm with Chase—cherished and safe, and undeniably wanted.

As my sleepy thoughts shift into awareness, I remember what he told me before falling asleep last night. I'm torn between memorizing the lines of his chiseled face and closing my eyes to keep cuddling for a little longer. He's leaving Friday; less than a week away. It feels too soon, like we have too much to figure out between now and then. I don't even know where to start. Apart from deciding to continue seeing each other once I head back to school, we haven't talked about any kind of logistics. Between my internship, his new job, an hour-long distance, and whatever else life tries to throw in, there just seems to be a lot of obstacles. My mind races through everything that could go wrong. Trying to control the spiral before it takes hold, I look back up at the peaceful face stirring next to me. I trace the line of his jaw, the hair on his face tickling my fingers as I go.

"You having fun?" Chase smiles with his eyes still closed.

"And what if I am?" I tease, jumping as he tickles my side.

"Well, by all means, don't let me stop you." He moves my hand back to his face, keeping it in place with his own.

I slip out of his arms, sliding my legs over his until I land in his lap. Running my fingers through his wavy hair and down his cheeks until I reach the muscles in his jaw, I lean forward to caress his lips with my own. Morning breath be damned, I just want to melt into him and ignore my racing thoughts.

Chase's hands find my waist, his touch gentle and firm—possessive, but tender. These moments where it's just us—no diner, no family or friends—make me want to freeze time and stay suspended with him in our own little world. This tiny island of happiness is the best thing I never knew I needed. I pull away slowly, keeping my fingertips on the edge of his jaw as I fight the urge to dive back into his comfort.

"Wake me up like that every morning, and I might just have to keep you around..." he mumbles. His hands travel up the back of my dress, making my skin prickle in response to his touch. I want so badly to tangle my legs with his, hoping to keep the morning at bay. A moan escapes my lips as his warm hands rub circles on my back.

"I have to go," I say, biting my lip, fully enjoying the way his fingers dance across my skin.

"Mmm, nah... I don't think so..." He pulls me down toward him, his lips finding my neck.

"Baby, I have to go do some research before my shift."

"Mmm, see, you just called me *baby* again. That adds another hour, I think…"

I sink against him, my giggles melting into sounds of indulgence as he moves his lips slowly up my neck, around my chin, and to my mouth, pulling on my lips with his own. "Chase… baby—"

"That's two hours now." He flips me down onto the bed. The motion is smooth, the surprise of it stealing my breath while he nuzzles his lips against my neck. As much as I want to continue, there's something more pressing for us to be doing.

"You're leaving, and we need to talk about it," I whisper, voice shaky from pleasure and something else. Something raw and vulnerable. I'm scared to lose him, but even more scared to tell him I'm scared of losing him. Telling him would give him the power to hurt me with it, and I don't think I could make it back from that.

He pauses, breathing a sigh into my shoulder before sitting up on his knees. I prop myself up against the headboard, and we stare at each other, unable to speak and unable to look away. After what feels like an entire minute, he places my hand in his.

"I have to report to the office on Friday morning, and I'll be there the entire week before the shareholders' event. After that, I'll have two weeks of freedom before staying in San Francisco permanently."

"And what does this mean for us?" I break eye contact, suddenly not sure I'm ready for this conversation. I don't want him to see the apprehension in my eyes, but he lifts my chin with his finger and lowers his face until we're nose to nose.

"Whatever you want to do, that's what we'll do. I want to be with you, Kayla, in any way you'll let me. Just tell me what you want, and I'll find a way to do it."

My mouth falls open as the entirety of his words filter through my wall of anxiety. His stare is intense, but I can't look away this time. My breath catches in my throat when I try to speak. He smiles before kissing me softly, gently grazing my cheek with the pad of his thumb. It's slow and deliberate, speaking volumes to my heart beyond what he's already said. He's not just willing to find a way for this to work, but determined to find a way that it will. He's all in with me. With *us*.

My thoughts swirl as my heart pounds in my chest. Words that danced around possibilities before now seem to cement assurances into the very makings of my soul:

> *Sometimes*
> *What you've lost, you'll find*
> *And you'll fall in kind*
> *To some kind of forever.*

A tear slips from my eyes, rolling onto his fingers. His look of concern as he pulls away takes me back to that morning in my best friend's bedroom, where my lack of communication caused him to question my feelings for him. Not wanting to make the same mistake again, I wipe my face and clear my throat of the intensity that has settled there, touching my head to his. Backed by the consuming emotions I don't yet trust myself with, I speak the first words accessible to me. "I just want you."

He smiles. "Then we'll spend as much time together as we can this week. And next week, I'll text, and call, and video chat with you so much you get sick of me." I giggle as he nuzzles my nose. "And when I come back here, I'll help you get settled at school, and we can maybe explore San Francisco together before I start working. The rest, we'll figure out as it comes. How does that sound?"

"It's perfect," I say, before leaning in to kiss him one more time.

IT'S A SLOW SUNDAY AT THE DINER. THE STARK difference from the onslaught of new faces at the end of May versus the end of July is a little jarring. If I wasn't using the slowdown to prepare my portfolio, I would be restlessly recleaning appliances and bugging Bert over in his corner. Tourists still come to Fort Bender through September, but those visitors are usually retired and prefer a slower pace. Most families have moved on to more exciting places to round out the end of their summer vacations before school starts.

I consider two types of formal catering attire as I study the portfolio sketches on my tablet. I've already finished my renderings of the venue color scheme—complete with tablecloths and floral centerpieces. The formal place setting ideas were easy, too, once I brushed up on the placements of silverware and dishes. I've even added a few extra touches—a table numbering system and waitstaff tracking cards—just to show the internship board I'm willing to go above and beyond. I've almost decided on a basic black uniform when three of my favorite people walk into the diner. So much of my summer has been spent laughing here with Ashlie, Hunter, and Chase, and I'm just now realizing how much I'll miss this scene when we all leave.

"Hey, babe." Chase comes behind the counter and wraps his arm around my waist, kissing my cheek quickly before dropping his chin to my shoulder. "Whatcha working on today?"

"The catering uniform for now, and then I just need to create the menu before I can turn it all in."

"It looks amazing already." He kisses my temple and moves around to the other side of the counter, where Hunter and Ashlie are in full swing with one of their ridiculous debates. They must have worked out whatever had them not talking to each other. I tried to pull it out of her, but she's been a steel trap on the issue.

"There's no way..." Hunter shakes his head emphatically.

"I'm calling a professional. That way, I know it's done right." Ashlie rolls her eyes at him and stretches a hand toward me. I think she wants me to help with her side of the argument, but I don't know what they're bickering about now.

"Is this your way of telling us you didn't want Bryan's ashy babies because he couldn't change a tire? Because that makes complete sense." Hunter's signature smart-ass smirk spreads across his face as Ashlie pushes his shoulder.

"Back me up here, Kay." Ashlie turns back toward me. "You get a flat tire in the middle of nowhere. Are you calling your boyfriend or roadside assistance?"

"Um, neither." I shrug. "I would just change the tire."

"You wouldn't call me?" Chase asks, jutting his head back in response to my third option answer.

"You're stranded, Kayla. *Stranded*," Hunter says, shaking his head again like I don't understand the hypothetical situation.

"I wouldn't be stranded because I can change a tire. I'd change it and be on my way."

"I forget we've got Miss Independent over here. She's probably been changing tires since she was five years old," Ashlie says, folding her arms and leaning back in the stool.

"Six, but close enough," I say, glaring back at her.

"So...you wouldn't call me to come help you?" Chase's face is scrunched as he asks the same question as before, clearly not understanding my position.

"Help me do what, exactly? By the time I called and waited for you to show up, I could have had the tire changed already."

"That's not the point..."

"What's the point, then?" I curve an eyebrow up and cross my arms, waiting for his reply.

"The point is that you wouldn't call me to help you when you're stranded," he speaks slowly, forming his words carefully.

"I wouldn't *be* stranded, Chase," I answer again as I watch him pull his lips together in a line, biting off any additions he had for this budding argument.

"I think we're witnessing their first fight," Hunter whispers loudly, nudging Ashlie with his elbow.

"Speaking of ashy, get your dry ass elbow away from me," Ashlie teases, pulling lotion out of her bag and handing it to him.

"That's just my white half showing," he jokes, rubbing some of the cream on his arms. The tension between me and Chase slowly fizzles as our friends continue to joke around, and finally, I'm relaxed enough to grab water and menus. We spend the rest of lunch laughing about one thing or another. When it's time for them to go, Chase pulls me in close, as usual.

After they leave, I make the final decisions on the attire spread for my portfolio and then pack it up. Before I can work on the menu, I need to combine my digital sketches with images from my idea board. Luckily, my boyfriend and new brother just so happen to be good with technology, and they've offered to help me combine it all after my shift. Checking the clock, I have about two hours before I can hang up the apron.

CHAPTER THIRTY-FOUR

KAYLA

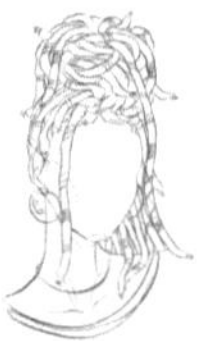

I pull up to The Bluffs in time to see Mr. St. Clair and Maggie talking in the driveway of the fourth rental house. The man's pale face is as unpleasant as it was last night, and I don't have any desire to have another encounter with either of them.

It's not that he's ugly by any means, but the frigid look in his eyes combined with his rigid posture lets you know upon first meeting that he's a snooty man. I clocked it from the pathetic handshake he offered last night. All my internal warning systems were telling me to get out of there. It's easy to see where Maggie gets it from. She gives her dad a hug before he dips into the back of a waiting, jet-black luxury car. Once she's back inside the house, I grab my tablet and head to the door.

"Kayla!" Artemis nearly knocks me back down the stairs as she tackles me with a hug. Her curly hair bounces when she tips her head back to smile at me.

"Hey, Artie." I grin, patting her on the back. "What you been up to today?"

"We went to the museum after lunch to see Ashlie, and she gave us a behind-the-scenes tour! *And then*, her boyfriend surprised her with flowers and cookies—"

"That's not your business to tell, Artemis..." Hunter says

from the door, shaking his head. I lift an eyebrow, just now learning this bit of information. "Bryan showed up at the museum after lunch with grand gestures and an apology." He shrugs.

"So how is it *your* business to tell but not *mine*?" Artie huffs, scowling.

"Just get inside. *Per-son-al bu-bble.*" They roll their eyes at each other as we walk into the house. Artemis joins Avery and Hadley outside on the deck after she makes me promise I won't leave before saying goodnight. I tuck my museum questions aside, making a mental note to text Ash about it when I get home tonight. But watching Hunter kick at a scuff on the floor has me wondering how he's taking it. I still don't know the details about him and Ashlie, but I assume Bryan showing up makes it all more complicated.

"Hey, you okay?" I bump his shoulder.

"Yeah, why wouldn't I be?"

"Because ashy Bryan is back..."

"He's not ashy. His *babies* are going to be ashy." Hunter smirks, using his sense of humor to try and deflect from the vulnerability in his eyes. He clears his throat, changing the subject as we move toward the couch. "Let's see that portfolio."

Chase joins us from the kitchen, bottles of water in hand, with a big smile on his face. Standing behind the sofa, he tosses the bottles on the empty cushion next to me and wraps his arms around my shoulders, kissing my cheek before turning his attention to the tablet in my lap. I show them the problem I'm having with adding pictures from my idea board to my sketches, and then I show them an example of how I need the presentation slides to look. Wordlessly, they get to work. Chase swipes on the tablet, arms still around me, while Hunter grabs a wireless mouse, keyboard, and glasses I've never seen him wear before. They've turned my tablet into a mini computer, backing up my sketches and moving files around so fast my eyes cross. I watch in awe at how quickly they anticipate each other's thinking, picking up where the other left off like a well-oiled machine.

"Think you could switch me spots?" Chase says distractedly, still clicking away.

"Sure..." I say, handing the tablet to Hunter and moving off the couch as Chase climbs over from the back. Standing there, looking at these two in their element for the first time, I'm struck by how much I still have to learn about them. My brother and my boyfriend—two things I didn't have at the beginning of the summer.

Sensing I won't be needed for a while, I grab a water from the couch and slip out the back door to see what the girls are doing. The sun beats down on the dark blue patio, and I take in the beauty of the waves crashing into the ocean bluffs.

"Hi, Kayla!" Hadley greets me while she mixes something together in a large bowl.

"Hey. What are you making?"

"I'm making a non-Newtonian fluid out of cornstarch and water that I'm going to put on the subwoofer over there so the sound waves will make it dance."

"...Why?" I ask. She spoke so quickly, I'm only half sure I know what the words in her sentence mean strung together in the way she said them.

With a bright smile, she responds, "Because I can."

"Is it like slime?" I ask.

"It's *better* than slime." She sticks her tongue out of the corner of her mouth as she stirs.

"And you have permission to do this?"

"Well, nobody said I *couldn't*...today. But it's totally safe."

Artie drapes plastic wrap on an overturned subwoofer while Avery drips food coloring all over the surface, and I'm only partially convinced of the safety of this experiment.

"Alright, girls, are you ready?" Hadley asks, looking around at us before scooping a spoonful of white goo onto the well of the speaker. "Hit it, Av!" She points, cueing her sister to play some music from the phone in her hand. The pop tune has a nice beat, and we all crowd around to watch the sound waves at work, bopping our heads together to the rhythm. The goo starts rippling, like a puddle surrounded by heavy footsteps as the beat drops in the song. Little rounded globs peak and dip with the music, like gnomes having a dance party. The colors mix, making a mesmerizing display of hues as everything swirls and blends into a colorful rave.

"I see they roped you into a science experiment," Kendall says from behind me with a chuckle.

"Yeah. That was so cool! I've never seen anything like it." I smile as he walks over to stand next to me.

"The boys showed me your portfolio in there... I hope that's okay."

"Oh, yeah, that's fine. It's not private or anything."

"Some people don't like sharing their work until it's completed. I didn't want to mess with your flow." He holds up his fingers, placing the word *flow* into air quotes. "You've got a good eye for detail. It looks amazing."

"Oh, thank you." My face flushes at the compliment. Navigating this new father-daughter aspect of our relationship makes me feel a little clumsy. Neither of us really knows where to begin, which leads to long pauses and nervous laughter.

"You're welcome." He takes a beat, letting an awkward silence settle in between us. "I wanted to run another thing past you, if that's okay?" He waits for me to answer, which is something I'm learning to appreciate about him.

"Sure, what's up?"

"I don't know if you already have plans with your mom, but how would you feel if Artemis, Hunter, and I visited you at Salima State over Labor Day weekend? We thought it could be nice for you to show us about your life there and spend some quality family time. Only if you want to, of course."

I guess this is the next step in getting to know them all better, seeing as summer is quickly coming to an end. I've been so focused on navigating this new dynamic with them around here, I haven't considered what we would do once we all got back to our lives. And Mom is a whole other issue. Aside from a few messages with her checking in, we haven't talked about any of this mess. She'll still be traveling when I go back to school, and if I'm the Princess of Avoidance, she's the Queen.

"I think that sounds nice," I say, offering him a smile.

The smile he returns is just as big as he nods. "Okay, good. I'm looking forward to it." We stand in another uneasy silence before the door behind us creaks open.

"Hey, Kayla, we need you..." Chase says from the door, running his hands through his hair.

Hunter leans back on the couch with his fingers laced over his torso, glasses resting on his tipped-back head like he's just gotten home from a long day's work.

As soon as I'm over the threshold, Chase says, "The images from your idea board needed to be decoded from their proprietary format and then reconverted to the word processing format. We made a template and formatted it with every feature you said you wanted. Hunter's going to show you how the different features work inside the template. He'll have you try it to make sure you're comfortable with the sketch transitions, and then you'll be ready to insert everything and upload it into the presentation software." The words flow from his mouth quickly and efficiently, like I have any idea what he's talking about. My mouth drops as I try to translate the tech speak.

"What—why are you looking at me like that?"

I snap my mouth closed, but my eyes stay narrowed as I try to keep up with how fast he's talking. With a nervous chuckle, I respond, "I've just never seen this side of you before. Either of you."

"Your girlfriend just called us nerds, bruh," Hunter says from the couch.

"Hey, she's *your* sister..."

"I did not! It just took me by surprise. It's impressive."

"Nerds, dorks, dweebs…" Hunter mocks, turning his hand into a talking puppet.

"Okay, sit, so there's time to snuggle before you have to leave." Chase motions toward the couch.

Hunter shows me the template, re-explaining what the problem was and how to place the photos next to my sketches where I wanted them. I quickly insert my photos, and they watch as I create the page spreads in the presentation software. "All you'll have left is uploading the menu, and then you should be good to send it off," Hunter explains. He grabs the keyboard and mouse and disappears upstairs.

Closing the cover of my tablet, Chase slides it on the coffee table and turns to me. "Oh, hey, baby. When did you get here?" he teases, taking his tech persona off and slipping back into boyfriend mode.

"So you *do* remember me? I thought I'd lost you there for a second…"

He pulls me in close, nuzzling my nose with his. "Never gonna happen." His kiss is soft and slow, like he's savoring every bit of it, committing the feeling of my lips to his memory. Tingles surge through my core, making me shiver as he pulls away. He flips on the TV, landing on the new detective show I've been wanting to see. I snuggle into him, and he slides my legs across his lap, rubbing his hand over my thigh. Apparently, the TV was just a front, because in no time, we're making out like it's the only activity that makes sense.

"What about the show?" I ask on a breath.

"I've already seen it," he says distractedly, lips continuing to occupy mine.

"But it's new…"

"Then I'll stream it later." His voice comes out muffled as his lips move down my chin.

"Okay…but what if…*I*…wanted to watch it?" I mean for it to come out in a teasing manner, but the way my body is reacting to his touch makes my breath hitch enough times that the message is lost.

"Then watch it," he says with a chuckle, leaving a trail of kisses down the column of my neck and back up. "I'm not stopping you."

"You're...distracting me though..." A giggle slips out of me as his breath tickles my ear.

"Sounds like a personal problem," he whispers as his eyes meet mine. Leaning back in, he wiggles his eyebrows playfully.

I bite my lip and shake my head.

"Okay, fine," he concedes. "We can watch this, but I get to make up for lost time during commercial breaks. Deal?"

I give in to one last steam filled kiss, running my hands through his hair and trailing fingers down his jawline, pulling away once I'm convinced he'll be aching for more. Simple payback for making me miss the beginning of the show. "Deal."

A groan rumbles in his chest as he nuzzles my nose with his. "You're gonna be the death of me, Kayla," he whispers.

"Maybe. But not until the next commercial break," I tease, giving a wink.

"You win." He props his chin on my shoulder as we try to catch up on whatever we missed on the show so far. We stay like this—whispering in between scenes, kissing during commercials —until it's time for me to go. I make a brief stop next door to find Artie, just like I promised I would, and then Chase walks me out to my car.

When we get outside, he presses me against the passenger side door for one last goodnight kiss, accidentally kicking the tire as he comes in close. He pulls away suddenly and drops to look at something. I tuck my satchel closer to my body so it doesn't hit him in the head.

"Uh, everything okay?" I ask, confused why I was just deprived of one of my favorite things. I don't care if we just spent an entire evening making out, I want my goodnight kiss.

"You have a flat tire," he says with an amused voice. I bend to look, and sure enough, my tire is squished all the way to the ground.

"Great." I sigh, hitting the trunk button on my car remote and walking to the back. He moves right along with me, and before I can stop him, he reaches into the trunk. "What are you doing?" There's a slight edge to my voice, the same irritation creeping in from the conversation at the diner earlier.

"Changing your tire…" He digs around the trunk, looking for the jack and spare.

"No, I got it." I lift the jack out of the back and lay it against the curb.

"Don't be ridiculous. I'm right here. Just let me do it."

"I'm not the one being ridiculous. I told you this morning I can change my own tire."

"I don't doubt that you *can*, but babe, you don't have to. Let me help you."

"I don't need help with this."

"Why won't you let me help you?" he asks, furrowing his brows.

"Don't act like I didn't just spend the evening getting your help on my portfolio." I cross my arms, annoyed he won't move out of the way so I can get started.

"That's different. It's what I do for work," he says, shaking his head. "You don't have to do this by yourself, Kayla." He touches my shoulder with one hand and points at the spare in the trunk with the other. The rage that ignites and courses through me under his hand comes as a surprise to me.

"The only *difference* is that your ego has deemed changing a tire as something a girl needs a guy to do for her. I don't need you to save me." I clamp my teeth together as I try to lift out the spare without bumping into Chase.

He puts his hand around the wheel, stopping my momentum. "…I'm not…trying to save you. *God*, you're so hard to figure out sometimes. I'm trying to help you solve this problem. Can't you just let me take care of you?" His voice edges on frustration as he lets go of the tire and puts his hands behind his head, puffing out an exhale.

"I'm not some problem that needs to be solved, Chase! I've been taking care of myself my whole life. I don't need someone taking care of me now." It comes out louder than I mean it to, but I double down anyway. I'm overreacting. I know I am. But the frustration in his voice paired with my indignation makes it hard for my brain to care about the consequences of prolonging this fight. I'm seeing red, and my pulse pounds in my ears. All my defenses are up, while all my instincts are telling me to get out of here.

He drops his hands, looking at me with his mouth gaping. "I didn't say *you* were the problem, but you're being so damn stubborn right now—"

"This is who I am. If you don't like it, then—"

"Leave? Is that what you were going to say?" His voice is intense. He's not yelling, but it's enough to ignite my already overstimulated senses. "I don't do that, Kayla, you do. When things get a little too vulnerable, when I get a little too close, you push me away, and you run." He stuffs his hands in his pockets, the muscle in his jaw twitching as he grinds his molars together.

"I don't push you away." I look away from him.

He dips his head to look into my eyes. The frustration is there in his gaze, but there's something else too. It's raw and unexpected, threatening to extinguish the anger I'm feeling. *Hurt.* "What are you doing right now, then?"

I'm hurting him, and I don't know how to handle it or how to stop it. Desperately trying to slow the air I'm pulling into my lungs, my eyes dart around, looking for any kind of escape. I just need to get out of here. Shaking my head again, I drop the tire back in the trunk and turn to walk down the sidewalk. "Whatever. Change the damn tire, Chase. It doesn't matter," I say over my shoulder.

"Where are you going? Kayla—" He starts after me, catching up in a few steps.

"I'm walking home."

"No, you're not." His hand wraps around my elbow to get me to stop walking.

I snatch it back, glaring up at him. "You're telling me what to do now? Don't touch me!"

"Kayla, just let me get my keys and I'll drive you home."

"No. I leave, remember? So let me leave."

He covers his face with his hands, a frustration-filled groan escaping his mouth. But he lets me go. He lets me walk away. I allow my anger to propel me forward, down the hill, to the main road. My bag swings wildly against my hip with each step, reinforcing the determination I feel to walk my ass across town. I almost make it to the end of the street before I hear the car behind me.

"Get in the car, Kayla," Hunter's voice says from behind the wheel of Chase's car. I turn, confused for a split second before I remember everything that led to me getting here. My rage surges all over again.

"No. Go home, Hunter." I continue walking.

"Naw, I can't really do that. Dad and Chase would have my head if I let you walk home alone this late."

"I'm not getting in the car."

"Then I'll follow you like this until you get home." He drives slowly beside me for another block, his stubbornness matching mine like it's built into our newly discovered sibling DNA. The speed in my pace slows, and suddenly, my face is wet. Fat tears roll down my cheeks, and I can't seem to stop them. The adrenaline from the argument drains from my body. All I'm left with are heaving sobs.

"Kayla, get in the car," Hunter tries again, with sympathy rounding out the concern in his voice. I can't look at him, but I trudge to the passenger side door and plop down in the seat. He's quiet as we drive through town toward my house. The only sounds in the car are my sobs as I play back the scene in my head repeatedly. I overreacted. I hurt him. I left, and he let me leave.

"What happened?" Hunter asks once we pull into my driveway.

"He wouldn't let me change my tire. I'm fine." I sniff, talking through the congested sound of my voice.

"You're crying, so you're obviously not fine...and neither is Chase, by the way." He pulls out his phone to show four missed text messages, all from Chase. "He sent me after you because he didn't think you'd get in the car with him." His phone buzzes in his hand, and he shoots off a quick text before shaking his head and dropping it in the cupholder.

"I..." I'm not even sure I can explain to myself why I reacted the way I did, let alone explain it to someone else. I hide my face behind my hands, feeling the rough, salty trails left by my tears.

"Look, I'm cool if you just want to sit in here for a while before deciding, but I think you should come back with me and talk it out."

"I have to open the diner tomorrow," I croak, shaking my head.

"I hear you. But do you really think you're getting any sleep tonight, like this? I know he's not..."

I shake my head again, trying to disrupt the negative thought spiral threatening to take over. My finger scrapes away at the cuticle on my thumb. He's right, of course. I should go back and work this out. Try to make it better. I hang my head, the war between my stubborn independence and a longing to be back in my boyfriend's arms raging through my mind.

"Go inside and pack a bag. If you two can't work it out tonight, I'll drive you to the diner in the morning myself."

I take a couple of minutes to decide, and Hunter doesn't rush me. He doesn't pull out his phone either, which is odd enough that I notice, even through the battle waging between my head and heart. Sitting with me in the silence, he shares his calm while I spiral in the passenger seat.

CHAPTER THIRTY-FIVE

KAYLA

Slowly, I undo my seatbelt and grab my house keys from my purse, leaving the bag as a signal that I'll be back. I don't bother turning the living room light on, preferring to slide my hand down the back of the couch until I reach the hallway. Flipping on the little desk lamp in my room, I grab my backpack from the closet and stuff my Patti's Place shirt and some black work pants inside, along with undies and my hair scarf.

I get body wash and my toothbrush from the bathroom, and just before I turn off the light, I catch a glimpse of myself in the mirror. I look...*sad? Worried? Tired.* Maybe all three, but especially tired, and not in a needs-a-good-sleep way. This is something more complex. Exhaustion of the soul. I'm tired of fleeing from myself and from what I know will ultimately make me happy. I feel like I'm on the precipice of a life-altering decision, where I can slink back into what's familiar, albeit lonely, or I can try something different. I can hide from the confrontation and tell Hunter to leave, or I could pivot into change, making the choice to move through this conflict without running from it. Avoidance hasn't helped me at all, I see that now. And I don't want to shrink back inside myself. Not with Chase. Not after everything he's seen me through this summer.

Hᴜɴᴛᴇʀ ᴘᴀʀᴋs ɪɴ ᴛʜᴇ ᴅʀɪᴠᴇᴡᴀʏ ᴀᴛ Tʜᴇ Bʟᴜғғs ᴀɴᴅ shuts off the car, waiting for me to move first. "Thank you," I whisper, biting the inside of my lower lip to keep the tears at bay.

"Hey, what are big brothers for?" He nudges me with his elbow before asking, "You ready?"

I nod, and we start a slow trudge to the house.

"Is she okay?" Chase asks as soon as the door opens. His voice sounds tired and muffled.

"Ask her yourself..." Hunter shrugs, moving away from the entryway. He steps past Chase, who's sitting on the stairs, before jogging up to his room.

Chase's elbows are propped up on his knees with his fingers covering his mouth. His hair looks like it's been raked through a thousand times, to the point where it limply falls into his eyes. He watches me for a few seconds before standing and walking over to the wide-open door behind me. I hold my breath as he reaches around me to close and lock it.

His movements are cautious, as if he's worried I'll turn tail and run at any sudden move. Slipping his hand around the strap of my backpack, he slides it down my arm and slings it over his shoulder without a word. When he walks toward his bedroom, I follow quietly, not daring to speak first. Dropping my bag on the chair in the corner, he turns around slowly, his eyes trained down at the floor.

He slides his hand through his hair before stuffing them in his pockets. Taking a step toward me, he chances a look into my eyes. "Can I touch you now?" he asks. He doesn't move until I nod my approval, and even then, his steps remain slow and methodical. Bringing his head down to mine, he gently places his hands at my waist, breathing a sigh as we move closer. "I don't like fighting with you..."

"Me neither," I whisper back, tears brimming in my eyes.

Chase brushes a finger over my cheek, catching one before it runs. He pecks at my lips softly once, twice, and a longer third time before reaching behind me to close the bedroom door. When he guides me over to the bed, we sit facing each other, knee to knee.

"I'm sorry, Kayla, about everything. You told me more than once that you didn't want or need my help, and I wouldn't listen. You were right, about the ego part."

"I-I'm sorry, too, for pushing you away, and for leaving." I bite my lip. He was right about what he had said earlier. I run. I followed the formula exactly as he said I would and left.

"Thank you for coming back," he whispers, reaching up to stroke my cheek with his thumb.

"Thank you for letting me." I cup his face in my hands and lean in to feel his lips on mine. He sighs into me, and I just want to feel close to him again, feel like this thing between us is a little less fragile. He pulls back, looking into my eyes as he nuzzles his cheek into my hand.

"Can we talk about it?" he asks, moving his hands over mine.

I nod, biting my lip, unsure of where to start.

"Baby," he says. "I didn't change the tire." He squints sheepishly, and I cover the unexpected laugh that escapes my mouth from his change of pace. He smiles while brushing a stray loc out of my eyes. "I sat out there for a good twenty minutes staring at it, deciding if I wanted to dig a deeper hole, but I couldn't get myself to do it. It wasn't worth it."

"So you're saying I have to walk to work tomorrow anyway?" I tease, nudging his knee with mine.

"Too soon..." He grimaces, shaking his head before tugging me to him. I rest my palms on his chest, and the serious look in his eye combined with the pain etched on his face drains all the humor out of me. "Watching you walk away was worse than falling out of that tree."

"I know it looked like I blew up over a tire, and I'm sorry for leaving. I don't mean to be hard for you to figure out, but I want to explain something."

"Go ahead."

"I've had to learn how to do a lot of things on my own. My mom worked long shifts at the hospital, and my great-granny, before she died, needed a lot of help doing things. She could tell me what to do, but she didn't have the hand strength to do it herself, once her arthritis got bad."

Chase shifts, leaning back against the headboard, taking me with him so I'm propped up over his chest. "You haven't told me much about her, besides what you shared at the museum. What was she like?"

"She was a potter who loved making ocean and redwood inspired ceramics. Granny built a name for herself in Northern California, and the pieces you saw at the museum are just the tip of the iceberg. She has installations in museums up and down the coast. She took my mom in at the age of five, and then helped raise me when I came along, teaching me so much.

"Granny was the strongest person I've ever known. When she couldn't move at the end—couldn't do the things she loved doing —it was devastating. Watching her wither down to nothing put a fire inside of me to always do what I'm capable of doing. I feel like I know my limitations and I ask for help when I need it, but some-thing about accepting help when I'm easily able to do it on my own feels like I'm willingly handing over parts of myself to wither away too."

He studies my face, our eyes bouncing back and forth as we stare. "I've watched you work so hard this summer, and I just want to help lighten the load whenever I see an opportunity. You're too competent to need saving, Kayla, we both know that. I just..." He pauses, his thumb caressing my cheek. "I want to be the one you want around when something goes wrong. Even if you don't need help or don't want me to fix it, I just want to be there. To me, that's what the tire was about, trying to force my way into that position when I shouldn't have."

I nod slowly, appreciating how honest Chase is with his vulnerability. I never have to wonder whether he's being upfront with me, and he never makes me guess what he's feeling. He's been himself from the start, and it's one thing I love most about him.

Love...love?

The word pings around inside my mind as I stare up into his ocean blue eyes. So much has happened this summer. So many things could have given him a reason to say goodbye, but he's remained constant through it all. Facing everything head on, right next to me, and giving me a boost when needed. *My blue pebble.*

I sit up, draping my knees on either side of his hips. Running my fingers through his hair, I tug him closer, kissing him feverishly as I try to erase the pain of the last few hours. He grabs my waist, holding me to him like letting go would cause a drop into the deepest abyss. Pulling back briefly, I deliver the message that's been on my heart since I left my bathroom mirror.

"Baby, I don't want to run anymore," I whisper, nuzzling his nose.

He tips his head to mine, and a smile breaks across his lips. "You finally letting me catch up to you?"

Biting my lip, I nod. "Yep. It must be your lucky day..."

I squeal as he swiftly flips me onto the bed, pinning me while his lips dance down my neck. His hands roam over my shoulders and down my sides until they find the skin peeking out from the raised hem of my shirt. I sigh into the feeling of his hands on my body, relief washing over me that I didn't lose this. Lose him. Just when I melt into his touch, he pauses and looks down at our feet.

"What's wrong?" I groan, trying to catch my breath.

"Just making sure we don't have socks on," he says. With a gleam in his eye, he stretches to open his nightstand.

God, I hope that means what I think it does. I'm ready to put this fight behind us. He's everything I could ever want.

Tossing the condom on the bed, he wiggles his eyebrows playfully and lowers his body onto mine. His kisses tickle my neck, and giggles turn to delightful moans when he slips a hand under my shirt, brushing his thumb over my pebbled nipple. With a gasp of pleasure, my back arches, fingers clutching the soft strands of his hair as he twists and tugs. I reach to unbutton his jeans, suddenly unable to contain myself. *I want him. All of him. Right now.*

His whispered breath in my ear sends goosebumps scattering across my skin. "Uh-uh, baby. You come first." Deft fingers dip into my waistband, sliding rhythmically against my clit.

"Chase," I whimper, my hips chasing the friction, rocking to match his pace. "Don't stop..."

"God, you're beautiful like this, Kayla." His eyes lock onto mine with a desperate heat that threatens to make me come undone. He slips one finger inside me, pumping slowly before gliding it up to circle my sensitive bud. I cry out his name, and a mischievous smirk slides across his lips as he dips in again. "So fucking beautiful."

"I'm—*oh, God...*" My core tightens as his slick fingers twirl around my clit, my eyes squeezing shut so tightly I see fireworks. His kiss devours me, swallowing every single moan as he sends my body spiraling into oblivion.

"I'm so glad you came back," he whispers in my ear, stroking me slowly while I come down from my high.

"If this is what a reunion is like, maybe I should leave again," I tease breathlessly.

"Don't you dare." He smirks and slides his hand from my pants. Unbuttoning his own, he tosses them on the floor. His shirt goes next, and he grabs the condom before leaning against the headboard. I hurriedly tug off my clothes.

Guiding me onto his lap, he smiles up at me, and I'm struck by how easy it is to be with him. Even after a horrible fight, we were able to work it out. *Is this how love is supposed to feel?*

He caresses my cheek as he brushes his lips against mine, sighing the same way he did the first time we kissed. We unravel slowly, deeply, in a paradise of our own making, until, at last, we melt together.

CHAPTER THIRTY-SIX

CHASE

These first few days in San Francisco haven't been too bad. Trevor, the other manager, and I have been working with the corporate trainers—Mike and Marla—since Friday. We've been undergoing leadership training as a team. Besides helping us build our field and office teams, they're guiding us on conflict management, tracking traveling expenses within the team, and conducting performance reviews. Today, we're on the second half of an intensive two-day HR training with the six associates.

We break for lunch, and once I'm in my mostly empty office, the first thing I reach for is my phone. It's been five days since I left Fort Bender. All I want is to see my girl and hear her voice. We were back in a good place by the time I had to leave on Friday, spending the day before snuggled up on the couch at her place, and the night before tangled up in her bed. It took everything I had not to tell her I loved her when I left her house Friday morning. Something about saying those words for the first time before leaving her for a week just didn't sit right with me. She'll be staying with me after the shareholders' event in a couple of days, and I think I'll tell her then.

For now, I lean back in the chair in my office and press the video icon on my phone, bracing for her sweet face to appear on my screen.

"Hey! I was wondering when you were going to call today." She grins. I see the walls of Patti's Place behind her as she steps out of the dining area and hurries down the hallway to the back office.

"Yeah, we broke for lunch a little late today. I've got thirty minutes just for you." We quickly fell into a habit of doing video chats during lunch and right before bed, with a constant stream of texting in between. Looking at her on the screen is a poor substitute, though, and I can't wait until I can wrap my arms around her again.

"How's training going?"

"It's good. I think we've got some nice cohesion within the different teams. We'll see how they do while working together to gather the projected sales numbers. What about your portfolio?"

"I got it all turned in yesterday. I'll hear about the internship right before the event on Friday."

"You're gonna get it, baby. Your portfolio was top tier."

"I hope so! Patti's running around like a chicken with her head cut off, trying to prepare everything for the event, and it's driving me nuts."

I can just imagine Patti flitting around the diner, moving everything out of place, with Kayla cleaning up behind her, cursing under her breath.

The rest of our conversation touches on my new apartment, plans for the evening, and a promise to talk again later before she has to get back to work. Those three little words hang off the tip of my tongue as my screen goes blank, and the *I think I'll tell her this weekend* turns into an *I know*. I don't care about the number of weeks on the calendar anymore. I love her, and she deserves to know it.

"Hey, Chase," Marla greets me as we merge into the hallway from opposite directions. The dark brown curls framing her heart-shaped face bounce along with each footstep. She's friendly, and an absolute powerhouse with teaching corporate strategy. "You ready to finish up your nap in the back row?" she teases, referencing the dozing I succumbed to earlier.

"Nap? Me? During that very important and not at all dated HR slideshow? I'd never do that. Must be thinking of Trev."

"What'd I do?" An auburn buzz cut with sepia skin-tone emerges from the doorway.

"Just napping during the last session," I rib, clapping the former military man on the shoulder as I pass through the door.

"Oh yeah, that was definitely me." He nods with a chuckle, folding his tattooed arms across his chest.

"You two are a mess!" Marla smiles, shaking her head before joining Mike at the front of the room. The rest of the associates file in shortly after, and I feel my eyelids droop as soon as the slideshow starts up again.

KAYLA

Patti and I just pulled up to the venue. Wish me luck!

ME

Good luck, baby! I can't wait to see you. Still good for lunch?

KAYLA

Yep! See you soon.

FINALLY, SHE'S HERE. AFTER WHAT FEELS LIKE THE longest week of my life, my girl—*my love*—and I are under the same roof. She doesn't know it, though. I'm in the ballroom at Trancy Hall, setting up the projector equipment for tonight's presentation, and plan to surprise her ahead of our scheduled lunch date.

I've dimmed the lights in the large room and positioned the

wheeled projector over the burgundy fleur-de-lis carpet so it points toward the curtained stage. Testing the focus on the screen, my mind drifts to how I want today to go. I'll take her back to my new apartment for lunch, and maybe that will be a good time to confess I'm head over heels in love with her. Or maybe I should wait until after, when the stress of finding out about her internship has passed. Either way, I need to tell her before my head hits the pillow tonight. Even if she isn't ready to say it back, I can't keep this inside any longer.

Circling my way around the large room, I double-check speakers, charge microphone batteries, and test the sales presentation twice, making sure everything is cued and ready to go for tonight. Glancing at my watch between each task doesn't make the clock move any faster, but I can't help it. I need the hands of time to speed up so I can wrap my arms around Kayla. When I can hold her, all will be well in my life again.

I walk down the dimly lit hallway toward the large Victorian styled dining area with a few minutes to spare. Peeking through the glass of the double swinging kitchen doors, I look for the one person I've wanted to see since I left her in Fort Bender.

"Hey, Chase," Patti says from behind me. I turn, half expecting her usual flour-stained apron and hair piled on top of her head. This isn't Diner Patti, though. This is Business Patti. She wears a navy pinstripe power suit and a simple string of pearls around her neck, with her hair pulled back into a sleek bun.

"Hey, looking sharp, Patti! I almost didn't recognize you."

"I clean up alright," she says with a chuckle. "What are you doing here?"

"Oh, I work for EdTechU. I had to set up for the presentation tonight."

"I see... Well, I don't know how I missed that tidbit of information, but Kayla's outside in the courtyard." She winks, turns on her heel, and disappears around the corner.

The glass doors to the courtyard are flanked by long tinted windows that dim the hazy morning sunlight, and I quickly stroll across the room. I walk out onto an open patio with a wide cobblestone walkway that leads down to a double flight of stairs. The courtyard at the bottom is enclosed inside tall magenta-flowered hedges, save for a wide arched opening where the stairs end.

In the middle of the courtyard, sitting on the ledge of a three-tiered water fountain, is Kayla. With her eyes closed, she tips her head back, a small smile scrolling across her lips as she basks in the hazy sun rays. The light around her casts that memory inducing glow, making me hesitate as I remember the times I've seen her like this before.

"Making a wish?" I ask, closing the distance from the archway to her. She starts, opening her eyes and looking over her shoulder. A smile spreads across her face as she stands from the bubbling fountain. I would give anything to feel that smile on my lips right now.

"Why would I do that?" Her head tips to the side as I wrap my arms around her waist. "All of my wishes have already come true," she teases, a nod to my cheesy line from our date at Crystal Beach. She weaves her fingers into the back of my hair, kissing me with lips that have gotten impossibly softer. If I never spend another week away from her, it will be too soon.

"I missed you, baby," I say, nuzzling her nose once we take our fill of each other.

"I missed you too." She smiles, pecking my lips one more time before adding, "And you're early..."

"Maybe I couldn't wait to see you. You think of that?"

Her eyes flash briefly as she pulls back to check her phone. "I got sidetracked out here. Give me twenty minutes, and I'll be ready to go." She takes my hand, and we make our way back up the stairs and into the dining area. When we get to the swinging kitchen doors, she turns to me, tips up on her toes, and brushes her lips on mine. "Twenty minutes," she says, squeezing my hand before slipping between the kitchen doors.

I lean against the wall and dig my phone out of my pocket to waste some time. It vibrates in my hand with a picture of Hunter, in a frilly apron covered with flour, flashing across the screen. Our kitchen from the rental is in complete chaos behind him.

HUNTER

Bruh, who thought it was a good idea to put me on sister duty?

ME

You know cereal exists, right?

HUNTER

You ever told Hadley you're not making her pancakes? The girl is downright scary in the morning.

ME

Good point. Maybe call Ashlie for reinforcements?

HUNTER

Can't. She's on her way to help with the event.

ME

Well, it was nice knowing you. At least you'll go out looking pretty!

Hunter: *middle finger*

I chuckle, silently wishing him luck as I continue scrolling through my phone. My hand drums against my leg while I wait for Kayla to finish. At last, she slides back through the doors with her purse in hand, blowing a forceful puff of air through her lips.

"Ready?" I ask, nodding slightly at her exasperation.

"Yeah, just a little overwhelmed," she says, sandwiching my hand between both of hers as I lead her out to the parking garage. "Where are we going?"

"Over to my place. It's not too far—about ten minutes with traffic. I'll cook lunch for us."

"*Cook*?" She looks at me, her eyebrow raising like I've said the most outrageous thing. With her working so much this summer,

I've never had the chance to show her my skills in the kitchen. Most of our meals have been at Patti's Place, save for the family dinners she's had at the rental and the few at her house.

"Hey, I can cook!" I chuckle, unlocking my car. When I open the passenger side door and she slips into the seat, I lean across her to steal a kiss. "I think..."

"Chase, I swear, if you give me food poisoning tonight..."

As I slide behind the wheel and weave our fingers together, I lift her hand to my lips before resting it on my cheek. "I'm joking. I can cook, and you're gonna love it. Might even ask for seconds."

She rolls her eyes and smiles.

I love you.

My mind shouts at me to release the words as I ease the car out of the garage. I clamp my teeth over my tongue. Not now. It can wait just a few more hours.

Stepping out of the elevator onto my floor, I'd be surprised if Kayla can't feel me vibrating with the anticipation of being alone together. She molds her body into my back as I unlock the door to my apartment. As soon as it closes behind us, I push her up against it. My hands tangle into the locs flowing down her back as she presses her lips into mine, pulling at my shirt to bring us closer.

"God, I missed you," I murmur against her lips.

"Me too."

She tosses her purse somewhere at our feet as I pull her with me toward the sofa, tripping over the corner of the rug as we go. My heart leaps at the sound of her giggling when we fall onto the cushions. *God, she's amazing.* I move my lips away from hers, peppering kisses across her jaw and down into the crease of her neck. That spicy vanilla scent that is distinctly hers sends fog clouds through my brain, and I let out a sigh as I'm swallowed up in her essence. *She's everything.* Her hands rove through my hair and across my shoulders, eventually gliding over the muscles in my back.

Nails digging lightly into my shoulders, she rolls her hips up to meet mine. "Baby," she pants in my ear. "I have to be back in an hour."

"Gimme twenty minutes," I whisper into her neck, smiling at the shiver running through her. She pulls my head back up to hers, our tongues twirling together in a frenzied waltz before shifting into something slower—more sensual. *Mine.* My hand finds its way to her hip, and my thumb just barely grazes the warm exposed skin on her side when a loud ringing sounds across the room. We both go still until the second ring, and Kayla shifts underneath me.

"It might be work," she explains, biting her lip. I let out a charged sigh and give her a peck before sitting up. She scrambles from the couch to get to her phone in time. "Hey, Ash," she says, moving into the open bedroom down the hall.

Running my hand through my hair, I breathe out the last few sizzling embers of our interrupted steam fest and get to work in the kitchen. By the time Kayla comes from the room, the pasta is nearly done and the roasted vegetables have about five more minutes.

"It smells good," she praises, sliding into the stool at the counter. I rinse the soap from my hands, drying them quickly before moving around the counter to wrap my arms around her shoulders.

"Told you." I smirk. "Everything okay?"

"Yeah. Ashlie's filling in tonight for one of the servers who got sick. She got lost after a detour. I had to navigate her into the city, but she made it to the venue."

"I didn't know Ashlie worked in catering..."

"She doesn't, but Patti was freaking out at the diner yesterday, and since Ashlie has waitressing experience, she volunteered."

I place a kiss on her cheek and move back into the kitchen to drain the pasta and pull the veggies out of the oven. Kayla watches me with her head tilted as I toss everything in a bowl with a white sauce and other seasonings. I dish up two plates and slide one over to her, deciding to lean against the counter in the kitchen instead of sitting.

With her eyebrow raised, she takes a bite, and her eyes instantly roll back in her head. "Okay, so you can cook," she says between bites.

"Yeah, Mom wasn't about to have a son who couldn't cook. She had me in the kitchen before I was five."

"I'll have to remember to thank her later." She flashes a smile and wipes her mouth with a napkin. My eyes flick down as she licks her bottom lip. "Nuh-uh, don't look at me like that. I have to get back for setup, and *you* are trouble."

"You can't lick your lips like that after the entrance we just had and expect me not to look." I smirk.

Standing from her stool, she walks into the kitchen, right up to me, gazing into my eyes. I reach around her waist, pull her into me, and lean down to kiss her nose.

I love you.

I could tell her right now, get it out of the way before tonight, and it might be okay. It might be better this way, with a few hours for her to stew on it at work. "Kayla, I—"

Her phone rings again from her back pocket. "*Ugh*, sorry." She grimaces before placing a soft kiss on my lips and stepping away to answer. I lace my fingers around the back of my neck, my elbows coming around my ears as I exhale my frustration down toward the floor. Feeling the chance to spill my heart fizzle away, I shake the thought from my head, for now.

Tonight. I'll tell her tonight.

After a quick drive back, I park near the doors in the parking garage at Trancy Hall. "Thanks for lunch," she says, squeezing my hand as we walk back into the venue.

"Of course, baby. I'm glad you liked it. I'll make breakfast in the morning, too, so you know it wasn't a fluke." I smirk, bumping her shoulder before opening the door to the dining room. Spinning her around to face me, I reach up to stroke her cheek.

"I'll see you tonight," she says shyly, tilting her face up in anticipation. I press my lips to hers, the tips of our tongues greeting briefly before she pulls away and slowly walks toward the swinging doors. Holding onto her fingers, I wait until the last possible second before pulling her back in close.

I nuzzle her nose. "Tonight," I say, more for myself than for her. I nestle my lips against hers one more time before letting her go.

Tonight. So much hangs on tonight.

KAYLA

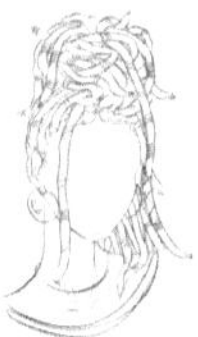

"Surprise!" Patti says from behind me. I turn to look at her, mouth gaping as I stand between the dining room and patio. I knew the internship board may use some of our ideas for the event tonight, but this is something else.

Every round table is covered with the exact royal blue scalloped tablecloths and warm yellow tea light center pieces I submitted with my portfolio. The large menu displayed in the foyer is a handwritten version of my own. Even the place settings, gold-leafed China, soft gold-colored silverware—*everything*—is how I'd imagined it in my head.

"Patti, what? This is—"

"Your portfolio," she finishes, grinning ear to ear. "The internship board was very impressed with your level of detail. The way you organized your presentation—showing your process of sketching and linking it to real-world examples—was excellent. They especially loved the tiered pricing structure you included and praised your use of comparison within each tier. From the small details like your table tracking cards for each server, to the logic you used when numbering the tables, it's all very well done. It's exactly how they would like event planning interns to present ideas to potential clients." She smiles expectantly as she looks at me.

"Event planning? But this is a catering internship..." My face scrunches as I try to make sense of what she's saying.

"We both know you don't want to do catering, Kayla, and it's clear you have exceptional skill with planning and management. I've been lobbying all year for the board to expand our internship program with you in mind, and *you* will be the first event planning intern for our EP division." She grins, watching as I take in all the information she's just dropped on me. I got the internship. No, I got a *better* internship, one that will directly translate to what I want to be doing with my life.

Looking up with tears in my eyes, I shake my head as I try to form words. "I...you... Thank you. I don't know how to thank you."

"Hey, you did the hard work. I've watched you go above and beyond for years to get here. You deserve this, Kayla." She smiles warmly, squeezing my shoulder before walking away.

My hands tremble as I look around Trancy Hall slack-jawed, fully appreciating all the time and effort I put in to get here. *I did it.* All the double diner shifts, camp counseling, management positions on campus, and even babysitting have paid off. Today might be the best day of my life.

The alarm on my phone snaps me out of my trance, signaling ten minutes until the start of the catering staff meeting. I scramble to the back of the kitchen and grab my uniform before finding a bathroom to change in.

"Hey, girl," Ashlie greets me as I reenter the kitchen, wearing an outfit identical to mine and the other servers. Her hair is securely out of the way, and she's wearing a white button-down shirt fitted with a bowtie, a V-neck pinstripe black vest with gold buttons lining down the torso, and black slacks with black dress shoes. We line up against the wall as Patti prepares to give her pre-event pep talk.

"There will be a lot of people here tonight who expect you to give them what they ask for quickly and accurately. No matter how unreasonable the request is, you will do what is in your power to meet it. We want Seaside Catering to gain referrals from everyone in this venue based on our customer service. Everyone here tonight has verified they are over twenty-one, so keep the drinks flowing until nine-thirty p.m. Things to remember: No drama, minimize conflicts, the customer is always right. And most importantly, all tips you receive are yours to keep. The doors will open in ten minutes, and the company has requested a mingling cocktail hour before dinner is served." She takes a breath and smiles at the staff lined up in front of her.

Patti's being a hard-ass tonight, which is expected considering this is her reputation on the line. It's empowering to watch her slip into boss mode when I see her young Mrs. Claus personality at the diner every day. She's mastered the art of balancing warmth and professionalism, something I try to emulate in my own professional persona.

"And now for the exciting news." Patti pivots. "I want to introduce our three newest interns. Ryan and Riley will be joining us on the catering team, and Kayla has been offered our newest internship, learning the ropes as an event planner."

Clapping bounces off the walls of the empty dining room while everyone offers congratulations to the three of us. Ashlie throws her arm around my shoulder in a side hug. This excitement still feels surreal. If I weren't looking around at my portfolio come to life, I'd have a hard time believing any of it. The clock chiming on the wall snaps me out of my celebratory daze, signaling the opening of the front doors.

In no time at all, people dressed in formalwear more expensive than the clothes in my closet combined enter the dining room. As the tables fill, our line of staff dwindles until we're all running drink orders back and forth between the bar.

I see Kendall, Russell, and Christine in passing as I work my way through the rapidly filling dining room. Camryn and Tamryn are hunkered down at a table on the patio, so I'm sure Maggie is somewhere around here too. I don't have time to worry about her, though, with the fast pace of the cocktail hour occupying all my thoughts.

Near the beginning of dinner, I run into Chase. He's leaning against a wall, hands in his pockets, wearing a navy-blue suit and tie with a crisp white shirt underneath. His hair is slicked back out of his face, and those ocean blues mixed with his crooked smile are threatening to distract me. He looks so damn handsome; I'm tempted to pull him into a closet somewhere.

Chase snags me by the elbow, tugging me out of the pathway of the other waitstaff. "I know you're working, but I wanted to say *hi* before you got too busy," he says with a grin. His fingers caress the back of my arm. "And I wanted to hear about the internship."

"Hi." I respond, my voice rushed as it mimics the pace in the dining room. "I can give more details later, but—"

Glasses crashing behind the bar shifts my attention back to the dining room. Patti rushes to the bartender's aid, giving me a few extra seconds to talk. I slide my eyes back to Chase, and we stare at each other for a few seconds, trying to keep our smiles polite and our distance professional since we're both at work. "I'll fill you in about the internship later." Stepping closer to him, I deliver a message I hope he thinks about until he takes me home tonight. "And I think you should keep the suit on when we get back to your place," I whisper, giggling at the way his eyebrows shoot upward.

"You got it." He winks, squeezing my arm before heading off toward the ballroom. My stomach flips over three times as I watch him walk away, heart thumping at the realization that he's mine and I'm wholeheartedly his.

I love him, and I'm his.

"Whew, I forget how good he looks in a suit," a cool voice says from behind me. I turn to see Maggie, biting her lip as her eyes follow Chase walking down the hallway. My first instinct is to sneer.

She's not going to ruin this night for me.

I reconfigure my scowl into a hospitable smile and ask her, "Can I get you anything?"

"Oh, I think I can get him myself. Thanks though." She saunters off toward the patio, and if it wasn't for the constant stream of orders coming in, I'd find a way to trip her smug ass.

After a thirty-minute presentation in the ballroom, we're ready for the dinner course, and I'm pulled aside by a staff member named Krista. "Table twenty-six on the patio has requested you as their server." My eyes move along with hers as she gestures to the table where Maggie and her friends sit. "They were adamant, and since we have to 'meet every unreasonable request,' I'll trade you for one of yours."

We pull out our table tracking cards, and I peel off my number thirteen sticker as she hands over the number twenty-six. I close my eyes and take a deep breath before nodding and trudging outside. *She's not going to ruin this night for me.* "What can I get for you?" I ask with a smile, unabashedly faking my way through the interaction. If I don't give them the satisfaction of my annoyance, I can get them what they need and get away quickly.

"We want full bottles of the house red and white," Maggie informs me, rolling her eyes like she didn't call me over here.

"Sure. Anything else?"

"Just the wine for now. I'll get some dessert later."

I nod and wind my way back inside to the bar. Once inside, I place the order and take a minute to look around the dining area. Chase's table is in the corner, and I've been avoiding looking over there to keep from distracting myself. Right now, though, I can't help but take a peek, just wanting to get another look at him in that suit. Glancing that way, I notice he's not there. I scan the crowd and see him bouncing between tables, laughing with almost everyone he talks to. The ease in which he talks to people is effortless, and I catch myself smiling as I watch him network. *My heart.*

The bartender hands over the two bottles of wine, and I steel myself, fixing my face before walking back outside to deal with the trio again.

"Here you go," I slide the bottles on the table before reaching into my apron for my corkscrew. Camryn and Tamryn whisper about something, while Maggie taps her foot, looking me up and down as I open the bottles.

"You know it's never going to last between you two, right?" she says as I place the newly opened bottle of red wine on the table and reach for the white.

"Can I get you anything else, Miss St. Clair?" I reply tersely, ignoring her jab as I place the second bottle of wine down in front of her.

She's not going to ruin this night for me.

"You two don't make any sense together. Chase is basically technology royalty, and you, well, you're just the help." Her smirk is smug, like she's delivered some kind of devastating blow that will knock me down a few pegs, where I seemingly belong.

Screw it.

Something in me snaps. Not enough to cause a scene, but just enough to flip off my hospitality switch while I deliver some devastating news of my own.

Leaning down so we're eye level, I stare at Maggie with my eyebrows pulled together, gathering as much faux pity as I can muster. "Oh, you haven't heard?" I ask, knowing full well she has no idea about the news I'm going to share. Everyone else at The Bluffs has kept my being Kendall's daughter a closely guarded secret for now, at my request.

Maggie's eyes narrow as she folds her arms across her chest and leans back, obviously disgusted that I would dare get so close to her face.

"Kendall's my dad, so I guess that makes me technology royalty, too, *cousin.*" I know she and I aren't technically related, but adding in the term feels like a nice way to drive home just how close our circles really run. The combined looks of rage, horror, and surprise on her face fill me with giddy satisfaction, knowing my message was received as intended. Standing up straight, I smile at the trio before turning on my heel. I walk back into the dining room, refilling the water glasses of my other tables as I go.

"What a menace," Ashlie says after I briefly recap what happened outside, leaning against the wall at the back of the dining room. We've hit a lull, with the guests wandering around the venue, admiring the Victorian architecture and the beautiful garden outside in the courtyard. "Cape Cod and Tampa just sat there and didn't say anything?"

"Nope, *Camryn* and *Tamryn* were whispering back and forth, like usual."

"Switch tables with me, just this once." Ashlie cracks her knuckles. I bump her shoulder with mine, snorting at her implication.

"The night's almost over. They'll be off to New York and we'll never have to see them again."

"Well, *I'll* never have to see them again. You, on the other hand, have a dad and siblings who she's related to. I think you'll have to deal with her periodically. Why not put her in her place now?"

"Because this is work, and I'm a professional," I say, stretching my back as the ache from being on my feet all evening sets in. She's right, though. I will probably run into Maggie again at some point, and the call to set her straight gets louder each time I interact with her. "Besides, she's harmless."

"She's annoying is what she is, and she wants your man."

"Yeah, but still harmless." I raise my eyebrows in an attempt to get her to let it go.

"Okay, okay, you're right. It helps that your boyfriend is a Golden Retriever personified. That boy is crazy about you, girl."

I smile, biting my lip as I remember Chase pulling me aside earlier. He looked so damn good, and in a few short hours, I'm going to enjoy getting up close and personal with that suit he's been wearing all night.

The bell sounds in the kitchen, signaling us to begin preparation for the dessert course. Ashlie and I grab trays and turn in opposite directions to our assigned regions. I'm bent over a table on the patio, stacking plates and glasses, when I feel someone brush my arm. Expecting another server, I turn distractedly, keeping my eyes on the table before meeting a pair of piercing blues.

Straightening my vest, I stand and smile. "Oh, Hi, Mrs. Wilmington. Can I get you anything?"

"Now, Kayla, you know good and well I want you to call me Christine," she says with a smile.

"Okay. Christine, can I get you anything?"

"Not at all. I wanted to tell you how great of a job you did here. Kendall was telling us how he remembered seeing a lot of the design elements tonight on your portfolio. Everything here looks amazing. You have quite the talent."

"Thank you," I say, beaming back at her. "It's taken a lot to get here, but everything looks better than I could have ever imagined."

"Well, I don't want to keep you. I just wanted to say congratulations, and I'm so happy Chase found you." She squeezes my arm and makes her way back inside.

Taking a deep breath to bolster the sense of pride I feel about this event, I look around the courtyard. Guests mill around the shrubs and flowers, and my eyes meet a dark-haired ballerina with a perma-scowl. Maggie stands at the arched entrance alone, wineglass in hand, smirking at me like an evil little pixie. I straighten my back and give her a smile with a little finger wave before turning to grab the tray stacked with dishes.

As the night has progressed, guests have shed their fancy jackets land shawls. The dining room now resembles that of a business dinner crowd, with alcohol lending to loud laughter and people sitting wherever they choose. Slowly, my colleagues and I are beckoned to refill drinks and swap out dessert choices. I glimpse Chase slipping out of the dining room, mingling with another table or three full of people outside.

Guests have started to make their exits the closer we get to ten o'clock, and I'm making my rounds with pitchers of water, when Camryn comes up to me. Her voice is high and nasally, so I know for sure she's Camryn. "Tamryn needs a refill," she tells me, and whips around without another word. There's no clarification, no indication of what exactly needs to be refilled. She just turns on her heel and walks back across the patio like she expects me to follow. Trying hard not to roll my eyes, I brace myself for the return to table twenty-six to see what else they could possibly need.

"Did you enjoy dessert?" I ask, looking around at the three untouched slices of cheesecake while I move around the table to fill their water glasses.

Giggling, Tamryn turns to me, and with her much deeper voice says, "Oh, I think Maggie's enjoying a different kind of dessert right now." She juts her chin toward the courtyard. Without a second thought, I turn to look over my shoulder.

I go still as stone.

Down the stairs, through the courtyard archway, on the ledge of the water fountain, sits Maggie. Except she's not sitting *on* the ledge, she's sitting *on* Chase's lap, her fingers tangled in his hair, kissing him while his hands rest on her leg. They whisper something back and forth before turning and looking right at me. And somehow, I'm no longer serving ballerinas on the patio. I'm transported back to my freshman dorm room, looking at Evan and my roommate.

Alone, together.

CHAPTER THIRTY-EIGHT

CHASE

"What the hell, Maggie!" I pull my face out of her hands and drop her foot.

"Oopsie," she says with a shrug. "I think your girlfriend saw us kissing." She turns to look up the stairs, wearing a triumphant smile on her face.

Following Maggie's gaze, I lock eyes with Kayla on the patio, wide-eyed and shaking her head. I've never moved so fast, trying to get across the courtyard and up the stairs, taking three at a time. By the time I reach the landing, Kayla is weaving quickly through the jigsaw of tables on the patio, trying to make it inside. Someone stops her for a quick water refill, and it gives me enough time to catch up to her.

"Kayla, that wasn't what it looked like," I say, panic coursing through each word as they leave my mouth.

"I know what I saw, *Evan*." Her hushed voice trembles as she continues her weave through the patio.

"Evan?" *Shit*. "Kayla, no. This wasn't like that. I—"

She maneuvers around chairs and shareholders, trying to get away from me while the requests for refills continually slow her down. "It doesn't matter," she says, her voice low as she crosses the threshold into the dining room. More people have cleared out of this room, making for less obstacles in her race to the kitchen.

"It *does* matter. Kayla, please, let me explain," I plead, grabbing her elbow to turn her around. "Will you just wait? Please?"

"*Don't* touch me, Chase." Whipping around, she stares down at my hand on her arm before jerking it away. She reaches the swinging doors of the kitchen with me right on her heels as I follow her through them.

"Please, Kayla, I LOVE YOU!"

"I'M WORKING!" she fires back, looking at me for the first time. I said it louder than I intended, and the moment wasn't anywhere near what I'd imagined telling her would be like. The coldness in her eyes is a near perfect match to the hostility in her voice, and it's enough to knock me back down to earth as I slowly become aware of the space we're in. I look around at the catering staff volleying glances between the two of us and realize I've made it halfway across the kitchen. The hiss of the water sprayer and clang of pots and pans from the dishwashing station becomes more evident the longer I stand here.

She drops her eyes, her chest heaving as she holds the mostly empty water pitchers down at her sides. The full weight of the last ten minutes settles in around me. This is her job. Her future rides on landing an internship based around this event. As much as it pains me to let her think what I can only imagine she's thinking, this is not the time, or place, to hash any of this out. I turn around and slip back through the swinging doors without another word, heading down the hallway to find a place to be alone.

Thankfully, the ballroom is deserted. Trevor was in charge of packing up the presentation equipment, and it appears he's already done so. I sit in one of the empty burgundy velvet-tufted chairs, loosen my tie, and take off my suit jacket. It feels like I'm roasting. As my thoughts spiral, I undo the buttons around my wrists and roll my shirt sleeves up my forearms.

Trying to organize the chaos in my mind to come up with a game plan, I start with the facts I know. One of the twins flagged me down to help with Maggie. I tried to coax her down from her drunken dance on the edge of the fountain when she twisted her ankle and fell. She asked me for help removing her shoe, and like the helpful idiot I am, I moved her leg onto my lap to reach the strap. She grabbed my face and attacked me with her sloppy, wine-soaked lips. Kayla saw it and thought...what? I don't know what she thought, just that she saw it. I told her, shouted at her, really, that I love her. And I potentially ruined her internship chances. Cool. *Fantastic.*

Breathing out a heavy sigh, I tip my head back in the chair, covering my eyes with the heel of my hands. The more I think about how it looked with me and Maggie at the water fountain, the more agitated I feel. This is bad...so bad. Kayla called me *Evan*, that asshole who broke her heart. That's what this looks like to her, that I strung her along in the same way he did. It's not the same, not in the slightest, but that's how it *looks*. I pull out my phone and send a text that she'll hopefully read when she's done working for the night.

ME:

Please text me when you're done.

Please... I'll wait for you by the catering van.

I don't expect her to answer right now, but I stare down at my phone anyway, watching for any glimmer of hope—bouncing dots, a middle finger emoji, *anything*—signaling she's still willing to talk to me. Eyes plastered to the screen, I tap with my thumb anytime the light dims so I don't risk missing a message. After a full ten minutes, there's nothing. I turn the screen off and run my hands through my hair as I lean my head back to stare at the ceiling. I don't even know how to fix this, but I know if I can get her to talk to me, or stand still long enough for me to talk to her, I can figure it out. *We* can figure it out.

I don't know how long I've been sitting here, battling every single thought that enters my mind, but I apparently don't hear the door across the ballroom open or shut.

"There you are…" I jump at the voice coming from behind me. Sitting up, I shake my head, not wanting to look at the face belonging to that voice. "I was worried you'd left," Maggie says sweetly.

My skin crawls as the tang of bitter rage coats my tongue. The utter disgust scrunched up in my expression while she walks toward me is only matched by the one I had when talking to her dad that one night on the deck. I try to choke down the burning in my throat as I realize she has no limp while she walks, and the strap of her shoe is back around her ankle.

"Oh, don't look at me that way, Chase. It had to be done. You were getting too attached to that waitress."

"You mean my *girlfriend*? What the fuck did you do, Maggie?" I screech, almost knocking the chair over when I stand. My pulse pounds in my ears as rigid resentment sets into my shoulders and heat flushes up my neck.

"Daddy said you might need a little push, so I pushed. Camryn and Tamryn helped get her to the right vantage point, of course. But it all worked out, so why does it matter?" She steps closer, and I instinctively move back.

"Are you even hurt?" I point down at her feet, shaking my head as I realize I already know the answer.

"I'm a dancer. Do you really think I don't know how to balance on a wide fountain ledge?" Her look is condescending, like she's talking to some naive child. And maybe I have been naive, but right now, there's nothing harmless about her. With one destructive pirouette, she just blew up my life.

I grit my teeth, livid heat engulfing me as she explains how she orchestrated this whole mess. I knew she could be devious, but this—making it seem like she was hurt and in need of my help just to get me close, recruiting her friends to make sure my girlfriend watched—this was intentional. This was diabolical.

She takes another step toward me, reaching out to touch my arm. "Now we can be together, Chase."

I flinch away. "We're never going to be together, Maggie! You need to get that through your head. There is not one single point in time where I would ever consider being with you. It makes me sick even looking at you right now, knowing what you just did." I grab my jacket from the chair and shrug it on. "Stay the hell away from me," I say over my shoulder as I turn to walk away.

Once I'm safely in the hallway, I scrub my hand over my face to try and ease some of the tension. I pull out my phone to check the time, but mostly to check for a new message. The notifications are blank, and the time reads ten forty-five p.m. Kayla should be done soon, so I walk down to the parking garage, helplessly hoping to find her there. When I reach the catering van, Patti is arranging the supplies in the back.

"Hey, Patti..." I say cautiously, not sure if she knows what happened in the kitchen earlier.

"Oh, hi, Chase! Did you enjoy your evening?" she asks, smiling as warmly as she ever has.

"Yeah, it was great. Have you seen Kayla?"

"Oh... She left with Ashlie about an hour ago. Said she wasn't feeling well."

"Left? Do you know where?"

"Back to Bender, I think." Her voice drops as she softly says, "Hey..." Her tone has changed, and a look falls across her face, her eyes telling me she might just know exactly what happened in the kitchen. "I'm not saying don't go after her, but I've known Kayla for a real long time. Whatever is happening between you two, give her some time to process it..." She knows. Of course she knows. I only yelled it out for everyone in the kitchen to hear.

I nod, considering for a moment that she might be right as I back away from the van toward my car. "Thanks, Patti," I say, before turning to jog the rest of the distance. The clock reads ten fifty-five when I start the car. If I go the speed limit, it should take a little over three hours to get from here to Fort Bender. I doubt I'll be going that slow. Shooting off a text to Hunter, I let him know I'll be back tonight and start my drive, hoping with everything I have that Kayla will see me in the morning.

CHAPTER THIRTY-NINE

CHASE

I tried to sleep when I got into the rental around three this morning, but my brain has been wired since last night. Forgetting to account for the construction detour, I made it back into town later than I expected. I exchanged my crumpled suit for sweats and climbed right into bed. Most of the dark morning hours were spent tossing and turning, sitting up to check my phone each time I changed positions, and lying back down to toss and turn some more.

Kayla hasn't answered my messages from last night. I called her phone twice on the drive back into town, and it went straight to voicemail each time. I even got so desperate that I called Ashlie, getting nothing in return. Now I'm sitting up in bed, waiting for the morning to progress enough for me to go over and knock on Kayla's door because I don't have the courage to call again.

As soon as eight a.m. hits, I grab my keys and head out to my car, moving quietly so I don't wake the sisters sleeping upstairs. I don't actually know if Kayla came back to Bender, but I feel like going to her house is the best chance I have at getting her to listen to what happened last night. I pull up to her driveway in no time, and a sense of relief floods over me when I see Ashlie's red hatchback in the driveway. *I can fix this.* Parking behind it, I take a deep breath, scrub my face in my hands, and walk to the front door. Hoping to see Kayla's face, my heart pounding in my chest, I knock lightly.

"You need to leave," Ashlie says, closing the door behind her as she steps onto the porch. Her arms cross, and despite her tiny frame, I recognize the enormous barrier for what it is.

"Is she awake? Ash, I just need to talk to her."

"She *just* went to sleep. You need to leave." Her scowl has never been directed at me before, but it is withering. "Do you know what it's like to have your best friend sobbing in the seat next to you and not know what's wrong for three hours? She was crying so hard; she couldn't tell me anything until we got here. And then to find out she's so upset because you were kissing Maggie... *I* don't even want to be talking to you right now. How could you do that to her, Chase?"

I blink at her, not sure what to touch on first. I'm grasping at straws, trying to catch hold of the explanations swirling through my thoughts. They all slip through my fingers. In my flustered state, my anxiety riddled brain latches onto the most cliched excuse. "It wasn't what it looked like."

"So she's lying? She didn't see you kissing Maggie?" She glares, challenging me, ready to attack in protection of her best friend. I think anything I say at this point will be the wrong thing.

"Will you please just tell her to call me when she wakes up? Please?"

"She doesn't want to talk to you." She pokes her finger into my chest. "Give her some space. I'm serious." Ashlie whips around and walks back through the door, closing it quietly, leaving heaps of fierce indignation in her wake.

The lock clicks into place, like a deadbolt sliding into a solid steel door. I'm knocked back down to a position where I can't reach through to Kayla, and this time, her friend is the brick wall. Feeling completely dejected, I hang my head, and with slumped shoulders, I do the only thing I can right now. I get back in my car and drive across town, back to The Bluffs Estates.

Hunter's in the kitchen eating a donut over the sink when I open the door. He stares at me for a few seconds and wordlessly slides the box across the counter, nodding for me to sit on the stool. Eating is the last thing on my mind right now, but I pluck a donut out of the box anyway, needing something to do besides worry. We sit in silence, the only sounds coming from the whirring fridge.

He pours two glasses of milk, and I let the coolness coat all the heavy words stuck on my tongue. This is Hunter, my best friend since birth—basically my brother. He may not know how to be serious all the time, but he knows how to sit in someone's pain with them, letting them process without needing to explain anything, and that's something I appreciate right now.

"Maggie kissed me last night," I start, covering my eyes with the heel of my hands.

"Ew," he whispers. I can imagine the disgusted grimace on his face. "No wonder you look like shit..." he jokes, and I look up in time to see him shake his head. He doesn't push, though, waiting for me to continue if I want to.

"I didn't get any sleep. I don't even know how it happened. Everything moved so fast," I say, lacing my fingers behind my neck. I explain drunk Maggie and her scheme, her ankle, the kiss, seeing Kayla from the patio, me chasing her through the venue, and unintentionally yelling to everyone in the kitchen that I love her. "That was the only thing I could think to say that would get her to stop and listen." I cringe. Recalling everything out loud makes it all sound so much worse than I remember.

"And you went to Kayla's house this morning? How did that go?"

"It went nowhere. Ashlie wouldn't let me past the front porch."

He nods, leaning against the countertop with his fingers splayed wide on the marble. I dig my phone out of my pocket, checking it for the thousandth time before opening my messages app.

"Bruh." He shakes his head, swiping his hand under his chin in a cut-it-out motion. "Look, I'm not taking sides. You're my best friend. She's my sister. I can't. But even I know Kayla well enough to know *that*"—he says, pointing to my phone—"is a bad idea. Give her some time."

I know he's right. I knew Patti was right last night, and I knew Ashlie was right thirty minutes ago. As much as I want to force this—make Kayla sit and listen to my version of the night—I know I need to wait. She'll see I've called and texted, and I guarantee Ashlie will tell her I came over. I need to give her the time to decide to talk to me. So I'll wait, and hopefully, she'll come.

"Chase?" Avery says sleepily, coming down the stairs. "I thought you weren't coming back until tomorrow."

"Aw, did you miss me, Av?" I tease, trying to force the worry off my face.

"Whatever." She scrunches her nose before walking over to the donut box. "*Ugh*! You guys ate all the good ones. All that's left are the nasty custard filled."

Hunter shrugs, smirking over at me. "Chase ate yours."

"*Ugh*, you're so annoying, Chase." She turns around, stomping up the stairs and slamming the door.

"Thanks for that. Let's just piss off every girl in my life," I say, shaking my head and standing from the stool.

"Eh, she'll be alright."

I flop down on the couch, turn on the first thing that looks interesting, and kick my feet up on the table. Hunter lands next to me, scrolling on his phone. I'm tempted to grab mine from my pocket, but knowing I'll click right to my messages, I leave it alone. Forcing my eyes on the TV, I give in to the trance-inducing colors moving across the screen.

CHAPTER FORTY

KAYLA

Last night should have been the pinnacle of the summer. I landed the internship of my dreams. I got to see my portfolio come to life. My boyfriend told me he loves me.

Right after getting caught with someone else.

The biggest night of my life, permanently marred by the image of my boyfriend tangled up together with the girl he told me not to worry about.

Why would he kiss her?

Seeing them left me feeling so small, and all I wanted to do was crawl into the deepest hole. Him yelling "I love you" in front of everyone just added to my embarrassment, like being loud about it would erase everything he did. But it didn't. I *saw* them, and I can't just ignore reality, no matter how much I wanted to say it back.

I love him, but I need to love myself more.

Blinking rapidly, I take a deep breath in through my nose and choke down a sob, remembering the two of them on the fountain. *No more tears.*

The girl looking back at me in the mirror is all cried out. A three-hour car ride's worth of sobbing and several more hours in my bed was enough. I didn't sleep well, but at least it stopped the waterfall. There will be no more.

I'm done.

My red-rimmed eyes ache as I scan over the puffy remnants in my reflection. With a sigh, I drop my eyes and slide my hand behind the shower curtain to turn on the water.

I can't believe I fell for it...again.

The charm, the eyes, the convincing words. Chase laid the bait, and I fell for it all, hook, line, and sinker. My danger sensors were blaring at the beginning of the summer, but I cut the plug on all of them, even after seeing Maggie's infatuation.

Maybe Maggie planned this...

No. I know what I saw, and I only have myself to blame.

Stupid.

I strip and climb into the shower, hoping the scalding cascade burns into my skin and seeps some sense back into my body.

Stupid.

That's the only explanation I've been able to come up with. Work and the internship should have been my only focus this summer, but I let a stupid guy get into my stupid head, and he ended up doing the exact same thing the last stupid guy did.

What's worse is that I told Chase all about Evan. I let go of my better judgment and trusted him with my heart. I trusted him to treat me differently because he made me feel special. And I wanted to believe, for once, that I was special. I gave him the power to devastate me.

And he did.

It's my *own* fault for trusting him. I should have known better. I *did* know better. The common factor in both instances of heartache is me. Me and my stupidity. But that stops here and now.

I'm done.

So I wash the memories away. I cleanse the caresses from my face, scrub his touch from my skin, and wash all his lies down the drain. I strip him from my hair and from my life.

When I get out of the shower and look back at my reflection, I recognize who I see. This Kayla, guarded and safe, just like I was at the start of summer, is familiar. This is the girl who's going to push this mess to the back shelf and move on. She's the one who's going to march into the bedroom, slap a look together, and tie up her hair. This is the Kayla who's going to drive across town and stick up for herself.

CHASE

Opening my eyes, I blink several times to figure out where I am. Hunter kicks my leg, dressed differently than he was this morning. A twinge shoots through my neck as I push myself up on the couch cushion. The TV is still on, and I don't know how long I was asleep, but the sun has made its way to the other side of the house. I tip my head off the back of the couch and close my eyes again. Apparently, I needed the sleep and could go right back into it if Hunter would stop kicking me.

"Naw, you gotta wake up." He shakes me again. "Kayla's out on the front porch."

Like a zap of electricity straight to my system, my brain comes online. I straighten up, scrub my face with my hand, and run it through my hair. "What time is it?" I ask, willing the grogginess to leave my voice. Kayla's here. She came. I can fix this.

"It's almost three. Look, I convinced her to wait another five minutes, and it's already been two..."

I jump up at that, stretching briefly before making my way to the door. With a breath, I step out into the afternoon light and try not to squint against the brightness. Kayla sits on the bench under the front window, looking toward the edge of The Bluffs. Her hair is pulled back, locs braided to the side and draped over the shoulder of her olive-green zip hoodie. The tip of her pointer finger scratches at her thumb, and my fingers twitch, wanting to wrap her hand in mine to calm her nerves. Even in this strained chaos, my breath hitches at the beautiful sight of her.

"Did you want to come in?" I say softly, not wanting to startle her.

She goes still before crossing a leg over her knee and putting her hands in the pockets of her jacket. Shaking her head, she looks down at the ground. I step slowly, worried she'll bolt off the porch if I move too quickly. When I sit down next to her, she leans farther away, turning her gaze back toward the street, clearly not wanting to be close. The foot hanging from her crossed leg bounces quickly, and I reach over to touch her arm. When she flinches away from me, it's like I can feel the hairline cracks in our connection fissure, and I wonder how we'll be able to make it back from this.

"Kayla, last night, what you saw, it wasn't real..." *That's not what I meant to say at all.* My hand taps away on the side of my knee as I try to organize what I want to say to her. I try again. "What I mean is, I was helping her with her shoe. She hurt her ankle... Well, I *thought* she did, and then she kissed me and that's what you saw. I didn't... I would never—"

"Do you know how ridiculous you sound right now?" She turns toward me but doesn't look. Her eyes are still fixed down to the ground.

"I... Yes, I do. But that's what happened. She set up the whole thing, and—"

"You're going to say it was all her? Chase, I *saw* you. You were holding her leg as she sat in your lap. Her hands were tangled in your hair. You were—"

She stops abruptly, closing her eyes tightly, unable to finish the last word in her sentence. *Kissing.* She thinks I was a willing participant in this, and from her perspective, I can see there's not much I can do to convince her otherwise.

"I know it looks that way, but I need you to trust me… Will you look at me? Baby, please?"

Shaking her head, she bites the inside of her lip. I squat in front of her, trying to meet her eyes, but she turns away from me, taking her hands from her pockets to push herself back against the bench. "No."

"Why?" It's more of a statement than a question. I'm so frustrated right now, trying to get her to let me back in. She's completely shutting me out, and I don't know how to stop it. There's only so much I can do when she won't even look at me.

"Because if I look into your eyes, I might believe your stupid excuse, and you'll reel me back in. I can't do that to myself. Not again."

"Kayla, I love you." I take her hands in mine, holding on tight as she flinches against it. "I didn't mean to say it how I did last night, but it's not any less true. I love you." Rubbing my thumbs over the back of her knuckles, I hope the skin contact will convey the truth in my words. "I love your drive, your confidence, your determination. When you're stubborn and challenge everything I say, and when you're sassy and playful. I love your heart, your smile. *God*, Kayla, your smile, it lights me up inside. I know it's too soon, and I don't need you to say it back. I just…" I hold my breath, waiting for her to say or do anything. She hasn't moved her hands from mine, but she hasn't looked at me either. "Baby, please look at me… I love you."

"It doesn't matter," she whispers as a tear rolls down her cheek.

I reach to brush it away, but her hand beats me to it. She pulls her other hand from mine, and her words slowly traipse through my head. *It doesn't matter*. I told her I love her, and she said it doesn't matter.

"I told you I was tired of running, and I am. When this happened before, I didn't stick up for myself. So this is me, facing everything instead of avoiding it," she says. The last glimmer of hope sparks inside of me as I wait for her to finish, just wanting to get past this so I can hold her again.

"I want to be very clear so there's no misunderstanding between us," she continues, wiping her face. "I don't want to see you, Chase. I don't want you to call me, or send me messages, or come over to my house. I don't want to be with you anymore." She looks at me then, her green eyes sparking with the determination I just told her I love. Her words are thick with resentment as she places the final brick on top of the wall she's been constructing between us since I stepped outside. "Stay away from me. Please," she whispers.

She stands, forcing me to scoot back so we don't collide, and walks down the stairs. The roar of her car's engine becomes the musical score to the squeezing I feel in my chest. My squatting has transitioned into a full sit as I lean against the railing, using my knees as a chin rest, unable to watch her drive away. My mind goes blurry, and I sit there until my legs tingle from numbness. When I stand, I trudge across the porch and into the rental. I go straight to my bed, and I stay there.

I DON'T EVEN KNOW WHAT DAY IT IS. MY STAGNANT muscles are stiff and my head hurts. Aside from getting up to use the bathroom, I've just been here, wasting away in bed. Hunter's come in a couple of times, but I fake sleep until he leaves. As I hear my door open now, I slam my eyes shut, purposely slowing my breathing. I just want to be left alone to sink so deep into the abyss that it doesn't hurt anymore. If we're talking tree scale, this feels like absolute hell.

"Get up, Chase," Mom's voice says from the doorway. I don't move, hoping she'll give up as easily as Hunter and leave me alone to decay in this bed. "You think I don't know when you're faking sleep?" She walks around the bed and slams the curtain open with a flourish. Bright light sails in through the double doors of my balcony, and my arm jumps to cover my eyes on instinct. "You've been in this bed for three days. Hunter's freaking out. He's never seen you like this before. What happened?"

With a sigh, I sit up, not bothering to catch the hood of my sweater as it slides backward. I look at her, unable to say anything because, what's the point? She can't do anything about it, and talking about it feels like a waste of time.

"And another thing…*Maggie*, Chase? Really?" she asks.

"Sounds like you already know what happened." I shrug before lying back down on my side, barely recognizing the flat tone of my voice.

"Get *up*!" She whacks my knee. Her arms cross, and she gives me the look that says she isn't going to repeat herself. I sit up again, leaning forward with my elbows on my knees. "There's food on the table," she says, not moving from her spot in front of me.

"I'm not hungry."

"I didn't ask. Now go." Arching her brow, she taps her foot, waiting for me to move. I know she's not above climbing into the bed behind me and kicking me out of it.

After another sigh, I stand and hobble past her out to the hallway. All the blinds are open, and I squint against the light as I drag myself to the kitchen.

A stack of chocolate chip pancakes sits at the head of the table, still warm from the pan. My stomach rumbles as steamy tendrils reach my nose. When I sit, my eyes focus on the front porch through the window, and I cringe. My stomach turns over as I remember everything that was said out there. *It doesn't matter. I don't want to be with you anymore.* Definitely worse than falling out of a tree.

Any appetite I had when I first smelled the pancakes has disappeared. I push the chair back, moving to the stool at the counter and leaving the plate where it is. My forehead hits the cool marble countertop as I lay my head down. I just want to crawl back into bed. A sliding sound next to my ear makes my head fall to the side as Mom pushes the plate toward me. A clanging fork and knife land next to it.

"Eat," she commands, walking around the island to stand across from me, keeping her eyes on me the entire way. When I sit up, my thumb immediately shoots to my temple, grabbing at the dehydrated pounding. I hear some clinking and open my eyes to a glass of water.

"Thanks," I croak. My slow sips turn into hearty gulps as I guzzle the cold water down. Reconsidering the stack of food next to me, I pick up the fork and wedge off a small piece. It goes down easier than expected, so I reach for the knife and move the plate in front of me. Each bite is better than the last until I've made it three-quarters of the way around the stack.

"What happened?" Mom asks again. She hasn't stopped watching me since she forced me out of bed this morning. *Is it morning? I don't even know what time it is.*

"Where is everyone?" I try to change the subject, not wanting to crack open the freshly buried box that is my heart.

"Chase, what happened?"

"You already know what happened, Mom!" I snap. The frustration in my voice comes out quickly, my head pounding at the surge of adrenaline.

"I want to hear it from you. Tell me."

We stare at each other for what seems like forever before I look down, sighing. Maybe she put something in the pancakes—some kind of truth serum—because I tell her everything. It all comes out, from the moment I picked Kayla up for lunch until the instant she walked away from me on the porch, with a side plot of scheming Maggie. By the time I'm finished, my eyes are red and my voice is shaky from reliving it all. This is infinitely worse than falling from a tree.

"I don't know what to do to fix it," I say, shaking my head.

"I don't know that there's anything more you can do. Some-times, life throws you two conflicting truths, and you just have to figure out how to live with the discomfort of it all. She experienced it her way, and you experienced your version."

"So I just let her walk away? I just let her believe what she saw?"

"Yep. You do it because that's what she asked you to do. If you love her like you say you do, then you have to respect her decision. I know you're looking for the solution to the problem, but you can't fix this right now because there's nothing to fix. You just keep moving—one second, hour, day at a time—until you move on." She comes around to my side of the island and wraps her arm around my shoulders, laying a kiss on my temple. Before walking out to the deck, she stops at the door and says, "Just remember, life has a track record of working itself out."

I nod, and she turns to leave. With a deep breath and a bleak foreseeable future, I head to the shower to drown out my thoughts and watch my last shreds of hope circle the drain. *You can't fix this because there's nothing to fix. It doesn't matter.*

CHAPTER FORTY-TWO

KAYLA

HUNTER

Dad's parking. We'll be in shortly.

ME

I'm at a booth in the back.

HUNTER

thumbs-up

I tuck my phone in my back pocket, craning my neck to look at the door. The first few weeks of school have flown by, and Labor Day weekend came up way too quickly. Pretty soon, it'll be October and I'll be starting my internship with Patti.

"Kayla!" Artemis yells from the door, running between the tables. I stand from the booth bench just in time for her to wrap her arms around my waist.

"Hey, Artie." I smile, rubbing her shoulders. "How's your new school?"

"It's so awesome! I don't have to wear a uniform, and they play music over the speakers at lunchtime." She shakes excitedly, her curls bouncing behind her as she looks up at me.

Looking back toward the door, I give Hunter and Kendall a little wave as they walk toward us.

"Hey, little sis!" Hunter gives me a side hug as I roll my eyes at him. He always finds a way to throw in the fact that he's older, I'm younger, or some combination of both.

Kendall beams over at me, keeping his distance. We're not at the hugging stage yet, he and I, but our conversations are a lot smoother than they were before. "This place is pretty cool. I like the underground vibe," Kendall says.

"Yeah, it's one of my favorites. I found it my first year and come here about once a week." We're at this little basement pizza place called The Wall where the lighting is dark, the music is loud, and the walls are covered in customer-made graffiti.

"Why don't you come help me order?" Kendall asks, and we leave Hunter and Artemis at the booth. "What are your favorites?"

"Definitely the cheese bread, tortellini Alfredo, and this white sauce pizza with chicken and olives called the *Owl's Nest*," I say excitedly. He chuckles as I rub my hands together at the thought of my favorite pizza.

"Alright, let's get all of that and a large garden salad," he says to the guy behind the register. We move over to the pickup counter and wait for our food. "So tell me about this new internship. Hunter was saying it's different than the one you were initially going for."

"Different, but better!" I fill him in on all the things Patti revealed to me at the shareholders' event, trying to ignore the pinging in my heart that happens whenever I think about that night. "I start next month, planning a Halloween party, and the internship runs through May. Then I have a provisional position the year after graduation."

"That's amazing, Kayla. I'm so proud." He pauses, scrunching his face a little. "Is that okay for me to say?"

I smile back, seeing a little resemblance between us, around the eyes. "Yeah. I think it's okay."

"Good." He bumps my shoulder playfully with his. We gather our food and head back to the table where Hunter and Artemis are bickering.

"Kayla, can I sleep over at your apartment tonight?" Artemis asks me hurriedly, like she's expecting to be interrupted.

"Don't feel like you have to say yes," Hunter says, rolling his eyes. "I already told her you might need your space."

"That would be fun," I turn to Artie. "As long as it's okay with..." *Your dad? Our dad? Kendall?* I still don't know what to call him sometimes, but I look toward him for approval.

"That's fine by me. A little sisterly bonding would probably be a good idea."

Artie's excited squeals are enough to lighten the mood again, and we dig into the food, laughing as Hunter tells us a story about his new roommate's sleepwalking habit. Kendall fills us in on exciting happenings at EdTechU, including an expansion overseas.

"Kayla, I wanted to invite you to the Reed Tech Gala in LA at the end of the month. It's a fancy black-tie event showcasing the year's best of the best in technology," Kendall says. "All expenses paid, including a plane and a dress for you and Ashlie."

"Ashlie's going? My friend Ashlie?"

"Only if you are." Hunter smirks. "She said she'd be your date if I could convince you to come." Since when does Hunter know something about Ashlie before I do? I know they talk occasionally, Ashlie's let on to that much. But the way he so casually slid that in there, like they talk every day, makes me wonder how much my best friend has been keeping from me.

"Yeah, and Dad and Russell are getting an award. Chase should be there too," Artemis chimes in, cheeks stuffed with pizza. Her eyes widen as she watches the smile fall from my face.

I clear my throat, reaching for my glass of water. Hunter and Kendall glance at each other.

Kendall sighs, "Come on Artie-girl, let's go check out the

jukebox and have a little chat…" He stands and holds his hand out to Artemis.

Hunter waits until they're out of earshot before saying, "Look, I've tried to stay out of this, but as your big brother—"

"You're only three months older, Hunter. We're basically twins," I say, rolling my eyes and sitting back in the booth.

"Still older. And since I'm older, and therefore, *wiser*…" He flashes a smart-ass grin, looking right into my eyes. "I think maybe you should talk to him."

"About what? There's nothing to talk about. Is this why you want me to go to that gala? Because Chase will be there?"

"Naw, Dad really wants you to go. He's ready to charter an entire plane just to get you there and back, and he *is* receiving an award. It's usually a pretty fun night. I just think talking to Chase wouldn't be the worst thing in the world. Maybe get a little closure for both of you. By the time the gala rolls around, it'll be, what? Two months? Emotions have cooled and heads have cleared…"

"Closure? Everything was *closed* the second he kissed Maggie." I shake my head as the image threatens to creep back into my mind.

"That's not how it happened, though. Maggie's a master manipulator, and Chase wouldn't hurt you—"

"I'm not talking about this, Hunter!" Folding my arms over my chest, I scowl at him. "It's over."

"Damn, okay. Touché. Just…promise me you'll think about coming. For Dad. You don't have to say yes right away…*but* there will be swag bags." Hunter waggles his eyebrows in what I assume is an attempt to add some humor to his request.

A smile edges its way onto my face. "Fine, I'll think about it. The gala part, not the Chase part."

"That's all I ask," he says, throwing his hands up in the air.

Pressing my thumb and pointer finger into my eyebrows, I try to soothe the sudden headache settling there. I've done a good job of zapping Chase from my thoughts, sticking him on a shelf in the back of my mind and diving right back into the distracted campus life I had before the summer. While I try not to think about Chase much, there are still those sneaky little quiet moments where a memory creeps into my mind. I shake them as soon as they come, but they still come, and probably will for a while since I love him too. I shake the thought from my head.

Loved him. Past tense.

It took everything I had to walk away from Chase that day on his porch, especially after seeing the sadness in his eyes, but I had to do it. I had to stand up for myself, even just to prove that I could.

ARTIE CHATTERS A MILE A MINUTE THE MOMENT SHE enters my studio apartment. She hasn't stopped smiling since she got here, bouncing as she sits on my worn beige-colored couch in her fuzzy pajamas. Right now, she's telling me about her new teacher, a young Black woman with curly hair just like hers, and it's hard not to smile back at her excitement. She's different than I was at her age—happier, more naive. I was a serious and practical child, while she's free to play around and be a kid.

"So, Artie, what should we do first? I've got movies and snacks. Or we could make cookies. Play with makeup?"

"Ooh, makeup! I'm not very good at it though..." Her shoulders droop as she looks down at her knees. She has these moments of self-consciousness that seem out of place for a ten-year-old, like someone has sprinkled morsels of doubt throughout her adolescent psyche that spill out whenever she's feeling a little too confident.

"That's okay. Neither am I. We can practice together."

She hops off the sofa, and I show her back to the bathroom, pulling out my limited collection of eye shadow, lipstick, and blush. Looking at her wide-eyed reflection in the mirror makes me chuckle as she reaches for pink lipstick and an eyeshadow brush.

We take turns being used as a canvas, with me adding warm, neutral colors to her eyes and cheeks and her using the brightest neons on mine. On the count of three, we turn toward the mirror to see our masterpieces.

She gasps as she moves her face closer, touching her cheeks gingerly with the tips of her fingers. "I look so pretty!" Her incredulous voice breaks my heart a little bit.

"That's because you *are* pretty Artemis, makeup or not. And anyone who says otherwise is just a hater."

"Maggie's a hater then..." Her voice is low, and while I don't disagree, I feel like this is something I should investigate further.

"What do you mean? Did she say you weren't pretty?" I already know the answer to this. I've heard some of the out-of-pocket things Maggie has said to Artemis, and I just know she's said something horrible here too.

"She said I looked like a clown with makeup, that I'd be prettier if I stayed out of the sun."

My mouth drops as I stifle every single cuss word in my throat, regretting each time I turned down Ashlie's offer to tag team the ballerina bitch and her friends. How anyone can look at this sweet girl and say such nasty things is beyond me. I kneel on the fuzzy bathroom rug and look my little sister in the eye.

"Maggie's wrong. If she ever says something like that to you again, you call me and I'll take care of it, okay? That's what big sisters are for."

Artie nods, and I wrap my arms around her shoulders, squeezing just as tight as she squeezes me. I don't have a lot of practice, but I like doing this big sister thing. Artemis is adorable, and if I can help her keep her confidence, even a little bit, it will do wonders for the little girl living inside of me too.

Over my shoulder, Artie's muffled voice says, "If I show you something, will you promise not to be mad at me?"

I pull away from her to look at her face, where tears are welling in her eyes. "Of course. Why would I be mad at you?"

"Because I didn't show this to you before..." She takes her phone out of her pocket, sniffling while she scrolls to a saved video. "Everyone always tells me to mind my business... I didn't tell her you were my sister, I swear. But sisters are *always* your business, and she wasn't saying nice things about you."

"Artemis, who are you talking about? What—"

She presses play, and I recognize the back patio of The Bluffs. I can't see faces, and half of the video is covered, but that blue deck is as undeniable as the voices that come through the speaker.

Maggie: I've decided, girls. I'm going to kiss Chase at the event in San Francisco and finally make him see that we belong together. Artemis, you can't tell this to anyone, okay? Cousin secret.

Tamryn: It's about time! If he won't make the first move, you have to take matters into your own hands.

Camryn: What about the waitress?

Maggie: What about her? She's just a bitchy obstacle in my way. You two can distract her while I take care of Chase.

Artemis: I like her... She's nice.

Maggie: Girls like her are trouble, Artemis. You really shouldn't use her as a role model.

Artemis: Why not? She's nicer than you are. That's why Chase likes her instead of you.

Maggie: Mind your business, you little brat! The only reason I let you hang out with me is because your mom asked me to take you under my wing. Don't push me.

The video cuts off, and I trace the patterned floor of my bathroom with my eyes as I sit back on my heels, trying to make sense of everything I just heard. My heart pounds, almost as quickly as the thoughts racing in my head. Chase's highly unbelievable story was the truth? Maggie planned the whole thing. What I saw at the fountain was orchestrated to do exactly what it did—break us up. My thoughts swirl as wetness drips on my arm. I look up to see Artie's eyes full of tears as she clutches her phone. "When did you take this?" I ask.

"The day we made the goop." Her breathing stutters, and she erupts into tears as she rambles, "I kept forgetting to show you, and then I was going to show you after you got back from San Francisco, I swear. But then you stopped coming over because you were mad at Chase, and I didn't want you to be mad at me too."

"I... Come here, Artemis," I pull her down to sit on the floor before throwing my arms around her neck. "This is not your fault, and I'm not mad at you. We're sisters now, which means you're stuck with me no matter what."

She hugs me back, and eventually, her sobs quiet down to sniffles and whimpers. I grab wipes from the vanity and free her face of the makeup running down her cheeks. Reaching for another, I clean off my own, letting the coolness of the cloth slow the pounding in my chest.

"Why were you recording Maggie and her friends anyway?"

"I want to be a spy when I grow up." She shrugs and holds up her phone, scrolling through the videos and pictures she's taken over the summer. Some are dark and grainy, some clear and in full sunshine, but all of them are taken from far away with some kind of obstruction.

I giggle at her ten-year-old logic, shaking my head. "You'd make a pretty good spy. But you probably shouldn't record people anymore without them knowing about it. Deal?"

She nods. "Deal. Can we watch a movie now?"

"Yep." I stand and hold out my hand to help her. "Totally."

She picks a cute movie about a group of friends who start a

babysitting business. While it's easy to follow, I find my mind wandering back to the video and everything that happened in San Francisco.

CHAPTER FORTY-THREE

CHASE

My office door creaks as it opens and snaps my attention away from the sales proposal I've been reviewing all morning. In steps Trevor, leaning against the doorframe. His arms are crossed like he means business, and it's convincing, except for the friendly smile on his face.

"Oh, good. I caught you before you left. Were you able to take a look at those numbers from CellularSpeak? I was hoping to get back to them by end of day."

"Yeah." I turn in my swivel chair to the stack of papers on the shelf behind me, pluck a blue folder off the top, and hand it to him. "Everything looks good on our end. We should be able to move forward at the start of fourth quarter."

"Nice. Thanks. You excited to be going home? Your dad's getting an award, right?"

I nod, eyes shifting back to my screen briefly. I want so badly to turn back to my computer and brush him off, but I don't. Trevor's a good guy. It's not his fault my interest in small talk, or anything else, really, has disappeared. I plaster a grin on my face, the new facade I present to everyone at work lately, and drum my fingers on my knee. "Yeah, it should be a good time."

He takes a beat, looking around my office before standing up straight. "Well, I won't keep you," he says, slapping the side of the door frame. I feel bad as he turns to leave, knowing full well he was trying to be friendly and connect.

"Hey," I call after him. He slides his head back into the doorway, eyebrows perched with interest. "You still seeing that mystery girl of yours?"

"Uh, yeah." He rubs the back of his neck as a goofy smile spreads across his face, lost in a memory I'm glad I can't see.

He doesn't know I know this, but he's hooking up with Marla, our corporate trainer. I saw them cozied up in a corner at the shareholders' event.

"And you're not going to tell me who she is?" I ask, playing along as I save the proposal file and power down my computer.

"Nope. I don't kiss and tell." He tips his finger toward me before walking off down the hallway, shouting, "Have a good one!"

The speaker crackles overhead as the pilot announces our ascent into the sky. *Finally.* It's the last bit of permission I need to drop the "friendly guy" mask from my face. Being an early Friday afternoon flight, the plane is empty enough that almost every row has a vacant seat between passengers. I could use the space. Scrubbing my face with my hands, I take a deep breath before pulling out my headphones.

With almost two hours to zone out before landing in LA, I just need something loud in my ears to drown out the thoughts a quiet plane would likely lead to. It's not getting easier yet, that part where I'm supposed to slowly stop thinking about Kayla every minute of every day. If I'm not actively trying to shut thoughts of her out of my brain, her face occupies everything. Forcibly trying to forget her feels uncomfortable and miserable, so sometimes, I give in and let her memory seep back under my skin.

It doesn't necessarily feel any better, but at least it doesn't feel wrong. The only thing I've found to completely drown out everything is music where the bass is heavy enough to reorganize the atoms in my body.

The flight is so quick, I almost slip into a relaxing doze before we're heading back to the ground. With only a carry-on and my laptop, I make it to the pickup lane outside in no time, squinting against the bright sunshine as the busy sounds of the city come to life. I take a deep breath, preparing myself for this weekend of pretending around my family.

"Chase!" Dad waves from several cars to the right of where I'm standing. Hitching my bags higher on my shoulder, I walk toward his car as he opens the trunk wide. He has a giant smile as he claps my shoulder, making it easier for me to slip that mask over my face.

"Hey, Dad," I say, tossing my bag in before climbing into the passenger seat.

He slides behind the wheel and stares at me for a few seconds, eyes assessing. "Hey, kid. How was your flight?" He pulls into traffic, driving through the shadow of a departing 747 on its way up to the waiting skies.

"It was good. Short." I shrug.

"Speaking of short." He rubs my head. "Look at you with your new hotshot haircut over here. I haven't seen it this short since you were little."

"Yeah, yeah," I say with a chuckle, running my hand through the mussed-up strands of my new crew cut. "It was time for a change."

He turns his head, continuing his assessment from before until traffic moves again. I look out my window, not wanting to entertain any conversations about how I'm doing. "Well, your mom has us on a tight schedule for tonight. She's so nervous, I wonder if she thinks she's the one getting an award."

"That sounds about right." I shake my head, snorting as I imagine her running through the house, panicking about speeches she doesn't have to give and stages she doesn't have to walk across.

"We're headed straight to the tailor, where we'll meet Ken and Hunter for final fittings on tuxes. Then, home to get ready. The car will pick us up at five o'clock. Can you let them know we're on our way?"

I nod, blowing out a puff of air and looking at the clock on the dashboard. It's just before one-thirty now, meaning we'll be running all over town until after the gala. I'll be lucky if I get any rest this weekend before my flight back on Sunday. The seatbelt digs into my collarbone as I lean to the side, reaching for the phone in my front pocket.

MOM, DAD, AND I WALK INTO THE CAL CONVENTION Center a little before six p.m. From the outside, the white granite building looks judicial, with the columns of pillars surrounding the front. Mom stops to check her jacket, her long, black sequined dress swishing behind her as she and Dad walk across the white marble floor to the coat check attendant. A sweeping staircase opens up in front of the entrance, and I smooth my hands down my black velvet tuxedo jacket before climbing to the second floor.

I continue into the banquet room, following an usher as he escorts me to a table close to the stage, reserved for the Wilmington and Jackson families. Using the few minutes I have to myself, I breathe deeply, taking in the dark room. Centerpieces with white tea lights glow at every table, and blue and white silk drapes from the ceiling artfully. A projector illuminates the wall behind the stage, welcoming everyone to the Twentieth Annual Reed Tech Gala.

It all looks fancy and magical, and yet, I can't seem to care about any of it. I don't want to be here. It's been a long day. My face hurts from fake smiling, and I just want to go home and go to bed. I check my phone for the time, starting an internal count-down for when it will be acceptable for me to leave. Being jostled from the side snaps me out of the little pity party I'm throwing for myself.

"Bruh, you good?" Hunter asks after sliding into the seat next to me.

"Yeah, I'm fine. Why?" I say flatly, finding it hard to throw that mask back on my face.

"You just look sad, man."

I look at him, unable to say a thing. He's not wrong. I am sad, and the more tired I get, the harder it is to care about how I look. I nod and shrug, hoping he'll leave it alone.

"So it's probably not a good time to tell you Kayla's walking through the door right now, is it?" Hunter gestures with his chin, and my head turns before I can think better of it. There are people standing in front of the entrance, filling up the tables behind ours, but as they sit, I see her. Sandwiched between Kendall and Ashlie, she's dressed in a black velvet floor-length gown. Her hair is twisted intricately around her head, landing in a swirl over her shoulder. She's even more breathtaking than I remember, and if we were together, we'd look like a matching pair. But we're not, and my stomach drops to the floor.

"*What the fuck*, Hunt!" I grit my teeth, rubbing my forehead as my pulse pounds in my ears. "Did you know she was coming?"

"Uh, yep. I invited her. And you're welcome."

"Why the hell didn't you tell me?"

"Because it wouldn't be a surprise if I would have told you. You wouldn't have come either. Look, just talk to her."

"I *can't*," I say, shaking my head. "She doesn't want that." My scalp prickles with sweat as panic floods every nerve in my system. A lump forms in my throat, and I try to swallow it down to no avail.

"How do you know?"

"Because she fucking told me, man. She… I can't…" I scrub my face, groaning as I realize we'll be at the same table all night long. I want to throw up, knowing I can't take seeing that look in her eyes again—the cold repulsion mixed with resentment. I'm barely hanging on as it is.

"It's been months. Things change."

"Not this… I need a drink," I say, scooting my chair back from the table. I walk in the opposite direction, toward the open bar. Whiskey. Maybe I can lessen the agony of being this close to her with whiskey. Or Bourbon. Hell, maybe both. I'll try anything.

Leaning against the bar, I knock back a shot, and then take a glass on the rocks back to the table. Mom and Dad have found their seats, and I try my damnedest to keep my eyes from straying across the table toward Kayla.

"Hey, Chase," Ashlie says, putting her hand up in a small wave. I raise three fingers off my glass in return, keeping my eyes on her face, successfully avoiding the jade eyes next to her. That wasn't so hard. Maybe I *can* do this. Hunter kicks me under the table to get my attention, and I kick the asshole back without looking.

I manage to make it through dinner by keeping to myself. The conversation around the table is light and fluffy. Since no one asks me anything directly, I don't offer up anything. The ice in my third drink has all but melted, and I'm tempted to go grab another when the lights dim.

The noise level in the room drops significantly as the host for the evening introduces the history of the Edward Reed Award. But all I can think about is how much time I have left at this table. I've fixed my gaze on the corner of my place setting the entire night, except for when I look at the stage. It's helped give me something to focus on, but it's not sustainable. Every time I hear Kayla's voice or listen to her laugh, my neck twitches and I have to make a conscious effort not to raise my eyes in her direction.

Dad and Kendall accept their award, giving speeches I couldn't tell you a thing about. I watched the whole thing—their walk across the stage, each taking turns at the mic—but my mind was elsewhere. They make their way back to the table with everyone around us offering whispered congratulations as they pass. My knees feel like loaded springs as I anticipate leaving. I just need some air, and space, and another fucking drink. There's one more performance standing between me and freedom.

A Black, middle-aged songstress walks across the stage, the lights twinkling off her silvery dress as she croons. The song's opening notes sound familiar, with her sultry voice starting low and slow, ebbing and flowing like the waves of the ocean. I'm overtaken by the memory of ocean waves, me and Kayla, hands wrapped together casually as I drive to the beach. And another, listening to Kayla singing karaoke after the train ride. The performer sings the words, and I know exactly where I've heard this before:

> *Sometimes*
> *What you've lost, you'll find*
> *And you'll fall in kind*
> *To some kind of forever.*

I do it. I look across the table at the only person I've wanted to see for months, and she's looking right back at me. Kayla bites her lip in the way she does when she's feeling self-conscious, and so many things rush at me at once. My heart fully pounds out of the little box I've wrapped it in. An army of butterflies invades my core, and my fingers twitch as I think about how it would feel to hold her right now. I let myself wonder if her velvet dress feels as soft as that spot on her neck, just below her ears.

It doesn't matter. Taking a deep breath, the sobering hit of oxygen catapults me back down to earth. My eyes drop to the table, all hope pulverized by the echo of the last words she said to me.

When the music stops, thunderous applause fills the room around me. The MC announces the start of dancing and partying, gesturing to a small doorway across the room. I shoot out of my chair and loosen the jacket button at my waist, tugging at my tie as I race for the door. I'm suddenly roasting in my tux. I need air...and space. And another fucking drink. Hurrying through the tables of guests, I manage to snag a half-empty bottle of booze from the open bar on my way out.

The convention center is home to a small botanical garden, and I step through an ivy-covered archway that opens to a secluded koi pond. I collapse onto one of the large boulders surrounding the pond with a huff. Reaching up to scrub the tension from my face, I let out an audible groan. After a few swigs from the bottle, I close my eyes, shaking my head like it will expel everything out of it—Kayla, here, looking amazing in that dress, the song, all of it. I just want it gone.

Gravel crunches to my left, and I open my eyes to find Kayla, standing under the archway, as beautiful as ever. "Hi," she says quietly, taking her time walking toward me.

I take another hit of liquid courage to get me through whatever comes next. She's close enough for me to see the little floral details on her dress, close enough that it would only take a few steps for me to reach her. She's close enough that I can hear her phone buzzing in her hand.

"So your phone *does* work..." I hear myself say in a bitter tone. I slipped up a couple of times and texted her, just to see if we could talk. She never answered.

Kayla nods, looking down briefly before fixing her eyes back on me. "You cut your hair..." She smiles, stopping a couple feet away.

I take several seconds before answering, mulling over which cards to throw on the table. *It doesn't matter.* "Really, Kayla, that's what you go with? First time seeing each other in months, and *that's* what you want to talk about? My hair?" I shake my head, looking away from her. "Yep, I cut my hair." Asshole card it is, I guess. The bitterness coating the words as they slip out of my mouth doesn't sound like me, but I can't figure out how to sound any different right now. I'll probably regret it in the morning, but I admit, in this moment, it feels satisfying.

She takes a deep breath before saying, "Chase, I feel sorry... I feel so bad—"

"Good." I glare at her before taking another drink. The burning in my throat only adds fuel to the storm brewing in my head. Oh, great, *pity.* She feels sorry for me, and that isn't any better than resentment. At least she feels bad about something.

"Good?" She knits her eyebrows together. "You *want* me to feel like this?"

No, I hate it. I love you—It doesn't matter. My brain is swimming with so many things I could say right now, but that last thought is what hangs on and propels my anger forward.

"I told you I loved you—*twice* if we're getting technical, and you said it didn't matter. Not that you didn't love me back, or that you needed time, but that it didn't fucking matter." Heat creeps up my neck as the level of my voice increases. "Do you know what that felt like? It fucking broke me, Kayla. So excuse me if I'm not worried about you 'feeling bad.'"

Several emotions cross her face as I stare her down. I want to see how my words have landed, want to see her feel a percentage of how I've felt these last couple of months.

"I'm sorry," she whispers, looking down at the ground.

I shrug my shoulders while taking another slow sip from the bottle. "It doesn't matter..."

She nods quietly, eyes still on the gravel, and walks back through the archway without another word.

As soon as she's gone, I regret everything. All the resentment and angst leave my body, and I just feel empty. And drunk. I hate everything about this night. My head falls into my hand as a tear slides down my cheek. This isn't even on the tree scale. This just fucking sucks.

I don't know how long I sit there, but I periodically tip the lip of the bottle to my mouth, letting the spicy liquid drain down my throat just to feel something—anything.

"Chase, what the hell is wrong with you?" I hear stomping across the ground toward me, and two Hunters appear as I raise my head. "Gimme that." He snatches the nearly empty bottle from my hands and sets it on the ground by his feet.

"Leave me 'lone," I groan, swaying briefly before I steady myself on the rock with one hand.

"So you can fall backward into that pond and drown like an idiot? Naw." He shakes his heads, and I close my eyes briefly to keep from getting more dizzy. "Here, drink this," he says, cracking open a water bottle and shoving it at me. "What is wrong with you? You're wasted."

"I'm *fiiine*," I slur, sloshing water out of the bottle as I try to find my mouth.

"You're not fine, Chase. You've been drinking all night. I hand-delivered Kayla to you on a silver platter, and all you've been is an asshole."

"She didn't come here for me." My bottom lip puffs out as I shake my head in disbelief.

"She *did* come here for you, dummy. She knew you were going to be here. She wanted to see you—to talk to you, and you've been acting like she's not even alive. What are you *doing?*"

"She thinks I'm a cheater, man. She said she feels sorry for me. That's all this was." I slap a hand over my eyes, trying to force the tears back inside my body. I'm a bumbling mess.

Hunter blows out an exasperated breath. "Bruh, no. She doesn't feel bad for you. She feels bad that any of this happened. Look..." He sits next to me and shoves his phone in my face before pressing play on a video. I move his hand back, trying to focus on the image on the screen.

Recognizing Maggie's voice, I ask, "What is this?"

"Proof that Maggie planned it all. Kayla knows the truth."

I half watch and fully listen, closing my eyes when the video shakes a little too much. There's not much to see, but here it is. A full confession, right in my lap, and I have no idea what to do about it. I'm feeling a little less woozy and a lot sicker to my stomach as I realize how unbelievably idiotic I've been tonight.

Kayla was here, *right here*, close enough for me to touch, and I let her walk away—I pushed her away.

Hunter sits next to me for a while, not saying much except to remind me to drink the water in my hand. Feeling sobered up enough to have a rational conversation, I turn to him. I'm sure I look as bad as I feel because the sympathy on his face is something I haven't seen since I fell out of that tree when we were kids.

"Thanks, man," I say, dropping my eyes to the ground.

"Sure. You'd do it for me. The question is, what are you going to do about Kayla?"

I shake my head, struggling to answer the question of the hour. San Francisco may not have been my fault, but tonight sure is. I acted like a petty asshole out of spite and fear, and I have no one to blame but myself.

"Do you want to be with her?"

"More than anything," I croak, my voice low and gruff.

"So what are you going to do about it?"

"I don't even know." I shake my head again, at a loss for how to handle any of this. It feels like a lost cause. I have no plans, no motivation. All I have is sorrow...and a headache.

CHAPTER FORTY-FOUR

KAYLA

The red-rimmed eyes I see in the mirror belong to the same face I left behind in my bathroom months ago. Despite looking like shit, I look like cleaner shit now that I've washed off the mascara that was running down my cheeks. I think I cried the entire hour-long drive back to Ashlie's apartment, plus another thirty minutes on the couch as she showered and changed. I don't feel tears on the edge of falling anymore, but I still feel terrible.

Tonight was an absolute disaster. I expected a little bristle from Chase, but he full-on ignored the fact I was sitting at the same table as him. He wouldn't even look at me, and I'd know because I was staring at him all night long.

And the pond.

Ugh.

That whole conversation is one I'd like to scrub permanently from my brain. Seeing him like that—resentful and closed off, completely opposite of the guy I spent the summer falling in love with—was heartbreaking. And I feel horrible, learning what I said that day on the porch had that kind of effect on him.

"Girl, did you fall asleep in there? I have to pay that water bill." Ashlie's banging on the bathroom door snaps me back to the present. I turn off the water, completely forgetting it was running. She sounds annoyed, but when I open the door, her face is full of worry lines and sympathy.

"Sorry..." Tears well up in my eyes again, and she pulls me forward into a hug.

"If you don't stop apologizing..." she whispers, squeezing me tighter as my shoulders shake. She leads me over to her bed and prompts me to sit on the edge. "None of this was your fault, girl."

"I know."

"Then why are you still blaming yourself like it is? You did your best based on what you saw. When you learned new information, you tried to make it right. He was the one acting a fool tonight, not you."

"I know that, but if I would have listened to him—"

"Then what? You'd be in a relationship with a guy you didn't really trust? We both know that's not true. You saw what you saw, you were just missing part of the equation. You didn't know what you didn't know. That's not on you."

"But I hurt him, Ash. I really hurt him. I love him, and he won't even look at me." My cheeks are on fire as the fresh tears roll down the same raw trails the previous tears traveled before. I'm really tired of crying, but clearly, I'm not the one in control here as a new wave pours from my eyes.

Ashlie sighs, turns on the TV in her bedroom, and clicks to our favorite comfort show. "Let's get into this third season, see if we can take your mind off of it for a little bit."

I move toward the headboard, curling up on one side of Ashlie's queen size bed. Staring at the TV, unable to see what's on the screen through the blurry wetness that steadily streaks down my face, I contemplate closing my eyes, hoping sleep will overtake me. The buzzing of my phone on the dresser across the room makes me freeze. I turn to Ashlie, eyes wide and heart pounding.

I'm terrified.

I don't know whether I'm more scared of it being a message from Chase, or it *not* being a message from him.

"I'll check it," she says, rolling off her side of the bed. She taps my phone screen and shakes her head with a smirk on her face. "It's Hunter. You want it?"

I nod and she tosses my phone across the bed.

HUNTER

How you holding up?

ME:

Best. Night. Ever. Top 10, all-time favorite *sad face*

HUNTER

Hang in there, sis.

Dad wants to know if you and Ash want to meet us for breakfast tomorrow.

ME

Who is us, exactly?

HUNTER

LMAO! Just me, Dad, Artie. No Wilmingtons allowed.

ME

thumbs-up

Turning to Ashlie, I start to ask, "Do you—"

"I already told him we'd go. He just wanted to check up on you," she says without looking away from the TV screen, like they casually talk all the time.

"So are you two... What's going on there?"

"We're your best friend and brother who are worried about you. We're just friends. That's all." Her eyes narrow at the TV, and the way she's avoiding looking at me lets me know that's not all of it. This must be the distraction I need because my eyes are suddenly drier than the Mojave Desert. Her drama trumps my drama.

"Ash, I saw the way you two were looking at each other on the dance floor tonight. His hands were a little too low on your—"

"Okay, fine. We talk, but that's it."

"Like, how much talking?"

"*Ugh*, why are you in my business?" Ashlie groans, pausing the show. She unlocks her phone and tosses it over to me. I pick it up and scroll through her messages with Hunter. They talk all right. Several times an hour, day and night. I abruptly stop swiping as I realize I might see some things I don't want to see.

"I'm gonna give this back before I see any spicy pics that will require me to have to gouge my eyes out." I shiver, scrunching up my face.

"He wishes." She snorts, taking her phone back. "It's not like that. We talk all the time, about everything. But he knows I'm a relationship girlie, and I know he has several girls on his roster, so we don't cross that line."

"So best friends who have a thing for each other?"

"I...guess? We spent a lot of time together this summer." Ashlie shrugs, grabbing for the remote. "And he was there when I broke up with Bryan...both times. But we can't ever be together. We're too different. Now can we watch this? I don't want to spend the whole night talking about Hunter."

"Just talking *to* him all night, then?" I arch my eyebrow and smirk at her. Her phone buzzes between us, and her hand flinches to reach for it, before drawing back. "It's Hunter, isn't it?" I nod toward her phone.

She rolls her eyes, sucking her teeth while crossing her arms over her pink nightgown. Her phone vibrates again, and I fold my hands under my chin and smile at her. We both know I'm right. A third buzz has her snatching it up from the bed, biting her cheeks as she tries not to smile.

WE PULL UP TO HONEY BRUNCHES AT SEVEN A.M., EARLY enough for me to make it through LA traffic and to the chartered plane by ten. I see Artemis bouncing in her seat through the red bricked restaurant's window, her mouth moving a mile a minute as she talks away at Kendall. He's so patient with her. The smile on his face is warm and loving, and I can't help but wonder what it would have been like to grow up knowing him.

"Hey, didn't you win an award yesterday?" I tease Kendall as I slide into the booth next to Artemis. The cozy café music lends to the whirring drips of the coffee machines in the background, adding to the relaxed vibe of the brown and black accented restaurant.

"*Oh. My. God!* Can we have your autograph?" Ashlie fans herself dramatically, playing along. She sits next to me, and the disappointment that flashes over Hunter's face makes it obvious the feeling between them is mutual.

Kendall chuckles, shaking his head as the people at the table next to us try to decide whether he's famous. A set of short fingers wiggle between my back and the seat as Artie snakes her arms around me, giving me a tight squeeze.

"Hey, sis," I say, hugging her back.

"Did you take a picture of your dresses?" She bounces, smiling up at me. "Hunter said Ashlie looked beautiful."

My head whips over, first to Hunter, who has his head buried in his menu, then to Ashlie, whose eyes are wide as she stares at him.

"Oh, did he, now? What else did he say?" I ask Artie, eating up this best-friend-new-brother drama. I hand her my phone to see the pictures, flashing her a smile.

Hunter clears his throat, eyes narrowing at us. "Naw, that's not how it happened. You asked me if she looked beautiful in her dress, and I said yes."

"How's that any different?" Ashlie baits him with a sassy head tilt.

Hunter opens and closes his mouth several times before Kendall leans toward him, whispering loudly, "You might want to quit while you're ahead, son. You're no match for these three."

I cover my snort with my hand as my shoulders shake against my best friend next to me. Ashlie knocks into me, and I can't hold the laughter in anymore. Pretty soon, Kendall's laughing along with me and Ashlie catches the giggles. Hunter sucks his teeth, trying not to smile.

"Man, teasing big brothers is *fun*." I laugh, rubbing my hands together, feeling proud of myself.

"Yeah." Artie nods. "Just wait until you find out about his collection of—"

"Artie, I *swear to God…*" Hunter warns through his teeth.

Kendall clears his throat, and my two siblings roll their eyes, going back to their corners and burying their heads in their menus.

After finishing breakfast, and with a few more promises to see them during the holidays, we're all headed to our respective cars. I hug Artie first, then move to give Kendall one of our newly accomplished, awkward side hugs. Finally, stepping in front of Hunter, I wrap both of my arms around him, holding on tight. He freezes, but relaxes just as quickly and hugs me back. Despite how horribly everything happened yesterday, I'm so very grateful to have someone like Hunter in my corner.

"Thanks for trying," I whisper into his arm.

"Hey," he says, pulling back. "Don't give up on him yet, okay?"

I scrunch my lips to the side and shrug, at a loss for what to do about Chase. He made it clear last night that he didn't want anything to do with me. I'm not in a rush to redo any parts of that heated conversation by the pond. I just want to get on the plane, go back to school, and forget this weekend ever happened. Hunter hugs me again before climbing into the passenger seat of Kendall's SUV. Waving, I slide into Ashlie's hatchback.

When we pull into the airport, I take a deep breath before looking over at Ashlie, ready to leave LA, this weekend, and Chase right here. Since I'll be the only one on the eight-seater, I'm giving myself the hour-long plane ride to cry and get it out of my system. Then I'll box up what's left of the tattered shards in my chest, wrap it up nice and neat, and pack it away. My internship starts on Monday, and I need to leave this all behind in order to focus.

Ashlie wraps her arms around me, hugging me as well as she can over the center console. The tears I've been holding in all morning fall. For every one I brush away, two more replace it, and I have to pull away just to catch my breath.

"You decided, didn't you?" she asks with a somber voice.

I nod my head, trying to get some control over my breathing.

"You're not going after him."

"Nope," I whisper, shaking my head slowly as my blurry eyes look at the gearshift between us. This feels different than it did on the porch at The Bluffs Estates. Before, it felt like a decision had been made for me. Like my hand was forced by circumstance and I had no choice but to follow through with ending things. This is something else. This is all me, my choice.

The decision is mine, and I'm choosing to move on, leaving the messy parts tangled up how they are. Maybe someday I can look back on the good things from this summer, but right now, I just need to forget.

"Let me know when you get back. And hey," she says, looking into my eyes. "It's okay to take some of those tears with you when you get home. Don't feel like you have to leave them all on the plane."

I sit back against the window, puzzled by how she knew what I was planning to do.

"Girl, don't look at me like that. I know you, and I'm just saying, it's okay to feel sad about this for a while."

We sit in silence, with Ashlie squeezing my hand as I take in her advice. I don't know if I'll follow it, but it feels nice to consider it. It feels nice to have her give me the permission I won't give myself to cry for as long as I need to.

With one more deep breath and another wipe of my face on my sleeve, I grab my weekend bag from the back seat and head inside toward the private jet terminal. I just need to make it onto the plane before I can fall apart again.

Check-in is quick, and after they escort me back for a brief security screen, I'm ushered through the doors and onto the tarmac. With each step I take toward the plane, my body slowly comes undone. My shoulders slump, my footsteps slow, and the tears brimming behind my eyes threaten to release.

My seat.

I just have to make it to my seat.

I repeat it over and over in my head, to no avail. My foot touches the first step of the plane, and the floodgates open. I frantically try to wipe them away, looking at my shoes to keep from falling while hiking my bag up higher on my shoulder. Making it onto the threshold and inside, I swipe at my cheeks to clear my vision enough to find a seat in the middle of the cabin. My eyes move up the aisle to gauge how far I need to go, and I freeze.

Next to the seat I would have collapsed into stands Chase, one hand in his pocket and the other holding onto a small bouquet of pink lilies.

"Wh-what are you doing here?" I ask, my voice hitching in my throat. My feet feel stuck. I'm unsure if walking forward, toward him, or backward off the plane is the best course of action.

He bites the side of his lower lip and takes a breath before moving a step toward me. "I needed a quick flight back home, and Kendall offered me a spot on the plane."

"But this isn't flying to San Francisco..."

"Yeah. I know." He takes another step forward, and I would take a panicky step back if only my feet could move. "I wanted to apologize for last night and figured an hour-long flight was a good way to do that."

Chase takes another step forward, and I let out a shaky breath. He did all of this just to apologize to me for being rude? After all this time lost, all the hurt and pain I feel halfway responsible for, he's the one standing in front of me with grand gestures?

"I was an asshole. I wasn't in a good place, and I took it out on you." He takes his hand from his pocket and closes the gap with one last step forward, putting the flowers on the seat next to us. Reaching up, he slips my bag from my shoulder and drops it in the seat opposite the flowers. "I don't want to see you hurting, Kayla, and I'm sorry I said I did." Timidly, he laces our fingers.

Chase's eyes meet mine, deep dark blue enshrouded with guarded anticipation as he watches me. Waiting.

It's my choice.

He's waiting for me to decide what happens next, and I'm frozen. I had made up my mind, resigned to let him go and here he is, asking me to reconsider.

I want to reconsider.

I want back what we had before LA, and Maggie, and San Francisco. To accept the words he said to me on his porch, when he told me all the things he loves about me. However it looks, whatever form it takes, I want some kind of forever with him.

Chase looks down, and I feel him releasing our knitted fingers as he pulls away.

No.

I cup his cheek in my hand. With a sigh, he closes his eyes and nuzzles his face into my palm, and it's like I can hear him silently releasing a long awaited, *finally.*

I lean in, brushing my lips against his, and his hand presses at the small of my back, pulling me closer. The kiss is soft—hesitant, nervous—as we give in to one another. Piece by piece, we knit the fragile fabric of our hearts back together, giving and taking what we need to feel whole again.

When he pulls away, his forehead rests against mine, and it feels like coming home. We stand entwined, just us two, alone together.

After several minutes, he leads me back to the middle row of seats, pushes the armrest up, and pulls me in close. "I missed you," he whispers, fiddling with the ring on my thumb.

It's my turn now. This guilt that has been eating me up since seeing the video, the guilt from last night, seeing what my words did to him, refusing to believe him, it all feels like this is my fault.

"Chase, I'm sorry. I should have believed you, trusted you—"

His lips are on mine again, briefly, before he pulls back, shaking his head and looking into my eyes. "No. You believed what you saw and trusted yourself. I can't be upset at you for that."

"But all of this could have been avoided if I would have just—"

Chase lands another kiss to quiet me, this one more determined than the last, before pulling away. "Stop. It doesn't..." He shakes his head and takes a deep breath. "*This...*" he says, reaching for my hand and placing it over his heart, securing it with his own on top. "This is what matters to me."

The speaker overhead clicks as the pilot's voice crackles through, prompting us to buckle up for takeoff. Chase lets me go long enough to secure his seat belt and reaches for my hand again, trailing the tips of his fingers back and forth across my open palm. The soft tickle of his fingertips on my skin is a feeling I've missed more than I realized. If he never stops touching me, never stops holding me, I think I'll be just fine.

We watch the clouds pass by the window as the plane takes to the skies. As soon as it reaches altitude, Chase unbuckles to move closer to me. I lean in, angling myself to rest my head on him, my breathing slowing to match the rise and fall of his chest.

"Did you get the catering internship?" he asks quietly.

"Nope. Well, not exactly..."

His body stiffens, and I turn to look at him, his eyebrows pulled in with worry. "Because of what happened in the kitchen?"

"No, nothing like that. I got a different internship—a better one. I'm the first event planning intern for Seaside Catering."

The look of relief on his face puts a smile on mine, and I turn back into our snuggle. "That's amazing. You're going to be great at that, ba—Kayla..." He buries his face into my shoulder, settling there for several minutes before asking, "Can we spend the day together? I'll have my work buddy drive me back home tonight, but I don't want to leave you yet."

"Do you have to leave tonight?" I ask.

"No, I don't have to. I just didn't want to assume anything…"

I pull out of his arms and turn to face him again. After all the miscommunication we've had, I need him to hear me say this and see that I mean it. "Chase, I want everything back that we had before San Francisco." I place my hand on his cheek. "I want you. I want to be with you, and I want you to stay tonight. Please stay."

A smile, one I haven't seen for far too long, stretches across his face. He reaches for me, pulling me in to smother me with the sweetest of kisses. Rubbing my nose with his, smiling as big as the day we met, he says, "I'll stay, baby. As long as you want me, I'll stay."

CHAPTER FORTY-FIVE

CHASE

I slip out of Kayla's bed a little before seven a.m. Grabbing my shirt from the chair in the corner and shrugging it on, I look back to see her sprawled out on her belly, her hair scarf threatening to slip away from her forehead with the next roll of her body. Seeing her there, dressed in an oversized SSU athletic tee and apple pie pajama shorts, her hand splayed where I was moments ago, I'm struck by the casual beauty of it all. I could wake up seeing her like this every morning and it would never be enough. Slipping into the bathroom, I do a morning refresh, and then I get to work.

I'm determined to have a do-over of the night that was ripped away from me in San Francisco, and I want to catch the grocery delivery before they knock on the door and wake her. I want to tell her I love her—again—my way, and it's happening this morning with breakfast. As I turn the outside of the knob and press the bedroom door closed to avoid the latch clicking, I slip my phone in the pocket of my sweatpants. Before moving to her tiny kitchen, I check the grocery delivery progress on the app.

The lilies I got her are still wrapped up on the countertop, and with five minutes to kill, I search her cabinets for a cup to fill with water. When we landed yesterday, she showed me around campus.

We talked about work, and I filled her in on Trevor's workplace tryst. She told me about her new internship and how excited she is to be doing what she loves. We ate at her favorite places, walked around the quad, and I spent every spare minute reaching for her to steal kisses. By the time we finally made it back to Kayla's apartment last night, we were ready to fall asleep, too tired for an apartment tour or anything else. Yesterday was perfect, but this morning will be better.

Unwrapping the bouquet and using a steak knife I found in a drawer to trim the stems, I arrange the flowers in a plastic cup and set it in the middle of the countertop. My phone buzzes in my pocket, notifying me the delivery driver is pulling up to the apartments. I hurry to the front door, cracking it in hopes of avoiding a knock, and in a minute, a short middle-aged woman appears with bags in hand. After a quick *thank you*, I get started in the kitchen. I'm turned toward the stove, my hand about to twist the knob, when I hear the bedroom door creak open.

"What are you doing up so early?" Kayla yawns behind me.

Looking over my shoulder, I see that she's lost the scarf, allowing her locs to fan around her shoulders. *My God, she's my favorite thing to look at.* She shuffles to the kitchen and sits at the lone stool, and I abandon the thought of turning the stove on. I lean across the counter and reach for her hand, kissing her fingers before holding them to my cheek.

"Morning, baby." I smile, watching her rub the sleep from her eyes.

"Yeah...*early* morning..." She yawns again, looking around at the mess in the kitchen. "What are you doing?"

"Well... I promised you breakfast a few months ago and never got to deliver," I say.

She blinks at me, holding my gaze for a while, resting her chin in her hand. There's none of her anxious tells. No lip biting or thumb scratching. No face scrunching or shifting in her seat. She just stares, unreadable.

"What?" I ask, suddenly feeling paranoid.

"I love you too..." She says it casually, like she's telling me it's Sunday morning and the sun is rising. My heart kick-starts, and relief I didn't know I needed floods over me.

"You do?" I ask, feeling the smile spread as I look into her eyes.

She grins, finally, and the thing lights up her whole face, igniting me in the process. "I do."

I move around the counter and pull her out of the stool faster than anything, pressing my lips to hers. She smiles against my mouth, and I smile back, my heart cracking wide open.

"Well, that's just not fair..." I say, tracing her lower lip with my thumb.

Her face scrunches as she replies, "What's not fair?"

"I had this whole thing planned," I say, trailing my fingers over her shoulders. "I was going to make you crepes—"

"Crepes, huh?"

"—and you would tell me how amazing they were..." My hands slide down her back, stopping on her waist.

"So I liked the crepes, then?"

"You did. And then I would profess my undying love for you, and you'd swoon."

"*Swoon?*" She laughs. "Those are some pretty lofty plans there, Mr. Charming..."

"Yeah, but now you ruined the surprise."

"You can still make crepes, Chase... I'll even tell you how good they are. But I can't promise any swooning," she teases, squinting her eyes.

"Nope, it's ruined," I insist, shaking my head. "Now I'll have to give you a different surprise."

"Like...?" she asks, raising an eyebrow at me.

"Like this," I say, sweeping her legs out from under her and cradling her in my arms.

"Chase!" she squeals, wrapping her arms around my neck.

I walk her back to the bedroom, and the breath from her giggles tickles my skin as she buries her head in my shoulder.

Dropping her onto the pillows, I arch over her to pepper quick pecks down her neck as she giggles even more. Her hands splay around my shoulders, and she smells so damn good that I can't help but linger, the playful pecking melting into soft kisses. She moves her hands around my face, pulling me up to meet her lips. *I swear they've gotten softer in the last two minutes.* I melt into her, wishing there was a way to get even closer.

"Baby..." she says between kisses.

"Hmm?" I moan in response, more to her calling me *baby* than to provide an answer.

Kayla pushes on my shoulders, staring into my eyes with that jade-colored gaze that left me frozen in the beginning. She dips back in, almost to my mouth, before smiling and whispering, "Take your socks off."

Catching me all the way off guard, I chuckle into her shoulder before sitting up on my knees and pulling the socks off my feet. When I turn back to her, the sultry smile she bites lights my entire soul on fire. *She's everything.* My lips are back on hers so fast that a gasp slips from her mouth in surprise.

"I love you, Chase," she whispers, and I know anything I could have planned this morning could never feel as good as this moment does.

"I love you, too, baby."

FIVE YEARS LATER
KAYLA

The elevator dings as it rumbles to a stop on the fourth floor, hovering slightly before settling with an audible thud. I grip the green reusable grocery bags around my wrists when the double doors slide open. Hefting them up, I turn sideways as I exit, shuffling down the hallway on my kitten heels. To avoid smashing the bread and eggs against the door, I shift the grocery bags onto the sleeves of my black power suit and punch in the code. Four beeps and a sliding lock later, after kicking the door closed with my foot, I've successfully loaded everything onto the kitchen island.

I'm halfway to the pantry with a jar of peanut butter when my phone rings in my purse. I hurry to set the condiment on the shelf and turn on my heel to dig through my bag before it goes to voicemail. There's only one person who calls me, refusing to get with the times.

"Hey, Mom," I say, pressing the speaker icon and placing my phone down on the counter. I reach for the loaf of bread, pausing briefly to hear what she's saying.

"Kayla, hey. Real quick, are you still coming for Thanksgiving? I'm trying to get my time off requests approved for the holidays, and I wanted to make sure."

"Yeah…" I say, hearing the door to the bedroom open.

Chase shakes his disapproving head at me, still wearing his blue EdTechU polo and black trousers from work. He grabs the bread from my hands, kisses my cheek, and walks to the shelf.

"Yeah, Mom, we'll be there for Thanksgiving. We've both requested the time off already," I assure her. It took a couple of months for Mom and me to talk things out about the Kendall secret, and things were uncomfortable for a little while. But now, I split holidays between both of my families with no love lost. Sometimes, she'll even join us for Jackson family outings.

"Oh, good. Okay, I'll handle things on my end," she says.

I rummage through another bag, grabbing apples, and turn to open the fridge.

"Don't you dare…" Chase says quietly, eyes narrowing as he takes the apples out of my hand.

"Hi, Chase!" Mom yells from the phone. "Is Kay giving you a hard time?"

"Oh, just refusing to let me help her with the groceries again…"

"Did you just *tattle* on me?" I whisper.

"Kayla, you better let that man help you…"

He shrugs, leveling me with a brow raising stare. "Hey, Ms. Harris," he calls with a cheery tone. "How did your last week in New York go?"

"Oh, I have so many stories. Nursing in New York is a different world than California, but I'm glad to be home." Something beeps on her end, muffled yelling coming through a second later. "Hey, I have to get back to work, but I'll see you both next month." She hangs up before we can say goodbye, and I shake my head, imagining her running down the hallway to a patient's room, her curly ponytail flying behind her.

"You are in *so* much trouble…" Chase says, leaning against the counter and tsking at me. I squint at him, putting one hand on my hip while reaching for a tub of yogurt with the other.

"*Don't...*" he warns, reaching me in two steps. I drop my hand, abandoning the yogurt on the counter.

"You're acting like I changed a tire..." I tease, looking up at him. He wraps both arms around my waist, leaning in close.

"Too soon..." he says, leaning down for a kiss. "You were supposed to text me when you got in the parking garage..."

"It's five things. It's fine."

"Baby, there are ten bags on this counter. And your wrists still have marks on them from hauling it all inside." He gives a look, daring me to say he's wrong.

I roll my eyes, knowing he's not going to let this go, and raise on my toes to give him a peck. He holds me tighter and stares me down until I roll my eyes again, wrapping my hands around the back of his head and pulling him down into a proper kiss. With a smile against my lips, he melts into me, fully forgiving my rebellious streak of independence. He knows we'll have this same argument next week, and I know he'll forgive me afterward.

I pull back, biting my lip to try and leverage a deal. "How about I let you put everything away and we can forget about this little lapse in judgment?"

"*Or...* We could keep doing *this,* and let the groceries handle themselves." He presses his lips to mine, his sigh making me heavily consider his suggestion.

Chase has been pulling late nights at work, and this is the first he's beaten me home in a couple of weeks. Some nights, I've fallen asleep on the couch just to see him for a couple of minutes before going to bed and doing it all over again the next day. His EdTechU team is trying to recruit a big account from Chicago to here in San Francisco, and he's been working himself ragged to get it done. I haven't heard him complain, but I know he's exhausted. We're almost to the weekend, when we'll both get some rest, relaxation, and quality time.

"If we do *that,* the ice cream will melt. Do you really want me to go back to the store?" I lift my chin expectantly.

"Good point…" He presses a kiss to my forehead before reaching behind me for the yogurt and cheese. When he turns back toward the fridge, I stretch my arm across the counter for the bag of tortillas.

"Kayla *Marie* Harris…" Chase says, not bothering to turn around from the fridge.

"Fine!" I huff, putting my hands in the air. I drop the bag and step away from the counter. Apparently, living together for three years hasn't taught me anything because we still battle with the groceries weekly. He wants to help me bring everything in, and I can usually get it all in one quick, albeit heavy, trek. There isn't much we butt heads on anymore, but tires and groceries will do it every time.

Kicking off my heels with a groan, I lean against the island, watching him work. Chase's phone rings in his pocket as he sticks the last of the reusable bags on the hook inside the pantry. He scrubs his face with one hand, taking a heaving breath before reaching into his front pocket. "It's work." He keeps his eyes down at the screen, turning to head back into the bedroom. "Hey, Trev," he says as he closes the door behind him.

I hang my bag on the hook by the front door and slip my shoes in the basket underneath. Grabbing my laptop, I shuffle over to the couch and peek out of the large glass window of our high rise, watching the golden hour of light fade as I go.

Patti has me working with her on a party in LA on Friday, and I have a few more workups to send out for approval before my flight tomorrow. Chase is flying down with me to make a weekend of it. I haven't seen everyone in a few months so after the event, we'll spend the rest of the weekend with our families. I'm looking forward to some much-needed downtime.

Pulling up my work email, I review the new messages from Joan, my engagement party client in LA. She's Patti's oldest friend, and the story of how she and her fiancé got together is adorable—high school sweethearts reconnected in their sixties. Joan has been a pleasure to work with, loving everything I've sent over, trusting my professional opinions. Her style is reminiscent of mine, which makes the process that much quicker. I can envision myself in the space, pretending like this engagement party is my own, at times, to fully embody her vision. Blush pink and golden champagne colors will cover every inch of the venue, with pink lilies and white peonies as the floral arrangements. The only thing I would have different from hers is losing the tacky At Last banner she insists on having. It's a little too on the nose for my taste, but this party isn't for me.

Not yet anyway. Chase would have married me after the first year if I would have let him. I blame the idyllic relationship he grew up seeing between his parents. I've wanted to wait, building our lives—our careers, our futures—to make sure we have solid ground to stand on. We have ensured, together, that our bond is unbreakable. I wouldn't change one bit of the last five years. He's my everything, and there's no sense of urgency to sign a paper saying we are what we already feel we are. That's not to say we won't do it, there just isn't any rush.

The bedroom door clicks open as I'm moving pictures around my screen, trying to finalize the table centerpieces for Friday. Fully distracted, I don't glance up until Chase sits next to me on the couch. His hand caresses my knee as he waits for me to get to a stopping point. When I finally look at him, he's got his head leaned over the back of the couch.

"How's Trevor?" I ask with a slightly sarcastic tone. They just saw each other at work a few hours ago. He doesn't answer right away, so I move my computer to the coffee table, giving him my full attention. "What's wrong?"

"Uh…" He scrunches his face, and I know he's got bad news. I wait, watching as he rubs his thumb in between his closed eyes. "So, I have to fly out to Chicago on Friday…"

I blow a breath through my lips, trying to tamp down the disappointment before it starts. "I thought Trevor was going…"

"He was, but he just called saying he's got a fever and chills. He can't go and infect everyone in Chicago and expect us to land the contract. Baby, I know we've been looking forward to this weekend, but this is something I can't get out of. It's either me or we lose the account." He turns toward me and wraps his hands around my waist, pulling me closer. A look of regret falls over his face as his blue eyes peer into mine.

"It's fine," I say, trying to make myself believe I don't feel sad. It's work. I know better than anyone that sometimes you just have to put work first. "We can have another weekend. It's fine."

"It's *not* fine," he groans. He stands and places one hand on either side of the sofa around me, before planting a feverish kiss on my mouth. It's needy and firm, full of the pent-up energy long working hours brings. He's missed me, and I'm one more of those steamy kisses away from forgetting about my work and showing him how much I've missed him too. "I'm sorry. I'll make it up to you," he whispers.

"Right now?" I ask, biting my lip.

"I can make it up to you right now if that's what you want," he says, standing to do whatever it is I'm about to ask him. He turns toward the kitchen, and I just know he's expecting me to ask for the ice cream in the freezer.

"Oh, I definitely *want*..." I look up through my lashes, my eyes traveling from his belt, up his torso, and finally landing on his mouth while I wait for him to connect the dots. I lick my lips, and by the time my eyes reach his, I find my longing reflected back at me. Unfolding my legs from the couch, I stand in front of him, moving close enough that our chests touch. Reaching up, he grazes his thumb across my chin, and I move back, biting the smile spreading on my lips. He cocks his head to the side, and I take off for the bedroom, slipping past his fingers with a squeal as he tries to grab my waist. Chase groans behind me, a clear sign he's too tired to play games tonight, but he gives chase anyway.

Entering the bedroom, I move right to the mirrored dresser, taking off earrings and loosening my locs from the tight spiral on top of my head. I slip off the tennis bracelet from my left wrist, an anniversary gift from my love, leaving only the rose gold band on my thumb. When I look back at my reflection, Chase is watching me through the mirror from the doorway. His hip is propped against the side of the doorframe, with one hand holding the top. I stare back, raising an encouraging brow to see what his next move is going to be as I slowly reach behind me to unzip the back of my skirt. That's enough to get him across the room.

"Nope," he whispers in my ear, removing my hand from the zipper, kissing my neck from behind. He eases the zipper down, moving his hands past the waistband around my hips and letting the skirt fall to the floor before pulling me flush against his body. I loosen the buttons on my shirt, fumbling on the second one as his breath fans over the sensitive parts of my neck. "Take this off," he murmurs, nudging the collar of my shirt with his nose to kiss my shoulder.

"Baby, I'm trying..." I answer breathlessly, closing my eyes in a moment of pleasure, silently kicking myself for wearing a buttoned blouse today. Chase laughs quietly and moves his hands from my hips, circling around my ribs to grip the sides of my shirt. With one firm tug, buttons fly across the room, making me gasp in surprise. "My shirt—"

"I'll get you another shirt," he mumbles against my skin, sweeping my hair to the side before easing the sleeves down my arms. He presses kisses along my shoulder, and I shiver as his fingers slide up my torso, swiftly turning me around to face him. His eyes are deep blue flames, burning trails in my skin as he takes in every inch of me. In all the years we've been together, he still looks at me just as intensely as the first day we met. It's easy to let myself get lost in those eyes. I reach for him, lacing my fingers around the back of his neck to guide him to my lips. He wraps his arms around my thighs, lifting me up, and I hug my legs around his waist as he walks us to the bed.

Chase lays me on the pillows, tugging my tights and panties off before standing to whip the polo over his head. "Socks," I tease, propping up on my elbows.

He looks at his toes, realizes they're already bare, and squints at me before smiling. "I'm never going to live that down, am I?" he asks, kicking off his pants.

"Never." I smirk, shaking my head as he hovers over me. My hands move up his firm biceps, resting on his shoulders as he leans in for another kiss.

"I've missed you, baby," he whispers into me, lips trailing down my body. The delicious burn of his stubble brushing against my skin elicits a moan as he presses soft kisses along my thigh. I shiver, spreading for him as he inches toward my center. The way he's memorized me—anticipating the moves my senses will respond to, covering me with the lightest of his touches—has me reeling.

"I love you," I sigh, losing myself in the tingling warmth of his tongue. Savoring this small moment of connection, I fully give in to his touch and sink into the comfort of his love.

With our chest's heaving, I roll over and prop my chin on his shoulder, staring up at him. His eyes are closed as he moves his hand to rest on top of mine, mindlessly flicking the ring on my thumb while catching his breath. "How's the engagement party coming along?" he asks, coming down from his high.

I take a couple of breaths before answering, letting the passionate haze dissipate. "It's good. Joan's really excited, and I'm satisfied with the way everything came together so quickly. I'll send you pictures before it starts."

He nods, still playing with the ring on my thumb. "Do you even want to get married?" he finally asks.

"Chase Wilmington, if this is you proposing—"

"It's not," he says quickly, smiling. His eyes are open now, staring at the ceiling fan above us. "We haven't talked about it in a while, and I just thought I'd check in. It's okay if you don't. You already know there's no one else for me, and I'm pretty sure you like me at least a little bit." I nudge his shoulder, and his grin turns wide as he squeezes my hand.

"Yeah, someday. To you even…" I tease, moving myself up on my elbow to fully see his face. "I just don't feel any rush. But I know we'll get to it sooner or later. Whenever it happens, it happens."

He nods, locking his eyes to mine. We watch each other for several seconds, just staring.

"What?" I ask, tilting my head.

"I love you." He smiles, and I could melt. I already have melted. He gets all my soft and gooey parts, all my stubborn and feisty parts—everything. He loves everything. He *is* everything.

ALMOST ALL OF THE SUPPLIES HAVE BEEN DELIVERED— flowers, food, even the DJ is set up in the corner. The only thing we're waiting on is that stupid banner. It was the one thing Joan was adamant about. If it doesn't show up, I might flip a table. We have less than an hour before the guests arrive, and I keep looking out the window for the delivery truck.

After a prolonged goodbye at the airport with Chase, I landed in LA yesterday. I'm staying with Ashlie until I leave Sunday, much to the disappointment of Chase's mom, Christine. Chase boarded one of the EdTechU company planes this morning for Chicago. I was still bummed about losing time together this weekend, so Ashlie took me out to lunch today before dropping me off here at the venue.

I'm wrapping champagne-colored satin ribbon around the centerpiece vases, trying to finish up the table decorations, when Patti calls me from the kitchen, using her we-have-a-problem voice.

"What's wrong?" I ask, smoothing out my pink floral dress and moving to the back of the kitchen. Working for Patti has been seamless. She hired me right out of the internship, and being quick on my feet earned me the senior event planner title I hold today. I haven't met a party planning obstacle I can't solve, and we're not going to start today with this VIP Client.

"Well, it looks like the bakery sent over one hundred mini cupcakes in boxes instead of fifty regular cupcakes. And they forgot the three-tiered stand." She flips open one of the white bakery boxes, waving her hand over it with a flourish. "Oh, and they're smashed."

I look over her shoulder where the tiny pink and white frosting-covered pastries sit scattered inside two large sheet cake boxes, with no stabilizer to keep them from toppling into each other. The bottoms of the cupcakes are all bare—the baker didn't even bother using cupcake liners. What a disaster.

I sigh, looking at my watch as I try to think of how to salvage the mess-in-a-box in time for the event. I also make a mental note to never use this bakery again. Closing my eyes, I think of what my alternative cake stand could be. The boxes won't work, and I don't remember seeing any cake stands when we took inventory of the kitchen.

Remembering the silver serving platters I saw tucked away in a cupboard, I pop my eyes open and maneuver around the counter to pull out three of the shiny dishes. I take them with me and walk back into the main room, not speaking as I let the cogs in my brain propel me to work through this solution. Double-checking that it's marked *food safe*, I grab the extra pack of center-piece doily paper and get to work. The lacy paper is just smaller than the space within the trays, making it a perfect fit. I take my armful of supplies back to the kitchen.

"Whatcha got?" Patti asks, watching my process.

"I need food gloves, and skewers or toothpicks." I say distractedly, searching through drawers. She joins in, starting with the drawers on her side. We meet in the middle, finally coming across a half-empty box of long toothpicks and a full box of short ones.

I wash and dry the serving trays, slip on some thin disposable food service gloves, and get to work centering the doilies on the trays. Patti follows my line of thinking with the toothpicks, skewering two mini cupcakes straight through the middle with the long sticks and one cupcake on the short. We both arrange the pastries on the trays, salvaging all but four, and I stand back to look at the new display.

"Nice work," Patti says, nodding with her hands on her hips. "I knew there was a good reason I hired you." The boss is satisfied, and so am I.

I check my watch again. Twenty minutes till showtime. "Thanks Pat," I say before scurrying back to the main room to finish tying bows around flowers. I make it with seven minutes to spare, rushing around to clean up what little scraps are still lying around the room. Patti has already moved the cupcakes to their designated table, and I give the room another once-over, snapping a couple of pictures before disappearing into the kitchen. I send the pictures of my work to Chase, the first I've been able to text him all afternoon.

ME

All finished.

CHASE

It looks great, baby. Proud of you!

ME

How's Chicago?

CHASE

Windy *winky face*

Tucking my phone into my dress pocket, I hear the first guests arriving. We like to give guests twenty minutes to settle in before we step out of hiding, ensuring we aren't a distraction at the beginning of events. Patti nudges me on the shoulder, holding her hand up for a high five. I slap it, and then my eyes widen.

"What's wrong?" Patti asks, looking around the kitchen.

"That stupid banner!" I groan, reaching for my phone. I check the delivery app, and it still shows *out for delivery*. "*Ugh*, it's the only thing Joan wanted!" Rubbing my hand across my forehead, I feel a dread filled twinge pulse in my temples before turning toward the door.

"Wait!" Patti shouts, stopping me in my tracks. She grimaces at the surprised look on my face as realizes how loud she yelled out in her panic. "I'll talk to Joan," she says sheepishly. "Just, stay here and breathe. We don't need both of you freaking out." She moves to put herself between me and the door, hurriedly peeking over her shoulder to see out of the glass window.

Something's not right here, and Patti looks nervous. She doesn't get nervous at events. "Patti..." I say, squinting at her. "What's going on?"

"Nothing." She purses her lips, checking over her shoulder again. "I'm just watching for Joan."

"Patti, what don't you want me to see?"

"Nothing," she says again, more confidently.

"Then move over and let me see."

"No."

I laugh, shaking my head at her. "Patti..."

"Kayla, not yet! Just wait five more minutes."

"For what?" I cross my arms, raising an eyebrow.

"For...the banner..." Patti says hesitantly, flashing a nervous smile. I walk toward her, planning to look over her short frame through the glass when she jumps up in front of me.

My mouth falls open, my reaction stuck between surprise and trying not to laugh.

"Okay. Don't get upset, but the banner is here. It's not a big deal. It's just...wrong."

"*How* wrong?" I ask, watching her closely. She grimaces again, and I shake my head. "I'm going out there," I say, pushing past her and opening the door. Looking around the room at the decorations, I skim over the faceless guests in my panic, and everything looks the same as it did when I took pictures. The cupcakes are on the table, the DJ is set up in the corner, everything is dripping in blush pink and champagne, and the centerpieces are all adorned how I would have liked them to be if this were my own party. My eyes move up to the trim above the window where a pink banner with muted gold script hangs, reading: Chase and Kayla, At Last.

Why does it say that?

I look over my shoulder at Patti, utterly confused. She smiles back and nods toward the room, prompting me to look again. Turning, I look closer at the tables and see Hunter sitting, wearing a dress shirt and tie, with his arm draped around someone I've never seen before. Trevor, in a navy suit, stands near the drink table talking to Ashlie, who's wearing a champagne-colored dress a few shades lighter than her curls. Patti nudges me through the doorway, and I happen to see Artie, my dad, my mom, and Chase's parents, all sitting at another table talking and laughing. They're all dressed up too. All my people are here, but I have no idea why.

I walk slowly toward the middle of the room, taking in more details I hadn't before. Ashlie's sister, Willa, clicks a few pictures of a couple of the junior planners from work. Hadley cruises by the cupcakes, snagging one and popping it in her mouth before anyone else can stop her.

When Ashlie notices me, she clears her throat. A series of hushes go around the room as everyone turns to me. I'm looking from side to side at all of these faces I know and love, trying to figure out why they're at Joan's engagement party. And where is Joan? *And why does the banner say that?*

That's when I see him—Chase, wearing a tan suit, blush pink tie, and the biggest smile I may have ever seen on him. I halt, and he closes the distance between us, walking with his hands in his pockets.

"Hey, baby," he says softly, reaching for my hands.

"Wh-what are you doing here?" I ask, looking at him here, in front of me instead of in Chicago.

"Well, you've been saying how much you miss everyone, so I thought it would be a great opportunity to get everyone together for our engagement party."

"For our *what*?" I ask. My forehead scrunches as I look around the room again. Everyone's smiling, and I notice a videographer in the corner who wasn't there before.

"Kayla…"

"Hmm?" I glance up at him, but he's no longer there. My eyes travel downward to see him on one knee, smiling up at me, holding both of my hands in his. My mouth falls open as I finally realize what's about to happen.

"Kayla, I know you don't believe in love at first sight, but I think we can all agree that I was drawn to you from the first moment I laid eyes on you. You are my greatest adventure, the only one I want to explore the mundane and extraordinary aspects of life with. You make my world feel vibrant and new, just by being you, and I will forever cherish the love you have given me."

Tears flow down my cheeks at his words, blurring my vision. I don't wipe them away, needing to hold on tightly to both of his hands so I don't fall over from the waves of emotion surging through me. My love—my blue pebble, the constant light in my often-stormy world—is pouring his heart out to me in front of everyone we care about, and I'm pretty sure I'm in shock.

He continues, "I love the life we've built, and if our life together never brings anything more than what we have right now, I will still be the happiest man in the universe because I have you."

He reaches into his jacket pocket and pulls out a small black box. When he opens it, my breath hitches at the pink, pear-shaped morganite stone—haloed, set in a rose gold infinity band. "I love you with everything I have. Will you m—"

"Yes! Of course!" I lean down, holding his face in my hands as I press my lips to his. I can't see him through the tears, but I feel his smile against my mouth. He stands, lips still pressed to mine as he wraps one arm around my waist, holding the ring box in his other hand. When he pulls away, he reaches for my left hand and slides the ring on my finger, despite my trembling. It matches perfectly with my granny's ring on my thumb. The tears slow, and the room erupts into cheers as everyone *awws*.

"How did you pull this off?" I ask, looking around the room again.

Chase pulls me close, placing one more soft kiss on my lips. "Lots of late nights at work and frequent phone calls," he admits, squinting an eye. "I had to use Trevor as the fall guy anytime someone called about this. Everyone helped in one way or another, and they all knew if I answered with, 'Hey, Trev,' they would need to give me a minute to make sure we weren't in the same room."

He's talking fast, something he does when he's trying to squash his nerves. "And that bakery, they almost refused to deliver boxes full of smashed cupcakes. Hunter had to go in there last night and offer them double just to convince them we wouldn't leave them a bad review."

"So Chicago was—"

"All a ruse. I needed a good excuse for the planning meetings without you getting suspicious."

"But... Joan. I've been talking to her for weeks. Phone calls, video chats..."

"Yeah..." He smirks. "Joan *is* one of Patti's friends, but the only way I could make sure you had no idea about any of this was to make you the party planner. Ashlie gave Joan the details for colors and flowers, and *you* handled the rest."

"And what if I would have said no?" I ask with a breathy laugh.

He shrugs, stroking my cheek. "Then we'd have a fancy party with our friends and family, and smashed cupcakes."

"Oh God, I probably look like a mess!" I say, dabbing at my eyes. He grabs the handkerchief from his jacket and wipes the remaining black marks from my mascara.

"You look beautiful, baby." Leaning in close, he nuzzles my nose before drawing me in with his lips. I move my hands to his shoulders, still half dazed he pulled all of this off flawlessly. He breaks our kiss, tilting his head as he looks at me. "If our moms shoot any more eye-daggers in my direction for keeping you to myself, I don't think I'll make it to the wedding." He laces his fingers with mine and pulls me with him toward the tables.

As we near them, I get a closer view of the scrolled font above the window. "That banner is so bad," I whisper as we walk to the table where our family sits.

"I know..." He wrinkles his nose, nodding at our smiling mothers. "You can thank them for that. They wouldn't let it go."

COMING SOON

Want to know what happened between Hunter and Ashlie? Catch up with them in the second book of the Fort Bender series, coming early 2025.

ACKNOWLEDGMENTS

This book has been a long time coming, and none of it would have been possible without the support of my family. To my husband, Mr. James, thank you for encouraging me to follow my dreams, no matter how lofty they may be at times. To my kids, you're the best cheerleaders a mom could ask for! To my dear friend, Kenzie, thank you for hyping me up every step of the way.

I'd like to thank my editors, Kourtney and Jessica, for making sure my story flowed on the page as effortlessly as it did in my head. I couldn't have done it without you!

To my beta readers, Kathryn, Anna, Riya, Olive, Melissa, and Samantha, thank you for being the first eyes on this story and giving me the courage to actually put it out into the world. Your insights were invaluable.

Last, but not least, I want to thank my writer's club for being the best resource and support group an author could ask for!

ABOUT THE AUTHOR

Contemporary Romance author Layna James writes love stories with swoon-worthy banter, HEAs, and just a little angst. Her stories feature diverse characters who navigate the complexities of life while falling in love.

She lives in Texas with her family and an anxiety-ridden Rottie named Ruby. Layna loves fuzzy socks, most types of dessert, and all genres of music.

9 781963 567014